The Faithless Wife

Jo Eames

First published in 2010 by
Peach Publishing
The Peach Barns
North Aston
Bicester
Oxfordshire
OX25 6HX

British Library Cataloguing in Publication Data:
A catalogue record for this book is available from the British
Library

ISBN 978-1-907672-01-9

Cover: Healthy Bodies, Harper's Bazaar, July 1935 © Estate of
Martin Munkacsi, Courtesy Howard Greenberg Gallery, NYC

Typeset by Regent Typesetting, Hackney, London
Printed and Bound by TJ International, Padstow, Cornwall

www.peachpublishing.co.uk

For Hamish

So I took her to the river
Believing she was a maiden,
But she already had a husband.

Federico Garcia Lorca

1

On the edge of the cliff I lean all my weight against the wind. A less ferocious wind would relent from time to time and then I'd fall. But this is the north wind, *la tramuntana*, the one that sends people crazy in the head, so the islanders say, and it does not relent for a moment. Not out here on the headland where the storm is striking land with dizzying force for the first time in a hundred and fifty miles.

Far from letting me fall, it is doing its damnedest to push me away from the edge. I daren't even spread my arms wide in case it picks me up and dashes me down somewhere back amongst the broken rock and scrub. Instead I hug myself tight and lean into its raw power, exhilarated more than terrified. Of course, the wind could always choose to let me fall and, if it did, I wonder if I would recognise the moment of no return. I wonder if I would struggle and flail and fight my way back towards a solid footing, or if I would simply accept its will and embrace the drop.

Though half-blinded by the stinging rain, I stand and stare at the angry sea for a long time. The wind's roar is so loud it batters my ears and fills my head but I feel oddly at home in the maelstrom, oddly comforted.

And beneath me the waves continually heave themselves up into great grey rolls before smashing down in a confusion of spray. The base of the cliff shakes under the repeated assault and, as I finally turn to go, white water comes arching over the cliff to my left where the sea has worn an almost circular cove. The wind tries to hurry me away now but something makes me want to look down and see how the water surges around the arc it has spent so long in carving. A slab of granite at the back of the cove tilts steeply towards the cliff edge, dangerously slick with rain and spray, and I find myself kicking off my sandals before placing first one foot and then the other on the cold wet slope. My toes grip so tight to avoid slipping that my calves begin to tremble. It seems that today is not the day.

Down below, the waves roll in and around the cove until they run up against three jagged rocks, where they detonate into white fireworks. Roman candles and rockets explode in the air, water droplets sparkling as they separate from the solid wave. Spray spatters me at the top of the cliff even before the wind can snatch it away, and I lick salt from my lips. All is confusion, black and grey and white water roiling together and scraping clean the little crescent of pebbles that is normally cluttered with driftwood, plastic bottles and old tyres. There is nothing on the shore now. The sea has reclaimed its motley treasure to bestow elsewhere.

Yet even as this thought occurs to me, the sea throws something back. It lies on the shingle for a moment until the next wave covers it and smuggles it away. I toss my head to fling the dripping hair out of my eyes. What was it? A seal, a dolphin, a sack of rubbish, a coil of rope? My stuttering heart tells me it was none of these things, but all I can do is wait and see if it is carried ashore again. Something rolls in the waves that is not a wave itself, but the sea is playing a rough game and refuses to let me see what it has in its grasp. Now and then I catch glimpses of a brown barrel shape, paler at the ends, that flops and dips. It has mass, weight, but no momentum of its own. Whatever it is, it is at the sea's mercy.

My teeth are beginning to chatter, but I can't move

until I know what the thing is. And then suddenly the sea loses interest. It tosses the thing onto the shore a second time, with such a heave that the next waves cannot reach far enough up to drag it back into the water. So there it lies, a brown barrel shape with pale extremities, arms flung out now as if to grasp dry land, the grey head bare, one cheek nestled against the cold pebbles, legs and pale feet still pounded by the surf.

It is not a dolphin, or a seal, or a sack of rubbish or a coil of rope. It is what I'd known it would be, from the first glimpse. A body. Dead. And in the very place I expected it.

I stand for a moment longer, looking down at a sight I have imagined a hundred times, but never thought to see for myself. Then I turn my back to the tramuntana and run with the wind.

2

I should have realised last night that there was a storm coming. Normally the fishermen go about their business without saying much to each other but last night they were gathered in small knots on the landward ends of the jetties, arms folded, talking and looking at the sky. One took his boat out onto the mooring in the channel and brought his old dinghy back to shore. Even the kid's brother lengthened the springs on the Alba, letting her swing free of the jetty.

I should have caught the sense of anticipation. It was certainly there in the unusual animation of the fisher-men's chatter. The tramuntana is the old enemy here, the wind that sweeps down the Gulf of Lions and across the Mediterranean with all the barbarity of a foreign invader. Up near Cap Cavalleria, the whole landscape appears to run before it. Buckled layers of sandstone and shale slant to the south and low-growing myrtle and juniper curl over the upper slopes of the hills like spume on wave-tops. Ancient fortified farmhouses turn their backs both to the wind and to the pirates it once blew here, doors and windows huddling together on the south side of the building, while the northern flanks stand bare.

So I should have sensed what was coming, like the locals do. But I am not a local, and it only dawned on me when I woke to the dry rattle of palm fronds beyond my balcony, a breeze blowing down the *cala* and out to sea the clouds moving like a fleet of airships across the horizon.

Sometimes the wind blows itself out before it reaches the island, so that the only sign of it is a heavy pounding sea that takes two or even three days to return to calm. But the tramuntana did not fall short today. In half an hour the pleasant maraca tune the palm tree was playing had become a wild thrashing voodoo dance and the wind was howling in the chimney. Then came the rain. Not the sandy rain that the xaloc brings from North Africa but clean cool rain from the north. It began to fall in torrents, hammering the sea, slapping against the windows and plopping down the chimney onto the driftwood I have piled in the fireplace against the onset of a winter that seems almost unimaginable on long hot summer days.

Like the needles on a battery of compasses, the boats swung as one to face the head of the cala. The storm would do its best to tear them free but these moorings have endured many tramuntanas and so have the steady, dauntless men who maintain them. It was not a day for fishing, or for a pleasure trip and so the jetties were deserted.

The wind and the rain kept up their terrific pace all through the morning and with each hour the sea was stirred higher and higher into a state of matching fury. The howling in the chimney grated on my nerves worse and worse until I had to get away from it – even if the only place to go was into the storm itself.

Running back from the cliffs now, all I can think about is reaching the shelter of my house and stepping under a steaming shower. I skid down the rough drive that drops from the ridge to the shoreline and am about to turn right to the house, cold and numb, only my ears burning, when I see the kid's boat.

There's little to be done. Water is almost up to the gunwales and all his paraphernalia is either sunken or floating, barely penned in by the rim of the boat. No good to try and bail. The rain is falling faster than I could empty it out and anyway the boat is so near loss of buoyancy that even the turbulence of bailing might be enough to swamp it.

The boat is an old wooden dinghy with a seventy-five horsepower outboard engine. Too young for a car or a motorbike, its owner drives it with a casual recklessness. I have watched him as he pulls away from the jetty, standing in the stern and pushing the tiller of the outboard right and left, carving turns in the water, avoiding the Alba's mooring, steering round shallow patches of sand and weed until he reaches the deep channel in the middle of the cala. The handle isn't designed to be used standing but he disdains to sit and leans down with his back bent, planting his legs wide to balance against the swell.

Once upon a time the boat was painted white outside and blue in but the paint is old, shabby, abraded until the bare wood shows through. The bottom of the boat is always littered with useful debris: snorkel and flippers; polystyrene floats; buoys made from plastic bottles; lengths of pole that could serve as fishing rod or boat-hook or harpoon; a red and black football; a petrol can. A galvanised steel anchor lies in the bows attached to a length of frayed yellow rope. The ship's equipment is so plentiful that the ship's company has to pick a way through it, ankle-deep, carefully.

It is the kid's boat, no doubt of that from the proprietorial way he fiddles with the outboard engine and the way his friends stand hesitant on the jetty, waiting for his word before clambering down and squeezing in amongst his junk. Only his little sister, dark as he is fair but still his sister – *claro* – from her confident manner, climbs aboard as if she doesn't need permission and I can tell that it galls him. There might be two years between them and she tries to keep up with him, sharing or copying his loose-limbed walk. They are an exceptionally handsome pair: he tall and slim with fair straight hair cut blunt and a little too long, so that he looks like a Hollywood child star nearing the end of a short career, a step or two away from the Viper Room; she smaller but still tall for her age, her hair straight like his but coal-dark and her skin darker too. They are strangely self-assured, at ease in a world that, as yet, contains nothing that is incomprehensible to them.

I don't know the boy. Don't even know his name. That's why I think of him as the kid, the nonchalance of which suits him. But I have watched him often from my balcony and I know he loves that boat. It strikes me suddenly that I want to do something. And, since in this case there is certainly no time like the present, I run to the edge of the surging water and wade in. I may not be able to save the whole thing from sinking, but what I can try to do, what I resolve to do, is to save his engine.

I reach the boat's stern thigh deep in the surf and try to remember how to unship an engine. It's been years since I did it myself but I've seen the kid do it a few times and recall him leaning down over the back fiddling with something. The engine is submerged to the top of the propeller shaft but I'm almost sure the water has yet to find its way into the workings. The normal thing to do, I think, is to tip the engine forward into the boat but if I do this now I shall sink the lot. Instead, I grope about under its body and grasp a metal pin. I pull it and as one side comes free the engine lurches and I feel its weight. Then I wonder if I have over-reached myself. Will I be able to lift it, keep it out of the water and carry it to shore? I look around, but all the houses are shuttered and empty. It is too early in the season for holidaymakers and, apart from the fishermen, the locals only come down to their places at weekends. It is, I'm almost sure, a Tuesday. There is not a soul around.

I plant my feet as firmly as I can among the sand and weed and, putting one arm right around the prop shaft so that the haunch of the engine is over my shoulder, I give the pin another tug with my free hand. With a grinding wrench the pin pulls free and the engine bites into my collarbone. I stagger under the weight, which is even greater than I expected. Then I steady myself and shuffle round to face the shore. It is only five yards or so but the storm has churned up the water with sand so that I cannot see my feet and the waves are surging in and back, pulling at my knees. The engine settles deeper into my shoulder as I stand there, undecided, and the sand drains away under my feet till I begin to lose my footing and have to run, top-heavy, staggering drunkenly to shore where I drop the engine with a thud onto the wet sand and fall next to it.

The rain keeps on lashing down and it is too cold to lie on the sand for long, despite an awful tiredness that aches in every bone. Besides, lying here I feel too alike to that other figure on that other beach. I drag myself up and the engine after me, gripping it under what, if it were a man, would be its armpits into the shelter of the boathouse the kid's older brother, the fisherman, uses. There I prop it under an old tarpaulin. While my back is turned, the dinghy sinks silently to the sand.

I don't want to go into the water again but it seems like spoiling the ship for a ha'p'orth of tar so I wade in to collect flippers, snorkel masks, the oars, as they roll around in the waves. The red and black football swirls away as I lunge for it and at last, inevitably, I'm swimming. It's warmer in the water than out but with waves crashing in confusion against the supports of the

8

jetties it's not the day for a swim. The anchor seems safe enough on the seabed, marked by its plastic bottle buoy, so I pile up the rest of my salvage beside the engine and turn for home.

The hot shower stings and steams and is generally the most reviving thing I've felt in a long, long time. With warmth and dry clothes comes a sense of elation, smugness almost. I have saved something from the storm. Not the lost soul at the bottom of the cliffs, but something. The tramuntana has not had everything its own way.

Late in the afternoon the rain stops and, still wrapped in the glow of my achievement, I go back out into the wind. I have with me a note that I have written in Spanish, a plastic bag and a safety pin. I pin the note in the bag to the tarpaulin that lies heaped over the kid's engine and hurry home before I can have second thoughts.

3

In a small town at the heart of the island a woman lies awake, listening to the wind rage overhead. She sleeps less, and more fitfully, with every passing year, but her wakefulness tonight strikes her as out of the ordinary. There is a different quality to it – a restless anxiety – that is unfamiliar. It can't be that she is afraid of the tramuntana – after more than eighty years? Absurd. Nevertheless, she feels the urge to get up and look out of the window. But for what? For whom? No one comes to visit her at this time of night and her neighbours in their quiet street will have been long in bed.

When sleep will not come and the urge will not go, she slides her heels inch by inch towards the edge of the bed and then lowers her legs stiffly to the floor. She feels for her slippers and gets the first one on, but the second slides away from her crabbed toes and she curses quietly. What she wouldn't give to be able to swoop down, snatch up the recalcitrant slipper and slip it onto a pretty, slender foot. What she wouldn't give to be seventeen again.

Everything. Anything. Just for a day. Just for an hour. With him.

She stops fishing about the floor for the slipper and ponders. Is that what this is about? Is it an anniversary of some sort that she has forgotten? She runs through them in her head. Not the day they married. Not quite yet the day the war started, which was July. Certainly not the day it ended – bitter February. Not even the day he came up to her in the market place. The best day of all. The day she put down her basket to take his hand and turn her back on everything that had gone before.

She smiles at the memory. So long ago. Nearly seventy years and she can see him now as clear as if it was last week. He is walking towards her with his old ruck-sack over his shoulder, hair unbrushed, his boots scuffed at the toe and his trousers bunched up by a thick leather belt. But there is such energy to him, such life. Far too much ever to be buttoned-up in smart clothes and proper behaviour. He doesn't see her at first, or perhaps he doesn't recognise her, after eighteen months. From fifteen to seventeen a girl can change a great deal. More than she ever imagined possible. Her heart sinks as she thinks perhaps he won't recognise her. Has she altered that much? Is she so like one of them now that he will simply fail to see her? She swaps the heavy basket of tomatoes, potatoes and bread from one hand to the other and stands beside the butcher's stall, watching him come closer. She will not call out to him if he passes without seeing her. She has too much pride for that, though she knows it will break her heart a second time. Determined to take it on the chin in the way she's been learning to take everything, she stands up straight and watches and waits.

Then he sees her. He stops dead, so suddenly that the person behind cannons into him and knocks him a few steps forward, but she can see that he doesn't even feel it. His eyes are locked on hers and the look in them is so deep, so strong, so incandescent that she instantly fears for anybody who steps across its line, in case they should be burned through by the intensity of it.

And she knows. Even before he closes the distance between them and speaks to her, she knows. And she exults in the knowledge that now he sees, now he realises that he loves her just as she has always loved him.

Once, she would have been angry, but her anger has worn itself out, somewhere in the last terrible year. She doesn't care any more that he couldn't see what she knew eighteen months ago. Perhaps it was absurd to expect an ambitious young man – especially one whose head was filled with Marx and Lenin and the dialectic – to take a fifteen year old girl's infatuation seriously. She doesn't even care any more that by turning her away he drove her to an act of terrible stupidity. None of that matters now that she has seen the look in his eyes.

"Catalina?" he says, as if he is still unsure that it is really her, in her neat and sober grown-up woman's clothes. She nods and he puts out his hand:

"You have to go away with me."

And she puts down her basket of shopping, the food for her husband's supper, and walks away from it without a second thought.

4

There is a knock at my door early the next morning. I go slowly down the stairs, cursing yesterday's stupid expansiveness. The silhouette beyond the opaque glass is taller than I expected and for a moment I wonder if it is the older brother, the fisherman, who has come to see me. But when I take a deep breath and open the door it is the kid standing there.

We look at each other and I see that this is the first time he has noticed me. I have been watching him from my balcony for weeks but not once have I caught him looking over in my direction. I had wondered if his perfect indifference was faked, if he had actually stolen a look or two from under that long fringe, and wondered who I was. But now I realise I have indeed been thoroughly invisible. He doesn't exactly seem as if he wants to be here on my doorstep even now and perhaps no one ever does like having to say thank you for an unsought favour. Maybe he's ashamed, too, that he was not enough of a seaman to keep his boat safe from the storm.

"Is it okay?" I ask him in Spanish.

"*Sí*" he says. "*Sí*. Jes."

From which it's clear that he knows I'm English. So either my accent is unmistakable or perhaps my presence has been noted on the cala after all.

"Come in" I say and stand back to make room on the stairs.

He hesitates and then says: "*Muchas gracias*" though I can't tell whether this is in response to the invitation or the salvage of his stuff. I wait a moment but still he doesn't move and I regret the note even more completely. I haven't had my morning coffee yet and my desire to be thanked, my craving for conversation, evaporates in the face of teenage taciturnity. I turn to go upstairs again, hoping he'll grasp his chance to back out of the doorway and go, but I've only moved up a few steps when I hear his tread behind me, light but definite.

"*Café?*" I say, when we reach the kitchen. I turn just in time to catch a nod. I go to fill the kettle and above the sound of the tap running I say: "What's your name?"

"Billy" he says and water sprays off the side of the kettle and up my arm as I swing back to look at him. Billy. The Kid. It seems the funniest thing and I start to laugh but then I see his face. He looks hurt. Indignant too.

"My name is Biel. But my father, he is Biel too, so I am called Bielet at home and my friends call me Billy."

I can see it, the casual corruption of the Spanish diminutive into something American, glamorous, a little bit tough. I can see why he would like it and I wonder if it was his friends' idea or if it was his. I think I know the answer.

When the kettle has boiled I take the coffee pot and two mugs out onto the balcony. The kid – Billy – follows and we both lean on the rail in the morning sunshine. The storm is gone, the palm tree is silent again and only the sound of the sea still crashing against the rocks at the entrance to the cala stops me from thinking I imagined it all. There is one other piece of evidence. I glance down towards the spot where the kid's boat usually rides beside the jetty. He follows my gaze, then drops his head and I think I see his perfect, even tan redden slightly.

"Where is it?" I ask.

"*Por allí,*" he points and now I can see it, upturned

under a tamarisk tree on the shore. There's a streak of wet sand from the shoreline where he must have dragged it and I wonder if he hauled it out all by himself.

"Is the engine alright?"

"*Si, gracias, señora.*"

I bridle slightly at the *señora* before admitting to myself that it is only waiters in hope of a tip who call me *señorita* any more and I certainly can't expect it from a boy. I wonder how old he thinks I am.

"How old are you?" I ask.

He looks at me with suspicion, taking the mug I'm holding out to him with obvious reluctance.

"Fifteen."

It wasn't what I wanted to ask at all. What I wanted to ask was whether he'd heard anything about a body being found at the bottom of the headland. But how would that sound? Come in, have a coffee, by the way, any dead bodies washed up lately? He'd think I was a madwoman, or worse. No, there simply isn't a way to introduce that subject into polite conversation, not without admitting that I saw a body and didn't report it. Which is frustrating. Ever since yesterday I have been listening out for sirens, or the whir of helicopter rotor blades. But there has been nothing. There's a possibility, I suppose, that the sea did rouse itself enough to reclaim its booty and has taken it out into deep water, to toy with a while longer. Or forever. These things happen. Those left behind can wait a long time for the sea to give up its dead.

I decide to try and come at the subject from an oblique angle:

"It was a bad storm, that one."

He puts the mug to his lips and eyes me over the rim, wondering how to respond to this statement, or question, he's not sure which. So he just shrugs.

"Do people often get hurt, in tramuntanas? I mean, if you got caught out at sea, or even on the cliffs, the wind is so strong ..."

He shrugs again. I don't appear to be striking any chords with him. But, as I open my mouth to ask something else, he rouses himself to answer my last question:

"People, generally people know when a tramuntana is coming. They stay indoors, they ..." He stops and hangs his head and I immediately guess what he was going to say. "They make their boats safe." Except he hadn't and we both know it. No way of rescuing the conversation now. He avoids my eye as he gulps back his too-hot coffee and puts down his mug. It is clear that he wants to go. But then another idea strikes me and I have asked the question before I've thought through exactly why.

"Will you take me out on your boat?"

He looks startled: "Where?"

I shrug: "I don't know. Swimming? Snorkelling? Wherever you go."

I know he sometimes goes off round the headland, because I've seen him there, anchored in the entrance to that very same cove in calm weather, fishing with his friends.

His obvious desire to refuse struggles for a moment with his sense that he owes me something. To my surprise, the better impulse comes out on top.

"*Vale*. Okay. But not until the sea settles. Two days, maybe three. I need to get my boat fixed up, also."

Now he feels entitled to go, and he does, ignoring or simply not seeing the look of impatience on my face. The slap-slap of his flip-flops echoes as he lopes down the stairs and out into the sunshine. I watch him from the balcony as he heads along the shore towards the village.

16

He runs with his usual long stride, but there seems to be more than the usual urgency in it. He doesn't look back.

5

The young girl raced over the hot flagstones of the Ciudadella streets, late for a meeting, late for the most important meeting of her life. She has had to wait for her mother to finish brushing out her long dark hair before bed. The brushing took longer than usual because her mother wanted to talk to her, to plead with her to be reasonable and listen sensibly to her father's plans for her. As soon as her mother had gone, shaking her head at Catalina's stony response, she plaited her hair again as fast as her fingers could pull the thick strands into place and sneaked down to the wine cellar. A secret passage led from the back of the cellar out to a tiny door beside a neighbouring church. Theirs was an old house, re-built in the sixteenth century after the Turks sacked the town, and Catalina's ancestors had built the passage in case they ever came back. Not that the Turks had allowed anyone to take sanctuary in a church the first time, thought Catalina. Still, she was grateful to her unknown forefather. The passage gave her the freedom to come and go as she pleased. Her parents would never in a month of Sundays have given her permission to go out alone, let alone to political meetings.

It was already gone eight in the evening, but it had been a hot day and the paving stones in the main streets retained the heat the sun had poured into them. Afraid of being spotted by one of her parents' friends, Catalina darted off down a side street as soon as she could. It was cooler in the narrower lane, where the houses leant across almost touching at roof level. Her heart beat fast, not just from running but from knowing that in a few minutes she would see him.

She wondered if he would be speaking tonight. He was already a good orator, making up in passion what he lacked in eloquence or education. He wasn't all that much older than her, but he seemed so grown up. Her father would call him a peasant, would say there was no reason to waste education on him, when his place was to work the land for his betters. But the old system was gone now. There was a new Spain since the election, since the king abdicated and the republican government came in. A government for the people. Not just for the aristocrats and for old families like hers, whose only talent as far as she could see was for holding on to what they had.

Although she was fond of her father, she already recognised that he had little talent for business. Theirs was one of the oldest names and one of the oldest palaces in Ciudadella, but she knew it was a struggle for him to keep it up in a style to match the other leading families. Nothing much seemed to go right for him, especially these days. Trade was bad and he blamed it on the new government, the Red bastards he called them even in front of the children, although he was a man who very rarely swore.

Catalina couldn't quite bring herself to wish for her family to lose their house and the things they owned, but she believed that everyone deserved a chance to own the fruits of their labour, to rise on merit. She looked at Lluís, who declared without shame that he came from a poor family of farm labourers near Sant Agueda, and in him she saw the future, a strong, capable man who would lead others to a life of freedom and sufficiency in the new Spain.

For herself, she had ambitions. Maybe she could train

to be a doctor. Another thing her father called a waste, education for women. He had one plan for his eldest daughter, one only, and it was being pressed on her harder and harder. That was what her mother had been trying to talk to her about in her room – the very suitable young lawyer her father had found for her. Already going places, already making an impression, even if his family wasn't quite what one might have wished. There was money though, to make up for lack of pedigree. And looked like being more before long, if young Mascaró was as canny an operator as he appeared. If only, her mother said, repeating her husband's mantra, the new government didn't totally stifle the chances for trade.

Catalina had seen Joan Cintas Mascaró at a party – and didn't care to see him again. She recognised him instantly, with his straight back and his greased hair already beginning to recede, shoes polished to a shine. She saw him duck his chin to her father and mirror his every mannerism as they talked. He wasn't interested in a new Spain. He was interested in being part of the old Spain, in keeping hold of what he had and getting more, no matter at whose expense. She had tried to skulk in the corner of the salon but her mother found her and dragged her over to be introduced. She felt herself looked over like a brood mare whose blood-line was faultless but whose temperament was still unproven. She would have liked to show her teeth and whinny at him, but her father was giving her a warning look so she just stared at her shoes instead.

She hoped her sullenness would put him off, but the following week her father called her into his study to tell her that he had received a most gratifying offer for her hand in marriage. She told him he could go to hell and take his friend the lawyer with him. For good measure she told him that everyone knew lawyers were leeches on the people and she would sooner die than marry one. Especially when he was an old man twice her age.

Her father tried to hide his anger and reason with her. Told her thirty was a good age for a man to marry, and fifteen was an excellent age for a girl to settle down and think of babies. It was best for a girl to have her babies young, when they came easily, with no dangers. He only wanted her to be settled, he said, settled and secure.

And happy? She'd asked him. What about happy? But he'd only looked at her and said that happiness would come from doing her duty to her family, to her husband, to God and to the children He blessed her with. Then he sent her upstairs before she could think of another retort.

She thought of plenty up in her room. Settled and secure? He mean tied down and locked away. With no chance of freedom just when the whole of Spain was changing. It wasn't what she wanted, marriage and babies. A quiet life? No. She was going to be somebody, travel, help her fellow citizens build a nation with freedom and equality for all, be with Lluís.

Be with Lluís. That was the main thing. Go where he went. She was fifteen years old, had been nowhere and knew nothing, but she knew she was in love with Lluís. Had known it almost the first time she saw him. A girl knows, she told herself. Juliet had known as soon as she saw Romeo, and she was only fourteen.

The meeting was in the backroom of a bar near the port. Catalina pushed her way through the fishermen and dock workers gathered drinking and smoking in the front. They stopped talking and stared at her, shocked to see a woman, a girl, in such a place. Catalina just swung her plait and headed straight for the door at the back. It gave her a thrill to do something so daring, and alone. When she pushed open the door, there was even

21

more smoke, everyone in the room seemed to be dragging furiously on roll-ups made with the cheapest tobacco. Catalina suppressed the urge to cough and felt her eyes sting. There were about fifteen people in the room, one or two fierce looking women, but mainly men. There was a table at the front, behind which someone had erected a large red banner with the hammer and sickle on it. Three men sat behind the table and faced the rest of the audience through the smog.

One of them was Lluís. Catalina slipped into a seat on the second row. Another man was on his feet, speaking. Catalina tried to pay attention to what he was saying, but could only think of Lluís. He gave no sign of having seen her come in, was listening intently to the lecture. He sat leaning forward with his arms on the table, big square hands balanced on the balls of his fingers. The collar of his shirt was open and she could see where his neck was tanned from working in the fields.

A thrill ran through her as she looked at him and she thought:

"I love him. I'm not going to let them marry me off to some old man. I'm going to run away with him."

She didn't hear a single word of the meeting, not even when Lluís stood up to speak. She leant forward then, and saw him notice the movement and register her presence with a flicker of a grin, but still she didn't hear what he said. She just thought:

"See, he loves me too," and waited for the meeting to end.

When it finally did, she stood up and waited for him to come over to her. He lingered talking to the other speakers for a while, but she could tell from the way he angled his shoulder towards her that he knew she was waiting, and that he was waiting to be with her too. At last, the discussion broke up and he walked over towards her.

"*Salud*, comrade," he said, with a smile. "Did you have problems slipping away tonight? I didn't see you come in."

She nodded.

"I'm in trouble at home."

"I'm sorry to hear that," he said. "What is it? Have you been neglecting your piano practice again?"

She blushed, with annoyance rather than embarrassment:

"You don't always have to treat me like a snotty kid. I'm not, you know. I'm old enough to be married!"

He laughed, a strong rough laugh that seemed to come up from his belly. Normally, she liked it but tonight it infuriated her.

"Married? You? I'd like to see the man brave enough to try that, comrade. Even Stalin might not be man of steel enough for that job."

"Well, maybe if it's so incredible you should come round for dinner on Sunday. See the man my father has lined up for me. He's a lawyer, thirty, all his own teeth, most of his own hair, quite up-and-coming, according to my father."

Lluís raised his eyebrows and ran a hand through his hair:

"You're not serious? You're getting married? I don't suppose he's even on the left, is he?"

She was pleased to see that at least she had shocked him into looking disappointed.

"I'm deadly serious, but I'm not getting married. Not to him, he's the worst kind of capitalist lickspittle. I've seen him once and I don't care if I never see him again as long as I live. That's why I had to come tonight, before my family gets any further along with their stupid scheme."

He looked at her, puzzled:

"I'm sorry, comrade, what do you expect us to do? I don't suppose a delegation from the Party is likely to carry much weight with your father."

She shook her head, impatiently:

"Don't be stupid, Lluís. This isn't about the party. It's about us, you and me. I'm not going to marry that ... donkey my father found, because I'm going to be with you. I love you. And you love me. Take me home with you tonight. Marry me. Don't marry me. I don't care. I just want us to work together, for Spain."

As she finished, she wanted to raise her fist in the workers' salute, but thought it might be heretical to invoke solidarity for such a private matter. So she stood with her hand clenched at her side and watched his face, waiting. But whatever expression she had expected to see appear there did not come. And after a minute, she realised. He didn't know. He didn't have a clue what she was talking about. He thought she was just a spoilt little girl and he was a young man whose head and heart were filled with nothing but politics.

It was the greatest humiliation of her life. She had thrown herself at a man, told her she loved him, worse, told him he loved her, when she now realised he'd never even looked at her with anything other than amusement. It had all been a dream, a fantasy.

She turned and ran, knocking over a chair as she bolted for the door. She heard him shout her name behind her, but she didn't look back. She flew through the bar to a chorus of male laughter that she took to be aimed at her and burst into tears as soon as she hit the clean night air. She ran all the way home and slumped in the dank tunnel of the secret passage, panting and sobbing at the same time, wishing that the ancient walls would cave in and bury her, where no one would see her stupidity and shame.

But the ancient walls stood firm and at last she had no choice but to stand up and creep her way back through the cellar and up the stairs to her room.

6

I scour the local newspaper for five days (during which time there is no sign of Billy) before I find what I'm looking for. It is on an inside page, unable to compete with the headlines concerning the latest basketball win over San Sebastián and a proposal to turn a stretch of road between Mahon and Ciutadella into a dual carriageway, with all its burning environmental consequences. It is only a small piece. Two short columns and a photograph barely bigger than a postage stamp. The headline is incontrovertible: MAN FOUND DEAD AT BOTTOM OF CLIFF.

"*The body of an elderly man has been discovered in the sea close to Punta Pons. The body was recovered on Wednesday, after a day of strong winds and stormy seas, by an in-shore lifeboat from the naval base in Mahon after being spotted by a local resident. The dead man has yet to be formally identified. Cause of death is to be determined by a post-mortem examination. Police are appealing for witnesses to come forward.*"

So that's it. I have my answer, but of course it's no answer at all. What was I hoping for? Some explanation of who he was, how he got there and why? Life is never that simple. Why should death be any different? The photograph is terrible, blurred and dark. At first, I am not even sure whether it was taken in life or in death. The eyes are open, but stare blankly out of the page. The face is both lined and puffy and the hair is unkempt enough to have been dredged from the sea. But something in the jut of the chin and the very intensity of the blank stare suggests a willed stiffness rather than *rigor mortis*. So maybe the police do know who he is, after all. They're just not saying. And how could it matter to me anyway? Annoyed by my wholly absurd curiosity, I throw down the paper and go outside onto my balcony for a smoke.

The jetties are deserted now and I see that the kid – Billy – has finally been down to the cala whilst I was out today, because his boat has been re-launched and now rides silent on its mooring. The sun set an hour ago and the sky completes its last colour change, from gun-metal to black, as I finish my cigarette. It is time to go inside and light the lamps but I stay out on the balcony, filled with a fear I have not been conscious of before that if I leave this scene unwatched it will disappear. So I sit on and the kid's boat fades into the darkness. It is alike to twenty or thirty other dinghies moored to jetties or turned turtle on the shore the length of the cala. Yet it looks different to me from all those others, seems to tug more fiercely at the springs securing it, as if eager to be off round the headland with the kid at the helm. It isn't the boat though, is it? It's me, pining for some stimulation that my purdah can't provide.

A sharp pain stings my left forearm and my right hand smacks it hard, responding to some defensive reflex that is quicker than a thought. I turn my palm upward and there is a small smear of blood across the pad of flesh at the base of my fingers. The mosquito, body crumpled by the blow, still has its telltale proboscis embedded in my arm. Working by moonlight I pick it off, rub it between thumb and forefinger and drop it over the balcony. It is undoubtedly time to go inside.

Normally I would. The word strikes me as odd. Normality was something I thought I'd left far behind. But now I begin to see that anything can become normal, however outlandish by, well, by normal standards. There is a comfort to routine. Of the most basic kind. Here on the cala, a thousand miles from anyone who knows me, normally I light the lamps when it gets dark. Normally I eat something. Normally I wash the plate and sweep the breadcrumbs over the balcony for the little family of ducks that has come to expect them. Normally I go to bed. I don't normally sit outside trading blows with the mosquitoes and dreaming of new adventures.

A shiver goes through me although the air is still warm. This deviation from my routine is unnerving. Up until the last few days, the world beyond my balcony has been little more than a series of alterations in colour, and that has suited me fine. I know every shade of the day. Pink and orange at sunrise. White and grey just after dawn when the mist hangs over the water. Hazy blue at midday. Bright blue mid-afternoon. Clear clear gold-fringed blue in the early evening. Beaten copper at sunset. Mauve to violet to grey at twilight. I even tell myself the Spanish words for them, rolling the shapes in my mouth like a charm or a prayer: *alba, madrugada, mañana, mediodia, tarde, crepúsculo, la noche*. The beauty of the days has been comforting, but not as great a comfort as their predictability. The steadiness and sureness of them, bright tranquil Mediterranean days, with the constant promise of more of the same has been what mattered. It is only the body at the bottom of the cliff that has roused dormant dangerous senses in me: first, curiosity; now, this hankering after adventure.

Perhaps I knew that it couldn't last forever, my beautiful empty head. Still, I try to keep it that way. I can't stop the shivering though, as I clasp my arms around my knees and squeeze. And even when I put my chin down onto my knees I can still hear my teeth rattle. I'm not ready – nowhere near ready – to go to all the places where curiosity might take me.

I struggle to stay calm. The moon helps. A beautiful empty planet, so satisfyingly white and peaceful, it hangs silent and sympathetic above the houses on the other side of the cala and it draws my gaze up and then down to where it spreads a widening lane of light onto the water from the opposite shore to the end of the nearest jetty.

There is no wind tonight. And in a tideless sea there are only the barest traces of ripples to recall the on-shore breeze that blew this afternoon. If I concentrate hard I can just hear the water lap against the piles beneath the jetties and the hulls of the boats. The shining lane of moonlight flexes at the edges but does not break. And nor must I.

7

Lying out on the end of the jetty, the planks are rough and gritty with sand. I should have brought a towel to lie on, but I only came outside to keep an eye on the twins, who were bickering over whose turn it was to paddle the windsurfer. And then it was so hot I just had to dive off the jetty and swim across the cala and back. I can still hear the twins, carrying on their argument as they splash around in the water. I could see them too, if I raised my head off my forearm. And I will of course, if the tone of their voices changes to panic or fear or real pain. But for now they're just being kids, doing what kids do in the sea and the sunshine and I'm happy to be fifty yards off, too far away for them to bother annoying.

It's a perfect day, if I am being fair to it, especially with the breeze that's come up since lunch to make the heat bearable. Better than bearable. Delicious, actually. I can feel it stirring the hairs on my back, as if someone was lying next to me and blowing very gently across my shoulder blades. The thought makes me shiver. If only Johnny was here. But Mum and Dad had been very clear, the suggestion that I bring a friend this year had been definitely limited to girls. And nothing I could say about splitting the bed into two singles, or Johnny sleeping down in the boathouse, would shift them.

"You're fifteen years old, Katherine" my father said, in what the look on his face told me were his final words on the issue: "We're going on a family holiday. I'm not having it turn into a honeymoon for randy teenagers."

Of course, I refused to make the best of a bad job by inviting a girl instead, but four days into three endless weeks I'm wishing I hadn't been so stubborn. The twins are perfectly wrapped up in their own world, just as they have been since the day they were born. And out here even the parents seem to be in alliance, sneaking off together for afternoon siestas with furtive grins the meaning of which I don't even want to think about. Which leaves me playing the role of family spare part even more than usual. Feeling horribly sorry for myself, I let my forehead slump down against the planks and stare down through a gap in the woodwork into the green shallows below. The water is clear to the stones on the seabed and the surface ripples in the breeze, catching glints of the sun as it moves. The glittering motion makes my head swim and I close my eyes. When I open them again it takes me a moment to focus on the strange deliberate movement through the clear water, on the bulbous bag that is both head and body in one, on the rippling but somehow co-ordinated mass of arms. On the octopus that tiptoes across the slatted shade.

Then every salt-encrusted hair on my body stands on end. It isn't half an hour since I swam past here, walking up the sand of the slipway on my hands until my belly touched the ground. The thought that the octopus might have been here all the time, quietly watching me from its hiding place behind one of the rusty old iron supports fills me with fascination and horror. What if it had resented the intrusion? Or been curious? What if it had spooled out a tentacle and touched me?

I scramble up and run back along the jetty and then down the shoreline, shouting. The twins look round, glossy seal heads bobbing by the windsurfer. I wave frantically at them, but even from here I can see them giving me their twin stare, the one that says: "*Whatever it is, sis, it can't be as much fun as our game.*" And I head on towards the house, to fetch my father. But before I get there an old man emerges from a small white hut.

"*¿Que pasa?*"

I want to run on past, but the path's too narrow here, so I stop, panting, awkward and reluctant to answer. It isn't that I don't know who he is. In a fit of holiday neighbourliness, my father has struck up a kind of easy acquaintance with the old man despite them having no language in common. But I am a little afraid of him. This is the first time I have encountered him alone, without my family – without my unembarrassable father – to shelter behind. Whenever he talks, I can hardly tell whether he's speaking Spanish or the island language, Menorquí – his speech so guttural that it sounds just as though someone had thrown a shovelful of gravel into the barrel of a cement-mixer.

But "*¿Que pasa?*" is obvious enough, especially when he asks it again and cocks his head on one side in a way that says: "What's going on?" in any language.

I look around but there is no one else about. The old man is staring at me, waiting for an answer. I can't just run off, however much I want to, not unless I run back towards the octopus.

"Octopus" I say, in English, lamely: "There's an octopus."

He looks at me and says nothing, merely gives me an expectant smile, content to wait for a linguistic clue that he can follow. I dig about in my store of Spanish words, gleaned from restaurant menus:

"*Pulpo*" I say finally, wiggling my fingers in a ludicrous way.

The smile stretches into a beam.

"*¿Pulpo? ¿Donde?*"

I point at the jetty and he scuttles off down the shore.

The coast is clear now and I could escape back to the house, but I already feel possessive about my discovery and I want to see what the old man plans to do. A minute later he is back, disappearing into his hut and re-emerging almost at once with a heavy wooden paddle. Then he scampers off to the jetty again and wades down the slipway into the water. Intrigued despite myself, I walk slowly back towards the jetty too. He is bending down now, thigh-deep in the water, which is soaking the ragged hems of his old shorts. Just as I step onto the jetty he lunges forward and tosses something that lands like a heap of unwrung washing onto the planks and begins to beat it with the paddle. I stand there, unable to move as he crashes the paddle down onto the octopus's head. The despatch only lasts a few seconds but I feel sick and fascinated and a little bit thrilled.

When he is finished he grasps the creature by the flesh of one limb and brings it over to show me. The tentacles that had seemed so clever and so creepy as they felt their way over the seabed hang limp. Its head droops and the creature's shell-pink colour seems to drain away to greyness before our eyes. It is the deadest thing I've ever seen.

I want to feel sorry for the octopus, but I can't because of the old man. He is so happy with his catch, so proud, that I start to laugh. I can hear that it is odd laughter, with something panicky in it, but maybe that isn't obvious to him and he joins in anyway. We stand on the shore and laugh until the tears run down our faces and I don't suppose either of us knows why. When we calm down at last he pats me on the shoulder and heads back towards his hut. When he is almost at the doorway he turns and holds up the octopus, shouting something that I don't understand. I'm not about to go and ask him to repeat whatever it is, so I nod and wave and wander back towards our house.

The whole family is gathered in the main room of the house as the sun goes down. The twins are playing one of their endless, mis-named games of solitaire and the parents are up and dressed after a long siesta, drinking sherry. I am curled up on the sofa, resisting my mother's nagging to go and shower and rinse out my bikini and put on something nice before supper. Instead I am reading a rubbish book, a dog-eared unloved airport book that I found on a shelf, a book so truly rubbish that it is only by dint of fierce concentration that I can get from the end of one page to the next without giving in to the urge to fling it out over the balcony and into the cala. And if it weren't for the fact that that would give my mother another excuse to nag me, for being a litterbug, I would.

I haven't got round to telling anyone what happened with the octopus. The twins never bothered to ask why I'd been running up and down waving my arms about and by the time my parents roused themselves from their afternoon torpor I was wrestling with the bad book and not in the mood to talk.

So the others are even more surprised than I when there is a loud knocking at the door of the house and a shout of:

"¡Bon dia! Lluís."

A moment later the old man arrives amongst us carrying an earthenware pot of venerable age and blackness. In it, there is octopus stew. Still bubbling. Enough for everyone.

8

Lluís and the octopus are in my head as soon as I wake. I swing my legs out of bed with a strange feeling that it takes me a moment to recognise as a sense of purpose. On the way to the kitchen to make coffee, I scoop up yesterday's newspaper from the floor where I threw it last night. It is still folded over at the page. I read the column again:

"The dead man has yet to be formally identified. Cause of death is to be determined by a post-mortem examination. Police are appealing for witnesses to come forward."

I stare hard at the terrible little photo and try to subtract twenty years from the face that stares blankly at me. For a moment or two I'm convinced that the crazy idea I've woken up with is just that. And then I feel blood rush into my face and the paper starts to shake in my hand as the eyes in the picture grow unmistakably familiar. Despite the graininess of the photo I am suddenly absolutely sure that the dead man is my Lluís. Lluís of the octopus stew – and everything that came after. The change from twenty years ago is not that great after all: his face looked worn-out and empty like this for much of the time even when I knew it. Not always. There were times when it sparkled with laughter, like the day with the octopus, and you could catch a glimpse of a much younger man – a man whose life had once held possibilities. The possibilities are over now. The possibilities have shrunk to this: *cause of death to be determined by a post-mortem examination.*

I've always wondered if it's true that when you die your life passes before you. Always wondered if in fact what rushes before your eyes at the last (rushes away from you actually, out of reach forever) are all the things you haven't done, rather than all the things you have. The way I felt when the midwife said: "It's a girl" and one half of all the possibilities I had imagined for my inchoate child receded before my eyes like the view through a collapsing telescope.

Is that how it was for Lluís as he fell, if he did fall? All the things he hadn't done, and there must have been plenty, flying away from him. Or maybe he was unconscious when he fell. Perhaps he had a stroke. Or a heart attack. Was he even up on the cliff-top at all or did he get into the water somewhere else, from a boat maybe, and wash up there? I don't know and nor, clearly, do the police.

I read the scrap of newsprint again. It yields no more information than before. I dwell on what there is. Nothing about a date for a funeral, which isn't really surprising, when there's a post mortem still to perform. Nothing about a family either. I don't know where to find his family, if one exists, so instead I carry the paper out with me to the only place I know.

His old hut is still there of course, not far from my place and the house my parents rented all those years ago. It squats at the water's edge – a small white fortress with its door and window facing away from the sea and the tramuntana – just at the point where the path along the foreshore runs out into wet pebbles. The cala bends away from the open sea here, narrows and begins to turn into an everglade, with reeds growing in the muddy shallows where the fresh water of a stream meets the salt of the sea. The hut is freshly white-washed and the door is painted a glossy dark green. The mess of Lluís's old paint pots and rags that used to occupy the small yard beside the hut is gone.

There is a boat pulled up there instead – a new semi-inflatable rib with a big outboard. Not Lluís's. His boat was an old-fashioned Menorcan *llaud*, equipped with a small thump-thump of a diesel engine down among the bilges and wooden oars stowed together in rowlocks mounted high above the gunwale on the starboard side. I look up the cala, but the broken-down old jetty where his boat used to be tied up has gone. Some time in the last twenty years the village authorities have had a spring clean. Most of the flotsam and jetsam of old jetties made from rough planks, pallets and packing cases have been replaced by a regimented row of municipal efforts – part of the general smartening-up of the cala that has happened since I was a girl. I wonder when Lluís and his boat became too shabby for the authorities to tolerate. When he himself was tidied away to live elsewhere.

His hut is shut up tight and still, just as it has been ever since I first arrived back on the cala. I came here looking for him the very first day, not sure what I would do or say if I found him, not sure even if he would remember me, but unable to resist looking just the same. His place was immaculately empty, like all the other holiday houses, and I felt – I'm not sure what. Disappointment yes, but also, perhaps, relief. Relief that I would not have to explain myself to him, even though I had the feeling that he would understand what I was doing here, if anyone could. Or at any rate that he would be less likely to judge me than most people.

But he was not here and I assumed he had died. It was hardly a surprise. He seemed ancient to me twenty years ago. It was what I had told myself to expect. I certainly never dreamed he could be alive and yet not here. This was his place. The only place I could imagine him. For weeks I did half think to see him come stumping round the corner but I kept telling myself not to be stupid, that he must have been dead for years. And now it appears that only hours, maybe even minutes, kept us apart. I feel suddenly robbed, resentful.

I try to see inside the hut one last time through the single small window that gives onto the path but the wall is a metre thick and the glass set into the inner edge. It is like looking down a chimney when the fire is out. It is clear that Lluís has been gone for some time and now, unless I'm wrong about that photo, unless everything I feel in my guts is wrong, he is gone for good.

I stand on his little verandah for a while but the heat of the sun drives me back into the shade of the pines and tamarisk trees that still grow beside his front door. Sitting down on his step, with the whitewashed stone cool against the backs of my thighs, I find myself wanting to cry. That hasn't happened since I came to the island. So I shake my head and try to concentrate on Lluís.

It would be wrong to say that everything that has happened to me since I was fifteen is due to Lluís. That would make him responsible for all the choices I've made since, as well as all the twists in my fate that genes, environment and happenstance have raveled together. It's far too heavy a burden to place on anyone, and especially someone who only intended to do a good turn. But it is true to say that nothing that has happened to me since would have happened without him doing what he did. It seems suddenly unfair that I never had the chance to repay the debt and now I never will.

To calm myself, I wander out onto the jetty closest to Lluís's hut, scuffing the edge of each plank with the rope binding on the toe of my shoe. The cala is quiet today, especially here in the silted shallows away from the main channel. The water is a glass paperweight, inset with stones and the silver flecks of small fish. Sitting on the end of the jetty it seems easier to let the idea of Lluís go. And I do try.

9

The wedding was stiff, formal and attended by all the right people. Everybody Catalina knew who was anybody was there. And nobody she liked. The packed service in the Cathedral was followed by a reception held, like all major family occasions for generations, on the first floor *piano nobile* at her family palazzo.

The bride wore antique lace culled from the wedding gowns of her mother and aunt, so that every appearance of sumptuousness should be kept up, despite the slump that gripped the world in general and her father's business in particular. If the guests whispered that the food served at the wedding feast was of less than the first quality and in less than the most generous quantities, Catalina did not hear them. If they said that the bride looked pale and the groom looked like the cat whose bowl of milk had turned to cream, she did not hear them.

She was too busy listening for the sound she had been expecting all through the wedding mass, the sound of running feet on the cathedral flagstones. And a voice she loved, telling them to stop, telling them this could not happen.

But there were no footsteps, either in the church or across the marble floors of her father's house. No voice. No one to save her from her own petulant decision to acquiesce to her father's wishes. No one to save her from having to endure the hand of her new husband on her elbow, steering her around the room to accept the congratulations of Ciudadella society on her good fortune.

She caught sight of herself once, in the long gilt-framed mirrors that hung between the windows. She hardly recognised the ghostly figure of a young aristo-cratic woman wearing a small fixed smile. Her swinging plait was gone, her hair pinned up and covered by a lace mantilla fixed with a long-toothed comb. Even her eyes reflected empty like deep dark pools.

The figure at her side she tried not to recognise at all. But with his heavy black tail coat and dark, shadowed saturnine face he did remind her of someone. Of a line drawing in one of her school books: of Hades leading Persephone down into the underworld.

She had seen the ecstasy of delight on his face when she walked unsteadily toward him at the altar, when he realised that his ambition was actually going to be real-ised. He had patted her hand as they came out of the cathedral's incense-scented gloom and murmured some-thing about how privileged he felt, on such a wonderful day.

She had said nothing, hating that word "privileged", the worst he could have chosen. Now, the party ground on as if it would never end and she could not even get away from Mascaró for a second, so determined was he to keep her by his side. She began to feel as if he had in-corporated her into his wedding trousseau, like the right walking stick or the right shoes. She was a prize that he had won, and the fact that she was a living breath-ing person mattered not a bit. She already knew why he wanted to marry her, but knowing was one thing, being paraded around the room as if he was showing off a new horse, was quite another.

At last, hours after she thought she couldn't stand another second of meaningless remarks from meaning-less people, the guests began to drift away. It had been arranged that the newly-weds would spend their wedding night in one of the guest chambers in the bride's house. Mascaró was in negotiations for the purchase of a house for himself and his bride with a highly-respectable figure in the town whose commercial stock had fallen even further and faster than Catalina's father's. But the unwilling seller had not quite been screwed down to the price Mascaró had set by the time of the wedding, so the young man had been content to plant himself temporarily under his new father-in-law's roof.

As they stood at the door, saying goodnight to their guests, Catalina wondered if there was any chance she could sneak away back to her old room, but then her mother came to stand beside her:

"Catalina," she whispered. "Why don't you leave Joan to handle this with your father? You should be getting ready for your wedding night. I will come and brush out your hair for you. And there's something I want to say to you."

Catalina slipped her hand out from the crook of her husband's arm, where it had been resting for what seemed like an eternity. He looked surprised and tried to draw it back, but then he noticed his mother-in-law smiling at him. She gestured towards the stairs:

"Come up in a few minutes. Most people will have gone by then. She'll be waiting for you."

She said it in a coquettish voice, as if it would be she who was waiting for him, not the strained, silent child-woman standing next to her.

Catalina followed her mother up to the big old-fashioned room that had been made ready for the happy couple. A fire was burning in the grate, though it was not a cold night, and the best white linen was starched and stretched out over what she knew from childhood bouncing to be a fiendishly rutted and ancient mattress. Rose petals from the garden had been scattered over the pillows and vases of flowers stood on either side of the bed. A fine white lawn nightdress she had never seen before hung from the heavy old armoire, ghostly by the firelight.

She allowed herself to be led over to the stool in front of the dressing table and there her mother gently pulled out the comb and began to un-pin her hair. Catalina looked at herself in the mirror and realised finally what she had done. Her dreams were over. Lluís had not come to save her. She was a married woman and from tonight she would sleep every night in a bed with a man she didn't even like.

The tears came before her mother had dropped the third hair-pin into the little silver dish on the dressing table. She let them come and her mother didn't try to stop them. She just carried on with her task and when all the pins were out she picked up the hairbrush and started to stroke it gently through her daughter's long dark hair.

Catalina laid her head down on the table and sobbed. She felt her mother's hand replace the brush and smooth her hair away from her face:

"There, there," she said. "It's bound to be a little frightening, the first time. It'll be fine, though, when you're used to it. He's a very suitable young man, you know. Everyone says so. Just try to please him, Catalina. Try not to be too prickly for once. It'll be easier for you, you know, if you just make an effort to be a good wife. And don't worry if it hurts a little. It won't always, you know."

Catalina lifted her head and spoke through sniffles:

"If what hurts?"

Her mother patted her shoulder.

"Don't worry about it. It's all part of growing up, being a married woman. Now, dry your eyes and let's get you

43

into your nightdress. It wouldn't do for your husband to barge in before we're ready for him, would it?"

She started to undo the hundred tiny buttons fastening the back of Catalina's wedding dress and finally she was able to wriggle out of the sleeves and drop it down to the floor. As she stepped out of it she shivered, despite the fire. Her mother folded the precious lace over her arm and when Catalina had dropped her under-clothes onto the stool she held out the nightdress.

"Can't I wear my old one?"

"Indeed you can't! On your wedding night? What would Joan think?"

"But that one's virtually transparent!"

Her mother laughed and put the nightdress over her daughter's head, pulling her arms through the sleeves one after the other as she used to do when she was a very little girl.

"Like I said, it's your wedding night. Now, if you're shy get into bed and wait for him. Let him unwrap his present for himself."

She pulled back the top sheet and Catalina could see nothing for it but to slip under it. The bed felt cold and damp as a tomb and she pulled the sheet up to her chin. Her mother laughed again and bent over to kiss her forehead:

"I'll see you in the morning, darling. Everything will seem different then, I promise you."

10

There are two big rocks awash in the gap between this inlet and the next. Everyone who knows the waters here knows where they are but they aren't always easy to see, being so flat that in calm weather the waves slide over them without much fuss or splash. Generally, at the end of the winter they are marked with a buoy. But if the storms are bad and the buoy cuts loose it isn't always thought worth the trouble to replace it. And some years maybe they don't bother to attach it in the first place. Although the islanders are generally a correct and meticulous people they don't have much time for fools and fools are the only people who benefit from the buoy. Any sensible person knows about the rocks or can read a chart, so this is one piece of municipal housekeeping that isn't thought strictly essential. There has been no buoy on the rocks this year.

There is an even less obvious rock in the channel between *Illa Gran* and the tip of the shore. It is wide and flat and lies no more than eighteen inches beneath the surface. Passage between the islands and the shore is not advised except for boats of very shallow draft or for sailors who know the channel well and so this rock is never marked. I haven't been down this channel for twenty years and yet, when I see the grey outline of that rock slip past on the right hand side, I am back sailing a dinghy through the gap. And I can still hear the crash and feel the boat vibrate and stop as its keel slams against the rock.

We do not touch the rock today. The kid knows his

way too well to go over it or to stray too near the shallows by the island either. He steers the dinghy straight down the centre of the channel until all the rocks are behind us. Then, without reducing speed, he swings the tiller over and turns hard left so that we are running straight for the cliff of *Illa Gran*. In a few seconds it seems that we must crash into the outcrop of limestone. I glance back at him and immediately see that he wants me to be scared. His face is set in what he must hope is an expression of kamikaze intent. I turn from kneeling in the bow to sit facing him with my arms stretched out along the gunwale, ignoring the danger. He doesn't move and nor do I, except to give him a very small smile to show I'm not the right girl to play chicken with.

He throttles back, finally, as the high walls of rock pass me on either side and we cross the threshold of a small round bay. A rolling wave lifts the stern of the boat as our wash hits the rocks and carries us through the narrow entrance to the bay in a rush. With the engine in neutral, Billy runs forward and drops the anchor into a patch of weed five feet down. He reverses a way and I peer over the side to see the anchor catch and hold. I give him the thumbs up and he kills the engine.

"You knew", he says, partly disappointed, partly (perhaps) impressed.

I am tempted to say that I was coming here before he was born. But no one likes to be patronised, least of all the young, and so I just shrug. I like the fact that he has chosen to bring me here though, in settlement of his debt. Because I'd forgotten about this place, hadn't thought about it in years, and I'm glad to have the chance to see it again.

It's even smaller than I remember it, but just as extra-ordinary. An almost complete circle, the break in the rocks for the entrance not more than eight feet wide and almost invisible from outside unless you know it's there. On a calm day like today the motion of the sea breaks up and dissipates as it encounters the disruption of the rocks and the gap. The water inside the bay is flat and clear to the bottom. There is no beach but the shingle is ground very fine in places around the rim and I remember, when I was a girl, eating lunch on the miniature shore with towels spread on the stones. The seabed is a mixture of sand, flat rocks and weed and the water is so clear that the sharp little sea urchins stand out on the submerged rocks like five o'clock shadow. The biggest patch of weed is under the high rock, the one my father and the twins used to jump off when they wanted to frighten my mother. If everything else looks smaller, the drop from that rock looks much bigger. It seems that the changing perspective of age has its relativities like everything else.

Billy and I are alone in the bay and I remember the one unsatisfactory thing about it. It should have been an entirely secret place, where no one else ever came. It had a rare quality of separateness – the double isolation that came from being an island off an island – and of containment, the only view being of the sky. Yet, though it was only accessible from the sea and only visible from a certain angle it was well-known to the locals and often occupied by other boats. It was impossible to tell whether anyone else was inside before you entered from the sea and it was fear of that, rather than the narrowness of the entrance, that used to make us hold our breath as we passed in between the rocks.

Today, though, we have been lucky. For the moment at least, we do not have to share the bay with strangers.

I realise that Billy is watching me. I have become so used to thinking and not talking that I have almost lost any sense of how it must look.

"You want to swim?" he asks.

I nod and he tosses me a pair of flippers and a mask. I have a bikini on underneath my T-shirt and shorts but as I move to pull off my T-shirt I feel suddenly the strangeness of the situation. The enclosure of the bay makes me feel that we are in a private space, that what we are doing is clandestine, even illicit. Billy is sitting with his back to me, dipping his feet and the flippers in the water so that he can slide them on.

I turn away as I pull off my T-shirt, but I needn't have bothered. There is a soft splash and Billy is gone. I bend to pick up the spare flippers and follow him over the side. Water closes over me for a moment but isn't cold enough to take my breath away. The limestone bowl warms the water like the palm of a hand around a glass of rioja. If my memory is true, the only really cold water is under the surface near the entrance, where the open sea creeps in. I float on my back while I put on the flippers, which are too tight – his little sister's? The mask dangles from my arm in a loose bracelet. Billy is spitting into his mask and treading water a few feet away. He puts the mask on and sucks it to his face. Then he points to the area of weed under the high rock, duck dives and glides away doing silent breaststroke arms just under the surface of the water.

I sluice water in the mask and hold it to my face, smelling the old rubber and ozone smell. It jolts me back almost too vividly to my childhood and I hurry to put it on, stretching the strap round the back of my head and breathing in hard to make it seal. The world turns bleary and strange and the rubber rim of the mask bites into my face. I let my feet float up behind me and lay my face onto the water, perspex lens first. Rocks and sand and darting fish leap into focus and I give a kick that carries me forward a foot or two. I turn over an arm and then twist my head sideways to suck in a breath. The rush of memory drops away as I concentrate on the mechanical, kick my other leg, turn over the other arm and breathe again, tasting salt on my tongue.

Beneath me, the clean rocks and sand start to be smudged with weed and ahead I see a slow whirl of bubbles left behind by Billy's flippers. The weed is only two or three feet below my belly and I feel an old familiar tickle of panic that something in there might rise up and bite me. It's a strange kind of claustrophobia but no less real for that. Above me, a shadow falls across the sun-lit water and, glancing up, I see the outline of the tall rocks passing over my head. Billy swims deeper into the shadow and, although I don't really want to, I follow. The water grows colder with every stroke as the sun is eclipsed by the over-hang. At the same time the water turns from blue to grey. A shiver washes through me that even the change in temperature doesn't warrant. Then there is a new source of light ahead, wavering yellow in the greyness and Billy half-turns to me, gesturing with the torch I hadn't seen in his hand. We are in the mouth of a cave now, one that I never knew was here, and in a moment it changes the way I feel about the bay, adding a sinister dark angle to what I'd always thought of as a miraculous pool of bright sunlight in the sea.

As the kid swims deeper into the cave the roof hangs close upon our heads. I don't like it. If I were with some-one my own age I wouldn't hesitate to turn back and wait outside in the cove but some adult pride makes me not want to admit my fear to a boy. I purse my lips and blow out a long slow string of bubbles to control my breath-ing. When I next turn my head I see that he has stopped swimming and is treading water with the torch aimed upwards. He pushes his mask up onto his forehead and is smiling through the exertion of staying afloat:

"See?" he says.

I look up and I do see, a forest of stalactites that shine slick and yellow in the beam of his torch. I nod and float onto my back, pushing my mask up too. They remind me of all the other caves I've seen, in the Yucatan, in northern Spain, in Derbyshire. Scenes from another life. And then all at once they make me think of something else – of darkness and death – and in that instant I forget how to float and as I sink my arms begin to thrash and saltwater gags my nose and throat. The next thing I know I'm out in the sunshine again, clinging to the edge of the boat, breathing hard, water streaming off me into the bilges.

The side of the boat dips beside me as Billy grabs it with one hand and rolls his torch over the gunwale with the other.

"Okay?" he says in English and I wonder if he is going to be triumphant at having scared me after all. But when I feel calm enough to glance over at him he only looks uncertain, concerned even. In that moment he becomes a person to me, no longer a cipher, no longer the kid I've made up for my own entertainment. In that moment he becomes as subtle and sympathetic as anyone I've ever known, not the approachable blank I fancied he was, hermetically sealed in adolescence. I look down at where his fingers are gripping white against the gunwale of the boat and notice that he bites his nails. I can feel his eyes on me and it dawns on me that he is interested in who I am after all, just as much as any adult would be.

He opens his mouth to say something else, but I don't want to hear what it is, so I push away from the boat and float on my back, staring up at the sky, trying to get control of my breathing again. It is mid-afternoon and the sky is a perfect pure blue. Heaven. Pure heaven, to set against that terrifying glimpse of the underworld beneath the rocks. And I suddenly want to be up there, in the air, instead of down here, so I strike out for the shore, kick my flippers off on the shingle and start to scale the rocks. Billy swings round, one arm still holding onto the boat, and watches me for a minute, and then, with lazy beautiful strokes he follows.

The rocks are jagged. They cut into my feet, and I graze a knee as I pull myself up, but it's worth it when I'm standing on the top, looking down on the amphitheatre of blue water. It is definitely higher than I remember and either that fact, or the breeze blowing in-shore, makes the hairs stand up on my arms and legs. I stand straight and tall and take a deep breath. The air smells sweet and salt and the sun beats hot on my skin. I feel alive. Don't know when I've felt so alive. And I shut my eyes and step out into space.

The fall is short and swept away by the rush of bubbles and the cool water. I plummet down and my feet brush weed before I kick once and rise rapidly to the surface, coughing and flicking hair out of my eyes. I am still shaking my head when there is a great splash behind me and a wave washes over my shoulders. Then there is silence for a moment, before Billy erupts out of the water, laughing and snorting. I turn to face him but he takes one breath and dives back down. The sea is so clear that I can see his fair hair streaming out behind him as he parts the water in front of him with his hands and drags it past. It seems to be happening in slow-motion and yet it's only a couple of seconds before I feel his hands around my waist and he pulls me down under the water.

He kisses me until we run out of air. When we re-surface he pulls away and looks at me, as if he isn't sure that what was allowed in that dimension is still allowed in this. By way of answer, I pull him so close we can hardly tread water without kicking each other, so close that the last few millimetres of water separating skin from skin are squeezed out and I can feel the entire length of his body against mine.

We sink back down below the water and I'm not sure either of us cares if we drown. Taste and touch are the only senses that count as we cling to each other. We breathe each other's air. I feel his fingers pull at the knots at my neck and back and hips and my bikini drifts away. He kicks off his shorts in one convulsive movement and lifts me by the waist and then slides me down onto him. The dinghy drifts alongside us and Billy grabs the gunwale with one hand and presses the other into the small of my back, holding me tight against him. We look at each other for a moment, mouths ajar, panting. And what happens next is just what I need, fast and strong and unsentimental. Sex. Pure sex. No words. No tears. No love. The only need the need to come. And I do. And he does. And it feels like a baptism. It feels like the first time. It feels like I've just been born and I'm going to live forever.

11

There is a knock at the door. When the old woman opens it there are two Guardia Civil in their olive green uniforms on the pavement. They have their hats under their arms and sober, composed expressions on their faces. Nevertheless, she shudders slightly at the sight of them. It may be thirty years since the Civiles did Franco's bidding, but she still thinks of them as his henchmen.

"*Digame?*" she says, shortly.

"May we come in, Señora? We have something serious to tell you."

Immediately she starts to worry for her son or – worse – her grandson and she falls back from the door to let them enter. Once inside they offer her one of her own seats, but she declines and so they all stand awkwardly in the centre of the room. The older policeman clears his throat:

"We are very sorry to have to tell you, Señora, that your husband is dead."

She laughs. She can't help it. The sound just comes out of her mouth without warning.

"I should hope so," she says. "He's been in the cemetery forty years."

The two officers look at each other, puzzled. One takes out a notebook and flicks through the pages. Each is struck by the horrified thought that they are breaking bad news to the wrong person.

"Forgive us, you are Catalina Gallo Mascaró?"

"I am."

"And your son is Francisco Mascaró, living in Maó?"

She nods. Afraid once more that they meant son when they said husband. For their part, they look relieved. The notebook is buttoned back into a breast pocket.

"Then it was your son, Señora, who suggested we visit you. We had reason to believe that he was the dead man's next of kin, but when we informed him of the death he said that we should speak to you because legally you were still his wife, and therefore you are the next of kin."

"I don't understand," she says. But even as she speaks the words, it dawns on her who they are talking about and she sways and would fall if one of the officers didn't grab her arm and hold her upright. Still, she sags against his side and with his colleague's help he drags her over to her old armchair and sits her down. The other policeman goes off to find the kitchen to fetch a glass of water while the first fingers his mobile phone, wondering whether to call an ambulance.

But before he has reached a decision, before his partner comes back with the water, the old woman composes herself. Her back straightens, she raises her head and regards him with a calm gaze:

"You're talking about Lluís Sintes, aren't you?"

The policeman nods.

"How did he die?"

The man glances towards the door, wishing his partner would re-appear so that they can deal with this together.

"We're not entirely sure yet. His body was found near the foot of some cliffs, on the north coast. Some tourists out walking spotted it. The coastguard recovered the body from the water. We're not even sure exactly when he died. The post mortem results should tell us that."

"The day of the tramuntana," she says, quietly: "Tuesday."

The policeman glances at the door again, then squats down beside the old woman.

"How do you know that?"

She looks down into his face and speaks without expression:

"I felt it. Felt something give. Like a thread breaking. I didn't understand what it was at the time. I couldn't sleep, Tuesday, and I didn't know why. Something just seemed ... out of place. Now it makes sense."

"You must have been very close, to sense a thing like that."

She looks at him sharply, as if she suspects him of sarcasm, but says nothing. The policeman frowns:

"Your son, though, he didn't seem to be close to his father. He came down to identify the body, but he was adamant that any decisions about, well, the funeral and so forth ... should be left to you. We thought he would want to break the news to you himself, but he asked us to do it. We invited him to come with us, but ..."

He tails off, embarrassed at the implication of what he is saying, feeling that he may be rubbing salt into family wounds.

The old woman seems unusually calm, her voice steady as she says:

"Lluís Sintes was my husband many years ago. We were separated before my son was born. My son has always looked on his step-father as his true father, so no, they were not ... close. But I am surprised he would tell you that Lluís was still my husband. There was a law passed, many years ago by Franco, which invalidated marriages like ours. As far as the law is concerned, Lluís and I were never married."

The policeman, still crouched by her side, frowns:

"I think you're mistaken about that, Señora. In fact, I wouldn't have known this, but your son explained it to us and when we checked it out we found it was true. You're right that there was a law passed just after the War that annulled divorces and civil marriages performed at the time of the Second Republic, but that law was itself repealed in the 1980s. Your marriage to Señor Sintes has been valid again for the last twenty years."

She shakes her head in bewilderment:

"And it was my son who told you this?"

"Yes, but as I say, we checked it out because it seemed so odd, and it turned out he was right. Didn't you know?"

"No," she says, quietly. "I didn't know. But it wouldn't have made any difference. Lluís and I haven't spoken for sixty years."

12

Dad finds the Laser down in the boathouse. It is suspended from the roofbeams in a cradle of ropework, sails and rudder hanging beside it in bags, like a couple of hams in a butcher's window. I think he's trying to make it up to me – about Johnny. Trying to prove to me that I can still have a good time on a family holiday. Trying, maybe, to hold on to the last few moments of my childhood even though he must know in his heart that they have already gone.

Lucky for him, with no end in sight to the longest three weeks of my life, I'm desperate enough to give anything a go. At least with a boat to sail I can get away from the others for a while. So, after a good bit of trial and error, arguing over how we used to do it when we went sailing on the local reservoir, we manage to rig it up. He says he thinks he ought to take it out first on a test run. Standing on the end of the jetty, I watch him zig across the cala and zag back, timing his tacks to avoid the boats moored up and down the shoreline. He's out of practice and I laugh when he scrapes along the side of a fishing boat, hitting his head on an overhanging lobster pot. But then he reaches the open sea, hardens up the sail and shoots out across the water.

Until that moment there's something ridiculous about the little boat. And him in it. But as soon as the sail stops billowing in the swell and snaps taut there is nothing ridiculous about it at all. I can just make out my father, who had been hunched down in the cockpit while he tacked, leaning far out over the side now, with the boat

57

heeling. He's flying along and I know he must be shouting with exhilaration. I stop laughing and stamp the jetty planks.

"Come back Dad," I shout. "I want a go."

But he doesn't come back. In seconds he has disappeared from view round the rocks at the end of the cala and though I wait nearly ten minutes for him to reappear on the opposite tack, there is no sign of him. I wander back to the house, but even from the balcony I cannot catch a glimpse of the white sail anywhere.

More than half an hour has gone by, and I have long since slumped down onto a sun-lounger with the not-remotely-thrilling thriller, before I hear a shout from downstairs:

"Kate!"

It's Dad's voice, and I put my head over the balcony:

"Where did you go? You've been ages. I thought you were just going to test the rigging."

He is standing knee-deep in the water, holding the boat steady and he laughs:

"Oh, I've tested the rigging. Took her right round the islands. I've set a new record – thirty-five minutes, twenty seconds. Care to see if you can beat me?"

I shrug my shoulders, unwilling to let on that actually I am dying to have a go. But I throw down the book and run down the stairs to the boathouse, tying up my hair as I go with the hair-band that lives around my wrist.

"Life-jacket", he says as I emerge, screwing up my eyes, into the sunlight.

"You didn't take one."

"I'm old enough and ugly enough. You're too precious. Get a life-jacket."

"I'm a better swimmer than you are."

"That may be so, but if the boom knocks you out that won't help. Fetch a life-jacket, sweetheart. You're wasting the breeze. It'll die soon – and if you want to beat my record you'd better make the most of it."

I sigh and step back inside for one of the lumpen ugly yellow life-jackets that I know are hanging on a row of nails in the boathouse. The first one I pick smells stale and so does the second. I pull it on with distaste. I know it's going to ride up under my arm-pits when I get into the boat and hamper my movements when I tack. Worse than that, it makes me look and feel like a kid. I zip it up and then can't help but smile. At least it gives me cleavage.

Dad holds the boat as I climb aboard. It has been a year since we last went to the sailing club at home. Dad's been too busy at work to take us this season, the twins weren't really interested anyway, and I've had my O Levels to think about. Somehow, sailing is something that has just got dropped. Fallen through the cracks of family life and I hadn't even missed it. Except now I feel the stirrings of excitement as soon as I curl my toes under the webbing strap and reach out for the single rope that tightens and loosens the sail. The little boat bobs and jerks between the two neighbouring jetties like a racehorse in a starting stall, my father holding its head.

I glance up and smile at him, and it occurs to me that this may be the first time I've looked him straight in the eye in months. He grins back at me and without any warning gives the boat a mighty shove out into the cala. I rock back, off-balance, and squeal but I'm on my own now so I grab at the cord that drops the rudder and start to push down the centre board, not too far while I cross the shallows, then all the way into its slot when I reach the channel. And before I know it I'm sailing.

Looking over my shoulder before I make my first turn, I see my father is standing where I left him, a strange expression on his face. I lift my wrist and tap my watch face. The look dissolves as he smiles and gives me the thumbs-up to say he's already timing me. I turn my attention to the wake and the gentle furrow we're ploughing through the water tells me I have enough way on to make my first turn.

"Ready about," I tell the non-existent crew, from force of habit: "Lee ho," and I push the tiller away from me as far as it will go until I feel the boat begin to turn and the boom swing in towards me. I duck to let it pass over my head and shift my weight to the other side of the cockpit, catching the breeze in the opposite side of the sail. The little boat shivers with uncertainty for a few seconds before it gathers pace again. There is a speed-boat moored right in my path and I have to juggle, pulling in the sail, heeling over more than I like, to squeeze down the side of it. As soon as we're past I turn slightly into wind, the boat levels off and above the slap of the wavelets against the hull I can hear my heart beating.

It takes me three more tacks to reach open water. From the way Dad disappeared so quickly from view, I figure he must have sailed round the bottom end of the islands, up the far side and back home along the inner shore. With the wind blowing straight across the islands, it should be much of a muchness, going his way or the reverse. But I just have a hunch that the wind will be at its flukiest in the gap between the bottom of the islands and tip of the cala. And if that's right, I decide I'd sooner have what wind there is behind me, pushing me home, than in my face and having to turn this way and that to catch it in my sails.

Decision made, I point the boat just to the left of the breakers at the top end of the islands and haul in my sail. The boat tilts under the press of wind and, stabbing my toes against the wall of the cockpit, I shuffle my backside out across the narrow deck until only my thighs are inside the boat and the rest of my body is canted out over the sea flying past beneath me. This brings the boat back almost level, which feels less scary, though I know it means we're moving even faster through the water. Hair whips across my face and, as we crest a rolling wave and slide down its curling up-slope, I can't help but let out a cowboy's "Yee-ha!" and laugh into the wind.

It takes me three more tacks and a little boxy manoeuvre to get round the rocks at the top of the islands. The sea is rougher on the far shore but once I make the turn the wind is at my back and I can let out the sail. The boat flattens off as the boom swings out wider and the sail cups all the wind it can hold. Though we are probably moving at least as fast as before, all seems suddenly peaceful and I slip back into the well of the cockpit and snatch a glance at my watch. Eighteen minutes. Yes! I shout triumphantly. You went the wrong way round, Dad! I'm going to beat you!

At the bottom of the second island I enter the channel and turn for the cala and home. The wind is right behind us now, so I loosen the mainsheet altogether and the boom swings even further out to sit at right angles to the boat. Water rushes past the hull and the wake forms a perfect white-edged V behind us. Then just as I am thinking how apt the term "plain sailing" really is, the wind flukes and the sail flaps. The boom swings back towards me and our momentum falters.

I lean the boat into a gentle turn, feeling for the wind that was so present and correct a minute ago. Suddenly I find it and the boom flies out wide again, filling the sail with a loud crack. The boat lurches forward and I edge the steering back on course. But no sooner is the bow pointing back to the centre of the channel than the wind dies on me again. The sail billows and slaps at itself and the dinghy begins to rock end to end in the choppy swell. The channel is narrow here and I know there are rocks to one side, if not both. So I sit and wait, hoping that the wind is just taking a breather and will pick up again where it left off. A couple of minutes pass, though, and the boat is still stationary, jostled by the waves. I look at my watch again and realise that something has to be done if I really am going to beat Dad's record.

I move the tiller over, but because we're not moving forward the steering doesn't answer. The boat bobs and the sail ripples all along its length. Impatiently, I push the tiller harder and just as I do the wind sweeps back with a vengeance, into the wrong side of the sail. The gybe happens so fast I don't even have time to cry out. With a mighty rush the boom flies past my head, the tiller is wrenched out of my hand and suddenly I am not sailing but airborne, a very short flight that ends in a rush of cold water.

The life-jacket keeps me from going very far under and when I surface I lie there for a moment, taking stock. The Laser is on its side and the sail is flat on the water. I find that I still have the end of the rope in my hand, and when I flick it I can see it runs loose to the end of the sail. Good. Getting the main-sheet caught on something is usually what makes it tricky to get these things up again. I swim round to the far side, where the bottom end of the centre-board sticks out from the hull. Reaching up, I wrap my arms around the board and kick my legs to turn the boat into wind. When it's pointing roughly the right way I kick extra hard, trying to pull myself up on top. Damn life-jacket! Its bulk stops me getting my body up over the board. I try again, pulling up with my arms and straining my legs to kick as hard as I can. No good. But the third time I make it. At once, I feel the boat start to right itself and I reach up to grab the side and step over into the cockpit as my mounting-block disappears back under the water.

The wet sail flaps and spatters me with drops of water as I turn downwind again, gingerly this time. The boat picks up speed, none the worse for its dunking. I can feel the muscles in my legs and arms humming with the effort of righting the boat and I shake my head to clear soaking strands of hair from my face. My hair-tie has got lost in the crash and hair whips around me, blinding me and sticking to my mouth. I put a hand up to wipe it away. Perhaps that's why I don't see the rock.

I don't even know it is a rock at the time. All I know is that the boat stops with a shuddering blow that catapults me forward the length of the cockpit, tearing the tiller and main-sheet from my hands and slamming me against the mast. I can't quite follow what happens next. There's a moment when everything seems to hang in the air and then everything tips and I'm in the water again, with the sail wrapped around my legs. As I try to kick free I have the sensation of being in a box and the lid closing. The life-jacket is still holding me up but it's dark now, something is pressing my face down into the water and it takes me a while to grasp that the Laser has turned completely turtle and I am underneath it. My legs still caught up, I struggle to drag myself along the underside of the deck with my arms until I can push my head up into the cockpit space. There I cling onto the foot strap and breathe hard.

I try to think, but thinking doesn't come easy in the dark space under a sail-boat off a rocky shore. Choppy waves working their way under the dinghy splash up into my nose and eyes and there is a strange metallic reverberation in the hull, which might be the end of the mast hitting against the seabed. I don't know. I shake my head and force myself to concentrate. I have to get free, get out and right the boat. Now!

I kick my legs and wriggle to try and free whatever is tied round them. But it doesn't work so I have to take one hand off the strap and feel around to see how I am caught up. My ankle is tangled up in the rope, and the rope's free end must be caught round something else too because it's cinched tight round my leg. When I kick I seem to be lifting the whole weight of the boom and the sail flaps around me, catching at my other leg. I stop kicking and reach down to try and slip my ankle out of its trap but the rope is pulled too tight and I need to work at it with my fingers. The weight of the boom and the water-filled sail mean I can't lift my leg up very far, so I have to let go of the boat and go down under the water. I try it, and come up spluttering and grabbing for the strap. The bloody life-jacket is so big and so buoyant I can't sink deep enough to get a good grip on the rope. I strap-hang for a minute but I know what I have to do. The zip on the jacket is stiff and I shudder as cold water rushes in to replace the layer of warm water that had been pressed against my skin. I shrug the jacket off one arm so it floats up behind me. I try to go back down under the water but the jacket's buoyancy is still pulling me up so I shake it off the other arm too and, taking a deep breath, forget about it and let myself drop under the water.

The first breath doesn't last long enough for me to work the rope loose. Nor does the second. But as the water closes over my head for the third time I begin to panic – and panic gives me extra strength. I tear at the rope and finally manage to get a fingertip, then two, between it and my leg. I wrench with all my might and wriggle the noose over my heel and kick like I've never kicked before, a kick that sends me shooting up to crack my head against the inverted deck. I don't care. I'm free. I flail for the toe-strap and hang there, coughing and spitting sea-water.

Not for long though. I've spent too much time already in this dark cold box and I desperately need to see the sky again. The life-jacket is nowhere to be seen. I put one hand out to grip the side of the hull and dip under the water for what I hope is one last time, pushing the boat over my head. As I pop out into the sunlight it feels like being freed from prison, and I lie back and smile and then I see how close the rocks are and stop.

I still need to right the boat. Fast. The rocks are shattering waves only ten feet away and they will easily shatter us too if we drift onto them. I reach up to try and catch the centre-board but, because the boat has turned right over, the board is pointing straight at the sky and much further out of reach than before. After two or three fruitless leaps, I realise my only chance is to hook my toes onto the rim of the deck and throw myself as far as possible across the slippery hull to grab the board. But there's nothing to cling onto and I just keep sliding back into the water. Finally, I time my leap with a helpful wave that washes me towards the centre-board and I throw my arms round it. I cling there for a moment but the rocks are getting closer with each wave and I can't wait. Carefully, I climb to my feet and then lean backwards, holding onto the board. My weight should make the boat roll back upright again and it starts to come, but then it stops with a jerk. I bounce on the hull, rocking it gently at first and then with all my remaining strength but it will not shift. The noise of the surf is loud now and the rocks are right in front of me so I shuffle round to the other side of the board, trying not to slip down the slope of the hull, and lean the other way. The boat swings through its centre point. Then stops again.

Now I really do panic, because I know either the mast is stuck in rocks on the bottom, or the tangled rope is stopping the sail from emptying its weight of water and rising free. I can't be sure which, but it doesn't matter because either way I know I don't have the strength to go down there and sort it out and then climb back up here again. So I wrench and I wrench at the centre board, and I scream at it to Come on! but then my feet start to slip and as the board slides through my hands the hull leaps up to hit me in the face and ...

The next thing I know, a deep regular heart-beat is drumming in my ears. It takes me a while to think about what this means. The word: "alive" drifts into my head and lodges there. Thoughts begin to gather around it, like on-lookers, until there's enough of a crowd mustered to count as some kind of consciousness. I open my eyes and find myself looking at a pair of heroically gnarled feet. They are standing in a heap of fishing net strewn across dirty wooden boards. At the same moment my sense of smell kicks in (I mean, kicks) and I realise that the drumming noise is not my heart at all but a diesel boat engine somewhere underneath my cheek.

It comes to me that I am lying, tumbled like the day's catch, on the deck of an old *llaud*. The smell from its deck boards forces me to raise my head before my neck muscles feel ready to do it and then I see my rescuer. It is Lluís, crazy old Lluís of the octopus stew, and he looks at me and shakes his head and gestures me to lie back down. Which, despite the stench of fish, I do.

13

After the boat trip I keep myself to myself. The kid comes down to his boat most days, but I stay off the jetty, off the balcony. Once, I am downstairs doing some washing and I see a shadow pass the salt-streaked window. It is Billy, looking in, looking for me, and I freeze with my hands in the sink, waiting for him to knock or push open the door. But he doesn't have the guts for that and I watch as he looks up towards the balcony one last time, a smile ready and hopeful on his lips. I watch the smile collapse slowly and then he passes out of sight. I'm sorry for that smile but still I don't move. I even wait a few minutes before I wring out the washing, afraid that the sound of the water splashing into the sink will be audible outside and bring him back. But he has gone.

Then today, when I push open the door to the house there is a rustling noise and I can see that something is caught under it. I put my shopping bags down on the bottom step and stoop to pull out the piece of paper that is wedged under the door. It has concertinaed into a rough fan as I opened the door and its folds are gritty with dust and sand but when I shake it out the writing on it is legible. Appalling but legible.

There is no salutation on the note. Perhaps I never told him my name. I don't think I did. It just says in Spanish: "I have news of the old man." It is signed: "Billy" and then underneath in brackets and capitals he has written "(BIEL PONS)".

I had almost forgotten telling him about Lluís on the way back from the bay. The story just slipped out as we pottered home towards the cala. It was one of those moments when you can't help but say something personal, a gift, a token from your life. Marking one intimacy with another. I saw a film once where one character says to another: "Tell me something to make me love you." I ought to have known better. But that day I was feeling reckless, immortal, and so it seemed only natural to tell Billy the story of how Lluís saved my life.

The sliding window to the balcony squeaks as I push it back. Billy's boat is not on its mooring. His brother's boat is at the end of the jetty and the doors to their boathouse are closed. The brother rarely comes down to his boat before six o'clock in the evening.

My impression of him, from a distance, is that he couples the islanders' solemnity with the fisherman's natural wariness. He is a dour dark man who looks as if he goes out on the water not because he loves it, like Billy, but simply because it's preferable to staying on land where a man is likely to be harried, trapped and taxed. I've never caught him involved in a conversation that lasted more than a minute and even then his side of the talk seems to be mainly nods and shrugs. The most expressive thing I've seen him do is dip his head into his cupped hands to light his cigarette. It is his daily ritual as soon as he has backed the boat off the mooring and into the channel, leaning on the tiller with his thigh to free his hands and then tossing his head back when the cigarette catches the flame and letting the smoke stream away with the wind. It would be going too far to say that he looks happy then, but he looks as if life is momentarily bearable. He isn't a man I would care to approach with questions.

But there's no need because when I come out onto the balcony again a few minutes later the kid is back. He is on his own and, although he's busy with his engine and a petrol can, something about his posture tells me he's already seen my open door. He knows that I am here. Still, the minutes pass and he doesn't look my way. Clearly, he has made all the overtures he's going to make. I'm tempted to see how long he can string out his jobs around the boat before he has either to come looking for me or turn for home but then my eye falls on the note again and the bait – news of the old man – is too tempting to resist. Billy is nothing if not a talented fisherman.

Still, he doesn't look up until the toes of my espadrilles are squarely in his line of vision. He raises his head then and the sun must be directly behind me because he squints grotesquely.

"You're back," he says and I have a suspicion we're both relieved that he doesn't know my name. It might not be easy for him to call me by my Christian name and it would be absurd now to have him address me formally, using my surname as if I was his schoolteacher. Worse than absurd, it would be an admission that something transgressive had taken place, and I don't imagine either of us wants that.

"I'm back," I say, though I think we both know I haven't been away, and our conversation is shaping into a beauty.

Prepared for this contingency, I have brought two bottles of Coke from the fridge. I offer him one and he takes it as he climbs out of the boat and sits on the edge of the jetty. I sit down beside him and we swig from our bottles companionably enough with the hot afternoon sun on our backs.

"I got your note. Thanks."

He nods, and I wonder if taciturnity runs in the family, like flat feet or piles. I wait, but he just takes another long drink from his bottle, waiting me out.

"You said you had news? About the old man."

There hasn't been another word about Lluís in the paper and I thought that was the end of it. But maybe I have under-estimated Billy. Clearly, he has been making enquiries. Of whom, I've no idea. He seems in no hurry to share his findings, seems more intent on scraping the damp label off the Coke bottle with his thumb-nail. Finally, he plunders the family repertoire for a shrug and supplements it with a single word, as expressive of finality in Spanish as in English: "Dead."

My heart sinks. Of course he's dead. We know he's dead. The boy's an idiot, after all. A beautiful little idiot. I look up the cala towards Lluís's hut, his old vegetable patch, his path through the pine trees and the gorse scrub. He is gone, and I will never be able to re-pay him the debt I owe. Then the kid breaks in on my disappointment:

"He has a son though. I know where he is. I can take you to see him."

He stands up but this is going a little fast for me. It is my turn to squint into the sun.

"Who is he?"

"He is a lawyer in Maó. My mother knows a woman who works for him. I know where his office is."

Three sentences in a row leave me floundering in his wake. I wonder what grapevine has been tapped to yield with this information – and whether information has travelled both ways. Billy, clearly, is all prepared to go to Mahon right now to find the prodigal son. I am no-where near as ready. Stalling, I say:

"What sort of a lawyer is he?"

Billy shrugs sulkily. He didn't expect to be cross-examined and doesn't want to betray the limits of his knowledge.

Back inside my little house, the Yellow Pages from

the dresser are stiff with newness and the print smells fresh as I riffle the pages from the middle back to A for *Abogado*. The name that the boy has given me, Francisco Mascaró, is listed with an office in the Plaça del Princep in Mahon. He advertises himself in a discreet lined box as a specialist in property and testamentary matters. English is spoken, as is German.

Billy has followed me inside, though I didn't invite him, and is clearly waiting for me to reach for the phone. But I haven't used one in months, don't even know for sure whether the one on the pine dresser actually works, and when I do nothing more than write the lawyer's details on a piece of paper he grunts, unimpressed, and stands up. I think he is going to go but then he surprises me by taking from me the paper and the pen. I notice he fastidiously avoids touching my hand as he does so, and I'm glad. It will be so much easier if he understands that what happened out in the bay should stay there. He leans the paper against his knee and adds another number to the note, before handing it back:

"You can call me when you want to go to Maó. That's my phone number."

He pulls a small mobile phone out of his pocket to prove it to me. Then he slips off down the stairs and clatters the front door shut behind him.

14

It's not until I finally feel strong enough to pull myself up into a sitting position and can see over the side of the boat that I discover I'm not the only one Lluís has saved. There, behind us, tugging at the rope tied to the fishing boat's stern-post is the dinghy. Somehow Lluís has righted it and the sail is swinging loose, its black rope lashing in the wind. After a moment, I notice that the end of the rope is ragged and missing its knot, from which I deduce that the old man had to cut it loose from its tangle to free it. Apart from that though, the boat looks fine, ready to sail.

I twist round to check where we are. My first feeling is relief; Lluís is not a white slaver carrying me away to the Barbary Coast. The mouth of the cala opens out before us, and in a few more moments I shall be able to see our house. If my father is watching from the balcony he will soon be able to see us too. The thought instantly makes me feel safe, happy, and then a second later it dawns on me what that will mean. I groan and lay my forehead against the gunwale. But then a crazy idea occurs to me. Ignoring the pain in my head, I scramble to my feet and point at the dinghy. Lluís stares at me.

Can you … ? Please, can I … ? I want to …" God, if only I spoke Spanish, or the local dialect.

He stares at me some more and, glancing over my shoulder, I know I'm almost out of time. I can't think what to do except:

"Stop!"

He raises his eyebrows but reaches down to pull a

rusty handle by his feet. The note of the engine changes and the little dinghy surges forward and knocks into the *llaud's* stern. Lluís reaches out and pushes it away, then he turns back and points at it and says something to me I can't understand. I shake my head in frustration and do a completely hopeless mime of sailing.

He says something else, in a different-sounding language, but I don't understand that either. He shakes his head this time and tries a third language:

"Vous voulez arriver chez vous dans le p'tit bateau?"

He speaks it with a strong chewing accent, but it is definitely French. And French I can do, up to a point, although my schoolgirl's Parisian accent is very different.

"Oui, monsieur." I nod emphatically, though my head bangs with pain when I do. "Oui, s'il vous plaît. Je ne veux pas que mon père voit que j'ai souffrit un accident."

Lluís looks dubious: "Vous êtes sûr? Peut-être il devait savoir."

"Non!" I shake my head violently, and it hurts some more. He mustn't know, or he won't let me go out in the boat again. I shall be stuck ashore, between the twins and the bad books, for the whole three weeks. Then I really will have to kill myself!

"S'il vous plaît, monsieur. Je ne vais pas ..." I don't know the word for capsize. I settle instead on: "Je peut le faire." I can do it. I tuck my hair behind my ears in an attempt to look less bedraggled than I feel and gaze at the old man with a look on my face that I hope comes across as determined rather than concussed.

He stares at me for a while longer, then he shrugs and turns to untie the rope securing the dinghy. He hands me the end of the rope and gestures me to walk the little boat around the side to the lowest point of the *llaud's* side. At the same time he puts the engine into reverse and swings the boat into wind before dropping her back into neutral. Then he takes the painter from me and stoops down to catch the dinghy's prow and steady it.

"Allez!" he says, and holds out his other arm so that I can grab onto his hand as I step down into the little boat. I scramble round the mast and centre-board and drop down into the cockpit, the sail flapping round my head. Lluís keeps hold of the boat as I reach back and grab the flying main-sheet. I don't know how much of it he had to cut away but it is still long enough to run to the end of the boom and back to the cockpit with some to spare. My fingers stumble a couple of times as I attempt to re-tie a half-hitch in the end and, looking up, I see that Lluís is watching me carefully. I try to smile, but I can feel my lips tremble.

Lluís abruptly lets go of the prow, but keeps hold of the painter and ties it swiftly round one of the *llaud's* rowlocks.

"Attendez!" he says and lurches off across the deck. My heart sinks. He's decided to take me all the way home, after all, to face wailing and gnashing of teeth. Mum will blame Dad for letting me go out by myself in the first place, saying it was far too dangerous. The way she thinks everything remotely interesting is far too dangerous. She'll say I could have been killed and is that what he wanted and honestly, Andrew, sometimes I wonder if you've got any common sense at all. And, since this time she's been almost proved right, Dad will turn all sheepish and disappointed and it'll be years before I'm allowed to so much as row across a pond by myself.

"Voilà!" says Lluís in a voice so rough it sounds like a duck quacking. I look up to see him holding out a life-jacket. My life-jacket. He must have fished it out of the sea and thought to keep it as his salvage fee.

I take it from him and struggle into it gratefully, though it is sodden and clammy.

"Merci, monsieur," I say, as he stoops to untie the painter again. "Vous êtes très …" I search for a polite phrase from my French textbook: "gentil."

The old man laughs and shakes his head:

"Non, pas gentil. Jamais. Gentilhomme? C'est pour la bourgeoisie! Moi, je suis un conspirateur. Pour la liberté!"

With which he gives the dinghy's prow a great push that sends the boat spinning downwind so that I have no time to answer, just to concentrate on filling the sail and setting a course for home. And by the time I have a chance to look back, the fishing boat has turned and is heading out towards the open sea again.

15

Knowing he is dead is the strangest feeling. Completely different from the way she felt during the nearly forty years when she thought he must be dead. If he didn't come back for her, surely he must be dead. That's what she had thought, all those years. Yet she knows now that she never really believed it, because she never felt then what she feels now. This utter emptiness.

She sits in her armchair and wishes for death to come and take her too. She does not want to see another day end or another sun rise. There have been enough. And far far too many of them without him.

But death does not come. And though she wishes it with all that remains of her heart, she will not lower herself to pray for it. As if praying would make any difference.

There is a knock at the door and she wonders if it is the police, come back again with more information. They said they would telephone or write and she would prefer that. Still, she pushes herself up and walks slowly over to the door, feeling the weight of every one of her years on her shoulders. Whoever is outside raps again with the knocker and suddenly she knows who it is, from the sharpness of the taps, the fastidious separation between the two blows. She sighs and unlocks the door.

The sun is bright but her doorstep is darkened by a tall figure:

"Francisco," she says, and can think of nothing more. She holds the door aside for him to enter.

"Mother" he says and ducks his head to step inside the room. They do not kiss or embrace. She stands a moment longer with the door open, as if she wished to go out, or for someone else to come in. But neither happens and finally she closes it and turns to her son.

"Have the Guardia Civil been here?" he asks.

She nods.

"Yesterday. You should know. You sent them."

"I thought it was the proper thing to do. You are his ... were his wife, after all. According to the letter of the law."

"I never knew that, you know. But apparently you did. Did your ... did he know?"

"Not from me. As I said, it's merely the letter of the law. I don't believe it changes what I've always believed. In the eyes of God, you were only ever married to one man – my father. Just because I'm a lawyer, doesn't mean I have to agree with every stupid statute they pass in Madrid."

"So why tell the police?"

He shrugs, almost sulkily, and she knows that whatever he says about stupid statutes, it would be beyond her son's power to ignore a law any more than he can ever ignore his duty.

"I didn't want to have to deal with the old man's body. Arrange a funeral. He's your garbage. I thought you should deal with it."

"Francisco!"

Even though she is used to his bitterness, she is shocked.

"He was still your real father. After all these years, didn't you come to care for him at all?"

He laughs:

"I only had one father, just like you only had one husband. He died forty years ago, while the Red bastard

77

you always preferred to an honourable man carried on breathing all this time. It wasn't fair. He was nothing more than a tramp. What did he ever contribute? What did he leave behind? Nothing. I even had to pay his rent, the last few years. Arrange nurses for him."

"You didn't have to do that. I would have done that if you'd told me it was necessary."

"You? You couldn't even bring yourself to speak to him. You ignored him all these years. I shouldn't have been surprised. You never showed me any love. Or my father, who deserved it the most, who even kept you out of prison by taking you back. Out of the goodness of his heart. After what you'd done to him! I should have guessed that when the so-called love of your life finally turned up again you'd treat him just the same. There's something wrong with you. You're incapable of love. My father always said so. You have none of the proper feelings. And he was right. About so many things, he was right."

"I've always loved Ángel. You know that. You can't deny that. And I've always tried to love you, my son."

He nods his head, once, with sudden satisfaction, like a chess player who has just seen his opponent make a move he predicted:

"If that's true, then you'll do something for me."

"What?"

"You'll bury the old man quietly, when the authorities release his body. And you won't say anything to Ángel about him, even if he comes asking."

"Haven't I always kept my promise to you not to tell him about his grandfather?"

"Yes, but it's different now. I was out of the office when they first came to inform me and the fool policeman blurted it out to Ángel. Said they believed the dead man was my father. I've told him it was a stupid mistake, but that may not satisfy him. The boy's restless. Unsettled. I don't want you filling his head with nonsense. Not now, when the old man's finally dead. I've waited so long for the danger to be over, for my father's name to be safe from any more scandal. I want your word that you won't start telling him stories now. Especially not now."

She shrugs and sits down in her chair, turning her head away before she answers so that he cannot see the emotion on her face:

"What would be the point now? He's dead."

"Good," he says and turns to go. "Just one other thing."

She sighs:

"What?"

"Don't even think of burying him in the family plot."

There is silence between them and then she laughs, a dry, bitter laugh:

"Don't worry. I'll bury him where he'll find peace, not where he'd be bound to spin in his grave."

She doesn't look round again until she hears the front door closing. A shadow crosses the window and he is gone. She rests her head against the back of the chair and thinks about what he said. Was it true that she was incapable of love? If she had really loved Lluís, wouldn't it have been possible to take up again when he came home after all those years?

She remembers the way she used to look for him everywhere. The way she seemed to see him a hundred times a day – even in the restricted compass of the world Mascaró allowed her to occupy. Someone with the same build, the same way of waving. She remembered the sudden excitement of walking in the street behind someone whose hair lay in the same way on the nape of his neck. The way her heart leapt – and then fell – every single time. Could she really not have loved him, and still have looked for Lluís every day, in every street she walked down, for forty years?

She is about to acquit herself of the charge – until she remembers the day she finally did see him.

It was winter. A grey, bleak, windy day scattered with gusts of rain. Her son had come to pick her up in his car, to take her to Mahon. She doesn't remember why they were going to town, an appointment of some kind: dentist, optician. One of Francisco's duty calls. A son's duty, to look after his widowed mother's needs, even if there was no warmth between them, no pleasure in the association.

They were driving along in silence. Ángel was not in the car. She remembers that. If he had been, the atmosphere would have been happier. Such an irrepressible child he had been, so full of life. Sometimes he was even able to make his father smile, to create a bridge between the three of them. But he was not there that day. He must have been just old enough to be at school.

As they came to the narrow bridge near Son Tema an old man was walking by the side of the road up ahead. Francisco slowed and drove along the centre of the bridge and all the way across she could not take her eyes off the figure approaching on the other side. He was bent, warped and grey-haired, with all the fire gone out of him but somehow she recognised him. Even when he was still a hundred metres away, before she could see his face. Somehow, she knew it was Lluís and she began to tremble.

The odd thing was that for forty years she had been looking for the Lluís of 1939. He was strong then, vigorous, broad-shouldered – like a little bull. The old man on the roadside was nothing like him. And then she understood that somewhere deep inside she must have

80

imagined all the men he might have become in forty years and when her eye saw the old man by the roadside her mind recognised him. Her heart recognised him.

The car rattled over the rough stones of the bridge. She glanced at Francisco beside her and for the thousandth time saw no trace of Lluís in him. Just the heavy imprint of Mascaró's upbringing.

She knew she had to act, if she wanted him to stop the car, but she seemed to be frozen. Her hands gripped the large black handbag in her lap and her lips trembled as she tried to command them to say the word. All the time the old man and the car were converging. Her son and the father he'd never known. Her son and the father he would probably despise. The man whose name had been on the tip of her tongue every day for forty years and had never been spoken aloud.

Suddenly, she knew that she couldn't tell Francisco to stop. It would be too much of a shock for all of them. She wasn't strong enough to face it, to bear what either of them might say to her, or to each other.

The car sped up as it came off the end of the bridge. The old man shuffled on, looking down at the ground all the time they were coming towards him. He took no notice of the other cars that went past. Then, as they drew level with him, he looked up.

Their eyes met.

His mouth opened.

And then she looked away.

She was scared that Francisco would see. Coward! She had been scared for so long. Of Mascaró. Of Franco, and the terrible Spain he'd built. But they were both dead now. There was nothing to fear any more, but she learnt in that moment that all the courage she'd once had was gone. Used up. There was not enough left for a single clench of the fist in their old salute. Let alone for this meeting. So she just clutched her bag and stared out of the windscreen. She felt his eyes on her, just like she always could, through the side window. But still she didn't look back. Things might have been different if she had. If she hadn't added that rejection to the earlier one.

Now he was dead. He was dead and none of it could be undone. None of the terrible misunderstandings. His life, that had once held such promise, was over. He was gone and there was nothing left for her to do but wait for hers to be over too.

16

It is Saturday, a beautiful day, and the cala has come alive. Shutters are thrown back, cars and vans unloaded of food and bottled water and weekend gear, chairs set out on the foreshore and preparations made for two days of sociability. The water sparkles with splashes and cries of "¡Mira! ¡Mira!" from children playing in the buoy-edged swimming area. Boats are being prepared on jetties and moorings the length of the cala for fishing trips and picnics. The early fishermen who were out at dawn are already back, cleaning their catch on plastic boards at the sea's edge and tipping the guts back into the water to feed the little fishes that dart and flash about the shallows.

I lay my towel over the hull of an up-turned dinghy and wade into the water. It is cold but considerably warmer than it was a few weeks ago. Summer is definitely coming in. When it reaches my thighs I take a deep breath, topple forward and start to swim. During the week I head straight over to the far shore, dip my head under the string of weed-bearded buoys and climb up the metal steps to the concrete platform above. I lie there for a few minutes in the sun to dry off before I dive back in and swim home, feeling like I've been on an excursion, got out and about, seen the world.

But not today. Today there is a group of middle-aged women sitting chatting at the top of the ladder and half a dozen heads bobbing in the ring of buoys. So I strike out on a different course, almost directly out to sea. The water is shallow for a few metres, so shallow that my toes are tickled by weed as I kick. Then I am out over the channel and the temperature of the water drops from cold to exhilarating. I lengthen my stroke and make for the boats moored on the other side of the cala. I pick one of the larger yachts near the entrance to the bay and, when I reach it, puffing slightly, I grab onto its anchor chain and float on my back. The sky is a cloudless blue, the only blemish a con trail from a passenger jet banking down along the coast towards the airport at Mahon. I can feel the sun's rays warming my skin through the cool water and the contrast makes every nerve ending sing. I realise that I have no aches or pains anywhere, that I have rarely felt so well in all my life. And I wonder what I have been doing, all these years, when I could have been doing this.

On the swim back I have to stop and tread water three times to let boats heading in and out of the cala steer past me. The third one, a modern version of the old fishing *llaud*, passes between me and the end of my jetty. It is loaded with at least three generations of family and the family pet, a dog of uncertain provenance, stands proudly in the bows as look-out. He even woofs at me as they pass. I wonder if he knows about the submerged rock in the channel.

When the *llaud* has gone on by I move to resume my stroke, but something catches my eye. An unfamiliar movement at the bottom of the roadway. An unfamiliar figure. I feel an instant surge of resentment that someone should take advantage of my absence to invade my territory. I tread water a while longer and try to make out his purpose. He is too smartly-dressed to be a tourist. He could be an estate agent, in his sports jacket and chinos, but he isn't carrying one of those dapper little briefcases they invariably have and he isn't talking on a mobile phone so it seems unlikely. He looks uncertain, too, as if he isn't sure what he is looking for, or whom.

He has a piece of paper in his hand and he steps onto the foreshore and stares up at the row of boathouses, then down at the paper. Then up again. He stops outside my house and looks up at the balcony. The sliding doors are open and the front door stands ajar. I never bother to lock up when I go for a swim. There's nothing much to steal and I wouldn't especially care anyway. "Who steals my purse steals trash", right? Worse things happen.

But I'm not worried that this man is a burglar. No, that's not what makes me dive under the water and swim silently to the end of the jetty, where I hide in the cool shade. What scares me far more than the possibility that he's a criminal is the possibility that he's a policeman.

So I watch from my hiding place, not far from the spot where an octopus once lurked and watched me, to see whether my house is the one he's interested in. He consults his paper again and I hold my breath, heart thumping, as he approaches the door and knocks on the glass. No one answers. Of course no one answers. He stands by the step for a moment with his back to the door, looking left and right. Then he walks away towards the village, to an open boat-house where a man is mending a net. He shows the man the paper and the man points, with his wooden needle, back in my direction, but past my house, it seems, further down the cala.

The stranger nods and smiles and comes back along the hard, passing my front door without another glance. My heartbeat slows and terror subsides to curiosity as he passes my neighbours' houses too, ignores the jetties and disappears round the corner towards the point where the path runs out into wet pebbles.

Then my heart beat starts to race again because all at once I know what he's doing here. There is only one house beyond that point. Someone else is looking for Lluís.

17

I get away with it. Just. Of course I can't hide the fact that I'm dripping wet, but I claim I leant out too far whilst heeled over and got caught by a wave. It can happen that way, if the wind drops a bit and the boat flattens out before you can shift your weight. Suddenly, your backside's in the water, catching a crab, and you do get soaked. Dad laughs when I tell them, childishly pleased to have held the record, but Mum, standing beside him on the shore with her arms folded, glares at him until he stops. Here it comes.

"I honestly don't know what you were thinking, Andrew. Letting her go off out of sight like that. She hasn't done any sailing for ages, and never on the open sea. It's too dangerous. What if she'd got into trouble? How would we have known? She could have drowned."

"Mu-um!" I say. "Look at me. I'm fine. It was fun."

I keep the mainsheet gathered in my fist, so that no one sees the frayed end and I just hope that my face isn't going to be too badly bruised from where I smacked it against the hull. The whole of one side, from my forehead to my jaw, aches and some of my teeth are throbbing, but I obviously can't be bleeding or anything, because my mother would have noticed.

My father wades down into the water and holds the boat while I climb out. He knows there's no mileage in arguing with her. Better to change the subject and wait for better weather.

"Let's pull her up and then I'll take the mast down," is

all he says and together we run her up the sand until the hull grates on concrete. He unfastens the kicking strap and starts to haul the mast up out of the hull while I unclip the rudder from the stern. It's awkward, as usual, and he has already carried the mast, sail and boom into the boathouse and come back again before I've got it free.

"Funny!" he says, and I turn to see him running his hand down the leading edge of the centre-board, which he's just lifted out of its slot. It has a big chunk missing about two thirds of the way down and the wood above and below the bite mark is feathered into splinters. It's clear that what I hit was one hell of a rock.

"What is it?" asks my mother. "Something wrong with it?"

"Er, no," says my father, shooting me a look that I return with maximum innocence. "Nothing. It's just getting a bit worn, that's all. I might see if there's a plane in Ted's tool-kit. Smooth it off a bit. Give it a coat of varnish before we go. It's good of him to let us use his toys while we're here – I'd like to do him a bit of a favour back, if I can."

My mother tuts:

"We do him a pretty good favour paying the rent he asks. This place isn't cheap you know. You don't have to act as his handyman into the bargain!"

Dad shrugs.

"It's no trouble. It'll give me something to do, and I enjoy woodwork, you know. Just never get the time at home."

"You never get the time for anything except work and sleep these days. That's why I end up doing everything else."

I slip past them into the cool of the boathouse and make sure the end of the cut rope is out of sight until I can come back later with a knife and a cigarette lighter to neaten it off and seal it. Then I turn on the shower and put my head right under the steaming water, the drumming of which almost drowns out the sound of my mother tongue-lashing my poor old Dad.

It is several days before I see my rescuer again. In fact, he sees me first. I am standing with my feet cooling in the water, on afternoon guard duty watching the twins paddle their windsurfer in a roundabout course back from the opposite shore. From time to time I pick out a flat stone from the pile of water-worn slate chips I collected from a beach near the lighthouse, and stoop down to skim it out across the still water. My latest effort skips three times and then sinks.

"*Comme Menorca*," says a gravel voice behind me.

I jump and turn around to find Lluís approaching along what looks like a private path leading down from the top road. He is carrying a plastic carrier bag so old that its handles are stretched thin and the PVC is soft and opaque.

"*Quoi?*"

Close beside me now, Lluís sets down the bag, which is bulging with potatoes and a big bunch of mud-spattered flat-leaf parsley. He crouches down to imitate my skimming action. Then, pointing at an imaginary bouncing stone, he says:

"*Un, Ibiza. Deux, Mallorca. Trois, Menorca.*"

I look at him, no idea what he's talking about, expecting him to laugh and explain the joke. But he shakes his head, almost sadly:

"People always think they're the same. One. Two. Three. Three pieces of the same rock. Three mountains in the same range. But they're wrong."

I can follow his French, just, but not his meaning – so he tries again.

"The islands. The Balears. People think Menorca is no different from Mallorca. They think it's the same island, just smaller. That's the fault of the Romans. They called them Majorica and Minorica. But they're not the same at all. Here, standing here, do you know you're not even on the same continent as Mallorca? "

I shake my head, less in reply than in surprise at the weird choice of subject. He sees the surprise on my face, the doubt, because he laughs and wags his finger at me:

"It's better than that, in fact. People think this is one island. But it's not. It's two. La Tramuntana, that's the north – where we are. Es Migjorn, that's the south. Here, in the north, we're standing on the very last piece of a lost continent. Did you know that? A lost continent. Whereas everything south of the harbour at Mahon, and over in Ciudadella is only another little piece of Spain. Makes you think, eh?"

It makes me think he's just a crazy old man. Lost continent? Who does he think he is – The Man from Atlantis?

I kind of assumed that when I saw him again we'd talk about what happened the other day. I've been half-expecting a knock at the door ever since, half-expecting him to come and drop me in it with the parents. If I'm honest I've actually been avoiding him, skulking in the house at the times when he's usually about, nervous of seeing him again, expecting a lecture about my sailing, about lying to my folks. But now that he's here, now that he doesn't seem remotely interested in discussing my great escape, I have to say that I'm a bit miffed. He isn't acting at all like I expect a grown-up to.

"Are you going to tell them?"

It is his turn to look confused.

"Who?"

"My parents, of course. Are you going to tell them about the other day?"

He looks a little disappointed:

"No."

"Why not?"

He raises his considerable eyebrows:

"You want me to tell them?"

"No, of course not. It's simply that ..."

"You think adults can't keep secrets. You think secrets are for kids, eh? To keep things from their parents? No, my child, the adults have their secrets too. Here especially, on this island, there are many, many secrets. Too many. Alongside them, your little secret is nothing, believe me, nothing at all."

He pronounces "rien" as "re-eng", almost as if he is gnawing the word to pieces. His mood is very serious now, even a bit alarming. I wish I hadn't asked.

Suddenly there is a splash and a cry from the middle of the cala. Looking over, I see that the twins have tipped themselves off the windsurfer and (before they can show how good they are at getting back on) I shrug my shoulders apologetically at Lluís, run out along the nearest jetty and dive in.

18

I thought I had time to reach the house before the stranger finished prowling round Lluís's place, but he reappears when I am still knee-deep in water and a good ten feet even from the shelter of my towel.

I am always self-conscious, walking out of the sea. It's Ursula Andress's fault for setting too high a benchmark for how it should be done and how it should look. It's bad enough when you're alone. Even worse when a stranger is watching you. I try to do it now with my eyes focused somewhere in the middle distance, but the stranger isn't having any of that. He picks up my towel and holds it out to me:

"Yours?" he says.

"Yes," I say, and, without the least sense of gratitude: "Thank you."

"It was nothing," he says, and I don't disagree. Just throw the towel over my head, bend forward and rub my hair vigorously and at length, hoping that when I flick the towel back over my head and stand up straight he will be gone.

He isn't.

"It's a pretty spot you've found."

"I'm sorry, what?"

"I said it's pretty, this cala. Unspoiled. I've never been down here before. Everywhere is so built up on the south coast now. I forget there are still a few places that aren't ruined."

I can't help it, my interest is caught:

"You've never been here?"

"No. I was brought up in Es Castell – Maó. My father grew up in Ciutadella. We're from the south – Es Migjorn. This is La Tramuntana. We're very local people, Menorquins. We don't travel much. We don't have to. The world comes to us. Like you. You're not Menorquin. What are you, English?"

I nod.

"But you speak good Spanish."

"And the surprise is not to find it done well, but to find it done at all."

"I'm sorry?"

"It's nothing – something patronizing someone once said about women."

He looks offended:

"It wasn't my intention to be patronizing."

"No?"

I look at him and see he's telling the truth. He's far too earnest for that. For some reason I feel the urge to be conciliatory:

"Well, we are terrible at learning other people's languages. But it isn't absolutely impossible. I studied Spanish. At university."

"Have you lived here long?"

The question surprises me. I'm about to say that I don't live here. That I don't live anywhere. But I think better of it:

"Not long, no. A few months."

He looks disappointed and glances back towards where Lluís's hut is concealed in the trees. Calculating whether there is any point in asking me about the old man. At the same time, I am calculating whether to tell him. Up close, he doesn't look like a policeman. Doesn't have the swagger that the power of arrest seems to confer. Besides, I can't imagine a policeman in the world apologizing for being patronizing.

92

He finishes his calculation before I finish mine, scanning the cala as he turns back to face me:

"You know about the English invasion round here, I suppose?"

Maybe I'm wrong. Maybe he's not interested in Lluís after all. Perhaps he is one of those Catalan nationalist types – a local politician canvassing for an election. The look certainly fits. But if that's who he is, he's come to the wrong person. I'm not on the electoral roll.

"I know they own quite a few houses, but so do the Germans."

He is shaking his head, laughing.

"No, I mean they invaded here in the eighteenth century. They landed quite close to this spot. 1798. The Cormorant, the Aurora and the Argo, three frigates and I don't know how many troop ships. Can you imagine it?"

He steps onto the jetty and is pointing out to where the islands protect the entrances to two inlets:

"Can you imagine warships out there? Firing broadsides at the shore? You'd have been scared wouldn't you? You'd have been terrified."

I stand looking at his back. For a politician he seems a bit ... unfocused. He is walking now to the end of the jetty and is standing there, apparently scanning the empty blue sea for wooden-hulled sailing ships with open gun ports. There is something intriguing about him, something vaguely familiar. I wrap the towel around myself and, hugging it, walk out along the planks until I'm about a yard behind him. Close enough:

"I don't suppose there were many people here to be terrified in those days."

"There were shore batteries," he says, over his shoulder, "and I bet that house was here." He points across

93

the cala to an old white-washed boathouse with a crenel-lated wall and narrow windows in its south side.

Then he nods at the round tower opposite.

"That watch-tower wasn't here. The British built a whole string of those across the island right after that last invasion. But ..." he swivels on his leather soles and looks up and down the cala.

"That place. I bet that hut was here then."

Even without looking round to follow where his arm is pointing I know which hut he means. Instead of look-ing at it he looks at me, to see if I know whose hut it was. So I was right, after all. Whoever he is, he is here because of Lluís. But I'm still not sure it would be wise to admit that I used to know him. In fact, I'm sure it isn't wise. But I am tempted. I have to admit that. The demon curiosity is nudging me in the back again and whispering: "Go on!" but I'm not that easily led. I play for more time:

"You don't seriously mean there was a battle here, do you?"

He shrugs.

"I don't think you need to worry about fishing up any skeletons. I suspect the shore batteries fired off a few mortars and then withdrew. They wouldn't have been a match for three frigates. As far as I know the English landed eight hundred men here without any trouble. Scotsmen, I believe."

He looks pleased to be able to provide this titbit of added colour.

"So where was the battle?"

He looks slightly crest-fallen:

"Ah yes, well, that's the trouble with mercenaries. Men who fight for money are always keener on the money than they are on the fighting. The island garrison was mostly Swiss mercenaries at that time and they were supposed to fall back to the hill at Son Tema – I think," he pauses while he turns to look inland and consult his mental map again (the relief version), "it must be where the road turns towards Maó nowadays, near the petrol station. They were ordered to stop the British advance there."

"But?"

"But they sent to Mercadal for double brandy rations, drank them and then disappeared into the woods. The British marched straight to Maó."

"How humiliating."

As soon as I've said it I realise that it must have sounded condescending, jingoistic, crass. I'm out of practice at conversation. I've forgotten it's polite to avoid speaking the truth out loud.

"I mean …"

He glares at me sternly:

"What you have to understand about Menorca is that in the eighteenth century it never had a government of its own. The Menorquin people took the view that it didn't really matter whether the government of occupation was British, French or Spanish. Each had its advantages and disadvantages. So when the wind changed, we – they – tended simply to let it blow."

I have a sudden sense of déjà vu. He's like someone else, trying to educate me about the island. His manner is different though. He is bossier, less wistful. He doesn't feel it as personally as Lluís. When Lluís talked about Menorca's history, her geology, the temperament of her people he was almost Yeatsian, laying out the cloths of his dreams and asking me to tread softly.

He made me see that it wasn't just a simple place, a shallow, pretty, vacuous holiday destination – the nice place with nice people that my mother liked so much. It isn't simple. It isn't shallow or vacuous. It isn't even one island. It's two: La Tramuntana and Es Migjorn;

north and south; sandstone and limestone; old and new; Moorish and Christian; Spanish and British. And over the weeks he taught me how the two halves differ geologically, historically, architecturally, temperamentally. Not a simple place at all. He taught me well and I haven't forgotten.

Suddenly I want very much to see him again, to see the familiar unsteady gait coming along the shoreline, close to the water. But he isn't here and in his place is a stranger showing off what he knows. Are they all like this, the Menorquins, I wonder? Or just …

The realisation hits me so hard I have to bury my head in the towel for a minute and pretend to be drying my hair. Surely it can't be happening again, this sense of recognition. Maybe it's my brain playing tricks. Maybe that means it was a delusion the first time too. That the dead man wasn't Lluís after all and my response to the photo was just due to some weird short circuit in my brain, a blend of memory and loneliness and wish fulfillment. Or something worse. I hardly dare uncover my face to look at the young man, in case what I thought I saw has disappeared.

When I do lower the towel, he is still there watching me, with his head on one side and a slightly baffled smile on his face. And the resemblance is so strong now I know it can't be a mistake or a delusion. I should have seen it immediately, but I think the clothes blinded me. The old man I knew was always so scruffy, in an old T-shirt and torn shorts, whereas his son is immaculate. I suspect he even has his nails manicured and his hair, Lluís's coarse unruly hair, is not only brushed smooth but cut to suit his broad open face. He is about the same height as Lluís though, an inch or two taller than me, and the same stocky build as his father. His eyes are a deep brown and they are looking at me:

"What is it?" he says.

"What?"

"You look as though you've seen a ghost."

I know I should deny it, that I'm going to regret this, but I am so relieved not to be hallucinating that I can't help myself:

"Not quite a ghost. An image. You. You're the image of your father."

For some reason he finds this funny and shakes his head:

"Not at all. I'm nothing like my father."

Then he stops laughing and looks at me, his eyes serious and questioning:

"But I might, perhaps, resemble my grandfather."

19

It is Dad's idea to invite Lluís on our barbecue trip. The last night of the holiday has crept up on us just as I think we were all beginning to believe that the cala is real life and home is just a mediocre dream. Dad has got it into his head to sail round to one of the beaches you can't reach by car for our final barbecue. Mum, naturally, isn't keen, can't see the point, thinks it is a lot of effort and inconvenience when we have a perfectly good built-in barbecue at the house.

"Where's your sense of adventure?" asks my father, though he must have been married to her long enough by now to know the answer to that. If my mother ever had an adventurous spirit she lost it long before any memory I have of her. For as long as I've known her she has always acted as if the world is a place where the worst can happen, and often does.

"You can't sail in the dark, Andrew. There are no lights on that wretched little boat and besides, we won't all fit."

She is right, on both counts. But this is the way the yin and yang of their relationship works. Dad puts up an idea. Mum shoots it down. Dad puts up another. Mum blasts it out of the sky. It's like watching a marathon clay pigeon competition, where the only question is whether my father will run out of targets before my mother runs out of ammunition.

"We could ask the old guy if he wants to come. His boat has lights, and there'd be room for us all."

"Andrew, you can't. Whatever are you thinking? You can't even talk to him."

"Oh, I wouldn't say that. We get on pretty well, Lluís and I. Mostly nods and pointing, I grant you. But we make ourselves understood. And he and Kate get by with a bit of the old Franglais, don't you, girl?"

I nod, wondering when he has heard me talking to Lluís. We have become quite good friends, the old man and I, but our conversations almost always take place during the parents' siesta, when I am on twin duty.

"I feel a bit sorry for the old boy. He doesn't seem to have many friends. I don't know what that business was about last Sunday, but I didn't like it much."

He shakes his head and looks at me. I know exactly what he's talking about and I didn't like it much either.

Sunday had been a typically hot afternoon and I was slumped in a meagre patch of shade on the balcony, reading a book. A group of men had gathered in one of the neighbouring boathouses, the doors folded back and a table pulled out onto the hard-standing. Not a rare occurrence. Sunday afternoon seems to finds the locals at their most relaxed, their most cool. Sunday is the day the grandmothers hitch up their skirts and paddle along the water's edge with their friends. And it is the day when the men get together to drink wine from tumblers and sing.

Without paying much attention, I was actually quite enjoying the free concert. After two and a half weeks I had forgotten how much I hated it here. The men sang well together and their songs sounded cheerful, tuneful with a good momentum and rhythm. Music to make a body feel happy, at home, part of something. Only my dad, tinkering at something down in our boathouse, was kind of spoiling it by whistling along without the first clue where the tune was going.

Suddenly I heard a shout, and then another. I sat up and looked down from the balcony to see Lluís standing

99

at the end of a jetty thirty yards from the boathouse where the men were sitting. He shouted again, and again, a single word that echoed over the water: "¡Fascisti! ¡Fascisti!" He was pointing towards the open boathouse and then he clenched his fist and shook it: ¡Fascisti!"

The singing grew ragged and broke down. There was a clatter as a chair fell back onto concrete and then the singers were out there below me on the shore. They were all in late middle age, well-fed, pot-bellied. But the bon-homie and good fellowship that had been in their voices moments before was displaced now by something ugly.

Lluís seemed to hesitate for a moment when he saw them come out into the open, but it was just for a moment and then he raised his fist again and shouted that word. The men looked at each other and then one of them started to sing again. Quickly, the others took up the tune and together they began to advance down the shore towards the old man. This was a different song, harsh and triumphant and indisputably military, and despite their soft bellies and the sand underfoot they seemed to me to be marching. In a dozen paces or so the verse of the song gave way to the chorus and as they belted it out, first one and then the others raised their arm in what was unmistakably, even to me, a fascist salute.

When Lluís started to shout I thought at first that it was one of his jokes, or that maybe "fascisti" was a Menorquín word I hadn't heard before, but when I saw the men's faces and when I saw that salute it was as if a cold wind had swept down the cala despite the hot summer's day. The hairs stood up on my arms and I was suddenly afraid for Lluís. From my vantage point he looked small and vulnerable and soon he would be stranded with nowhere to go except into the sea. But then, just as I thought his line of retreat was going to be cut off, my father emerged from our boathouse and said:

"Now then."

"Now then!" as if he was Dixon of Dock Green feeling the collar of some young hooligans. I felt myself go red with embarrassment.

But it had an effect. Two or three of the men turned to look at him, and the song stuttered and died. It was enough of a distraction for Lluís to seize his chance and he scuttled down the jetty and away round the corner towards his hut, shouting defiance as he went. Two of the men made as if to chase him, as they might have feinted at a barking stray dog, offering to kick it, and as Lluís disappeared they turned to each other, laughing. But one of the others nudged them and the smiles faded. Quietly, they turned and walked back past the spot where my father still stood with a chisel in his hand. A couple of them even nodded good day to him, as if they were just out for a stroll. They went back into their boathouse, pulling the doors closed behind them. One man slapped another on the back as they went in and if I hadn't seen it all, if I'd just come out onto the balcony at that moment, I would have thought that they were a cheerful lot.

"I don't suppose it was anything at all, Andrew," says my mother. "You probably misunderstood it completely."

"You weren't there, Mum. They were really threatening him."

"Well, perhaps they're just tired of his mess. You have to admit he doesn't exactly raise the tone of the area. Everyone else is so neat and tidy, keeps their places so nice and then there's him wandering about like an old tramp."

"He's not an old tramp, Mum. He's just not bourgeois like the rest of them. He's an individual."

"You can say that again. And if by 'not bourgeois'

101

you mean 'not clean' I can only agree. Did you see the state of the pot he brought that stew in? It's a wonder we didn't all get gyppy tummy."

"We didn't though, did we?" says Dad. "It tasted pretty good. I'm going round to see him."

And with that he skips out of range, leaving her with the next shot on the tip of her tongue.

He is back a few minutes later, smiling, and shouts up to the balcony:

"He said yes. He knows a good spot. We're going to take both boats. Leaving at six. I'll go up to the shop and get more charcoal. Kate, can you take the twins along the shore and pick up some driftwood? Only the dry stuff."

My mother sighs. She knows she is beaten this time and retreats to the kitchen to pack meat and salad into Tupperware boxes, sealing her lips and their lids into matching air-tight lines.

But her silent disapproval can't prevent a carnival atmosphere developing down on the jetties as we prepare for our excursion. Dad's plan is that he and I will go on the Laser while Mum and the twins travel with Lluís on his boat. But the twins both want to come with us and, after an hour of stereo pleading, Dad caves in and agrees that one can come with us on the way out and the other on the way back. There is hardly room for the two of us in the tiny cockpit, so the third crew member will have to lie spread-eagled on the bow in front of the mast.

"It'll be wet," warns Dad, "and you'll have to keep your head down."

The twins don't care. They're already fighting over who gets to go first. David wins, as usual, and Richie goes off to have a weepy little sulk in the boat house, also usual.

Lluís turns up just as we are rigging the Laser. I am

amused to see that he has dressed for the occasion in a raffish straw hat, if "raffish" is the right word for something made of raffia then mashed over many years. As well as the hat, he is armed with a collection of nets, spinners and buckets from which it's clear that he intends to contribute to the feast with food caught along the way.

He climbs aboard his own boat and stows his gear before standing to attention to welcome my mother and Richie, still snivelling but belted so tightly into an orange life-jacket that he is unable to take the long shuddering breaths he would really like. She is carrying a large shopping bag, a plastic cool box and a pile of picnic rugs. Lluís helps her aboard and mimes a suggestion that she should take a seat on the flat top of the engine housing, which is upholstered in a piece of old carpet. Mum shakes out one of the rugs and folds it double over the carpet before resting about ten per cent of her weight on it. No sooner is she settled than Lluís remembers he needs to start the engine and has to shoo her off to reach down into the innards and turn the key. The engine catches with the usual shudder and cough and throat-clearing of water through the exhaust before dropping into a reassuringly steady thumping rhythm. He settles the lid back in place and my mother on top and, when he sees that the rest of the fleet is ready, gestures to Richie to cast off the rope and backs the boat off the mooring.

It is a gold-fringed blue evening with just enough wind to carry the Laser along at the same steady four knot pace as the old fishing boat. When we arrive at the little bay Lluís has chosen, Richie is smiling all over his face, sulk completely forgotten. Lluís has let him steer all the way, ignoring my mother's squawks and remonstrations by simply pretending not to understand. While

103

Richie helmed, Lluís has scampered round the boat setting spinners, watching them and hauling them in from time to time, so that by the time we reach our destination the bucket he has placed between my mother's feet for safe-keeping is writhing and flapping with life.

He drops anchor fifteen feet from shore and we sail past to ground on the sand. David and I hop off the dinghy and he runs away across the beach to explore. I go to pull the boat up onto the shore but Dad says:

"I'd better go and get them. Your mum doesn't look too pleased. Give me a push."

So I pull the bow round and shove him back out across the water. Seeing his brother getting first crack at some new terrain, Richie doesn't wait. He has torn off his life-jacket and launched himself with a mighty splash over the side of the boat. Which is just as well because there will hardly be room in the dinghy for three adults, let alone a full picnic and a bucket of fish.

In fact, when they return to shore it is with the sail flapping and my father in the water towing the dinghy by its painter while Lluís and my mother sit in the cockpit, knee to knee, like a pair of old duchesses with their baggage piled up around them. He pulls the boat up onto the sand in a rush so that the duchesses almost topple over sideways and then goes to hand his wife out onto dry land, getting only a wordless glare for his pains. Lluís hops out on his own and pulls the bucket of fish out after him. He points to a spot at the left hand side of the beach, sheltered under a cliff:

"Là-bas," he says: "C'est l'endroit pour la feu."

He himself stops by some rocks that stick out of the shallows, jams the bucket between them and takes a stubby little knife out of his pocket:

"J'aurai besoin d'un plat" he calls over his shoulder as he attacks the first of his fish.

"What did he say?" hisses Mum, as she stumbles through the fine sand in her espadrilles, heavy bags in either hand.

"He says there's a good place for a fire over by that cliff – and he's going to need a plate for his fish."

"Oh," she says, an uncharacteristically weak response and when I glance over at her, expecting something more, I see that she has stopped and is looking round at the deserted beach, the encircling cliffs, the sky that is deepening from pure blue into a purplish dusk. It's clear that the beauty of the place is working on her and my own spirits lift as I think maybe, just maybe, she's going to allow herself to have a rare good time.

The fire is easy to make, in the circle of flat stones that someone else has left for us. I lie flat on the still-warm sand to blow on the charcoal while my father builds a structure out of driftwood on which to sit a wire tray. My mother lays out the rugs and strips back the lids on the Tupperware. Meanwhile, the twins have gone exploring and are barely visible half way up the cliffs on the far side of the bay. It is lucky that my mother is busy organising the food because she will lay an egg when she sees how high they have climbed.

Lluís brings over the fish and Dad hands him a can of beer, which he accepts with a gesture of "Cheers!" Soon, the smoke signals from the fire bring the twins scrambling down off the cliffs to demand food and tell us what they've discovered:

"There are goats!" they shout. And sure enough, silhouetted on the sky-line a herd of animals stands staring at us. "And a Nazi gun emplacement!" says Richie, who of the two is the more obsessed with the Second World War.

My father laughs at him:

"I don't think so. Spain wasn't involved in the War.

There were no Nazis here. It must be something else. The goatherd's hut maybe."

"But Dad, it faces out to sea, and it's got a slit for the guns and everything. Look!"

He points up at the cliff and we all look, including Lluís, who clearly has no idea what we're talking about. It is hard to distinguish rock from rock in the dusk but after a few seconds I can just make out a shape that is too regular to be natural, a small square of rock with a horizontal black stripe across its front edge. Dad has seen it too, because he suddenly takes Lluís by the arm and points straight at it. Then he points at Richie:

"This one," he says, in his talking-to-foreigners voice: "thinks the Nazis" and he clicks his heels together and gives a little salute: "were here in the War. With guns." And he machine-guns the sand in front of him with as much enthusiasm as any ten year old. Then he laughs, and waits for the old man to laugh too.

But Lluís does not laugh. He shakes his head:

"*Nazis no. Communistas si.*" And he strikes himself in the chest:

"Lluís!"

Then he shakes his head again:

"*Pero ...*"

He turns to me and says in French:

"Tell your father: We built these defences during our war, the Civil War. But we were too weak to stand when the rest of Spain had fallen. So the Nazis did come here, in fact. Franco's Nazis. They were here for thirty-five years."

He cracks open his can of beer and takes a long drink without taking his eyes off the cliff. Then he turns away to the fire and pokes at his fish with a stick.

"What did he say?" whispers my mother.

I tell them both and they look at each other, the way

106

the English do when someone steps outside the parameters of polite conversation. Deeply uncomfortable, each hoping the other will have a bright idea for changing the subject.

Lluís, who is squatting down by the fire, helps them out by announcing:

"*¡Listos!*"

"What now?" hisses my mother.

I look at the old man, who is pressing a chicken thigh between unwashed thumb and forefinger.

"I think he's telling us it's ready," I say and when I pass him a plate he starts to fork the meat and fish onto it.

"Come on, boys," says my mother. "Just run and wash your hands in the sea. You've been climbing about on those rocks with those dirty goats."

The twins moan and drag themselves off to dabble their hands in the water before running back and hurling themselves wetly onto a rug, fighting for space in a flurry of sand.

Lluís hands them each a plate and they tuck in, ignoring the salad my mother is thrusting under their noses in plastic boxes.

"We'll have some afterwards, Mum" says David, through a mouthful of chicken.

"I won't" says Richie, and gets a kick from his brother that makes him yell.

"Stop it, the pair of you!" says my father. "Kids eh, Lluís? Ninos. You got ninos?"

My mother shoots him a warning glance, but it's too late.

"*Si,*" Lluís nods his head and holds up a single finger. "*Hijo.* Son."

My father smiles at my mother, to say: "See, it's alright."

"Marvellous. What's he called?"

Lluís doesn't understand and looks to me to translate:

"*Comment il s'appelle? Votre fils?*"

"Francisco. Not my choice. His mother's. The last name I would have chosen."

I translate this back to my father and he laughs:

"Well, tell him sometimes it makes sense to let your wife have her own way. Anything for a quiet life, eh?"

I pass this on, but it doesn't elicit the smile we all expect. Lluís just shrugs:

"I had no say in it either way. She left me for another man before my son was born. She probably chose Francisco to please him. To prove she wasn't a Red any more. Maybe it helped keep her out of prison."

My father is still smiling, but the smile fades when I tell him what I think Lluís just said. Mum gives him a glare and shakes her head, then digs grimly into her salad, only raising her eyes to give him another hard look when he says:

"Prison?"

Lluís doesn't need this translating:

"After the War, Franco's prisons were very full. He made it a crime, you see, to have supported our government, the one we voted for, against his military rebellion."

My father's curiosity is too much for him now. Good manners are forgotten.

"So, were you ... I mean, did you ... go to prison?"

Lluís looks at him for a long moment and then he looks at me so that I can get his answer clear:

"Tell him: no. Tell him: it was worse than that. Tell him: I ran away."

20

It was a hot day when they built the gun emplacement. A blazing late summer day, much hotter than the norm, the blue sky so pale with heat haze it was almost white. The lorry with the cement backed its way past the big house and down the track to the beach. A goat stood on the skyline and watched it jolt from side to side. Lluís, waiting by the shore, unslung his rifle and took aim at the goat, but it jerked its head and skipped out of view, probably the shrewdest and only survivor of its clan.

Lluís propped his rifle against some driftwood he'd collected to make a fire at the end of the day, regretting the goat that would have roasted on it so well, and went to help Juan line the hole they'd dug in the beach. The sand they'd excavated was heaped to one side and, when the tarpaulin was arranged in the hole, Lluís stood up and waved the lorry backwards to the edge. Then he held up his hand flat and the lorry lurched to a stop. As it did so, the passenger door swung open and Catalina jumped down.

"He says we can only have half his load. He has to go over to Cavalleria with the rest."

"Do you believe him? Or is he going off to sell it on the black market? Tell him I'll be going over to Cavalleria myself tomorrow and if he's not telling the truth I'll have him arrested for looting."

She nodded and stuck her head back into the cab, resting her elbows on the door sill. She kicked her leg up behind her as though she was chatting with a girl-friend, not accusing a man of profiteering. Lluís shook his head and glanced at Juan. He wanted to say: "That's my wife!" but he knew it would sound bourgeois, proud and individualist. Anyway, he suspected his friend envied him Catalina, and he didn't want to excite that envy any more. He felt that a good communist should not feel such possessiveness as he did for Catalina about any person or any thing. But he couldn't help it. Though it pained him to admit it to himself, and he would not admit it to anyone else, he loved her more than the Cause, more than the Party, more than anything on the island, which was as good as saying more than anything in the world.

She finished her conversation with the truck driver and slammed the door.

"He's okay," she said, as she walked to the back of the truck. "Angry enough at the suggestion to be telling the truth. Anyway, he's Tolo's cousin. They're not in the Party, but they're on the left. Good Republicans."

She started to undo the pins at the back of the lorry that held the tailboard and the driver jumped down from his cab to do the same at the other side. He glared at Lluís but said nothing, too nervous to risk offending a commissar. As the tailboard was lowered, a slew of grey cement powder slid out into the hole they had dug. When the landslide stopped, Lluís and Juan jumped up into the back of the truck with their spades and started to shovel more cement out into the hole. The driver had another big shovel strapped to the rear of his cab, but he just walked away to the edge of the water and lit a cigarette. Lluís glared at his back, feeling he ought to punish his lack of solidarity. But he didn't want to ruin the day, a rare day with his two best friends, working together to strengthen the island's defences. Doing something, for a change, that seemed useful, when most of the time he felt so impotent, with everything that was important in the War going on over the water on the Peninsula.

So he bit his lip and said nothing about the driver's insolence. Just dug and shovelled and felt the sweat run down between his shoulder blades and was glad of the sensation.

When the cement powder had been unloaded and the lorry had inched its way back up the beach and disappeared in a cloud of dust, the two men leaned on their shovels and panted, waiting for Catalina who had gone to fetch water to mix up the concrete.

The two of them watched her come tripping through the fine sand with a slopping bucket in each hand. Lluís stabbed his spade into the beach and ran over to help her. A second later Juan did the same and she laughed indignantly as they grabbed the buckets out of her hands:

"I'm not so weak and feeble, you know. But if you want to do the donkey work and leave the architecture to me, that's fine."

With that she ran off up the beach and started to climb the rocks up to the spot they had agreed on earlier as the best position for a gun emplacement. Watched by the lone goat, she stood surveying the view of the sea and the sky for enemy ships and planes, then she bent down and started to haul rocks about, setting aside small and medium-sized pieces that would make good bricks, rolling loose scree down the slope and trying to achieve a flattish base where they could build. A large rock stuck up in one corner of the area she'd fixed upon and she sat down on it, trying to imagine what it would be like to keep watch here, through a concrete slit, with only a machine-gun for company.

From her perch, she commanded a view of the whole bay, which was perfectly untouched by man. The rocks on the opposite side from her vantage point were so finely layered and buckled by time that they looked like the pages of a book, left out in the rain and then dried.

Sitting there looking at the view that nature had spent so long perfecting, she felt guilty at the thought of what they were trying to do there, at the sight of Lluís and Juan toiling away to build an ugly pill-box with the sole aim of spying on and killing their fellow creatures.

Perhaps it wouldn't be needed, she told herself. And then, when the war was over, they could come back and knock it to pieces, picnic on the beach and teach their children to swim in the calm blue water.

They worked all morning and all afternoon, dragging buckets of wet concrete up over the rocks and building as roughly and randomly as they could, to camouflage their little stone hide against the cliff. Only the rectangular slit for the guns, which they held open with a block of wood until the cement was nearly dry and then knocked out, betrayed the fact that man and not nature had been re-ordering the landscape.

The sun was going down by the time they finished. Lluís led the way back down the goat path to the beach, where he flung down the last bucket and his trowel, tore off his clothes and ran splashing into the sea, bending down to wash the cement dust from his arms and face and hair. Juan followed and Catalina wasn't far behind. The two boys, for they were hardly more, soon started up-ending each other, fighting and laughing, while the girl set off with clean elegant strokes towards the open sea. Lluís turned to watch her, and got a ducking for his inattention. He would have liked to follow her, but he could not because he'd never learned to swim, so instead he held his breath and grabbed for Juan's ankle, twisting it up so that his friend was yanked off his feet and fell laughing into the water.

By the time Catalina turned and swam back, the two boys were lying in the shallows with their backs on the sand, smoking. She stood up when the water was thigh-deep and walked towards them, water dripping from her high breasts and running down her too-prominent ribcage. Whatever they'd been talking about, they both forgot. She walked past their silent gazes and dried herself on her shirt. Then she threw on Lluís's shirt and pulled it down over her thighs. She rummaged in his pocket for the tobacco tin and came back to sit on the damp sand just above the water line. In the meantime, they had both turned onto their stomachs and were watching her as she rolled a cigarette with tobacco that was mainly dried rock-rose leaves and lit it.

The first drag made her cough:

"God, this stuff is disgusting! What I wouldn't give for a decent smoke! Do you think we'll ever taste proper tobacco again?"

Lluís raised himself on his elbows and smiled at her:

"When we win, my heart, we shall have endless fine Russian tobacco. The Ebro's just the start. Once we break through there, we shall push the rebels all the way back to the Atlantic."

"And if we don't win? If the news isn't actually as good as they make it sound? How long can a battle go on, Lluís? It started well, but that was over a month ago. What's taking so long?"

He picked up a pebble from the water and threw it at her:

"Women are so impatient. War isn't like … sewing a dress. Have faith in our commanders. Modesto knows what he's doing. This is the battle that will show the world a rightful government cannot be defeated by rebels. And when Hitler finally provokes the rest of Europe into war the French and the British will have to take our side because Franco sure as hell is on the other one. It's just a matter of time."

"I hope you're right," said Juan. "They'd better win

113

at the Ebro, because if we lose too many men there's no one left to call up – after the sixteen year olds and the forty-five year olds, who? Still, on the subject of tobacco, if we were to lose, I imagine they might let us have one decent smoke before they shoot us."

"You are such a pessimist, Juan. We are not going to lose. I'm telling you, it's a matter of time before the whole of Europe understands the need to destroy Fascism. And when it does, that's when Communism will have its true chance to flower. One more war and then the workers will free themselves once and for all. You'll see. Hitler and Franco – they're a blessing in disguise for the workers of the world."

Catalina and Juan looked at each other and shook their heads:

"It's a good disguise."

"Certainly fooled me."

"So what have we been wasting our time all day for, if you're so certain the Fascists are about to be pushed back into the Atlantic?"

Lluís shrugged:

"It pays to be prepared, doesn't it? The Italians are on Mallorca. Who knows what Franco will think of, when he can't win at the Ebro? He might think it's a good idea to turn his attention elsewhere."

"You really think he might invade Menorca?"

He shrugged again.

"It's our job to defend the island. Against whatever comes. That's what we'll do. Cap Mola, Cap Cavalleria, all around the coast. We'll see them coming, we'll fight them, and we'll take as many of them with us as we can."

"We won't stop an invasion though, will we? You have to admit, history's against us there."

"True, Juan, but this is different. We wouldn't be

defending Menorca for a king, or a religion, or a foreign empire. This time it's our land, our people's land. We're not mercenaries or occupiers. We've sworn loyalty to the Second Republic that the people elected, that we elected. And the only way I'm giving up this island to an invader is with my last breath!"

21

The Plaça del Princep is just up the hill from the fish market and the old cloister where the general market is held. The lawyers' office is marked with a generous brass plaque, well polished. It is in a smart old house at the head of the square. I push open one of the double doors, letting sunlight spread across a marble floor and the base of a wide sweeping staircase. It smells of wax polish and respectable prosperity.

At the end of the first sweep of the staircase I face another plaque beside another set of double doors, elegant mahogany with a hint of art deco flourish. There is a bell push and when I press it there is a pause and then a buzzer sounds. The buzzer makes me jump and stops before I think to turn the door handle. When I do, the door opens anyway and I am in a grand high-ceilinged room. This must have been a salon once, or at least a receiving room, an antechamber to the salon. Where once there might have been chairs and settees made in the English style from the pattern books of Sheraton and Chippendale there is now a pair of boxy sofas upholstered in tan leather and a smoked glass coffee table. Only the receptionist's desk and an ornate glass chandelier suspended from the high distempered ceiling might be survivors from the house's original décor.

The marble flooring continues up here and the window behind the receptionist's desk is almost obscured by heavy curtains. The chandelier is not lit and it is dim in the room and cold after the bright sunshine outside. The receptionist is engrossed in a telephone conversation but she conducts it in a hushed voice and I wonder whether this is so that her boss will not hear or simply the influence that this room has on people. There is something sad about it, something solemn – beyond even the normal gravity of a lawyer's office – something bereft.

Eventually the telephone conversation ends and my presence in front of the desk is registered. I give my name and she nods towards the sofas. The coldness of the marble floor strikes up through the thin soles of my one pair of smart shoes as I walk away from the spot where I have been standing and starts a long shiver running up my body. I wonder what I'm doing here. When Lluís's grandson asked me to come and see him at his office he didn't exactly say why.

He just said: "Please! You're the only one I've found so far who knew him. I need you to tell me about him. Maybe you can help me work out why I was never allowed to meet him."

"Why don't you ask your father?" I said then, but he only smiled and said:

"It's not that easy. You'll see."

I look at my watch. It feels strange to have it on my wrist, the first time in weeks. I don't need it on the cala, where I can tell the time by the sky and where, in any event, I have no appointments to keep. Lluís's grandson, he told me his name was Ángel, is late.

Finally, the door from the staircase opens and a man comes in. But it is not Ángel. It is a tall angular elderly gentleman with a beak of a nose and straight black hair surprisingly untouched by grey. Dressed in an old-fashioned black suit and highly-polished shoes. He glances briefly in my direction and then at the receptionist, who shakes her head and jerks it towards the ceiling, which I think signifies that I am a visitor for someone who works upstairs.

He crosses the room to a second set of double doors, opens them and goes through. Sunlight briefly floods the ante-room and I catch a glimpse of tall bookcases and a huge polished wooden desk before he turns and closes the doors behind him, fastidious in not meeting my gaze.

The cold in the waiting room seems to intensify. Certainly, Ángel Mascaró appears not to want to spend any more time in there than he can help. He sweeps in fifteen minutes late, laden with a pilot case in one hand and a slim leather portfolio under his elbow, and sweeps me out again, up another flight of stairs and through a single door into an office that is markedly less grand than the one downstairs.

"I must apologise," he says as he kicks the pilot case under his desk and places the portfolio (his briefcase of choice, I imagine) more carefully onto the desk surface. The case is highly polished and he is clearly anxious to avoid scuffing it.

"I was before a judge who simply would not do the sensible thing. I had no choice but to argue, and I hate arguing."

"I thought that's what lawyers did best." I say, and he looks put out.

"Maybe some," he says "but not me. I do not like conflicts. I prefer solutions. I like to make agreements. In the interests of my clients, of course. Perhaps – I should not say this to you but I am not cut out to be a trial lawyer. My father wants that I should be one. He, he has the nose for it, you see."

And I have seen, if the elderly man is his father. The perfect Roman juridical nose. Which his son lacks, having inherited Lluís's broad peasant nose.

"Is that your father downstairs?"

"You met him?"

"No, but I saw him. You're not really alike, are you?"

He laughs. Then stops. Then laughs again.

"No," he says. "Not really. We've never had much in common. Now we don't even seem to have the same ancestors."

"What do you mean?"

"This is the reason I asked you to come. Because you knew him, you see – Lluís Sintes. The man the police said was my grandfather. You're the only eye witness I've got. Well, no, there's one other. But it wouldn't help to call on her, not with my father. You see, he maintains that his father was Joan Cintas Mascaró, who died in 1960. But that's not what the police said when they came to tell him his father was dead. He was out the first time they came, so they told me instead. And, according to you, that's not what my face says."

"It's not what Billy's mother says either."

"What? Who's Billy?"

"He's a boy who lives on the cala near me. He didn't know Lluís but he asked his mother and she said Lluís had a son, a lawyer in Mahon. Francisco Mascaró. And in fact, now I think about it, Lluís himself did once tell my family he had a son. Called Francisco, and that ..."

I stop. Perhaps I shouldn't say the rest.

"And that what?"

"Well, if I'm remembering it right. It was twenty years ago and I might not have understood it perfectly. I was only fifteen. And my French wasn't perfect."

"You mean your Spanish."

"No. My Spanish was non-existent in those days. That's why we spoke French, your grandfather and I."

"Okay. So what was it you think he said about my father?"

"Well, I think he said that his wife left him before the baby was born. For another man."

"Joan Mascaró?"

"I don't know. It was a long time ago. I only remember it because it embarrassed my parents. They were making small talk and he ... well, your grandfather didn't go in for small talk. I can't remember exactly what he said – something about her not wanting to be a Red any more. I think it must have been during the Civil War. Could that be right? Was he that old?"

"I don't know. My father was born in November 1939. A few months after the end of the war."

I shrug my shoulders.

"Makes sense. Perhaps your father just never knew, if his mother left his father before he was even born, maybe this is as big a shock to him as it is to you."

"No."

"Why? Why do you say that?"

"Because I know him. There's been something he's been keeping from me for a long time. I've never known what it is, but I think this is it. Whatever he says, I think he knew all about my grandfather. And I need to know why he never told me. Come on."

He pushes his chair away from the desk and marches towards the door, expecting me to follow. I hear the sharp taps of his soles on the marble treads of the staircase, then the sound of a door being flung open and crashing back on its frame, a squawk of female surprise and then, fainter, the crash of another door being thrown open.

What have I done? I think it's time to leave.

Slowly, gingerly, as if by moving silently I shall be able to efface myself from the picture of confusion I seem to have created, I pick up my things and walk out of Ángel's office. I try to make my feet soundless on the steps and I try not to listen to the sound of Ángel's voice, rapid and urgent and angry, coming from the inner office.

I have passed the open door of the ante-room and have reached the head of the flight of stairs down to the front door when it strikes me. I can't hear the voice of Señor Mascaró senior. Just Ángel, firing questions into silence, then waiting, then firing the questions again.

My shoe squeaks as I turn. I hesitate on the threshold of the outer office and then I see the receptionist, her eyes shining with curiosity and pleasure, rapt at her desk. Clearly she has waited a long time in inclement conditions for this moment. I cross the frozen waste and stop at the second open doorway. They both have their backs to me. The older man is standing at a long window, looking out. Ángel is squarely in front of me, the fabric of his jacket stretched tight over the muscles of his back, his fists clenched at his sides, all his strength directed into the attack on his father's silence.

"I asked you a question."

His voice is almost hoarse.

"I said, I asked you a question. Who was my grandfather? Why have you been keeping secrets from me all these years? All that crap I've swallowed from you about the old man – how close you were. Was he even my grandfather? Was he?"

The figure at the window is motionless. Then he turns and, calmly, as though he were alone in his office, walks over to his desk and fingers some papers. I see Ángel's shoulders tense even tighter and he shouts:

"For God's sake!"

The older man's head snaps up.

"For God's sake? Don't, you little red hypocrite."

Hatred splatters like blood across the floor.

"You want to know about secrets? Ask your grandmother. She's the one with secrets. She's kept them long enough by now. Maybe she's ready to confess them to her own little Ángel."

I am near enough in line with his gaze, at Ángel's shoulder, to see the absolute coldness of it, the coldness of a death. Then he says his final words and I know they're directed at us both.

"Get out."

22

It isn't until we're in the street that I realise my hand is round Ángel's arm, above the elbow. I must have pulled him out of that room and down the stairs, through the heavy door and into the daylight. The warmth of the sun drives the lingering effect of that cold gaze out of my bones first. Ángel still stands frozen on the pavement but then the muscle beneath my fingers begins to twitch and the feeling of life returning there gives me a jolt like electricity. Looking down I see that he is clenching and unclenching his fists. I move my hand up and down his bicep, as much – if I'm honest – to feel the shape and length of it as to make a gesture of comfort. Then he turns his head to look and see who's there and I drop my hand from his arm.

It takes him a moment to recognise me, I think, and a moment more to summon something to say.

"That's the end for us."

The dismissal hits me like a fist in the gut but I am hardly surprised.

"I'm sorry. I shouldn't have involved myself. I'd better go."

His hand moves quicker than I would have thought possible and grips me by the wrist.

"Me and him. Not you and me. It's the end of me and him. I'm not sure yet about you and me."

"But it's my fault. I'm sorry. I shouldn't have said anything. It wasn't my intention to cause trouble between you and your father."

We are still standing in the street, his hand round my

wrist. I could shake it off and walk away into the holiday crowds but I don't. Logical or not, my curiosity about Lluís is back, as strong as ever. There's something else too, besides curiosity – a sense that there may be parallels between his life and mine.

I'm surprised to see a smile of sorts come so soon to those blasted lips and eyes.

"Not your fault. It's been coming for a long time. I told you, there's been something wrong between us for years and I've never known what it was. Maybe this is it. Amazing, isn't it? A week ago I was Ángel Mascaró, third generation lawyer, socialist grandson of a staunch *Franquista*. Now, I don't even know what my real name is and an English tourist is better acquainted with my family history than I am. Know what that makes me think?"

I shake my head, just relieved that he still thinks of me as nothing more than a passing tourist:

"It makes me think I need a drink. Expect you do too. Come on, let's go down to the port. It's quiet at this time of day."

He touches me lightly on the elbow to point me downhill and leaves his hand there as we walk. A hot afternoon is beginning to cool into a balmy evening. It is a quarter to six, the time when the Mahonese reclaim their town from the tourists. Most of the baby buggies have been wheeled back to villas and apartments and the streets are once again populated with people who know each other, who stop and greet each other with a quiet handshake, who linger in their shop doorways and exchange the news of the day. We ourselves meet two acquaintances of Ángel's on the way. He shakes their hands but hardly slows his pace, making it clear that he is on important business with me, though of what kind is probably less clear to them and to me than it is to him.

124

We take the wide shallow steps that criss-cross the winding Ses Voltes road like a ladder entwined with a snake and at the bottom he touches my elbow again to turn me east onto the Moll de Llevant. At a gap in the traffic he hurries us across the road and then we walk along by the water. A little way down, moored to the mole, there floats a broad square pontoon laid out as a restaurant with white draped tables and a smart blue and white striped awning. It belongs to a bar restaurant whose main building is on the other side of the road. He hesitates on the gangway and says:

"You don't suffer from sea sickness do you?"

I shake my head and he gestures for me to precede him. We are close on the narrow gangway and I can smell his aftershave. It is a little too generously applied, but not unpleasant. As I step aboard, the waiter comes towards us and clearly he knows Ángel. He shows us to a table, pulling out a chair for me so that I have a perfect view across the harbour towards the pretty villas that tumble down the hillside around Cala Llonga. The view is curtailed but not extinguished when my companion sits down opposite me.

"What would you like?"

It's been so long since I did this: "A glass of white wine?"

I look at the waiter. He looks at Ángel.

"Monopole," says Ángel and the waiter moves towards the bar.

"Smoke?" He taps a packet, one of those soft foreign packets I've always preferred to the stiff English kind, on the table and shakes two loose. I'm about to say no, when I wonder why. I've been smoking a lot the last few weeks. Why deny it? It's not as if I need to impress anyone or set a good example. I've enjoyed every cigarette I've ever smoked and, that being so, it seems rather

125

ludicrous that until now I've never taken up the habit properly. And why not? Only for the ridiculously trivial reason that I thought it might kill me.

"Thanks," I say. "Yes, I do." And he leans forward and lights mine for me, while the waiter arrives with an ice bucket that clips onto the side of the table and a tall slim sweating green bottle. He shows it perfunctorily to Ángel before opening it deftly and pouring us each a glass. Then he sinks the bottle into the iced water and is gone.

"So. Let's forget about me for a little while. What about you? You're here on your own. Not married?"

For answer I put the cigarette down on the ashtray and spread my hands out towards him, fingers pointing down slightly. We both look at them in silence. There are no rings on the fingers and they are evenly tanned. Even so, I can see a slight wasting between the second and third knuckles of the ring finger on my left hand.

"Why not?" he says and I clasp my hands together, absurdly pleased, as if I'd just been told I look younger than my age. Still, under the white tablecloth my left thumb searches around for the callus there used to be at the base of my ring finger where it met the palm. It isn't there any more and, just as suddenly as I felt pleasure, I feel a sense of loss. I reach for the cigarette, take a long drag and hold the smoke down until there's a little shiver round my spine.

"What about you?" I say, turning my head towards the water and exhaling the smoke, not because I'm interested but because I remember that this is the form and I'm enjoying playing at being able to do this.

"Oh, I've been married," he says and gives me a look that combines condescension with an appeal for sympathy.

126

A boat goes past, one of the fancy llaud-cum-gin palaces that only seem to live in the roads at Mahon. The pontoon lifts and settles and the ice clinks in the bucket. He's about to tell me about his marriage, or maybe more than one. And I'm about to let him.

23

The lawyer stands at his tall window and looks down into the square for a long time after his son and the woman have gone. His secretary glances in once or twice through the door that Ángel flung back on its hinges, but when she sees Mascaró, motionless, hands clasped behind his back, she thinks better of interrupting his reverie.

Though he would never seem it, he might be grateful if she did, for his thoughts are not pleasant. Yet again, he has let his anger get the better of him. Worse than ever. As soon as the words were out of his mouth, he regretted them violently. But it was too late. The boy was gone. He watched the two of them standing on the pavement below, that woman with her hand on Ángel's arm, the boy stunned at what he had said to him, then shaking it off and turning his attention to her.

He wonders who she is, this woman. There has been no one, so far as he knows, since the divorce from Antonia. Divorce. In the Mascaró family. A disgrace. And so unnecessary. If only Ángel had shown a little more ambition, a little more willingness to move in the proper circles, if he wasn't always so ... gauche. That was all she wanted, Antonia, to feel that she had married a man who was going places, to be part of the right level of society. He still missed her, the way she called him: "Papa" and came out with him to exercise the horses, while Ángel squeezed himself into that ridiculous shiny fabric and went hurtling off on his bicycle as if he was one of those drug addicts in the Tour de France.

Such a straightforward, proper girl, from a good Ciutadella family – just the sort of match his own father would have approved of. He couldn't help feeling the divorce was Ángel's fault, even though it was she who finally left.

If only Ángel had known his grandfather, perhaps things would have been different. The tragedy of his death, younger than Mascaró was now, still pained him like nothing else. All he had ever wanted since that day had been a son with whom he could have the same relationship that he had had with his own father, the relationship that had been snatched away from him far too soon.

But they have never had it, he and Ángel. Have never seen eye to eye on anything from when he was the smallest child. Not once can he recall the boy looking up at him with the devotion, the respect, the awe he remembers feeling for his own father. He used to love the smell of his father's polished riding boots, the way his hair stayed in combed grooves from the pomade he put on it, the neatness of his moustache, grown just like the one in the photos of the Generalissimo. He remembers how proud he used to be when his father called him downstairs to introduce him to his dinner guests, how he learned to stand up tall in his blue shirt of the Falange Junior section and say "Good evening, sir" and shake hands solemnly even when he was a very small boy. And afterwards, the next day, his father would tell him who it was he had been meeting, and why they were important and he would nod to show he understood, even when he didn't.

Ángel would never do any of that with him. Was always off climbing a tree or chasing after geckos, getting himself covered in dust and tearing his clothes, so that if the nurse did manage to catch him when his father had guests, he was usually quite unpresentable. And on the rare occasions she not only caught him but forced him into a respectable shirt and trousers he would only glare glassily at the floor in front of the assembled businessmen and mutter "*Salud*" under his breath until his father waved him out of the room in exasperation.

Or perhaps it was the boy's mother dying that had prevented things going right between them. Francisco had tried his best to find a suitable wife, but it was so hard without his father there to guide him. His mother refused to have anything to do with Ciudadella society once she was widowed and so it was left to him to court Consuela without any guidance. She was a good girl, everything he thought his father would have recommended: sweet, compliant, devout, a perfect angel of the hearth. Except for one thing. The one thing Francisco could not have known how to judge, with his lack of experience. She was not made for bearing children. Something his mother could have pointed out, if she'd cared enough. Those narrow hips. Something a woman should have noticed, and warned him off. But she never did. Just held herself apart, as usual. Until after Ángel was born. Once she had her precious grandchild, then she told Francisco he should leave Consuela alone, or let her take measures to prevent another pregnancy.

But he was her husband and they were both Catholics and the matter was in God's hands. That's what he told his mother. And she looked at him and said: "You know what I think of God, Francisco. She's your wife and, if you love her, you should protect her yourself. For pity's sake, don't leave it to God."

He bends his head now as he remembers. Then he stares down the hill where his son walked away and wonders what he will do next. He bites his lip when he thinks of what he said to him in the heat of his anger:

"Go and speak to your grandmother. See if she's prepared to tell her secrets."

Stupid! Unless she keeps her promise he may have brought down on his own head the very thing he's worked to avoid all these years. He cannot bear to think what will happen if Ángel discovers that the man he has always urged on him as an exemplar is not his grandfather in a strict biological sense and, worse, that his real grandfather was a worthless Communist renegade.

He turns from the window and looks at the spot in front of his desk where he first saw the old man, pulling a pile of papers out of a tatty plastic bag. Can still smell the sweat and seawater smell coming off his faded clothes, the white blotches on his old sandals.

His younger self is sitting in the very same chair he has now, fingers steepled idly, waiting for the old fool to get his argument together. He has only agreed to see him at the request of his clients, some property developers who think it might be possible to buy the fellow off, either with money or promises of some concession that will appease his opposition to their plans.

He has offered the man a seat, a coffee, but both have been roughly refused as if they were offers of bribes. Mascaró is beginning to think it was pointless hoping to reach any kind of sensible accommodation with him. The whole meeting is a waste of time, and he assumes the clients knew that, given that they have found better things to do than attend.

Finally, the fellow has ordered his papers and begins to read a long diatribe against Mascaró's clients and their proposals. The lawyer realises that he has a real old hard case on his hands. Not only does his list of complaints include the old Communist myth that property is theft and, by extension, that property development is aggravated assault, it also contains a number of quite defamatory allegations about the political affiliations of his clients. The lawyer picks up his pen and begins to make notes of the more outrageous slurs. Then he puts it gently down on the blotter, deciding not to warn the old man of his vulnerability to litigation. After all, if he chooses to make these allegations in a public forum, it will only undermine his objections and make everyone realise that he is unhinged. Why should he help him by pointing the fact out in advance?

So he listens until the polemic reaches its climax, which it does, predictably enough with a clenched fist salute. Mascaró smiles, and stands, and says:

"Finished?"

The old man, who has worked himself into such a frenzy that there is spittle at the corners of his mouth, nods, apparently surprised by his listener's calmness.

"Good."

The clients need not worry. There is no need to offer to cut any kind of deal with an imbecile like this. There is no chance he can carry the feeling of a public meeting with him. Not unless they all want to be associated with an obvious crank.

"Then my secretary will show you out. Good day."

The old man's fist falls to his side:

"Is that it?"

Mascaró dips his head:

"That's it. I've heard nothing to suggest that my client's proposals breach any of the relevant guidelines. If you had had valid objections then clearly we'd have been willing to discuss them with you, try to work out a mutually acceptable position but as it is ..."

He gestures towards the door. The old man gathers up his papers and shoves them back in his carrier bag. He turns to go, then he pauses and turns back.

"There's just one thing I'd like to ask you, Senor, before I go. There was another lawyer called Mascaró, in Ciudadella, years ago. Is he any relation of yours?"

Mascaró wonders, for a moment, whether he has been too harsh, whether, unlikely as it seems, this man was once a friend of his father's. His manner becomes instantly more respectful:

"Indeed he was. I am honoured to say that he was my late father. Did you know him?"

The old man looks hard at the lawyer, seeming to focus on him properly for the first time. Then he shakes his head slowly:

"No. I never knew your father. But I used to know your mother. Before you were born."

Francisco is still surprised. His mother, he knew, came from an ancient and noble Ciudadella clan and had been married very young. He had no idea how she would have run across a peasant type like this.

"Did you know her well?" he says.

And the old man laughs, a harsh croak of a laugh revealing primitive dental arrangements, and says:

"Not as well as I thought. Even though she was my wife."

Mascaró stares at him. He is even more insane than he had thought. The old man runs his hand through thick unruly grey hair and juts his chin out defiantly. There is something weirdly familiar in the way he does it. The lawyer blinks as a terrible thought comes to him. He glances down at a framed photograph on his desk. His teenage son stares up at him, thick unruly brown hair, so different from his own, ruffling in the breeze.

He looks up from the photo to the face opposite him. Flat and square, with a broad nose and deep brown eyes under the unkempt brows. The hands too, with short powerful fingers and wide palms. He looks down at the photo again and everything he knows about himself shrivels up and blows away.

Suddenly, an old playground taunt comes back to him. One he never understood. A boy he bested in an argument, walking away and shouting over his shoulder: "*Cabron Rojo*". Red Bastard. Some of the others had laughed and turned their backs on him. He'd always thought it was just a carelessly chosen insult, but now he realises it wasn't. It was the truth. He is a Red's bastard. And the father he loved so deeply is taken from him a second time.

24

If my head hurt like this for no reason, I'd be worried that there was something seriously wrong. But I have given it good reason. Too much white rioja and too many cigarettes, smoked too enthusiastically. I have pills somewhere, but none for a bad head. None for a head that is bad in such an uncomplicated way, that hurts with a healthy crushing grip.

The smell of brewing coffee wakes me up properly and everything turns for the worse. My head is thick and my mouth dry and sour. The floor is already hot beneath my bare feet and the sun strikes my poor head like a slap as I push back the door to the balcony. The light outside is white and scorching. It is a day that belongs farther along in the summer, in August not June, sent early to punish me. And I cannot hide from it. I am past the stage of being able to lie down and watch the sun stretch shadows on tenterhooks across the whitewashed ceiling as another day passes quietly by. For good or ill, I have to face the fact that my old friend Lluís has dragged me right back out of the shadows and into the light.

When the pot stops bubbling on the stove I pour myself a mug of coffee. I go to drink it on the balcony but the dazzling brightness beats me back. Down below, a flash of sunlight reflects off my car's roof. It is parked at an odd angle and I vaguely remember insisting that I was fine to drive. The clock on the wall tells me that it's ten o'clock and the heat outside corroborates the fact.

One sip of the coffee is enough to prove that I need my caffeine cold, fizzy and sweet this morning and the coolness in the stairway comes as a relief. For once, I'm grateful that the light in the old fridge is broken and I stand and drink the Coke in the gloom of the cellar. As my head clears, the events of the evening begin to gather and re-form.

It had been easy enough to steer my friend, the lawyer, away from talking about me and back to a far more fascinating topic – himself. The story of his marriage, start to finish, took an hour, at the end of which it was easy to move him on from the subject of his ex-wife and her unreasonable expectations of his earning potential to the even bitterer subject of his father.

"To think," he said, "I've spent my whole life having my grandfather's close relationship with my father constantly thrown in my face as the example I could never live up to. And now it turns out his father wasn't even his father at all."

"It's not even as if he was so fine, the old man. I know my father worshipped him but my grandmother says it was only because he was desperate for his father's approval and I get the impression the old fascist was impossible to please."

"He was a fascist?"

He looked startled. Perhaps he wasn't conscious that he'd used that word at all. Perhaps he hadn't expected me to be listening that closely. Then he waved it away:

"We don't bring all that up. I shouldn't have said it really. But it's one of the things my father and I fight about. You heard him. He says I'm a damned Red," – he rolled the word "*Rojo*" slowly round his tongue like it was something hard or ice-cold and I had heard his father do the same and then spit it out – "especially when I speak Menorquin rather than Spanish. He hates

136

all that. He says that no one remembers what *El Caudillo* did for this country."

"*El Caudillo*?"

"Franco. Francisco Franco."

And he knew he shouldn't but he couldn't resist. His eyes sparkled with malice:

"My father was named after him."

My mind flew back twenty years then. To Lluís saying: "It's the last name I would have chosen."

Poor Lluís. It's hardly surprising he lived the rest of his life like a hermit. And I was just wondering what became of her, this pearl amongst women, when it came back to me what Ángel had said a few moments earlier: "... my grandmother says ..."

I sat up straight. I had assumed she was dead, or else why wouldn't Ángel be getting his eye-witness account of his grandfather from her? Instead of me, the original innocent bystander:

"She's still alive? Your grandmother's still alive?"

He smiled then, not seeming to notice my surprise, and I saw real feeling for another human being in his face for the first time.

"Oh yes. Forty years a widow. She could have remarried. She was still relatively young when he died, and must have been quite beautiful still. But it seems like one husband was enough to last her a lifetime."

He seemed to be forgetting about Lluís. But then, maybe they were never married. Did he refer to her as his wife? I try to think back to that night of the barbecue, but twenty years is too long. All I can recall is the gist of what he said:

"Where is she now? On the island?"

He laughed at the absurdity of the question:

"Of course. Menorcans don't leave, you know. Not unless they have to. It goes against the grain. She lives in Es Mercadal. She moved there from Ciutadella after the old man died. Said she'd had enough of all the hawk noses and the priests in Ciutadella."

"What did she mean?"

"Do you know Ciutadella?"

I shook my head. The town was over on the other side of the island. Only twenty miles or so, but a world away from my cala.

"It's different from Maó. Maó is ... arriviste. One of your countrymen, Richard Kane, made it the capital when the British came here in 1713. Because of the port and to take power away from the old families and the Catholic Church. Ciutadella was the main town before that. It was where the noblemen had their palaces and the Church had its base. It's still the centre for tradition, for snobbery, for sanctimony. At least that's what my grandmother says."

"And for fascism?"

He shrugged and frowned. Clearly, he felt he'd said too much about that and wished I would leave it alone. But then again, maybe breaking the taboo gave him a thrill. In any event he didn't shoo me off entirely.

"Ciutadella was less – how can I say it – enthusiastic about the Republican government than the rest of the island."

"So Menorca was on the Republican side then?"

He looked indignant:

"Of course. Right until the end. The very last place in Spain to fall to Franco in fact. Which happened just here."

He nodded at the water to the side of him.

"Here?"

"Yes, on a ship anchored here in the port. A British battleship actually."

He shook his head, as if bewildered by our continued fascination with his island. I am confused:

"But the British weren't involved in the Civil War, were they? Not officially. I mean George Orwell and all that. The International Brigades. But officially we were neutral, weren't we?"

He laughed again, at more absurdity:

"Oh yes, you were perfectly neutral. Just like the French and the Americans. Wouldn't sell our democratically-elected government so much as a bullet with which to defend itself against an armed insurrection, even though Hitler and Mussolini were supplying the other side. Still, give the British their due. They did turn up right at the end. To see fair play. Nothing at all to do with the rumour that Franco needed the Italians' help to invade the island. Mussolini had bombers, you see, and para-troops. Franco didn't have either."

"Well, the British got very excitable about the idea of Mussolini getting his hands on a deep-water har-bour in the Med. Especially one they still thought of as half theirs. They must have done, to risk their pre-cious neutrality by sending a ship with a messenger from Franco on board. His job was to negotiate a surrender with the island authorities. The British didn't like it, but they ended up ferrying a boat-load of refugees to Mar-seille. That was in February 1939. As I said, right at the end."

And his father was born in November. So where was Lluís by then? "I ran away" he said. That I do remember. Twenty years or not. It suddenly strikes me that maybe that's what we have in common, Lluís and I.

But he must have run further than our cala to escape Franco and his prisons. When I knew him he spoke French – in a way I've travelled enough since to see is the way a native speaks it – a Provençal French, using "veng" for "vin" and "domeng" for "demain". Not French you could learn out of a textbook or from tapes, even if the idea of Lluís with language tapes wasn't so completely absurd. No, the French he spoke you couldn't learn unless you lived there, somewhere in the South. Not too far from Marseille.

"Why don't you ask your grandmother about all this? You confronted your father – why not her?"

He dropped his head and stared into his glass:

"I should. I will. I just ..."

He looked up at me and I was shocked to see there were tears in his eyes:

"I love my grandmother. She's the only one I've always been able to love. If she did something terrible when she was young, I don't know whether I can bear to ask her about it. She's over eighty, and she's a very private person. She lives her own way. What if she told me to 'Get out!' also?"

He dropped his eyes and spoke quietly:

"Then I'd have no one."

There was a silence. I thought he would start off again, on another tack, but he didn't. I stared down at my wine glass, twisting the stem. I didn't want to look up. Experience told me it would be a mistake to look up just then. When I did I knew experience had been right. There was no misinterpreting the look he was giving me now. His eyes, already shadowed in the dusk, seemed to grow black with insistence. There was no longer any attempt to charm there, no humour, no flirtation. The well-cut sports jacket, the polished shoes, the expensive leather briefcase ceased to say anything about him. Everything he was was contained in the hungry unblinking look and its single question.

I could have gone with him, done whatever he wanted. After all, my encounter with Billy had been a great pick-me-up. What stopped me, this time, was that love he'd shown for his grandmother. If it hadn't been for that, if all I'd seen were his bitterness and self-pity I would have done what he wanted. Because what he wanted would have had nothing to do with me. But he'd ruined it for himself by showing me that vestige of feeling for another person. I couldn't risk him turning that on me.

So I said I had to go.

"Stay."

"No."

"At least have dinner with me."

"No."

"Why not?"

"I can't."

"Someone waiting for you?"

"It's not that."

"Then you can."

He signalled to the waiter and smiled at me, veiling the look, putting it away for the time being. I decided not to take it personally. We talked our way down another bottle and he seemed more relaxed, more likeable. So I was surprised, when I did get up to go, to find that he was churlish.

Dislike – of his vanity, his self-regard – boiled up in me then. Did he think he was the only one with whom life did not play fair? So I waited for a pause in the litany of complaint, leaned over, kissed the sulky mouth very lightly and said:

"Hasta la luego, Ángel."

Then I walked away.

25

Billy answers his phone on the third ring with a shouted: "*¿Si?*" There is noise in the background, the sound of an engine and voices.

"It's …" and I realise he still doesn't know my name. "It's me," I say, and I hear the engine die away. The voices recede too and I can picture him stepping aside and pressing the phone to his ear.

"*¿Que pasa?*"

"I need your help", I say. There is a pause on the end of the line, although I think we both know that he doesn't seriously have to think about it.

"Where are you?"

"On the cala."

"I'll be there when I can," he says, and I think we both also know that if I take the drinks out of the fridge now, they will still be cold when he gets here.

I open two Cokes and take them out onto the nearest jetty. I have hardly had time to find my place in my book before I hear the whine of an engine coming down the incline. It sounds like a motorbike, and none of the neighbours has one so I look up as it slews round in the gravel at the bottom of the hill. It is red, not a full sized motorbike actually, more of a trail bike with high mudguards and long springs. The kid is sitting astride it, grinning at me and I have to laugh. It suits him so well. Clearly, he wants me to go over and admire it and so I do, handing him the bottle of Coke.

"Are you old enough to drive that thing?"

He looks hurt.

"It was my birthday yesterday. I'm sixteen." Which doesn't exactly answer the question but I let it pass.

"It's very … red."

He knows I'm laughing at him and he doesn't care. He has his hands on something so cool that nothing anyone can say will knock him down. Now he has his independence on land as well as on the water. I feel a twinge of sadness for his boat, which has been his pride and his joy. Will he abandon it now for the flashier thrills of the road?

I glance over at the boat, which is floating there on its mooring. Billy follows my glance and also, perhaps, my thoughts. He swings his leg over the bike and kicks down the stand. Then he wanders out along his jetty, drinking as he goes, and sets down the bottle while he checks the ropes. He swings off the jetty one-handed into the boat and picks up the petrol can, swilling it from side to side to check how much fuel there is. He seems satisfied and stows it back in the stern. Then he gives the rubber bulb in the fuel pipe a couple of squeezes and pulls the cord. The engine grumbles and catches. A belch of blue grey smoke drifts over the water.

I pick up his bottle, wondering where he is going, and then I see that he is waiting for me.

"Do you want to come?"

Always, I think. But I don't say it. We'll see what happens. Instead I say:

"Where?"

He just shrugs. I look back at my open front door, at my book steepled upside down on the neighbouring jetty, and squat down to untie the ropes.

"We could go to Maó – except that I think you've already been."

It's an accusation – a valid one, as it happens, though I don't know how he knows – and I look up from the rope, my fingers still working at the bowline. He is waiting to meet my eye, indignant, self-righteous. Expecting what? An apology? One day he'll come to understand that life's too short.

"How did your mother know that the lawyer was Lluís's son?"

This is the second time I've questioned the quality of his information and he is instantly peevish, a trait usually attributed to the old but shown off to perfection in the young.

"I don't know. She seemed to know, that's all. She said he was a little bit crazy in the head. You don't say that if you don't know someone, do you?"

There is the beginning of a pout, which lengthens when I say:

"Can we go and talk to her?"

"My mother?"

Billy sounds incredulous and I am sceptical myself, though probably for different reasons. How am I to explain my interest in Lluís? What will I say if she asks me what I am playing at with her young son? The feline plague, curiosity, urges me on.

"Will she be at home?"

He shakes his head, still horrified at what I am suggesting:

"She works."

"Where?"

There is a pause.

"In a bar resto in Arenal."

"Will she be there now?"

He thinks about the answers he could give to this question and then imagines, perhaps, the alternative: me knocking at the door of the house one evening as the whole family sits down to eat. Knowing what I'm capable of he can't be sure I won't. He picks the lesser of the two evils and shrugs sulkily:

144

"For sure."

The last rope is free and I step down into the boat as she begins to drift away from the jetty.

"Let's go," I say and turn my back on Billy while I coil the ropes. There is silence, except for the idling of the engine and I wonder if he will have the nerve to refuse, to tell me to get out of the boat. But age must count for something and a projection of confidence, that powerful illusion, counts for the rest because after a few seconds he puts the engine in gear and backs off the mooring.

We head out down the cala and then swing northwest towards Arenal. The sea is calm this morning. It is too early for an on-shore breeze, although with the sun so fierce there will probably be one this afternoon. For now the boat creates its own breeze and I am glad of it blowing through my hangover.

The square white rear of the biggest hotel in the resort is visible on the next hillside before we leave the cala but then it disappears behind dark shale cliffs and fifteen minutes pass before the cliffs part to reveal the entrance to the bay. Billy turns off his course to give a half-submerged rock a wide berth and then throttles back so that we almost drift through the neck of the bay towards the wide semi-circle of land. It is a child's idea of a beach, a long curving strip of white sand that dissolves into weedless blue water. There are rock pools at either edge of the beach and the protecting arms of the cliffs hug the centre, securing it from wind and waves. Where the sand peters out on the hillside in what once were pine woods there stands a child's idea of a holiday resort – bars and shops selling ice creams, inflatable balls, plates of chips and video games, hotels with all-you-can-eat buffets, fancy dress discos and organised games in the pool.

Billy steers the dinghy carefully under the lee of the

rocks at the eastern end of the bay. It's as if he doesn't want to be seen and as he comes forward to grapple with the anchor his head is so far down between his shoulders that there's no doubt about it.

"Where are you supposed to be, Billy?"

He shoots me a quick glance:

"School."

"I thought you'd finished for the summer."

"I have," and he shoots me a grin to explain that the end of term has been the subject of a unilateral declaration.

The anchor drops into the water and Billy squats down in the bottom of the boat.

"Which one does she work in?"

He points round the corner of the rocks, towards a point we cannot see and from which, if the laws of physics count for anything, no one should be able to see us.

"There's a bar in the corner, up under the trees. She should be in there."

"How will I recognise her? Does she look like you?"

He shrugs, which I take as a reluctant acceptance that there is indeed a family resemblance.

"What's her name?"

There is a pause. "Esperanza", he says, scowling, as if when it comes to parents even their names are embarrassing.

"I take it you're not coming with me."

A shake of the head and a twist of smile.

"Will you wait? I could always walk back along the cliffs."

Another shake of the head.

"It's too hot to walk. I'll take you back."

Which I take to mean that although he doesn't want to go up there with me he will want to know what I have said to his mother and what she has said to me. He may have other reasons too.

The water is deeper than it looks when I slip over the side. It soaks the ends of my shorts and I have to wade very gently to avoid getting wet to the waist. As the water grows shallower it grows warmer too until the last four or five steps ankle-deep are like walking through clear soup.

The beach is strewn with parasols, sun loungers, sandcastles and little cairns built from towels and shoes. And bodies, still and in motion. A naked small boy darts into my path, skinny with a big potbelly and stubby little angel wings for shoulder blades. But then just as he reaches me he stops, looks to the side and runs away again, shrieking with laughter at the game. And his mother catches him in a beach towel and laughs over his head at me as she rubs him down. Everywhere I look there are families playing and arguing, eating and drinking, loving and hating each other on the sand. I turn my eyes on the sea for relief but even there fathers are batting balls and tossing children into the air, mothers are pedalling slowly round on pedalos with their teenage daughters and the bucket and spade brigade are toddling up and down the water margin building moats and dams and castles.

It is a scene that deserves its Lowry, its Breughel, its Hieronymus Bosch but the painter would find no place in it for me. I have forfeited my right to appear in any more family portraits and I still don't know if it was the right thing to do, or whether I shall ever be forgiven. My heart stalls in my chest and a glob of cold salty regret gags my throat. For a moment I can't breathe. Then it slides slowly down. I swallowed a raw oyster once. The sensation was much the same

I look for somewhere to turn and then I see the bar above me, a square patio with parasols of plastic straw over the inevitable white plastic chairs and tables. Lluís. Concentrate on Lluís.

Rough concrete steps lead up to the bar from the back of the beach and when I get there I run up them, not because they're hot underfoot – though they are – but to give my heart a reason to start beating again. By the time I reach the top my lungs hurt and my vision is blurred and I have to stand for a while with my hands on my knees before I can read the menu posted on the wall, a row of laminated photographs of grinning prawns and round-eyed eggs and chips.

I choose a table at the edge of the patio, as far away from any families as I can get. I glance out across the water but Billy has chosen his mooring well. His boat is hidden from view by the rocks. A waiter wheels over to me with a tray and an order pad. I ask for a beer and the menu and he wheels away. I look around for a waitress but I can only see two waiters. One of them comes back with my beer in a frosted mug. A thin sheet of ice slides down the dimpled side and I shiver when I grip the handle. The cold has taken away the taste but the beer feels wonderful as it slips down my throat. I think of Billy sitting in the boat in the hot sun and I raise my glass in salute towards the rocks. Then I see her.

She has come from inside with two plates of food for a table at the other side of the bar. She is tall and slim like Billy, but she looks more like his brother. There is something of the dourness of the fisherman about her. Maybe Billy will have it one day. Maybe it's the mark that life places on those features. She puts the plates down without a word, hands out cutlery wrapped in paper napkins and heads back towards the kitchen. Her legs are bare beneath her black waitress's skirt and her long dark hair is held back in an inter-locking plastic comb.

I leaf through the greasy plastic menu and then wave at the waiter. He is beside me quickly, hardly stopping on his way to the next order. I point at a photo of sardines, he nods, scoops up the menu and is away again: a study in professional perpetual motion. I feel as if I'm at a fairground, watching the gallopers move past me while I stand on the edge of the crowd. I need to jump aboard, to catch Billy's mother at the moment she comes closest to me, but I'm not sure I can do it. I shift my chair round so that I can watch the approach from the kitchen. She comes out once more with food but heads away from me. Then she is back with a single plate and I know this is my moment.

"Señora Pons?"

She looks at me, frowning, and shakes her head. Then I realise what I've done wrong. Pons is Billy's father's name, not his mother's. The Spanish order these things differently.

"Esperanza?"

She frowns again but nods her head this time.

"Biel's mother?"

She nods again and gives me a longer look.

"I'm the English woman who lives down on the cala. It was me who was asking about the old man, Lluís."

"Ah, yes. The English woman."

She looks at me as if I am not what she had in mind. Not unfriendly though, not hostile.

"You saved Biel some money with that engine."

That's why. I nod, slightly surprised that he owned up at home to his shortcomings as a boatman.

"Miquelet told me. Not Bielet. He wouldn't tell me anything he didn't have to. He's at that age. You got kids?"

I have to swallow hard before I can shake my head and then I say: "Miquelet?"

"My other son."

The fisherman is more talkative than I thought.

She looks back towards the kitchen and I can see my

149

waiter standing in the doorway with his arms folded. I get the feeling we don't have much time to talk.

"You told Biel that Lluís's son was a lawyer in Mahon."

She nods.

"Do you mind telling me how you know?"

She looks as if she would like to ask if I would mind telling her why I want to know but then her eyes twitch back towards the kitchen and she decides that it would all take too long.

"My father owned the boathouse down there that the boys use now. He knew Lluís."

"They were friends?"

"I wouldn't say friends. The old man used to talk to him about how things were before he left the island."

"To go where? France?"

"That's right. You knew that? Knew the old man, right?"

"I came here on holiday when I was a teenager. I knew him, a little. He used to talk to me in French, but he never said anything about being in France. I was just guessing."

Hoping, more like.

"Yes, well. He lived over there for a lot of years. So I was told. They called him the Frenchman in the village. That's why. He had an accent when he came back. The Catalan they speak is different from Menorquí, so they tell me anyway. But he was convinced he still spoke pure Menorquí and he would get angry when people would tell him that a word he used must be from France. He said it was they who had forgotten the old words, not him. He was a bit ..." she twisted her finger at her forehead and glanced back at the kitchen again.

"And his son?"

She shakes her head:

"Oh no, his son wasn't like him at all. Very respectable, the son. Very smart. They weren't at all alike. The old man was abroad when the son was growing up, I think. My father always said it wasn't like they were part of the same family. Still, the son used to come and take him out sometimes, when he needed to see the doctor. That sort of thing. But they were never close. His son was involved with all this," she pointed towards the sweep of hotels and apartments around the bay, "and Lluís, well he preferred the island the way it used to be. Before tourism. Before a lot of things."

"And you're sure that his son was Francisco Mascaró?"

She nods:

"Sure. My father even used him as his lawyer when he sold some land down on the cala to build new houses." She laughed. "Lluís never spoke to my father again."

"Why?"

"Oh, he didn't want them building on the cala. And he liked, I think this is what it was, he liked to have enemies. Some people think they're more dependable than friends."

There was a clatter of crockery on the next table as the waiter slammed down three plates of food and stalked off towards the bar. Billy's mother gave the waiter's back a cold stare but began to move away too.

"Señora? One more thing?"

She looked over her shoulder at me, her mind already back on the job.

"I saw Lluís's death reported in the newspaper. But I've seen nothing since. Do you know how they think he died?"

"Who? The police?"

I nod. Who else?

151

"Oh, I think they are saying it was an accident. That he tripped and fell over the cliff."

"Do you think that?"

She shrugs.

"It would be easy to do. It's rough ground up there. He wasn't so steady on his feet, even when he lived here. That's what nobody understands though, what he was doing on the cliff. Nobody had seen him round here for a couple of years. Most people thought he was dead already. Still, I expect the police are right. I don't suppose we'll ever know any different anyway. If nobody saw what happened …"

And at that she goes, with an unexpected apologetic smile that lights up her face and makes her look more like Billy. I am alone with my sardines and my questions. One has been answered: Francisco Mascaró was Lluís's son, and he knows it, whatever he tells Ángel. But now I have others. What made Lluís leave the island and why did he come back? Why does his son deny the connection? And if he did fall from the headland, how did he get out there in the first place? I fillet a sardine and lift out its delicate little backbone, which bends under the weight of head and tail. If only people were so easy to anatomize.

26

I feel guilty enough, when I finish my sardines and my beer, to buy Billy a can of limón and a ham bocadillo on my way out of the bar. The sun hits me with its combination punch of searing heat and dazzling brightness as soon as I step off the patio. It is half past one and the beach is slightly, but not much, emptier. A few sensible souls have dragged their sensitive Saxon skins indoors but there are plenty more broiling on the sand. I pick my way through a sea of reddening flesh and stand for a moment at the edge of the water, feeling the wet sand suck away under my feet.

I can see the boat now. It is empty. I search up and down the beach, careful this time not to let my eyes rest on any particular family tableau, but amongst all the shades of skin visible there is no sign of Billy's smooth brown tan and amongst all the movement I cannot see his easy loping stride. I look out at the boat again and then I see a buoy floating on the anchor rope. The buoy waves at me.

When I reach the boat he is still floating there in the bare foot of shade thrown onto the water by the dinghy's blunt prow. His feet are wrapped round the rope and he lies on his back with his arms spread. His skin glistens in the sunshine and his hair floats round his head in the water like a halo. He has no idea how beautiful he is.

"It's hot," he says.

"¡Claro! I brought you some lunch."

I lay the cold can on his bare stomach and he gasps with shock, splashes and sinks and then resurfaces laughing.

153

I step backwards quickly and wave the paper-wrapped sandwich at him, my insurance against a dunking.

He shakes his head and turns towards the boat. He reaches in and places the can on the seat. Then he hauls himself up on his forearms and twists and slips effortlessly aboard. He stands up and offers me his hand. I give him the one without the sandwich but then I need to grip the side of the boat with the other hand. He holds out his hand for the sandwich and as I give it to him he smiles and pulls me upwards and then slips his wet hand out of mine and drops me flat on the water.

The water folds over me in a rush of blueness and bubbles. When I surface, spluttering and brushing water and hair out of my face he is bent forward with his hands on the gunwale. He is ready to laugh but something in his eyes suggests that he isn't sure whether he has gone too far, that he isn't sure if he can really treat me as he would a friend or whether something is owed to my adult sense of dignity, my foreignness, my being a woman.

Without giving him any clues I reach up my hand and he puts out one of his to grasp it. I let him start to pull me up and then I jerk on his arm, not hard enough to pull him in, just enough to rock the boat. The smile leaps to his face and I laugh and he laughs too, more out of relief, I think, than anything.

He puts his hand out again – in a gesture of truce – and I take it. His hand is already bigger than mine, but only just, and I wonder how much growing he has to do, how much distance there is still between Billy the kid and Billy the man. The muscles in his arm are taut as he pulls me up out of the water and so well defined under the skin that I can almost see them corded around his bones.

As we leave the shelter of the bay the water grows choppy and my wet hair lashes around my head.

"Little bit of wind," says Billy through a bite of his sandwich and the boat bounces on a wave.

I am suddenly feeling nauseous and it scares me, because I never get sea-sick. I feel truly awful so I lay the back of my head against the side and let the motion of the boat and the sea combine to beat against my skull. Billy swivels in his chair to look at me from time to time but I can't move. The ancient dark cliffs of the north coast (so much more unforgiving than the pretty white limestone cliffs in the south) grind past as the wind and waves try their best to push the dinghy onto the shore. The motion is sickening and at least that means there's no need for explanation when I hurl myself to the downwind side of the boat and heave my lunch over the side.

It takes longer to get back, with the wind and the chop, than it did to go out. Finally, we enter the cala and I immediately begin to feel better, which makes my panic recede. Perhaps it was simply sea-sickness or the after-effects of last night, after all. The islands slip by over my shoulder and as the awning of the bar flaps into view I manage to get to my knees and pull myself forward to sit in the bows. Billy throttles back the engine and we move gently down the channel. Nearly home. And when we get there I'll think of something to say.

The Alba is on her mooring and so the view is blocked until Billy turns the boat for the shore. I am already sorting the ropes and I don't catch Billy's question first time. I look over my shoulder at him:

"What?"

"I said: who's that?"

He points towards the jetty. A man is sitting with his legs dangling over the end. He is wearing a well-pressed short-sleeved shirt and smart trousers in khaki drill cotton. His deck shoes are carefully polished. He is reading my book.

I open my mouth to tell Billy to turn back out to sea, but the man has looked up now and seen me in the boat. He smiles and waves and I have no choice but to wave back. Behind me, Billy hisses:

"Who is he?"

I turn to face him and he looks accusingly at me, clearly angry that I have brought someone else to the cala. God, why does everything have to be so complicated? Even when you start again from scratch. I sigh:

"That's Lluís's grandson. But I have no idea what he's doing here."

27

Ángel climbs to his feet and stands waiting for us to arrive beside him. But Billy runs the boat smoothly alongside his own mooring and we are both busy tying the boat up bow and stern by the time the lawyer has made his way back to shore and out along Billy's jetty.

I am unable to muster a "What a nice surprise" or a "To what do I owe the pleasure?" I am almost as annoyed as Billy. This is what happens if you give people the smallest morsel of information, show them the faintest glimmer of interest. They come looking for more. That's why I kept myself to myself all these weeks. So as not to have to say:

"*Bon dia, Señor Mascaró.*"

"Ángel, please. I'm sure we moved on to first names last night."

The boat sways as Billy gives a particularly vicious yank on the bowline he has tied.

"Ángel, yes. Sorry. Why are you here?"

I move to climb out of the boat and he is there instantly, offering his hand and planting his immaculate deck shoe on the edge of the less than immaculate jetty planking. I accept the hand and the boat jerks again as Billy tips the engine forward on its bracket with more than usual force.

"I was passing, on my way to Es Mercadal."

I hear a grunt behind me, an indication of what Billy thinks of the stranger's route planning. And so does Ángel. He looks at Billy for the first time and then at me. He can't work out the connection.

"Not your son?"

Fabulous. Just the reminder I needed that I'm old enough to be Billy's mother.

"Not my son. Biel is a friend. Biel Pons. Ángel Mascaró."

The two shake hands, Ángel leaning down into the boat and Billy reaching up, but they do not speak.

"So, Mercadal? Are you going to visit your grandmother?"

He looks surprised.

"Last night, you told me she lives in Mercadal."

"I did? You have a good memory."

"It's not always an advantage."

I feel tired and sick and this morning's headache is back with interest. The door to my house still stands open and I'm tempted simply to run for it and shut myself in. But Mascaró doesn't seem to notice that he's outstaying even his limited welcome.

"Oh, but it is. As a lawyer ..."

A wave of nausea flows through me and my patience runs out:

"I'm sorry. What do you want?"

Mascaró's face reddens. He looks from me to Billy, who is grinning, and I can see him wondering what is the precise extent of my friendship with a boy he's already pointed out is easily young enough to be my son. He clears his throat:

"I wanted to have another look at my grandfather's place, before I went to see my grandmother. I, well, I wondered if there was anything else you could tell me about him."

He is putting off the evil hour and we both know it. I could tell him to go away, but then he will only come back again. Maybe if I hand him everything I know, he will leave me alone.

I swallow down hard on a gush of saliva that has filled my mouth and take a long swig from the bottle of Coke I left on the jetty. The warm sweet liquid furs my teeth but at least it takes away the taste of bile. I feel a little better, so I push my feet into my old espadrilles and, without speaking, lead the way along the shore to Lluís's old hut. As I turn to check that he is following I catch sight of Billy, still standing on the jetty. He has his arms folded and his cap tipped back. He looks sullen, jealous even. Suddenly I see his brother in him, and his mother – Biel, Miquelet and Esperanza. Lluís, Francisco and Ángel.

Family. We kid ourselves that we're unique when really so much of what we are is shared, handed down and beyond our control. Which makes it vital that we know where we came from, doesn't it? Especially now that we're beginning to understand how our genes delineate us, how they predict our personalities, our strengths and weaknesses, even the diseases that will stalk our lives. Turns out there really is such a thing as destiny. What we do with the information, well that's up to us. We still have choices. But we have to know. Don't we? If Lluís's grandson wants to know, I owe it to Lluís to tell him. Don't I?

Ángel stops abruptly as we turn the corner:

"So this is really where he used to live?"

I nod:

"You have to forget the boat. That wasn't here. And he wasn't smart, like you. There were paint pots, rags, old bits of wood. It was a mess."

"He was a painter?"

"Yes, of houses though, not pictures. When he wasn't fishing, he used to do a bit of painting for anyone who'd pay him. Just down on the cala or in the village. He didn't have a car, at least not when I knew him."

Ángel is standing on the little verandah to the side of the house, where there used to be a table, where Lluís used to take his meals. I try to imagine the two of them sitting there talking to each other in Menorquí, exchanging a joke, but the younger man's neat town clothes and the tidy job of renovation someone has done on the little house conspire to prevent Lluís reappearing in the place that was once his.

"Come on," I say.

"Where?"

I am already walking along the shoreline, away from the sea, and when I turn to answer I see the broken patterns my espadrilles have left on the damp sand. The path peters out here and there is a choice: either to step from stone to stone where the water is a few inches deep or to cut away up the hill behind the first rank of pine and tamarisk along the remnants of an old path. The path is overgrown but still just visible and it is not until I hear Ángel's question that I know. This was Lluís's path. It is clear to see that no one uses it now and hasn't for a long time. Lluís's tracks are very faint indeed.

"This was his path, the way he used to go to his vegetable patch."

Ángel steps off the verandah to follow me. He slips as he crosses the wet sand to reach the path and when I hear an exclamation I look round expecting to see him annoyed at ruining his shoes. But what I see instead is a figure crouched down at the water's edge, the turn-ups of expensive trousers soaking in seawater, rubbing the leaves of a plant between his fingertips.

"What is it?"

"In Menorquí, *fonoll marí. Crithmum maritimum.*" The lawyer loves his Latin. "I don't know the English."

I squat down beside him. What has caught his attention is a low rounded bush, shaped like a lavender plant, but in appearance more like mistletoe, if mistletoe were made out of pliable green rubber. Flowerheads, like the umbels of fennel or angelica, are beginning to form at the end of thick green stalks. It is a strange plant and, growing at the water's edge, looks as if it belongs wholly neither to land or sea but partly to both, an amphibian. I recognise it. It grows all along the cala in the crevices of steps and round the base of jetty posts but most abundantly here beyond Lluís's place where the cala becomes wild and private.

"Samphire."

"That's it," he sounds pleased, "Samphire. You know it."

"I've eaten it once or twice. With fish."

"Here on the island?" He looks worried

"No, in England."

"You shouldn't eat it. It's too rare. On Mallorca it is almost extinct now. They pickle it in vinegar, you know."

He looks disgusted, though whether at the bigger island's environmental recklessness or at their fondness for pickling I cannot say.

"If they knew it was here they would probably come and take this too, to sell."

"Better resurrect the shore batteries."

"What?"

"To keep out Mallorcan marauders."

"It wouldn't be a bad idea."

He pinches a stem gently between thumb and forefinger, enough to bruise out its scent but not to injure it, and raises his fingers first to his nostrils and then to mine. I catch the iodine smell of the sea on his fingertips and remember the taste of samphire in a broth with red mullet. It was on my birthday, one year, in my last life.

My eyes must have been closed because when I

open them he seems very near. His eyes are dark, dark brown and they are watching me intently. I flinch at the scrutiny:

"What is it?"

"Nothing. It's strange stuff, though, isn't it? It seems prehistoric, not sure yet where it belongs in the ecological scheme of things, whether it's a plant or seaweed."

He laughs:

"I feel a bit like that myself. Not sure where I belong."

I look directly into those brown eyes for the first time, and see that he means it. Even the little I've been able to tell him about his grandfather has had the effect of tearing him out from the – admittedly stony – soil where he was planted. Clearly, he thinks I'm going to help him find somewhere new, somewhere more fertile to put down his roots. I hope Lluís will not turn out to be a disappointment to him. Because I almost certainly will.

"Come on."

The old foot-worn track that plots its meandering course up the hillside seems fainter than ever. The pines and gorse bushes it used to skirt have grown over it in places so that I have to push them aside to follow the path. The maquis thins towards the top of the hill where the sun dries the ground and the path disappears altogether from the gravelly surface but I can see, on the other side of the estate road, the square patch where Lluís – thanks to the generosity or forbearance of one of his neighbours, whose land it was – used to grow his food.

It's weed-strewn now, but the stones he set around the boundary of the plot are still there. Standing with Ángel beside me I feel that I have brought him not to an allotment but to a grave. A eulogy seems warranted and so I tell him about the vegetables his grandfather used to grow: aubergines, onions, peppers, the handfuls of parsley he would push into the top of the carrier bags, groaning with new potatoes, which towards the end of our stay he used to bring for my mother. Food was Lluís's way of expressing friendship: the vegetables from his plot; the octopus stew. They were his way of thanking my father for his pantomimed conversations and his gifts of beer. Billy's mother said that Lluís preferred enemies to friends but it wasn't entirely true.

When I've finished my speech he puts his arm around my shoulder and turns me so that his cheek is against my hair. We stand there, not moving closer or apart.

"Thank you," he says, his mouth close to my ear.

Then he jerks his chin back and looks at me.

"What is it?"

"I was just wondering how you'd react if I tried to kiss you?"

For some reason I completely fail to give this question the consideration it deserves. It's been a weird day. A reckless little whisper says: what difference can it make? And so I look back at him and smile.

I am still smiling as his lips touch mine and my mouth is just far enough open to leave undefended the sensitive inner part of the lips, behind the line of my lipstick. It is there that I first feel the warm stroke of his tongue. And the world slides. Instantly, I recognise that this is not like kissing Billy. This is not a clean and friendly engagement between two animals of the same species. This is human and personal. This is all wrong. And, as soon as I decently can, I step away.

Ángel kneels down to straighten some stones that have toppled out of line. Maybe he too realises it was a mistake:

"When was it that you knew him?"

Returning to Lluís is a better idea, which I latch onto gratefully:

"The mid-eighties, sometime. I was maybe thirteen, fourteen, fifteen. I can't say for sure."

I could actually, but some stupid vanity is making me want to fudge my age. And I'm instantly annoyed with myself, because what possible point is there to that?

"I was just finishing school then, arguing with my father over whether I should study law or botany, biology. I could have known him, the man you say is my grandfather, if only someone had told me he was here. I could have known you, come to that."

He smiles and climbs to his feet. The knees of his trousers are marked with reddish brown dust and the uppers of his shoes are crusted with white stains from the seawater.

"I don't think those are going to be smart enough for court now."

He looks down and then grins at me:

"Don't think I'm going to be going to court any more somehow. I never really was cut out to be a lawyer. Come on."

"Where are we going?"

28

Es Mercadal is a sleepy town, scattered at the foot of the only mountain on the island remotely worthy of the name. Monte Toro sticks up through Menorca's crust like a pie funnel and from its peak, with its whitewashed monastery and jumble of communications masts, the whole island is laid out for view. From the pointing finger of Cap Cavalleria in the north, past the close-lipped female funnel of Fornells bay, along the grey cliffs to Arenal and Addaya, past the slate moonscape at Favaritx to the deep slash that is the harbour at Port Mahon the defensive weaknesses of the island are revealed at a glance. The southern coastline drops away abruptly in sheer white cliffs to a dazzling blue sea and on a clear day the whale-like hump of Mallorca shadows the horizon. Finally, on the flat plain to the west buildings spill like cream across a tabletop to form at the island's edge the welling mass that is Ciutadella.

It is from Monte Toro that the watchers have kept a lookout, through the centuries, for ships: galleys from Carthage and Rome; triangular lateens from North Africa and Turkey; square-rigged sails from Spain and France and Britain. It is on Monte Toro that the first beacons have always been lit to warn of invasion. From here the message in fire would be kindled on hillocks and talayots across the island and beasts would be gathered in, shutters battened and farms and towns would take on the deserted appearance of a daylong siesta.

Mercadal sits languidly at the bottom of the road that

winds up the hillside. It is as if any energy or tension that might be generated at the top of the hill by its view of the wider world goes over the heads of the people living below. The islanders' fatalistic approach to foreign invasion seems to reach its apotheosis in Mercadal. It is too used to being marched through by victorious invaders on the way from triumph in Mahon to accept the surrender in Ciutadella, or vice versa, to expect to play an active part in events.

There is not much to see, and less to do, in Mercadal. My guide book says that the first British governor, Richard Kane left his mark here, *por supuesto,* in the form of a reservoir to supply drinking water to the town. But no one has made much impression since. The houses in the narrow streets are neatly whitewashed, with dark green doors, window frames and shutters. Unshuttered windows are protected from view by panels of white lace or drawn-thread work and old men sit in their dark doorways on folding chairs waiting in hopes that other old men will walk their dogs and stop to exchange whatever passes for news in Mercadal.

The street where Ángel's grandmother lives is between the church and the police station. It is closed to traffic and paved with red quarry tile and concrete planters. We drive past the narrow entrance and park a hundred yards away on the hump of a bridge over a long dry watercourse.

As he hauls on the handbrake Ángel says:

"I think you should stay here."

"What?"

"I mean, I think this is something I should do alone."

"So why did you bring me?"

"I don't know. Sorry. To stop myself from getting cold feet, maybe. I still don't know what I'm going to say to her. I want to know the truth, but she's my grandmother. How do you ask your grandmother something like that?"

He leans towards me as he pulls on the door handle:

"There will be a time for you two to meet, later."

"Will there?"

He nods and opens the door. Half way out of the car he leans back in and for a moment I think he is going to kiss me again but he just says:

"Whatever happens, I'm glad we met. I'm glad that you would tell me about my grandfather, when nobody else would."

He swings the door shut and walks quickly away. I sit there for a few seconds, wondering what to do with myself, then I get out and walk slowly after him. Not intending to follow him, exactly, but not knowing what else to do. It has been a while since anything I did was contingent on another person. I am out of the habit.

I reach the crossroads just in time to see him with his hand raised to the knocker of a house at the far end of the street. The door must open to his knock because he disappears from view. I dawdle down the street, pretending to look in shop windows and when the shops peter out I am reduced to glancing at doors and windows, pots of geraniums, until I reach the door he went in. The street is a dead end and I feel conspicuous but I find I do want to know what is going on inside. With an intensity I can't explain even to myself, I want to see this woman Ángel loves, whom Lluís must have loved once too. Before she left him and robbed him of his son. I want to see what a woman who has broken her family's heart looks like. I want to understand her story, and Lluís's, and how she came to have a son and a grandson so painfully different from one another that the air freezes between them.

What clues there are in the house front tell me only

that she is a woman of the island: neat, industrious, conforming. The house is white with dark green paintwork. The brass doctor's knocker on the door is finely polished, the drawn threadwork panels covering the lower half of the window gleam pearl white and the step is immaculately swept. She may be in her eighties but she is not letting standards slip. And whatever she and Lluís once shared, it was not a love of housework.

I am sorely tempted to try to see into the room beyond the window but something holds me back: fear of witnessing another scene like that between Ángel and his father; fear of being caught again and fairly blamed for meddling in something that is none of my concern; fear of making things harder for Ángel. In any event I retreat to the crossroads and take a seat at one of the outdoor tables of the bar which gives the better view up the street. I order a beer and wait.

Streetlights have begun to shine in the gloom before I look up to see Ángel walking back down the street towards me. Behind him, causing no more than a slight disruption to the straight white line of houses, is a small thin figure. She is standing in her doorway, watching her grandson walk away. I cannot make out her face.

In the car he is quiet and drives us back to my cala, without a word. It is fully dark, and the moon is up over the water, by the time he pulls in at the top of the hill. He has been so quiet that I expect him to let me out and then drive away, but when I climb out he gets out too and follows me down the slope. He stands silent whilst I unlock the door and when I start to climb the stairs I can hear him behind me in the darkness. Moonlight floods the main room and I push back the sliding doors and gesture to the chairs on the balcony. He sits down and I wonder whether he is sleepwalking.

I run down to the fridge for a cold bottle of wine

and when I come out onto the balcony with the opened bottle and two glasses he looks at me but I am still not sure if he is awake.

"What's happened?"

He shakes his head, though whether in denial of my question or in confusion I cannot tell. I hand him a glass of wine and he holds it in both hands, resting his elbows on his knees.

"Drink!" I tell him, and he raises the glass to his mouth obediently and takes a long swallow. Then he shivers and looks up at me.

"She wouldn't tell me anything. Not even whether it was true. Yes or no. I hammered at her for ages, but it did no good. She just turned her face away and said I should ask my father. But he wouldn't tell me. Would he?"

He looks across at me, wanting me to give him some hope that his father might take pity on him. But the look on the older man's face isn't easy to forget:

"He seems to be an awfully cold man, Ángel."

"Maybe it's not his fault though, is it?"

"Maybe it's not. Do you think she's the one to blame for that?"

He looks out over the cala and I wonder if the moonlight floating on the water will comfort him as it has sometimes comforted me.

"I don't know. Why won't anyone tell me what happened? My father, that's not a surprise. But I thought my grandmother loved me. She's always been the one person who did."

He looks back from the water to me and I see that he is crying.

29

"The baby came early."

That's what she decided to say. And in truth she didn't know exactly when it was due. Just that it must be a full month before the date Mascaró's doctor calculated.

In the end it was easier to convince them than she thought. The contractions started one evening an hour after they'd gone to bed. His fault, she screamed at him. His fault the baby would be early. All because he wouldn't let her alone.

She'd thought he would stop, as she grew bigger and bigger. But he was her husband, it was his right, and he always took everything he was entitled to. Always had. When he could no longer climb on top of her without hurting the baby, he made her bend over the chest at the end of the bed instead and held her down by the neck as he forced his way into her. Every night. Telling her to: "Shut up, red bitch. It's no more than you deserve, to be treated like an animal, after what you've done."

Now, when the contractions came and she screamed at him that it was his fault she saw fear in his eyes for the first time since the start of their second marriage. It was almost funny to see him trying to get his trousers on, yelling for the servants to call the doctor, call the midwife. She almost smiled, for the first time in months and then the pain gripped her again.

He went out when the doctor came. She was glad. She breathed easier when he was out of the house and she needed to breathe now. He didn't come back until it was all over. Someone must have run with a message to wherever he was hiding.

The midwife and the nurse were changing the bloody sheets on the bed for clean ones, rolling her from one side to the other as if she were no more than part of the bedding herself. She felt white and blank as a sheet herself and a lazy hope drifted through her head that they might roll up her up and carry her away from here with the rest of the laundry.

But they didn't. They stood back and admired their handiwork, chatting with the doctor who was washing his hands in a bowl at the foot of the bed. Then the midwife picked up the small white bundle that was lying on the chest at the foot of the bed and tried to place it in her arms. She held it out and waited for Catalina to reach for it, but her arms lay slack at her sides where the nurse had placed them over the clean linen and she turned her head to the side.

"Come on now," said the midwife gently. "Say hello to your son."

When the new mother didn't move, she clucked her tongue, unwrapped the bundle and laid the baby, still beetroot red and wrinkled with a slick of jet black hair, gently on her belly. Eyes still tight shut, he twitched and fidgeted for a moment at the unfamiliar feel of the cool sheet and the air on his skin, then he reached up with a tiny flailing hand and patted his mother on the breast.

The three professionals stood back and watched. For a moment there was no response and then the woman's hand lifted slowly off the sheet and she began to turn her head towards the baby. The tiny fingers waved uncertainly in the air again and his mother's hand reached out to touch his palm. But as she did so a door slammed heavily downstairs and footsteps pounded up the stairs.

The baby jumped and the mother let her hand drop

back onto the sheet and closed her eyes. A collective sigh issued from the midwife, the doctor and the nurse and a moment later Joan Mascaró burst into the room to take possession of his son.

The midwife observed that the woman in the bed seemed to fade further into the white sheets as her husband entered the room. He didn't give any sign that he noticed, striding over to the bed and lifting the baby off her belly without even looking at her.

He held it up under its armpits and laughed with jubilation:

"It's a boy. Do you see that, doctor? A fine boy."

"Indeed it is. And no obvious ill-effects from being a little premature. Mother did a fine job, though she is a little tired now, naturally."

"No ill-effects. Of course not. He's a Mascaró. Tough and smart as a whip. Just proving he's advanced for his age right from the off."

The doctor smiled:

"Undoubtedly that's the case, Señor Mascaró. My hearty congratulations."

"Thank you, doctor. Excuse me if I don't shake hands. As you can see, I have my hands full."

"Not at all. I must be going now. Your wife will be a little fatigued for a while. She needs plenty of good nourishment and little exertion. I know the food situation is poor at the moment, but the more milk, meat and eggs you can get for her the better."

Mascaró glanced down at the bed for the first time.

"I understand, doctor. Don't you worry. I'll make sure she has everything she needs to feed my son properly. There is food to be had if you know the right people."

"Then I'll leave your family in your capable hands Señor. Please give your wife my best wishes. I think she is having a little doze. Goodnight."

172

The doctor left, but Catalina was not asleep. She felt the bed sag as her husband sat down on it. She opened her eyes a slit and saw him staring intently into the baby's face now. He's wondering, she thought, he's wondering if he's really his. He stared at the baby for a long time and the baby, its head wobbling dangerously, opened its eyes and tried to stare back. Suddenly, Mascaró seemed to come to a decision and to her amazement she saw him give a sob and his eyes fill with tears, the first time she had ever seen him cry.

Something roused in her at that and made her want to take the baby back. She wanted to look at him herself, just as intently as Mascaró had done, to convince herself that whatever he had seen had been a lie. To discern Lluís in him instead.

She began to lift her arms from the bed to take him and her husband swung round at the gesture. The baby's head jerked with the motion and he began to cry. Mascaró looked down impatiently and handed him quickly to his wife.

"I've made a decision," he said as she cradled her son's head in the crook of her arm and felt a smile begin to tug at the corners of her mouth. She glanced at Mascaró, unguarded for a moment.

"His name is Francisco. In honour of the Generalissimo. Aren't you proud?"

The smile died.

30

Just because a man cries is no reason to sleep with him. But I do. Of course I do. And maybe it isn't just because he cries, and reaches out for me and pushes his face into my belly, like a child that has fallen and wants his mother to set the world right. Maybe it's also because I don't want to be left alone with my guilt at uncovering another woman's secret. To make someone question the one person they've always loved, is that the best I can do? If I could do it to her, maybe someone will do it to me, just as casually, with as little thought for the consequences. And that is something I just don't want to think about.

He is heavy to pull up out of the chair but once he reaches his feet he rocks once and then seems to regain control of himself. The male in him refuses to be led weeping to bed by a woman. And so the child becomes a man, cupping my face in his hands and kissing my eyelids as if I am the one who needs to be comforted.

The moon lights the path to the door of the bedroom and there is enough of its glow inside the room for us not to need to turn on the lamps. It is, anyway, a strange encounter, like two moles, each trying to escape its predators by burrowing deep. I learn something of his body by touch, the texture of his skin against mine, the taste of his mouth, the proportions of his limbs against my own. But I do not see him and nor do I think he sees me. It is almost possible, in the moon-shadowed darkness, to forget that this is Ángel, to cling onto the idea that what I hold in my arms is just the anonymous assemblage of parts that make a man, any man, and that this bucking shuddering meal we make of each other is just the assuaging of hunger by two starving animals.

Until morning comes.

He must have woken first. When I open my eyes and find that I am not alone, he is already waiting for me to turn and look at him. Immediately, I sense his satisfaction, his lack of doubt about his right to be here in my bed. I can feel the warmth of his body sprawled beside me, one arm thrown out above my head so that I am curled within the gallows of his arm and body.

A cold wave of panic rises up over me, from my toes to my throat, where it chokes me. How could I have let this happen? The sheet is wrinkled at the end of the bed and I stretch down to pull it over us, but his hand reaches lazily out for mine and stops it. He pushes his fingers between mine and lowers our interlaced hands onto my leg.

"Let me look at you", he whispers, and I think I'm going to scream.

My one thought is to get him out of here, to reclaim the bed, the house, the cala, as my territory. I have no idea how. So, reluctantly, I roll from my side onto my back and let him look at me. He props his head on the arm that was behind my head and looms above me. I look at his face – but not into his eyes – and see a smile of appreciation as he strokes the curve of my waist with his free hand.

Then the smile flickers, and the corners of his mouth droop, as he runs his index finger from one hip to the other, across the lower part of my belly.

"You have a child."

"No."

"But you have had one."

"No."

"*Si*. Here. It came out here."

I look down and watch in horror as he drags his broad finger with its spatulate nail back along a puckered line on my skin.

"No."

"An operation then. A big scar. Something serious."

"No."

I lunge down the bed and pull the sheet free, scrambling to get it round me and get out of the room. I can't bear him to look at me, to ask me these things. What gives him the right?

"What are you doing?"

He is lying on the bed, utterly uncovered, bemused. I don't want to look at him, at this hardly-known, unhappy man on the verge of middle age, at his slack belly and wrinkled pink cock, but I can't avoid it. Why is he here? How could I have let this happen?

If he won't go then I have to. My dress is under the chair and I pull it, crumpled and dusty and smelling of yesterday, over my head. The sheet is still wrapped around me, under the dress and, as I am bending down to look under the bed for my shoes, he leans over and starts to pull at it. Just as his pulling threatens to topple me back onto the bed my fingers close round one of my wooden-heeled sandals. I throw out my arm, perhaps to steady myself, perhaps not. There is a loud crack as the shoe catches him on the temple, hard. The shout he gives is of surprise, probably, as much as of pain. But his mood darkens. He lets go of the sheet suddenly and I stagger against the arm of the chair. He lies back on the bed, rubbing his head. Yet the blow isn't what has hurt him.

"Why have you been lying to me?"

I am trying to strap my shoes on but his voice is so different, so much harder than it's been before, that I look up.

"What?"

"Why did you lie to me, about not having children? Is it just me? Does everybody lie to me?"

I wish I was enough in control of myself to be able to say something to placate him but I'm not. Speech is beyond me.

"That's it, isn't it? Everybody lies to me. My father. My grandmother. My wife. Now you. What is it? Is it this face? Do I look like a person who enjoys being lied to? Did they lie to my grandfather too?"

I feel sorry for him, but I can't do anything to help him. Not a thing. I start to skirt around the bed, towards the door, but he sits up suddenly:

"No. You don't need to go. I'm the one who's going. I need to get out and see if there's anybody out there who'll tell me the truth."

He is out of bed now and pulling on his clothes, almost tearing them in his anger. I stand in the corner of the room and watch as he drags on his shirt, punching his fists through the buttoned cuffs.

"Perhaps I'd better start with strangers. Maybe ask someone the time. See if they lie about that. Think that'll work? Think that's a good start?"

In a few moments, which nonetheless feel like hours, the glass rattles in the front door and he is gone. As soon as the house is quiet I pull my dress off over my head, kick away my shoes and step into the shower. I stand for a long time under the showerhead, which bucks as the electric pump draws water from the well in fits and starts, and then I wash myself all over with a soapy sponge. As I pass the sponge across my belly I look down and see, under the trail of soap bubbles, the scar that Ángel found. I haven't looked at it for a long while, had almost forgotten it was there. It is old now, and faded almost to the colour of skin, only its keloid

177

shine and the way the skin either side sits puckered like a bad seam giving its presence away. Not like the other scars, the livid circle on the inside of my leg, just above the knee and the angry red line down my thigh. The new ones. The ones I couldn't let him see.

After the shower I dress in cala clothes and wander out onto the balcony. The day is still young, but promising. The only reminders of last night are the half-empty wine glasses on the ledge and I move to clear them away. But as I do so my eye catches a movement beneath the balcony. For a moment I think Ángel has not gone after all, and my heart stalls. I step back and look down fearfully through the railings and then I see that it is not Ángel, but Billy, who is waiting for me to get up.

I lean over the balcony, cheerful with relief:

"*¡Hola! ¿Que tal?*"

He looks up sharply:

"He's gone then, your boyfriend? He must have been in a hurry. He took my bike."

"Why? His car's at the top."

"Wouldn't start. He must have left the lights on. Window was open too. Cats have been in it."

31

It seems odd to have Billy sitting beside me in my car, when I am used to being with him in a boat, and used to him driving. Strapped into the passenger seat he seems diminished, younger, less independent.

We stop at the lawyers' office and I tell Billy to stay in the car while I get Ángel's address. I imagine it will be difficult enough to prise personal details out of the receptionist without a kid in board-shorts leering over my shoulder.

It is more than difficult. It is impossible. No, Señor Mascaró Menor is not in the office. No, she is not permitted to give out his address or his mobile phone number to … anyone.

I take a deep breath and ask to speak to Señor Mascaró Mayor. Her over-plucked eyebrows jump a little at the audacity of this request and then she calculates the entertainment it will provide and moves immediately to press the intercom button with a well-filed nail.

There is, she says, "a person" to see him. And she means it to sting.

Señor Mascaró comes out to see for himself what manner of person is calling on him. His face stays blank for a moment and then he recognises me from yesterday. His features stiffen, I don't know how exactly, something around the jaw and the eyes. He holds out a long corpse-like hand for me to press and then gestures with the other hand towards his room. I note the receptionist's disappointment as he shows me through and closes the doors behind him.

His sanctum is smaller than the outer office but clearly

a more important room, perhaps the place where the ladies of the family would once have sat to receive their favoured guests. Its light comes from two sets of full-length windows that open onto the square and onto the sunshine that seems to belong to another world. Book-cases line the alcoves on either side of the imposing fire-place and a single massive piece of furniture cuts off the top right hand corner of the room, between the fireplace and the first set of windows, Señor Mascaró's desk.

He goes behind it now and waves me to a straight hard chair on the opposite side.

"Who are you?" he says as I sit down, and for a simple question it is full of sub-text and connotation. He means, I think: "What are you doing here?", "Why are you med-dling in our lives?" and "Are you sleeping with my son?"

For anyone else, the simple answer would be to stick to the Geneva Conventional approach: name, rank & serial number. The simple answer is no good to me. I don't tell my name to strangers, especially strangers connected to legal systems and databases.

"I need to speak to your son." I say. "As he isn't here ..." I pause to see if there is a reaction to this. There isn't. "I wonder if you could give me his mobile number. His home address."

"He hasn't furnished you with them himself?"

He steeples his fingers and taps the apex against thin lips.

I shake my head.

"We only just met a few days ago. But I need to see him urgently. He has something ... belonging to a friend of mine."

He looks at me for a long moment and then stands up.

"I'm sorry, Miss ... I don't act as my son's social secretary. I'm sure that if he wants to ... contact you again he will do so himself. I'm afraid I cannot help you."

He walks towards the doors and opens one.

"He stole a motorbike."

He shuts the door abruptly. I wonder whether the receptionist heard me. If so, she will be beside herself with excitement. He turns back to face me

"He what?"

For the first time there is colour in his sallow face and I realise that he is angry.

"He took a motorbike belonging to a friend of mine. He was rather … over-wrought. I'm sure he doesn't mean to keep it but my friend is anxious to have it back. I thought he might have brought it back here – or to his home."

"He's not here. I don't know where he is. Such an impetuous boy. But to steal? He has been brought up to honour the law, not to break it."

"Then if you could just give me his address and phone number, I hope it won't be necessary to involve the police."

"The police?" He looks horrified. "I should think not." He reaches into a drawer and pulls out a black-bound address book. I realise that he doesn't know his son's address by heart. Now he puts on the pair of half-moon spectacles that hang around his neck on a black cord. The glasses accentuate the beakiness of his long narrow nose. Whenever I look at Ángel I see glimpses of his grandfather in every movement and every gesture. Staring at his father as he writes the address on a piece of paper it strikes me that not one thing about him reminds me of Lluís. Or of Ángel come to that.

When he stops writing he looks up and catches me examining him. I think we are both aware that I do not like what I see. He hands me the piece of paper and I stand up:

"It's on Carrer de Annunciavay. Not far from here. If

181

you find him there you might ask him when he proposes to honour us with his presence here."

It's on the tip of my tongue to remind him that it was he who told Ángel to get out only the day before yesterday. But I have caused enough trouble. The receptionist watches me go, disappointed that there were no more scenes.

The kid isn't where I left him. I jingle the car keys in annoyance and wonder where he can have got to.

"Any luck?" says a muffled voice behind me.

I swing round and there is Billy, carrying a paper bag and talking through what appears to be a mouthful of macaroon. He offers me one.

"What are they?"

He swallows.

"*Amargas*. I used to love them when I was a kid."

I start to smile but then he looks at me sternly and I remember his misappropriated bike and take a cake from the proffered bag instead. It is a macaroon, almond not coconut, crumbly and sweet, still warm from the oven. As soon as I bite into it I remember I haven't eaten breakfast or, now I come to think, supper.

We climb back into the car and he waits while I lick my fingers:

"There's a map in the glove box. Carrer de Annuncia-vay. Can you find it on there?"

The map of the town centre has a key and he finds it quickly, sending me right at the traffic lights and then left and left again down a narrow canyon of eighteenth century houses. Annunciavay.

"There it is!"

I think he has spotted the house number but then I see he has better proof of our being in the right place – his motorbike parked at the roadside.

He has the door open and is out of the car before I have stopped. I lean over to shout to him.

"I'm going to park the car. Then I'll be back."

He nods but doesn't look back, already has his hand on the bike's flank, patting it as a rightful master might pat his stolen horse. I stretch out across the passenger seat to pull his door shut and then carry on up the car-crowded street, looking for a parking space. Finally I find one a hundred metres further on, and change for the parking meter that stands fifty metres back in the direction I came from. A few minutes have passed before I get back to Billy and I can see that he is torn. Part of him would like to go in and confront the man, the lawyer after all, who took his bike. But another part of him just wants to re-possess it, to fold himself onto it and take it out onto the road where he and it will blend into one against the wind. And this is the part that is winning.

"Do you want me to come up with you?"

He makes the offer but already he's sitting astride the bike.

I shake my head.

"Better not. You go. I'll tell him you took the bike back."

He nods, but makes no move to go. Something is eating him. I wait but he says nothing, just looks at me until I turn away and then he spits it out:

"You gonna … ? With him?"

I stop, and sigh, and turn back:

"It's unlikely, Billy. But if I do, it's no concern of yours. Just as it's no concern of his what I do with you. Okay?"

He shrugs and starts the bike and walks it backwards on the tips of his toes until he can point it down the street. Then he pauses to think about what I just said and perhaps he finds some unintended encouragement in it because he gives me a hint of a grin and twists the throttle. The bike leaps forward and he flattens down over the handlebars, his hair streaming out behind him. Fifteen yards on he shoots a look at me over his shoulder and I am glad to see that even that small burst of acceleration has restored his mood entirely. Because the smile on his face now is one of pure joy, pure freedom.

Billy's bike was parked outside number 13, but this is an art gallery, on the ground floor at least. I pull the piece of paper with Francisco Mascaró's writing on it out of my pocket. The handwriting is clear, even elegant. Written in real ink with a fountain pen. There is none of the shakiness, the loss of confidence that comes with age. No. 20. Apartment 4. I walk up the street. Roughly half of the buildings have some sort of business on the ground floor. A few look as if they are still family houses. Most are sub-divided into apartments. Apartment no. 4 is the top bell at no. 20. There is an intercom. I am going to have to tell him who I am before he opens the door. Perhaps he won't let me in. Perhaps I hope he won't.

I press the bell, but the oak front door is solid and I hear no sound from inside. After half a minute of silence I turn my back on the door and look up and down the street to see what better use I might put my life to than standing here.

Then the intercom clicks and squawks:

"¿Digame?"

The voice, even through the walkie-talkie distortion of the intercom system, is Ángel's. But deeper than usual, weary, older.

"It's me."

There is a long pause, then a buzz and the click of the door lock sliding back. A push on the door swings it heavily open.

Apartment no. 4 is on the third floor and I am out of breath by the time I reach the top. The entrance hall is cold too, with its marble stairs, and dark and I feel a shiver as I raise my knuckles to knock on the cheap deal door. Then I notice that the door is slanting slightly, ajar, and I straighten my fingers and push at it gently. The room beyond the door is bright compared with the stairwell, and painted white, light coming in through two half-length sash windows. The furniture is a mixture of the cheap stuff that comes with a furnished apartment and a few pieces of good quality modern design – it looks like what it is, the aftermath of a divorce between a couple who had just started to be prosperous.

The only sign of Ángel is a jacket, the one he was wearing when I last saw him, thrown over the arm of a sofa. The intercom phone is by the door so he must have been in this room when he pressed the buzzer but he isn't here now. I could call his name but it sticks in my mouth and so I move deeper into the apartment, towards the doorway that stands between the living area and the galley kitchen. This leads to a short corridor with two more doors leading off it, left and right. Through one I can see a glimpse of shower curtain. I turn into the entrance of the other and I am back where I started the day, in a bedroom with Ángel.

He is sitting on the edge of the bed with his head in his hands. After a moment he says:

"What do you want?"

What do I want? He's not the only one who's confused. Less than three hours ago all I wanted was to get away from him, to get back to being on my own. I told myself I was only coming here for Billy's sake, to retrieve the bike. Once we found it, there was nothing to stop me driving straight home, back to the cala. But I didn't do that. Why? Why am I here, feeling like I owe him something? Does it really have anything to do with his father and his grandfather? Could I be getting involved with Ángel? I push the last thought away. There's no question of that. There can't be.

Last night was a mistake, but it was mine, not his. He wasn't to know what would happen if he came too close. I tell myself I just want to make things better for him, because he's Lluís's grandson:

"I went to see your father."

He doesn't look up:

"Why?"

"I didn't know how else to find you. I thought you might have gone back to work."

"I told you – I'm not cut out to be a lawyer. Turns out it doesn't run in the family after all. Anyway, what made you want to find me? Oh, the bike I suppose."

"Not just the bike. Although I did bring Billy with me. He's ridden it home. I don't think he'll press charges."

"I would have brought it back."

"I'm sure. Lawyers are known for their unimpeachable honesty."

Now he glares up at me.

"I would."

I put my hand on his shoulder.

"I know."

He shrugs it off and looks down at the floor again.

"Do you know what you've done to me?"

"I'm sorry. For hitting you. It was an accident. I get very claustrophobic if I feel trapped. I don't like to be cross-examined."

"I didn't mean that. The shoe. I meant, do you know what you've done to my life?"

"Oh. No. Was your life so perfect before?"

"It was a life I understood, at least."

"Was it?"

He runs his hands through his hair, then clasps them at the back of his head and tips his face upwards.

186

"No."

He looks across at me and there is the shadow of a smile on his face. Something shifts inside me. I feel something, but I hardly know what to call it.

"So, my father. Did he tell you anything of interest?"

I shake my head:

"Just where to find you."

"Well, that turned out to be true, at least. You're doing better than I am. Although actually, just before you arrived, I had an idea. I thought of something I read in the paper a few months ago. Someone who might have known my grandfather. Or known of him, at least. I was just about to go and see if I can track him down. You might as well come with me, now you're here."

32

The telegram arrived at the seminary in Salamanca late on a Saturday. Francisco was called to Father Ignacio's office just as he was preparing for bed. He wondered what he was in trouble over. He couldn't think of anything as he hurried towards the priest's office, his soutane tangling between his knees. Francisco hated to be found in the wrong and his heart was pounding as he knocked at the door.

Father Ignacio opened the door himself, which disconcerted Francisco even further.

"Come in, my son," he said and put a hand on the boy's shoulder. "Sit down."

Francisco wanted to ask what was wrong, but he just licked his lips nervously as the old man walked over to his desk. When the priest turned round he had the telegram in his hand. An arrow of pure and certain feeling shot through the boy: let it be my mother. Not my father.

"I'm afraid it's your father," said the priest and proffered the piece of yellow paper.

Francisco grabbed it and read the message:

"FATHER GRAVELY ILL STOP COME HOME SOONEST STOP MOTHER"

"There's no train until the morning. And it will be slow, I'm afraid, on a Sunday. Father Miguel will take you to the station."

He opened a drawer and took out a cash box, which he unlocked with a key from a large ring. He peered in and brought out a handful of peseta notes.

"Here is money for the train and the boat. I wish you Godspeed, my son. But remember, God is infinitely merciful and if it is his wish that your father be gathered to Him then you must find it in your heart to be grateful, knowing that he has gone to join our Father in glory."

Francisco held out his hand for the money and did not speak. He could not. Must not. He clamped his teeth shut and bowed his head and fled. For the first time since the age of eleven, when he had decided that he would be a priest, for the very first time he doubted that God was infinitely merciful and if his father died he knew he would never be able to find it in his heart to be grateful.

The journey home to Ciudadella was long and slow and torturous. When the ferry docked in Mahon harbour, Francisco did not wait for the great ropes to be fastened round the bollards or the ramp to be run out to the passenger gangway. He stood on the rail and leapt across the foaming gap onto the mole, ignoring the shouts of the landing crew. From there he ran up the hill and through the streets to the bus station. All the way across the island, he watched the changing landscape, watched the pine woods give way to olive and myrtle, watched it grow drier and whiter and felt home approaching. And as it grew nearer he felt the fear rise from his belly, through his chest until it hung in his throat as they entered the outskirts of the town. When the bus pulled into the station, he found himself not running but walking through the familiar streets, suddenly willing himself to believe that there was plenty of time, that it could not really be so serious that running would make the difference.

Finally, he came to the house. From the outside, everything looked normal. The brass knocker was polished to a high shine. The ancient door with its metal studs looked as impregnable as ever. Francisco put his hand on the handle and found it was lower than he remembered. It was nearly a year since he'd been home and he realised that he must have grown. He turned the handle and the heavy door swung inwards.

It was dark inside, and he stood, disorientated for a moment in the gloom after the bright sunlight outside. Then he heard footsteps and a maid he didn't recognise came scurrying from the direction of the kitchen.

"Can I help you, father?" she asked and he realised she didn't know who he was.

He shook his head and turned and ran up the main staircase. He had just reached the landing when his mother came out of her room. She stretched out her arms, though whether to greet him or bar his way he couldn't tell.

"Francisco …"

"Where is he?"

She didn't answer, just looked at him, so he pushed past her arms and ran now, down the landing to his father's room. The shutters were closed over the windows but he could see that the bed was empty, stripped, with the outer covers still puddled on the floor. He turned and ran back to his mother and gripped her by the arms:

"Where is he? Which hospital have they taken him to?"

"Francisco …"

"Which hospital? Tell me!" and he shook her so that her head flew back and he saw fear on her face. Still, she tried to put her arms around him but he pushed her away and flew back down the stairs and into the room where they had once laid out his grandmother.

There he stopped and all the terror and dread that had accompanied him on his two day journey forced its way out of his throat in a scream he didn't even hear. His mother heard it though as she followed him down the stairs. By the time she entered the room he had raised his father's body off the bier and was clutching it to him. She tried to comfort him, to draw him away, but he just shook her off and rocked back and forth with the body in his arms. And all the while sobbing and screaming and cursing God.

She sat in the corner on a straight-backed chair, waiting for the moment when his grief would ease up just enough for him to come back to his senses, but he never once looked in her direction and it was hours before he finally fell asleep and she called one of the servants, who half-roused him and coaxed him up to bed.

He stayed in his room then until the funeral, wouldn't eat, wouldn't speak to anyone. She couldn't tell if he had prayed or slept, but when he emerged to carry his father's coffin it looked as though he had done neither in several days. At the graveside, she was terrified that he was going to throw himself on top of the coffin, but the whole of Ciudadella was there and he had too much decorum for that.

The day after the burial he set aside his priest's robes and came downstairs in one of his father's suits. It fitted him perfectly. Even his father's shoes fitted him.

He sat down at the breakfast table and his mother moved to pour him some coffee.

"I shall not be going back to Salamanca," he said, as she filled his cup. "I see now where my duty lies. I refused to honour my father in life but I shall honour him in death. I'm going to train to be a lawyer like he was."

"You don't have to do that," she said, just as he'd known she would.

"I do, mother. I know my duty. Better than you've ever known yours. Anyway, don't pretend you wanted me to be a priest. You only went along with it because you knew it made him unhappy. You don't even believe in God. You don't believe in anything. I don't think you feel anything either. I don't suppose you're even sorry that he's dead, are you? Are you?"

When she shook her head, he didn't know whether it was a denial of his accusation or an admission. And he didn't care enough to ask.

33

When I was a child the market was different. Back then, fruit and vegetables were piled on wide trestle tables set between the columns of the church cloister. Butchers and cheese merchants occupied the niches on the cloister's outer rim. You entered their little square cells, ill-lit and rich with the smell of meat or Mahon cheese, under gothic arches decorated with the carved heads of saints or angels. There was a strong gender divide, I remember, the men in the niches selling meat, the women in the open at the tables serving fruit and vegetables. It was a cheerful busy place, robust with smells and conversation flowing from stall to stall.

They've improved the market since those days. The cells under the arches, once lined with cracked tile and sawdust, have been replaced with hygienic new catering units. The arches themselves have been plastered over so that the angels' heads protrude, like inquisitive ghosts, from blank toffee-coloured walls. The trestle tables have gone too, and with them the spirited old ladies who used to run them. In their place are cabins of polished wood and steel, with lockable shutters, as likely to sell CDs or joss sticks as lettuce picked that morning in the market gardens at San Lluís. The place is quiet now, quiet enough that you can hear the faint mechanical creak of the new escalator heading down to the supermarket and underground car park where the crypt used to be.

The map museum is on the first floor, up a twisting stone staircase that has been spared anything worse than sandblasting. At the top we come out onto a wide gallery with views out of tall arched windows onto the ruined square below. Let off the gallery are concert rooms, pottery studios and a small museum. It's quite new. And quite unfrequented.

"Have you been here before?"

I don't know why I'm whispering as we walk up to the modest glass door but Ángel just shakes his head and shrugs.

The man on the Reception desk looks up in surprise when we walk in. Surprise and delight. He looks at us both and offers us leaflets in Catalan and English. We take them, accepting our pigeonholes, but then Ángel asks him if he knows where we can find the man who is researching the victims of the War. The man looks slightly disappointed to find that it is not interest, pure and simple, that has led us to his door:

"You mean Juan Mercadal Triay? He's in the map room." And he points at a set of stone stairs with his chin.

The stairs are lined with maps of the Balearic Islands dating back centuries and as the island shapes morph through different cartographers' ideas of them I think of Lluís and his game of ducks and drakes: Ibiza, one bounce; Mallorca two; Menorca three.

The room at the top of the stairs is cut in two by a glass screen. The left hand half is lined with more maps, of Menorca only. I only have time for a cursory look but what stands out, from a sweep around the room, is the opposition of Mahon and Ciutadella, their two harbours like the mouths on two heads facing Janus-like in different directions. Beyond the glass divide there are a couple of large desks and, behind them, rows of bookshelves and cabinets that the leaflet says contain every published work that mentions the island. There is only one person sitting in the library, an elderly, bookish man working at a table piled high with papers.

"Is that him?" I whisper. He doesn't look a likely friend for my Lluís.

"I don't know," Ángel whispers back. We have both come down with a bad case of library laryngitis.

Our quarry looks up as we walk across the room towards him, an expression of mild inquiry on his face. I glance at Ángel and wonder what he's going to say, how he's going to start what is, after all, his third attempt to question someone about his grandfather. Because I'm busy watching him I don't notice the change in the old man, the blood that rushes into his face, the movement to take off his reading glasses.

I hear the glasses clatter onto the wooden table though and the squeak of his chair legs against the floor and as I look over he's coming round the table with his hands stretched out towards Ángel:

"Lluís."

And as he says it he takes Ángel by the shoulders.

"You're his boy."

I am shocked to see that there are tears in his eyes.

Ángel shakes his head and I realise he is shocked too by the effect he has caused because his voice is unsteady when he says:

"Not his son. Maybe his grandson."

It's the second time someone has made the same mistake and he must finally be starting to believe in this realignment of his ancestry. Even before the old man says, in a surprisingly strong voice:

"There's no maybe. Don't you think I would remember what he was like when we were both young men? You are his image. It's extraordinary."

I'm glad it isn't only me that can see it. The corroboration is a relief. Someone to share the burden of memory.

195

"You and he were friends?"

"Friends. Yes. But there's a better word. *Amigos-hermanos*. Friends and brothers. Truly."

He holds Ángel away from him, his hands on the young man's forearms, to look at him again. And slowly he nods.

"Could you tell us about him?" says Ángel, eagerness over-riding caution: "You see, I never knew him."

Lluís's old friend frowns:

"But he only died very recently. I saw it in the newspaper. Ah, wait, I think I see now. Forgive me, I'm getting slow. Trying to hold too many stories in this old head at once. I always understood that Catalina's son was Mascaró's boy. Until now. But it can't be. You are far too like Lluís for there to be any doubt about that. Well, well. It seems life always holds one more surprise. I suppose that's what makes it worth going on with."

He walks over to the table and spreads the pile of papers with the palm of his hand before picking out a photograph. It is a black and white glossy reproduced, I'd guess, from an old print.

"I came across this a few months ago, during my research. It was taken in the concentration camp at Argelès-sur-Mer. June 1939. God knows how it survived. That's your grandfather, second from the left. I'm at the far right."

Ángel and I stare down at a photograph of half a dozen men in baggy trousers and rough shirts standing against a blankish background that might be a beach. One of the young men in it looks familiar. I realise that this is the first time Ángel has seen a picture of Lluís at all. No wonder it quivers in his hands. He is gazing at his own face.

"And this is where you got to know him?"

The old man shakes his head and laughs:

"Oh, no. We knew each other here, on the island. Since we were boys. We were still boys then, more or less. I was twenty-three at the end. I think Lluís was even younger. But in war, it's what you've seen and what you've done that determine how old you are. We'd both seen plenty. Done plenty. Or so we thought."

"And how did you get to France? On the Devonshire?"

Ángel is so hungry to know that he dives straight in. Juan Mercadal gestures with his hand. "Sit down, both of you. I will also, if you will permit me."

I sink gratefully into the chair that is already placed in front of his desk and we wait while Ángel drags up a second chair, scraping it carelessly across the floorboards in his impatience to get started. Already it seems that the Mascaró fastidiousness is starting to wear off him. He picks up the photo again and leans forward with his elbows on the desk. The old man takes this as his cue:

"The Devonshire. You've heard of it. Yes. The British." He snorts. "We didn't have a choice. It was a question of exile or death. We weren't under any illusions about what would happen to us. And it turned out we were right. They shot nearly one hundred and fifty after the surrender, most out at La Mola. I still go and look at that place sometimes, across the water. Sometimes I think I can hear the guns of the firing squads. It's just my imagination, of course. But I still hear it."

He looks at us, to see if we are shocked.

"Sorry. Maybe you didn't come to hear about that. I find, trying to gather information for my book, that I think about it more and more these days. My wife tells me I'm becoming a bore."

Ángel shakes his head.

"Your book?" I ask.

"Yes. I am collecting together the names of every

Menorquin who died as a result of the Civil War. It's a kind of memorial. Not the kind you carve on a wall, just a way of making sure they aren't forgotten. I want to set down where they came from, what they did for a living, and how, when and where they died. Simple really, though it's harder than you'd think. The records are very patchy. You see ..."

Ángel interrupts:

"It's exactly what we came for. I saw a piece in the paper about you a few months ago, about what you are doing. I thought then that you were right – even before I knew it had any significance to me personally. I'm tired of people not thinking about that time, not talking about it. Then this morning, when I was racking my brain trying to think who might remember my grandfather I thought of you. You needn't be concerned about boring me. I want to know everything."

The old man looks startled, and then he laughs:

"It's not just your looks, is it? You sound like him too. "I want to know everything." That's exactly what Lluís would have said. So what do you want to know about? The Devonshire?"

Ángel nods.

"Well, she just appeared one morning. We didn't know she was coming. Suddenly there she was. We sent a boat out and the captain asked to see the Governor. We didn't know there was a messenger from Franco on board. We were preparing to resist an invasion and all of a sudden they were offering us terms for surrender."

"Why did they do it? Was it really because of Mussolini?"

The old man shrugs:

"That's what they say. Franco wouldn't have wanted to give Menorca to the Italians. But he did want the war finished quickly. And we were the last bastion. The last Republican outpost. That's why he was prepared to negotiate with us."

He stands up and walks away from the table. He is looking out of the window, down the sweeping curve of the harbour towards Cape Mola and the open sea. And I suppose he sees them now as he did in the light of a February dawn in 1939: death on the one hand; exile on the other.

"There were only supposed to be a few of us taken off on the ship, you know. Just the leaders, the commissariat. The British didn't want to take any. Scared of compromising their neutrality. Scared, also, that the French would refuse to let us land and then they'd be stuck with us. We didn't even know where they were taking us. And we were Menorquins. You know what it must have meant to us, to leave this island. You know it's against all our traditions. It felt like death. Defeat and death. It felt like cowardice too. We'd vowed to give our last drops of blood for the Second Republic and here we were sailing away. Giving up. They took our arms from us as we came aboard. I saw them collect three sacks of guns. We weren't soldiers any longer. We were refugees. The only thing we could do was tell ourselves that the fight wasn't over. One day we'd be back to drive Franco out. That's what we had to believe. It was the only thing that made it bearable."

I sense that he is about to stop talking but I want to know what happened between Lluís and Ángel's grandmother. Where it went wrong. Why she stayed behind.

"Was Lluís's wife on the ship?"

"Catalina?" He turns back to face us and his expression is curiously blank.

"No. Lluís sent word for her to come, but she never did. She was on the official list of passengers, like we were – but that meant nothing. The Italians had started to bomb Mahon and everyone who could get into a boat was heading out to the ship and trying to climb on board. It was the middle of the night, pitch black except for the fires burning in the town, and in every boat Lluís was frantically looking for Catalina. He wanted to go back to shore and find her. It was I who stopped him. I told him if he went back she was bound to be in the next boat. They'd miss each other. I was wrong about that though. She wasn't in any of the boats. The ship tried to leave when there were still boats alongside and people started jumping into the water. Lluís climbed down the nets and was pulling people up – the women especially – thinking one of them had to be Catalina. There were hundreds on the deck but by the time it was light enough to see for certain that she wasn't there we were half way to France."

"Where was she?"

He shrugs:

"I never heard, all these years later. Perhaps Lluís found out, but if he did he never told me. All I know is that when I came back to the island, when I got out of prison in fifty-four, I heard she was back with Mascaró. They had a son. Or so it seemed. Your father."

It is Ángel who spots the oddity:

"You said 'back with Mascaró'?"

"Yes. Joan Mascaró. Her first husband."

Ángel and I look at each other. The old man sees our puzzlement:

"It was, you'd call it nowadays, an arranged marriage. Set up by her father. She was very young, probably only fifteen or sixteen. But she had a mind of her own. Mascaró was utterly bourgeois and the marriage was not a success. She left him for Lluís, before the War. It was all legal at the time – her divorce, their marriage."

I don't understand, but Ángel is nodding as if he does.

I am infuriated when his next question leads us off in another direction:

"And what happened to you and Lluís? After you left the island."

"Twenty-four hours later we were in Marseille. The British handed us over to the French, who weren't expecting us, or at least only a tenth of us. And they put us in a camp. It was nothing, that place. Just barbed wire cages on the beach. No food, no shelter, nothing to wash with. And only two ways out. Either you died, or you joined a work detail. That's what we did. It was slavery, pure and simple. Don't let them tell you only the Nazis used slave labourers. The French were glad to do it. We got no pay. There were armed guards. We were prisoners. What else could you call it but slavery?"

"What work did they make you do?"

"Oh, the usual work of a chain gang. Mending roads. Digging ditches. Then after Germany invaded Poland they had us moved to the north to reinforce the Maginot Line. We were still there, still digging, when the Nazis came rolling past. They were too clever to come over the top, though. Such a joke. They drove around it – motored to Belgium and came through the forest, beyond the end of the line. The French sat in their forts and the Germans swept right past them and on to Paris and Dunkirk."

"Suddenly we turned round and the guards had gone. Just dropped their guns and ran. Lluís and I looked at each other. It was the best feeling we'd had since we left home. We threw away our shovels and picked up the guns. They were good guns too – not the antiques we'd left on the deck of the Devonshire."

"And what did you do?"

"We went to kill some Fascists. What else? The French didn't seem to have the stomach for it, but we did. We'd

201

waited years to get at them face to face. And let me tell you, it felt good."

"But we couldn't do much. So we formed up a sort of platoon and worked our way back down south. Laid low for a while. Then we joined up with the French Resistance. In forty-four – after D-Day – Lluís and I came back over the mountains into Spain. We thought it was time to finish Franco. The Fascists were losing all over Europe. We thought it was our time again. But we were wrong. Franco was still too strong. One of the local farmers betrayed the position of our camp, I suppose we were eating too much of his orange crop, and we were over-run by the army. I was injured, taken prisoner. Lluís was out on a raid when it happened and he got away, back into the mountains. I didn't see him any more for thirty years. Not until the dictator was dead. Natural causes. That's how useless we were. The bastard even got to die in his own bed."

"But you came back here before then."

"Yes. As I said, nineteen fifty-four. Convicted of 'adherence to the Rebellion' – what a joke! They were the Rebels. They, not us. But the winners write the laws as well as the history books and I was sentenced to thirty years in prison but they let me out after ten – subject to conditions. Restrictions. I wasn't eligible to vote. Not that there was anything worth voting for. There were jobs I couldn't get. But there was a woman who had waited for me, a few friends left who helped us quietly. I was still alive. I was home."

"And now, look around. See how things have changed. This building, you know, was my prison for a while. There were cells here. I used to look out through my bars down to Santa Maria and the Casa Mir. Now they make pottery here, hold concerts, sell washing powder. Innocent things. Times have changed. That's why someone has to record what happened. Soon the last ones who remember will die and it will all be too unimaginable."

"Lluís remembered, didn't he?" I say.

"Of course. But he didn't live here through the grey years, when everyone became anaesthetised. Smothered. It makes you dull, repression. You shut down or you go mad. Because he'd missed those decades, Lluís didn't feel that relief we all felt when the dictator was finally dead. He never understood the pact Spain reached with itself at that moment – not to look back. Nowadays, the fashion is all for 'truth and reconciliation' but in the seventies we settled on something different, the 'pacto de olvidado', the pact of forgetting. More and more I think that he was right and the rest of us were wrong. His name won't be in my book. But in a way it should. He wouldn't have lived – probably wouldn't have died – the way he did if it hadn't been for the War."

I can see that Ángel's about to ask something more about Lluís's death, but I am just as intrigued by the woman called Catalina.

"What do you think happened – with Catalina? Why did she go back to Mascaró, if she loved Lluís? Why didn't she go away to France with him?"

He shakes his head in true bewilderment.

"I don't know. I told you, when I came out of prison she was set up again as Mascaró's wife. He was a born Franquista, a successful lawyer in Ciutadella. I heard she even went to church with him, she who helped us to throw down the statues in Santa Maria and smashed their heads with a sledgehammer. God, she could swing a hammer, that girl! Such a firebrand! To change into that."

He shakes his head again.

"There didn't seem any point in going to talk to her. Plenty of people tried to forget who they'd been in the Second Republic. Of her I didn't expect it. No.

We thought she was Penelope and she turned out to be Clytemnestra."

He must see surprise on both our faces.

"We may have been communists, but we read other things besides Marx. Lluís had read Homer and he used to talk about it – not the Iliad so much as the Odyssey. The journey home. Menorca was our Ithaca. He used to say he was like Odysseus, waiting for the gods to show him the way home to his island and his wife Penelope. Only he had it wrong. He wasn't Odysseus. He was Agamemnon. And she was Clytemnestra."

"But Clytemnestra murdered Agamemnon when he arrived home, didn't she?" I remember the story from an old painting. "Catalina didn't kill Lluís though."

"No. Not absolutely. Just broke his heart."

He is quiet for a moment. Then he says to Ángel:

"Have you asked her? Why she turned against Lluís? I think I'd like to know that myself. Why she changed sides. I've never even thought this before, but maybe she changed sides earlier than we realised. How was it that she never had to face a firing squad? Or at least prison? I mean, everybody who was anybody went to prison. And Catalina was certainly somebody."

Ángel has, even more than usual, the bruised look of a man who has had his trust betrayed. He is finding it hard to hear his grandmother spoken of as a woman who broke a man's heart and abandoned her friends.

"Well, in truth that's why we came to see you. You see, I've only just discovered that Lluís was my grand-father and she won't speak about him to me at all. She just tells me to ask my father."

"So he knows too? And he won't talk either, I suppose? No. I wouldn't expect him to. Forgive me, I don't know your father personally but his reputation is not that of an ... expansive man. I hadn't thought of going to see your grandmother. She didn't seem likely to … in the circumstances. But maybe I should. For the book. See if she remembers anyone I've forgotten. You do, you know. Forget. It's not true what it says on war memorials. We don't always remember them. That's why I have to finish this work before the last few of our generation are gone."

He looks down at the piles of papers on the desk in front of him. There are index cards, photocopied registers of deaths, letters, postcards. And a pile of old photographs like the one he already showed us. Each represents a lost life that he is determined shall not be lost to memory too.

"We'll go."

Ángel looks at me in surprise.

"If you wouldn't mind lending us the photos. Maybe we can persuade her."

I hold out my hand for the photographs and, after a moment's hesitation, the old man gives me all that is left of the friends of his youth. I reach across the table and pick up the photograph of him, Lluís and the others in the camp. He watches me add it to the pile and I can see that he hates to let it go:

"I'll take good care of them."

He nods and looks me right in the eye: "Please," he says. And I realise that I have accepted an obligation to one more person.

As we are crossing the parquet floor to the stairs, I hear him opening one of the drawers in his desk and then he says:

"Wait!"

I think he must have changed his mind, but when I turn round he is holding out another piece of paper, another photo, folded in four, the paper dirty with age:

"Here. Take this one too. You might as well have them all."

34

We leave the old man to his research. I'm beginning to wish I'd never gone up to the cliffs in the tramuntana. Or at least that I'd left it to someone else to reunite Ángel with his lost grandfather. The whole thing is too exhausting for words.

When we reach my car, I absent-mindedly go to the right-hand door, as if it was an English car. Ángel laughs and holds out his hand for the keys and, though I don't know why, I hand them over. I had expected him to leave me and go home but now I climb into the passenger seat and let him drive me away from Maó. Towards, perhaps, a different past from the one he has grown up with.

We travel in silence, although I can almost hear the cogs in his brain turning violent revolutions. Just beyond the monument raised to Governor Kane by the people of the island – strange, that tribute by the colonised to the coloniser, stranger still for a people who have treated so many invaders with such indifference – Ángel slows down and turns left onto the road that a small battered sign tells us is the Cami d'en Kane. I understand why he wants to go this way – this old road always feels like a secret route across the island and we are in pursuit of secrets.

To turn onto Kane's Road is to take an immediate step back in time. The road is wide – exactly twenty feet was Kane's stipulation – and deserted. It is still hemmed in by the stout stone walls he specified so carefully nearly three hundred years ago, in places still overhung with the fig trees he recommended should be planted every twenty feet. Elsewhere the walls are supplemented or overgrown with hedgerows of wild rose and myrtle and all the way along the verges within the walls are dense with different grasses and the dry remnants of spring flowers. The sun is lowering off to the left of us and its warmth and colour both rebound off the stone walls. Corn stands high and dusty yellow in the fields on either side of the road and butterflies dance in the late afternoon heat haze. Ángel slows a little at each blind entrance and turn, anticipating the tractor or car that believes the road to be its own, but no one tries to wrest possession from us.

At Alaior, we pass the triangular plot of land with the yew trees and the public bench, where the town gibbet used to stand. There were road-works here just recently. The workmen have gone now, taking the venerable pot-holes with them, but the white limestone dust thrown up by their diggings is left behind. It coats the Aleppo pines and the myrtle bushes and the grasses in the verge, dulling them to a grey ghostliness that seems eerily fitting for the route they line between the gallows and the cemetery.

Beside the town cemetery, with its white-washed villas of the dead, I see Ángel look over and ask, with his eyes, is he there? I shake my head and shrug. Maybe there's only one person who knows, and we are on our way to see her. I feel in my pocket for the photos but as I do so we turn north towards the coast, not west for Mercadal.

Beyond Alaior the road is faster but still carries something of the spirit of Kane, although the walls on either side are hunchbacked, topped with a cap of white cement in the Minorcan style, a thing Kane could not abide. The road has wide swinging curves and long dips and rises and the car accelerates and falls into the rhythm of a roller coaster. The ride ends just as the sun's orange glow fades to pink over the cala.

Where the road faces the sea and divides, he turns left and the headland opens up before us. The road expires in a turning circle filled with grit and weeds and beyond it lies the wild view, the view I think of as Finisterre. It has that end of the world feeling. Face away from the cliffs and the village lays itself out before you with its square, its south-facing bars, its sheltered little beach – the seaside. But face the cliffs and the frothing green water at their base and you face the sea.

It is usually windy on the headland, even on the hottest day. As the climate is different from further down the cala so is the landscape. It never fails to surprise me that in the bare half mile from these limestone cliffs to the head of the cala the terrain can change from the dry scrub of the *maquis* to a green swamp lush with tall reeds, algae and lichen. Down there where the water grows brackish and shallow all is tropical decay and dragonflies flitting in the stillness. Here on the headland, by contrast, there is freshness and exhilaration in the sea breeze and the whiteness of the cliffs, in the liveliness and power of the sea and in the sense of being on the edge of the island with nothing to the north for hundreds of miles.

Ángel parks at the edge of the turning circle:

"I thought we were going to see your grandmother."

He shakes his head:

"Not today. I'm not quite ready to face her again yet."

"Well, you're taking your life in your hands coming back here," I say. "Billy lives just round the corner. I hope for your sake he doesn't have big friends."

"Why?"

"He was pretty angry about you stealing his bike."

"I didn't steal it. He offered it to me."

It seems unlikely:

"Why would he let you take it? He doesn't even like you. And why did he let me think you stole it?"

"Because I caught him listening."

"What?"

"When I went downstairs I caught him sitting on the step with the door pushed open. He was eavesdropping on us. So when my car wouldn't start and I told him I needed to call a taxi and he offered to lend me his bike instead. I think he wanted me out of there. Wanted you to himself."

"Don't be absurd."

"I'm not being absurd. He thinks you're his personal property. God knows how long he'd been there. All night probably."

Then he remembers last night. We both do. He looks north. I look south. Each of us sees the sea.

"So what are we doing here?"

"This is where they found his body, isn't it?

He walks to the edge and stares down a steep scree slope. Sixty feet below us the water washes and sucks at the base of the rocks. Ángel walks away again, following the line of the headland round from north to south. But I feel hypnotised, magnetised by the confused motion of the sea where it meets the irregular rampart of the cliffs and I wait for him to come back to me here.

Which he does and says:

"This must be it. The police said they found him lying on a sort of beach. And this is the only one. There are rocks all the rest of the way round."

He has identified the spot precisely and I wonder whether to tell him so. But then I would have to tell him how I know, and explain why I didn't report finding the body to the police. Which I cannot do. So I say nothing. He, meanwhile, is heading back towards the road:

"Where are you going?"

"We need a boat."

"A boat?"

"Yes, to go and look down there. Where does Billy live?"

"Billy?"

"Yes, Billy. Your *novio*."

"My boyfriend? Funny. That's what he calls you."

He looks at me for a moment, and then decides this is not the time to go into that.

"Where does he live?"

"You really want to ask Billy? I think I'd better come with you."

Billy's motorbike is parked on the terrace in front of one of the houses opposite the restaurant called *Sa Figuera*. The door is at the side and Ángel insists on standing beside me as I knock. I feel like a child asking if his friend can come out to play. I am relieved that it is Billy himself, and not his mother, who opens the door. He smiles at me, and then he sees Ángel.

"We need your boat," Ángel says.

Billy looks back at me as if I should know better.

"Nobody takes my boat out but me."

"Of course, I know," I say, to placate him: "Will you take us? We need to go round the headland, to look at something at the bottom of the cliff."

"It's dangerous round there. You can't go too close because of the rocks."

"But you can snorkel. I've seen you."

One day when I was walking on the headland I spotted his boat idling in the water beside the entrance to a small cave. Billy was busy setting his anchor whilst two of his friends dipped their feet in the water and put on

210

flippers. When he was satisfied that the anchor was holding he straightened and looked up, like the good skipper, to check that the sky and the wind threatened no dangerous surprises. That's when he saw me, watching from the cliffs above him. He had gone very still and I wondered if he was going to point me out to his friends. But he didn't. He just stood in the boat, ignoring the commotion around him, before raising his arm in a slow wave. I know that he remembers. It was one of those moments. Now he shrugs and pulls the door to behind him. Clearly, his diving activities are not for parental consumption.

"You need to go now?"

"Yes," this is Ángel but Billy looks to me for confirmation. I nod.

He turns and shouts something through the doorway to the interior and then comes out onto the step with us, shutting the door hurriedly before an answer can reach him.

"I'll go and get it. You wait on the mole."

Ángel and I walk down through the square, past the beach and out onto the mole. He sits down on the edge of the wall and swings his legs over the water. I stand beside him and look out for a small ship with a fair-haired skipper.

"What are you expecting to find?"

"What?"

"On that beach, what do you expect to find?"

He shrugs. "I just want to see it for myself. The spot where he died. It's the closest I can get to him now, isn't it? I can't believe I've missed knowing him by a lousy few weeks. All my life he must have been within a few miles of me and I never knew about him. Then no sooner is he dead than I find out he existed. It seems so unfair."

He's right. It does. I felt exactly the same when I recognised Lluís's photo in the newspaper.

"Did the police say how they think he died? Did he drown?"

"That's what they said. The post-mortem showed there was water in his lungs but he'd also been bashed about by the rocks, so they couldn't tell if he went into the water conscious, or hit a rock on the way down."

"It must have been an accident. Surely?"

"The police seem to think so. Although I didn't get the impression they'd put much effort into finding out. They thought he must either have fallen or been blown off the headland. There was a bad storm a couple of days before they found him."

"I remember it. A real tramuntana."

"Yes. But what was he doing up there on the cliffs in the first place? The police said he was living down in Es Castell, in an apartment."

"Lluís wouldn't have liked that."

"Maybe he didn't have a choice. His neighbour told the police his heart was bad."

"We always have a choice. Maybe he made his on the cliff-top."

"You think my grandfather committed suicide?" Now he sounds offended on behalf of someone he never even met.

"I don't know. Would that be so terrible? If he was ill and had no reason to carry on?"

His position on this vexed moral question goes unexplored because neither of us has noticed the approach of the old blue and white dinghy until it bumps alongside the mole by Ángel's feet. The bottom of the boat is strewn, as usual, with snorkel masks and flippers. Ángel jumps down into the boat and then offers me his hand and I jump down after him. Without a word, Billy backs the boat away from the wall and turns towards the channel. The sea is quite calm and it only takes five minutes

212

to motor round beyond the headland. Ángel points up
to where the front wing of my car is just visible on the
cliff top.

"Directly below there. There's shingle at the
bottom."

Billy nods:

"And three rocks right in the entrance. I'll take you
as close as I can but you'll have to swim in. Even that's
a bit dangerous."

"I'll be okay," Ángel says and the way Billy shrugs
his shoulders suggests that that isn't his major concern.
Then he looks over at me.

"She shouldn't go. She doesn't like tight spaces."

Ángel looks from me to Billy and then back. He realises that Billy knows something he doesn't and he is unhappy. He decides to make the decision his own:

"The boy's right. It's too dangerous. You stay here. I'll
go by myself."

It is Billy's turn not to like it, being called a boy, and
I think the sooner one of them is off the boat the better.
Billy swings the dinghy into the outer lip of the double
cove that narrows towards the cliff. The rocks he's talking about are twenty feet away, and he hurries forward
to throw out the anchor and drop the boat back out of
danger. Today he carries a second anchor and when he
is sure the first is holding he drops this over the stern.
There is a gentle swell from the north that carries under
the hull of the boat, causing it to rise and fall on its two
anchors. Half a minute after it passes under the boat
the swell breaks against the cliff in a froth of white and
drops back into blue water.

Ángel pulls off his shirt and his trousers and I catch
Billy looking with distaste at a body that is twenty
years older than his own. I feel a twinge of sympathy
for Ángel, who is too caught up in his strange quest to

213

notice the adolescent examination or his failure to pass it. He struggles into the flippers and dips the mask overboard. Then he stands up, a ridiculous clumsy figure in flippers, mask and boxer shorts, and steps over the side. The boat rocks violently sideways and Billy laughs out loud. But once in the water Ángel becomes surprisingly elegant. Maybe twenty years ago he was a kid like Billy, with a boat and a free existence among the rock pools and the birds' nests. I wouldn't be surprised.

Now he swims easily towards the shore, skirting the rocks. He kicks off the flippers when he reaches the stony ground and the two of us in the boat sit silently, watching him walk up and down the narrow beach, truly as if he expects to find something. Finally he stops and looks up at the cliff. He turns his head to survey the whole length of the slope that funnels down onto the shingle. Finally he stands at the edge of the water and stares out at the point opposite, trying to understand where debris washed in here might come from.

The swim back, against the swell, is harder and takes him longer. Billy pulls up the stern anchor before Ángel reaches the boat and it swings round towards him. He grabs the side and it dips down. I stand up to offer him a hand but he shakes his head and hauls himself up on his forearms. Water pours off them into the well of the boat and a moment later he is aboard. Billy starts the engine and nudges the boat forward. I pull in the main anchor and when I turn around Billy has thrown Ángel a ragged old towel and is backing the boat out into open water.

"Did you find anything?"

Ángel's head appears from within the towel.

"No. But …"

"But what?"

"I don't think he would have been washed in there. I

think he died there. You'll think I'm crazy but I could feel it."

With the torn scrap of towel around his neck and his hair wild he looks more like Lluís than ever and I'm inclined to believe that if anyone can sense what happened to the old man it is the grandson who never met him.

"Do you think he fell?"

"I don't know. He could have. If he didn't, somebody knows. Somebody always knows in a place like this."

And it occurs to me for the first time that he is not thinking of an accident or suicide, but of a third possibility. One that has not occurred to me. He is thinking that Lluís might have been pushed.

35

Everything is moving too fast. I feel tired. And sick again too. I realise I've allowed myself to be drawn too far in to other peoples' lives. What was meant to be a distraction is becoming consuming and exhausting. Maybe it's time to go back to sitting on my balcony or lying up on the roof, letting the sun beat down on me. It feels so life-giving, the sun. And yet I've never been a sun-worshipper until now, not since I was a teenager. There was always too much to do, too much to see and know and try, ever just to lie and bathe in the sun. To lie quiet and calm and soak it up. I never have had a perfect tan in all my life, just elbows and knees and nose that I forgot to protect and then burnt.

But out here, before I met first the kid and then Ángel, I had been working on the perfect tan. Up on the roof where no one except the birds can see me. Using olive oil for tanning lotion. Basting myself regularly and moving my ash-tray from side to side as I changed from front to back. I've been neglecting it the last couple of weeks. And I think I'm missing the energy the sun seems to give me. I think it's time to go back to watching the sky change colour hour by hour, like I used to, before I started running around after boys.

Except.

First, Billy catches me a fish. From up on the roof, I see him come in to his mooring and I can tell at once there's something he's excited about. He stoops down into the bottom of the boat and lifts it into the air, his fingers hooked deep in its gills. It's a beauty, flashing in the sunlight. Three or four pounds of shining sea made flesh, still twisting and arching in a desperate attempt to free itself but the kid has no qualms and no doubts. Whatever his fingers feel inside the body of the fish – softness, wetness, coldness, warmth, bone, fin, a beating heart – they don't frighten him or move him to pity. He is a fisherman and he has his catch.

Someone else might lose their footing as they climb up out of a rocking boat encumbered by a wriggling fish. Not Billy. He leaps lightly onto the jetty and trots to shore, his arms a loop hung with a silver pendant.

"¡Hola!" he shouts, kicking the bottom panel of my door, and I have no choice but to go down and let him in. He dashes past me and lopes up the stairs, dripping sea water as he goes. When I follow him into the kitchen he has tossed the fish into my sink, where it flaps its tail weakly and gasps for breath. I stare at the fish and it stares back, with panic in its eye. It knows it's going to die, soon, and I feel sorry for it. I think it's a seabass: *lubina*. Too pretty to be monkfish. Too long and slender to be *dorada*. Hake maybe: *merluza*. But I think it's a sea bass. How good it would be, stuffed with lemons and wild fennel pulled from the roadside verge, cooked on a hot grill. If only I could summon the appetite.

"Got a knife?" he says, and I pass him one and then turn away. He despatches the fish. "You want me to clean it?"

I nod and so he does, working expertly, slitting its belly and washing out the guts, heart and liver. He even scales it lightly, with the flat of the knife, and then holds it out for me to admire, hands under its belly, as if it is still swimming along.

"It's a beauty, Billy. Thank you. I'll cook it later." And I hold out a plate to put it on and place it in the fridge and shut the door. I can see he wants to stay, but I don't give him any excuse and so he goes. And I go into my bedroom, shut the door and sleep, all the rest of the afternoon and all night and most of the next morning.

When I wake, it is to the sound of footsteps on the stairs. I emerge from the bedroom, still woozy with too-heavy sleep, to find Ángel standing in my living area.

"Your front door was open," he says, as if that gives him the right to walk in.

I fetch two beers from the fridge and pass one to him, then I search in my bag for cigarettes. There's a mirror above the dresser and I glance in it and look away, shocked:

"Got anything to eat?" he asks.

I think for a moment.

"I've got a fish."

He looks interested:

"What kind of fish?"

"*Lubina*, at least I think it is. Billy caught it yesterday. It's in the fridge."

He hauls himself up off the couch and goes to see.

"Nice. The boy has his uses."

He looks at me sharply, to see if I'm willing to expand on what they might be, but I just step out onto the balcony and light my cigarette. He follows me with the plate in his hand.

"Shall I cook it?"

I blow smoke out towards the water and comb my hair with my fingers:

"If you like."

And off he goes, foraging in my fridge for lemons and then heading outside, coming back a few minutes later with a handful of wild fennel. Funny, that he's had exactly the same idea as I did on how it should be cooked. Next he cleans out the old barbecue set into the wall downstairs. I can hear him whistling as he scrapes at the

218

grill shelf with a wire brush and the rising smoke soon signals that he has it working again. I run the cold tap and splash my face with the water that comes up slightly salty from the well. Then I bathe the fish in the sink, turning it this way and that. I wash out its empty belly, a pink chamber of parabolic arches that I fill to the roof beams with wedges of lemon and fennel, and wrap the whole thing in foil.

I take the fish downstairs. To my surprise, Billy is there, sitting on an upturned bucket with a bottle of my beer in his hand, watching Ángel poke at the charcoal on the barbecue. He eyes my foil parcel suspiciously and I wonder if he is one of those fishermen who never touch fish.

"It'll be good," I tell him, "you'll like it."

He shrugs sulkily, from which it's clear that he hasn't come over because he's hungry, he's come because he's jealous of me sharing his fish with Ángel. He's come to make sure we don't have a good time.

I hand Ángel the fish and go back upstairs to find the makings of a salad. And then I take my book and the olive oil up to the roof to work on my tan, leaving the pair of them to glare at each other two floors below.

Of course, they can't bear to leave me in peace for long. A thin skein of fennel-scented smoke tells me that the fish is cooking and soon I hear footsteps on the stairs. Billy's head appears, complete with scowl, although the scowl changes to something else when he takes in the fact that I'm sunbathing naked:

"Er, he said to tell you it's ready."

"Okay," I say, "I'll be down in a second," but he doesn't go. In fact he takes another step closer, so I sit up and turn my back on him, reaching for my cotton kaftan. I can feel him watching as I pull it down over my hips. He doesn't even move as I walk over to the steps, as if it's beyond his power to do anything but stare. There's just room for me to pass him without touching, but the space between us buzzes with electricity. I'm almost past when he reaches out for my shoulder. Gently, he pushes me against the wall and pins me there with the palms of his hands. Then he leans in to kiss me. And I'm surprised, because the dreaminess of his movements hasn't prepared me for the fierceness of this kiss. His whole weight is taken, through me, on his hands and the rough plaster of the wall digs into my shoulders. It hurts, but I find part of me wants to be trapped there between him and the wall in the shadows where no one can see us. I don't even need to move. He will do everything. All I need to do is open up to him and let go of all the thoughts and questions and feelings that have been so exhausting me. His body pressing against mine offers another kind of distraction, the kind that will obliterate everything for a few minutes in a simpler quest with a simpler end.

But then Ángel shouts my name from downstairs, and I hear the glass rattle in the door as he starts to come up. A moment later my hand is against Billy's chest and I find I'm pushing him away, even as my fingertips register the delicious smoothness of his skin. As the kiss breaks off, his long lashes flicker reluctantly and his eyes open. He smiles at me conspiratorially, but I don't smile back. The realisation strikes me that I don't want Ángel to find us.

Even more than I want the other thing.

Because I can imagine the look on his face when he finds us here. It's a look I've seen already and I don't want to be responsible for causing it again.

In that moment I understand that something has changed. I'm not sure when it happened, I only know that I've broken my promise to myself. When I came here, it was to be alone. It was to have done with other people and their feelings. It was to act without care for the consequences. But I haven't been resolute enough. I thought that the search for Lluís was harmless. He was, after all, dead. But I failed to take account of the people he might have left behind. I should have taken one look at Ángel and walked away. I should have run.

"Coming!" I shout, to forestall him turning onto the last flight of stairs. Billy's head drops and he flings himself back against the opposite wall of the stairway, giving me a full-length view of what I'm turning down. A shudder of convulsed desire runs through me, and he sees it because he opens his eyes wide and starts to smile and reach for me again but I just shrug apologetically and turn away. Down in the kitchen I make myself busy, gathering up the salad and three plates and cutlery. Outside, Ángel is filleting the fish and, I have to admit, it does smell good. By the time I arrive, Billy is back on his bucket, staring at the ground and I drag a couple of folding chairs outside for Ángel and me. He hands round the plates and there we sit. I wonder if they've heard of the three wise monkeys.

The fish is beautiful, moist and delicately flavoured, and after three bites I can't face any more. I put down my plate and reach for my cigarettes. The other two exchange a glance and I see I've offended them both, fisherman and chef.

"Sorry," I say, "just not hungry, I guess."

"Do you ever eat?" asks Ángel, and the look he gives me is so anxious, so caring that I know I have to do something about it. Now or never.

I take a deep breath.

"I don't know who you think you are," I say. "You're as bad as each other. You turn up here uninvited, you hang around glaring at each other. You tell me where I can swim, and what I should eat. Who appointed you my legal guardians, that's what I want to know? I live on my own because that's the way I like it. Now, all of a sudden, I've got the two of you hanging around like stray cats the whole time. Well, I've had enough, you can vamoose, the pair of you."

I stand up and clap my hands at them, as if they really were a pair of stray toms, but they don't move. They just sit there with their mouths open, plates and forks still clutched in their hands. So I decide to leave them to it. I walk over to my front door and just before I slam it in their faces, I turn and say:

"Oh, and one other thing. The answer's yes. I know you're both wondering, and the answer's yes. I have slept with both of you. And neither one of you is now or has any chance of being my 'novio'. It was just casual sex, alright? So get over it."

And then I slam the door behind me and for once I even remember to turn the key.

36

To my surprise, they are as good as my word and vamoose they do. Billy's boat sits idle on the mooring and nobody comes nosing around Lluís's place. It is a relief. For several days it is a great relief.

I go back to my old routine, watching the tamarisk and the palm tree blow in the breeze, listening to the sounds of the building work that is always underway somewhere, the hammer blows that echo round the cala, the lazy whine of the circular saw, from eight until two and again from three thirty until five. The weekend noises are different. Car doors on a Friday night, excited voices, snatches of music, boat engines on a Saturday, the shouts of children in the water, the throaty island accents in unhurried neighbourly conversation during the evening *paseo*.

I listen to it all from my hidden roof-top and every day my basted body turns a deeper brown. I am strict about it. I don't try to read or sleep or polish my nails. I concentrate on the sun as it concentrates on me, lying first on one side then on the other, with one knee tucked up to expose the inner surface of my lower leg. Then I lie supine with my arms raised above my head so that my inner wrists and elbows and armpits turn the same even colour as my back and my belly. I even spread my hands out wide so that nothing, not even the webbing between my fingers, is missed. The tan, as it deepens, makes me feel stronger, as if I am turning from flimsy balsa into mahogany before my own eyes. It even seems to be absorbing my scars so that one day I look for them and

223

it takes me a moment. Without touching, I'm not sure anyone but me would be able to tell they were there.

The terrible tiredness begins to fade again too and everything returns to the way it was before I met Billy and Ángel. All thanks to the sun. Except that, as my batteries re-charge, my mind begins to gain in power too. Each day, as I lie on the roof, it becomes harder and harder to keep it quiescent. It wants to think. I tell it to lie quiet, along with the rest of me, but it is rebellious. It wants to think.

I forbid it, straight out, to think about Lluís, about Ángel and Billy. It tries to push the word "Catalina" into my thoughts, but I beat it back, distract it with a cigarette, watch a boat moving slowly across the water. This game, of temptation and distraction, goes on for several days until one morning my ally, the sun, deserts me.

I know something's wrong as soon as I wake. The window of my bedroom opens onto a tiny internal courtyard and normally sunlight is already bouncing off the white walls and into my room when I open my eyes. Today, the room is dark and the courtyard is filled with nothing but a dull greyness. From the balcony I see that the sky is filled with layer upon layer of cloud in every shade of grey. The cloud is moving slowly towards the sea, but inland, where it's coming from, the grey is denser, darker and promises rain.

It's astonishing how different the cala and, therefore, life feels without the sun. Its colours disappear. The sparkling blue water turns drab and uninviting. The white houses look instantly shabby and the boats on their moorings turn from jaunty to forlorn. It is almost painful to look at the view under a leaden sky. So I don't. I go inside and pull the doors shut behind me. I wander from room to room, feeling suddenly trapped.

My eye falls on a pile of photographs that lie jumbled

on the mantelpiece. They are the ones I begged from the old man at the map museum. I haven't even looked through them yet. He is probably wondering if he is ever going to see them again. Curiosity gnaws at me as if I am the bone and it is the dog. I reach out my hand to touch the pictures, but then I think better of it. I'm not going to get involved again. Am I? I shake my head and catch myself in the mirror doing it.

I should take them back, or better still, send them. Put them in an envelope and post them back to him. No explanation required, that way. He never heard my name. Wouldn't know where to find me. If he chooses to contact Ángel again, or Catalina, well that's up to him. They are easy enough to find and, after all, they are the ones concerned. Not me.

I search around in the cupboards of the dresser for an envelope to hold the photos. There is nothing useful. A few board-games in battered boxes, old maps of the island, a half-drunk bottle of Menorcan gin, a couple of unwritten postcards. I sit back on my heels. Then I have an idea. Under the bed in the spare bedroom is the bag I brought with me. I drag it out and unzip the compartment on the front. Inside, as I thought, there is a large manilla envelope. True, it has my name on the front but I can easily snip that out and cover the hole with one of the postcards.

Kicking the bag back under the bed, I carry the envelope out into the main room. Pleased with my ingenuity, I tip the contents of the envelope out onto the table. A slew of 50 euro notes falls out first and is then scattered across the table top by a pile of papers held together with a metal spring clip. Last, gliding down on top, is a photograph of three people. A man and a woman, flanking a girl, arms round each other, all smiling at the camera.

A family.

Mine.

My knees give and I grab at the back of a chair. How could I be so stupid? How could I remember the envelope and forget what it contained?

Slowly, I pull out the chair and sit down. I cannot take my eyes from that photograph, from the two faces I haven't seen for more than eight weeks now – the two faces I have tried, more than any others, not to bring to mind. I pick it up and hold it out and it shakes in my hand.

It was taken last summer and her hair is longer now. Was longer. When I left. Maybe she's had it cut again now. Would Peter have gone with her to the hairdressers'? Would he have been able to tell them how she wanted it? Or would she have got up the nerve to tell them herself? The way she always said she was going to when I took her, but then never did, sitting in the chair swamped in purple cape and urging me with her eyes, "Tell them, Mum. Please!"

So many things she's going to have to face for herself now. At twelve. Too young. Much too young. I look at Peter's face in the picture. So many things you're going to have to do for her now, Pete. He looks out at me, the way he used to look at the world. So positive, so trusting. A man who was never afraid to help out a stranger, or to ask for help either, believing always that there was more good in the world than bad. Peter, who was never dismayed when he left his wallet, or his glasses or his shopping bags in a bar or a taxi because he always believed there was a more than even chance an honest soul would hand them in – and was often proved right.

But it's been shattered now, that faith in the fairness of life. And I haven't seen a smile like that on his face since just after New Year. It was so much harder for him than

226

for me, to accept what they told us, because it meant everything he'd believed about life was unfounded. Something will turn up. Never say die. Things are never as bad as they're painted. All wrong. All useless when he needed them to be true.

It was easier for me, because I never believed any of that stuff. It was nice living with someone who did, because it made him optimistic and an optimistic person is easier to live with, most of the time, than a realistic one.

I knew, as soon as I saw the surgeon's face in the little operating theatre, when he looked at the thing close up. They should put you under, if they don't want you to see what they're thinking. It would be kinder to put you out for the duration than expect you to make small talk while they coolly cut holes in you.

The pathology would take two weeks. Peter was sure I was wrong to worry.

"It was only tiny," he said. "I had a good look at it when he'd taken it out. It looked okay to me."

I didn't point out to him that he had absolutely no idea what cancer looks like. Let him stay an optimist for two more weeks.

When we went back, they put us in the same room so that the consultant could take out the stitches. I heard his footsteps come striding confidently up the corridor. For a moment I thought I'd been wrong, that they weren't the steps of someone bearing bad news. Then they stuttered and broke stride, just outside the door. There was a beat, while he composed himself and took a deep breath, then he pushed open the door and came in smiling.

It was well done. I had to accept it was well done. Practice, I suppose. It fooled Peter, who squeezed my shoulder encouragingly, but it didn't fool me. I sat there

227

on the bed, with my skirt pulled up to reveal the black spider of stitches round the wound where he'd taken out the mole, and I looked straight into his eyes. Determined not to appear vulnerable, despite my pose, despite my situation. He looked back at me, saw that I knew, and sighed.

"I'm sorry," he said. "It is melanoma."

I nodded, as Peter gasped and lurched against me.

"We won't know how far advanced it is until we take out some more skin and do some more tests. It means a skin graft, I'm afraid. We'll schedule that in, some time in the next six weeks, I just need to …"

He came over and pressed his fingers into my groin, either side of my hip bone. First on the leg that we must forever afterwards think of as the leg with the cancer, then on the other side. He looked grim:

"I think it may be in your lymph nodes. I couldn't feel it before, but now …"

"That would mean it's penetrated through the skin and got into my bloodstream."

Peter looked at me, he didn't know I'd been busy on the internet, like every good modern patient.

"Not necessarily. Let's wait and see, shall we? Do the rest of the tests."

Peter cleared his throat. His voice still cracked as he said:

"What's the treatment, doctor? Is it surgery? Chemotherapy?"

I looked at him. So did the doctor. We avoided looking at each other. I wasn't going to tell him. You're the one getting paid to do this, I thought. You tell him.

"Quite possibly. It all depends on which stage it's reached. Let's take things a step at a time. Consider the options."

There might have been options. He was right not to

jump to conclusions. If the cancer had been confined to the epidermis, or even the dermis, there would have been options. Even if it had just reached the lymph node nearest the tumour site, radical surgery and chemo might have stopped it. But all the tests revealed that it was running free and clear, had already reached my liver and there were no options. None that appealed to me, anyway. None that held out any prospect of success or even meaningful delay. None that meant anything to a realist like me.

"Three months," said the surgeon, not quite meeting my eye any more. "Six weeks to three months. I can't say for sure. You need to talk to the oncologist. It's not really my department, dermatology, not any more."

I smiled at him:

"You must be hoping for a nice case of raging acne to walk through the door next."

He looked at my file for a moment and then he did meet my eye:

"To be honest," he said, "I am, yes."

I liked him, and I think he liked me. I think he was genuinely sorry and if someone has to tell you you're going to die, it is at least comforting to feel that they are genuinely sorry. He gave me my file, to give to the oncologists. But I didn't go to any more doctors, though I told Peter I would, told him I was waiting for an appointment. He still persisted in hoping, still insisted there was a battle to be fought when it was clear to me that the war was lost. Suddenly, living with an optimist wasn't so easy after all. Suddenly it was an ideological gulf that nothing could bridge.

My file is the one that lies on the table now. I can see the doctor's heavy black italic handwriting, his sketch of my leg with its black arrow pointing at the position of the mole. I brought it with me. Just in case somehow I missed my moment and grew too ill. In case I needed to show someone what was wrong with me.

That isn't going to happen though. I will not miss my moment. I owe it to them not to. I pick up the photo one last time. They can never know that I lived on after they thought I'd gone, not even for these few weeks. To them, I am already dead, and I owe it to them to stay that way.

I turn the photo over so that they will stop looking at me and slide it back into the envelope. Then I slide the medical file in after it and close the flap. I count up the fifty euro notes. There are still plenty to last me, but I don't put them back in the envelope. I put them in a box on the dresser and zip the envelope back into my bag, pushing it deep out of sight under the spare bed.

Coming back into the living room, I have picked up the pile of old photos from the mantelpiece before I realise what I've done. I hesitate when I find them in my hand. But only for a moment. Compared with thinking about my past, thinking about Lluís's seems positively innocuous.

37

The woman's hand is smooth and slender. Her long fingers curl around a child's ball and she wears a signet ring on her third finger. It is her left hand. A married woman then, a mother with a young child.

I lift the hand and it is surprisingly heavy, its brass solidity belied by the elegance of its shape and polish. It is cold too and any human sympathies I have ascribed to it drop away when it thuds, dull, against the door.

The door is opened just at the moment I have decided that she must be out. My first impression is that the grandmother is neat and small and very old. Although she is standing on a fairly high step I find that I am looking down onto the top of her head. Her grey hair is parted with straight-drawn severity from the crown and pinned back in a bun. She has not adopted the soft wave and pastel rinse of so many elderly women, even here. Nor has she chosen to spend her latter years in floral prints or man-made fabrics. Her dress is of black cotton and buttoned to the neck. Her face is heavily lined but her features retain the symmetry that must always have been their attraction and although I think age must have shrunken her it has neither stooped nor crushed her.

"¿Sí?"

Why do I have the feeling that she already knows who I am?

"Señora ... ," I don't know how to address her. "I am a friend of Ángel's." Though I was briefly somewhat more and am now infinitely less.

"La inglesa?"

"*Si.*"

I am slightly surprised that he, or someone, has mentioned me. She shakes her head and then takes a pace back. For a moment I think that she is going to shut the door but then I see that she is only standing aside so that I may step into the house.

When she has closed the door behind us the interior is dim and cool. It is the first time I have been inside a traditional island house and now the surreptitious glimpses through open windows and doorways coalesce into a complete picture. Immediately beyond the door is the main sitting room. The floor is paved with tile and the furniture is largely set around the edges, as if a dance was due to take place in the centre. There is a fireplace in one side wall and a single large armchair placed at an angle to it. A sewing bag and a pair of reading glasses sit on the arm of the chair and there is a radio on the mantelpiece. I cannot see a television set. A narrow stairway leads up from the corner of the room and beneath the stairs a door opens onto a dark passageway, which I assume leads to a kitchen and other offices.

The wooden furniture is warmly polished and the room smells of beeswax. There are a few small pictures on the walls and one incongruously large painting between the window and the door, a portrait in oils of a man in – eighteenth century? – uniform. I notice that there are none of the usual devotional items or images of the Virgin, very few ornaments of any kind. For the house of an old lady it is remarkably empty of objects of obvious sentimental importance.

"You're probably wondering why I've come to see you."

I get the impression she feels that to shrug would be undignified, though it is what she wants to do.

"Ángel is very unhappy."

Her gaze drops to the floor, and I am relieved to know that at least she cares.

"It's my fault, I'm afraid, for telling him about someone I used to know a long time ago, when I was a child."

She looks directly at me now, but still she doesn't speak.

"His name was Lluís. Ángel came down to my cala looking for the place where Lluís used to live. I showed it to him. Saw the family resemblance. Couldn't miss it actually."

"He's dead," she murmurs, as if she half hopes this will be the end of it, but there is a wistfulness about the way she says it that suggests the opposite too.

"The police also told Ángel that Lluís was his grandfather. But he – neither of us – we don't understand how that can be. Ángel has always understood that his grandfather – Joan Mascaró – died before he was born. You told him that he must talk to his father. But he cannot do that. Not at the moment. Did he tell you they had a terrible fight just before he came to see you? Maybe if Ángel knew what to say to him, what to ask. If you could tell him what he needs to know …"

She looks at me, quite steadily, then shakes her head. Nothing more. And starts to walk back towards the door to show me out.

"What about me? If you can't face Ángel, perhaps you could tell me what happened. Then I could explain it to him. It might be less painful for both of you that way. He'd have time to get used to whatever he needs to before he comes to see you again."

"What makes you think he'll be coming to see me again?"

"I know he will," I say, and she glances at me sharply, suspecting me of being a bringer of false comfort.

"How do you know?"

233

"Because he loves you."

"When did he tell you that?"

"Most recently? Just after he came to see you."

She takes in this information and begins to nod without taking her eyes off me. I can feel myself blushing. For a very old lady, she is a quick study.

"So you think you know him?"

"A little, yes. But it's hard when he doesn't even know himself."

She raises her chin, pretending that that didn't hurt:

"So I should tell you all the things I've never told anybody else in forty years. Just to help you get to know my grandson?"

"Not for my sake, no. For his."

Deep down, I know it isn't true. I'm not here for Ángel. I'm here for myself. To keep my mind off other things. The lie spills out so easily that I am afraid that she will see through me. But she doesn't. Her love for her grandson makes her want it to be true. The defiance fades from her face and she becomes an old woman again. She definitely hesitates this time. But then she shakes her head again.

"It's too late. Much too late for all that."

"Are you sure? Because I don't think so."

"Don't you? How would you know?"

"It's never too late for the truth, is it?"

She gives me another sharp look and I realise she is not the kind of person to approach with platitudes and clichés. I feel a pang of fellow feeling with her. She is no optimist either.

"Sometimes too late. Sometimes too soon. For some things there's never a right time."

"But there was for this?"

"I never thought so until he came to see me. Now I think that for Ángel maybe the right time was when his

234

grandfather was still alive. But it's no good now. I didn't take the chance then and it's no good now."

"But it …"

She holds her hand up and the fierceness of her look cows me into silence.

"I'm sorry. I'm about to go out now so …"

She gestures, almost points, to the door.

"Please."

I take the photographs out of my bag and hold out the top one towards her.

"Please look at this."

The once-glossy paper is so worn and limp that it collapses at the folds. It is in black and white, now faded to brownish greys. It shows a young couple leaning against a farm gate, a traditional Menorcan gate made from curved branches of olive wood. The creases in the paper divide the figures one from the other, vertically, and each from each, horizontally, at the waist. The girl is wearing a long gathered skirt and a white collarless shirt, open at the neck and rolled at the sleeves. There is a scarf round her dark hair. She is very young, slim and full-breasted and unmistakably happy, unmistakably in love. She is laughing with her mouth open, but it doesn't make her ugly, it makes her beautiful. The young man stands beside her, on the other side of the crease, a hand taller, broad-shouldered, in workman's trousers caught round with a thick leather belt. Like hers, his shirt is open and the sleeves are rolled up above his elbows, showing strong tanned forearms and wrists. He has a stalk of grass in his hand and he may have been tickling her with it. He is looking directly into the camera, smiling, sharing a joke with the photographer.

The resemblance to Ángel is obvious but so is the dissimilarity. The young man in the photograph (the very young man, hardly more than a boy) is at ease with himself, brimful with confidence, standing side by side with the woman he loves. When this picture was taken, Lluís knew who he was, in a way that I don't think Ángel ever has.

This is the photo Juan Mercadal gave me as we were leaving the museum. As soon as I unfolded it I knew what he knew, that if anything would work on her, this would.

She takes it from me with reluctance and drops it brusquely on the table as she hunts around in her bag for reading glasses, but when she puts them on she holds it up and looks at it for a long time. A long, long time. It shakes in her hand.

"Where did you get this?"

"From an old friend of yours, Juan Mercadal Triay."

"And where did he get it?"

"I don't know. He didn't say. But I would guess someone entrusted it to him for safe-keeping, maybe a friend when they were in exile together. He gave it to me because he thought it might mean something to you."

She re-folds it and tries to hand it back to me, but I make no move to take it from her. She takes off her reading glasses and drops them on the table, but I notice she does not put down the photo. Instead she walks over to her armchair and sits down. Then she shakes her head:

"What's wrong with you all? Why can't you just get on with your lives? Leave me alone. There's no point raking over things that can't be changed, that are almost dead and forgotten."

I bend down by the arm of the chair and lean forward, close to her face:

"But that's the point. Don't you see? You're one of the last. When you're gone, it really will be dead and forgotten. And then nobody will be able to unearth the truth."

I pause, then I decide to take a risk. I don't know why

236

it's so important to me to understand what happened between her and Lluís. I'm not even sure whether I want to know for Ángel's sake, or Lluís's or mine. All I know is that it matters, so I take a deep breath and say:

"But maybe that suits you. Maybe, in your case, that would be best."

She looks at me angrily:

"What are you trying to say?"

"Everyone knows the Civil War was a terrible conflict. You must have been very young. Maybe you chose safety over romance. It's understandable, especially if there was a baby on the way ..."

She starts shaking her head even as I am speaking and carries on shaking it as I peter out. Her eyes are dark with emotion:

"You have no idea. None."

"Then tell me. If that isn't how it was. If that isn't what you want Ángel to think, you're going to have to tell me."

She sits very still for a long time, looking at me with an expression that I cannot read. Her voice, when it comes, is a whisper:

"I can't. I made a promise."

I don't understand.

"A promise? To Lluís?"

She shakes her head.

"Then to whom? Your husband?"

She glares at me fiercely and shakes her head again, emphatically:

"Not to him. To my son."

"To Ángel's father?"

She nods.

"But it was he who told Ángel to come and ask you about Lluís, about your secrets. I was there. I heard him."

"Maybe you did, but a promise is a promise."

"I don't understand. Why would he send Ángel to see you if he didn't want you to tell him the truth?"

"You don't know my son. He is not straightforward like his father, his real father, and his son. Perhaps he thought it would make Ángel hate me, if he knew I had secrets that I wouldn't tell him. He's never liked the fact the boy and I are close. Thinks I'm a bad influence. And it wasn't a bad idea. It seems to have worked."

"If that's true, then you should break your promise."

She stares at me, hands tightening on the arms of her chair as if she might launch herself at me. Then something gives. The tension goes out of her and she gives a little shrug. I even think I catch the merest shadow of a self-mocking smile flit across her face.

"What good will it do?"

For a moment I am aghast at my own hypocrisy. How can I preach truth and reconciliation to the Mascarós when I have lied to everyone who loves me? She wants me to tell her what good it will do to break her promise to her son and stir up the past and I don't know what to say. For once, I decide to tell the truth too:

"Honestly? I have no idea. All I know is that your grandson is confused and unhappy and desperately needs to know who he is. Don't you owe him that, even if it means stepping down from the pedestal he's always had you on?"

She snorts and glares at me, with a sudden revival of energy:

"Pedestals are for saints," she says. "I've always hated saints."

"Then help me. Help us."

I take the rest of the photographs out of my bag and hold them out towards her.

"What are these?"

238

"The people Juan Mercadal Triay is trying to identify, to account for. The missing. He thought you might
know what happened to some of them."

At first, I think she's going to refuse to take them. But
then, very slowly, she lifts one hand from the arm of the
chair and touches the top photograph with her index
finger.

" Josep," she says, quietly.

"What?"

"Josep Quintana."

She looks up at me and I see that her eyes are
glittering.

"He was a mechanic. His wife, Anna, was my friend.
They had two little girls."

She opens her hand and I place whole pile face-up
on her palm. She gestures for her glasses again and
then stares at Josep Quintana for a long minute as I am
searching in my bag for a pen and notebook to write
down his name. Then she puts him to the bottom of the
pile. She shakes her head at the second photo but peers
long and hard at the third:

"Tolo? Not Tolo."

She looks up at me beseechingly, as if I have any
power to change the fate of people who died before I
was even born.

"He was only a child. Eighteen or nineteen."

"Who was he?"

"Bartolome Mir Salord. He was from Es Castell.
What happened to him?"

I look up from my notebook. "If he's in that pile, then
I guess nobody knows."

She shakes her head and looks up at me:

"I never saw him after … I never saw any of them. I
had no way of knowing. I assumed he'd got away with
the others. To France."

She touches the picture with her finger:

"He was the one Lluís sent to fetch me. We made it down to the port together, but then we got separated. He was ahead of me. I always thought he was safe."

Then she puts her hand over her mouth:

"Oh my God, he's never coming back for you. He thought … Oh, poor Tolo. It was my fault!"

"Because he got caught? And you got away."

She looks at me, and smiles wryly:

"Is that what you think? That I got away?"

I don't answer, but she nods anyway:

"You'd better bring him."

38

Bringing him would be easier if I hadn't sent him away. I prowl around the phone for half a day before I raise the courage to pick it up and dial the mobile number on his business card.

But in fact he makes it easy. He doesn't sulk or leave awkward pauses in the conversation. He doesn't even mention my rudeness and when I suggest we go to visit his grandmother together he offers to come and pick me up. I am surprised at how good it is to hear his voice, at how familiar it already sounds. When I put the phone down, I catch sight of myself in the mirror and see that I am smiling.

In Mercadal, Catalina's room is as it was before, save that a straight-backed settle has been dragged over to stand opposite her chair. She offers us a drink. Ángel shakes his head, but I am feeling hot, even feverish, despite the cool room, so I ask for a glass of water and she brings it and hands it to me, nodding at the settle. She brings nothing for herself but sits in her own chair and rests her hands for a moment on the polished wood of the arms. The hands are fleshless and the veins stand proud between bone and skin. She sees me looking and conceals them, clasped, in the folds of her skirt. Vanity reveals itself in the strangest places.

As we both look up from her hands our eyes meet and I realise why she is ashamed of their telling her age too accurately. It is because she is not an old woman at heart. My guess is that she dresses now as she has ever since she was widowed, and perhaps even earlier. Her body

241

may have made some concessions to age but she herself has not. She has decided not to become sentimental, doting, silly or helpless. She has decided to go on being the woman she has always been inside, to the end. And that woman is a resolute character, as determined now to tell her story as she was to withhold it before.

"I have been thinking what I could tell you that would make sense to you."

Ángel opens his mouth to say something but a sharp look quells him:

"I decided Juan was right after all. If we don't tell it now, the truth will die with us and the Right will have won its final victory. And anyway I am too old to be afraid of it any more. It's not as if I'm concerned about what St Peter will say. I don't believe in all that. I showed God what I thought of Him many years ago."

She rubs her hands together, washing them of God, and I realise she is actually excited about her decision to tell her story. She is more alive, suddenly, than when I last saw her.

"So. What to say? Well, my life, like any woman's life, has been driven by the men in it. There have been four men in my life. No, I'm wrong. There have been five men in my life. I was forgetting Franco. He's been as important as any of the others. But I won't tell you his story. You can find that out in the books these days. He has studied it."

She nods at Ángel.

"But the others, I'm going to tell you their stories. And then you'll know the whole of mine."

"So who are they, the four?"

"It's very simple. They are my husbands, my son and my grandson. This one here. If I was being logical I would start with the story of my first husband. But all my life I have been led to believe that women are not

242

bound by logic. So I don't choose to start with him. I never chose him freely in life. I don't see why I should be forced to choose him when he's dead. Put him to one side. I start with my second – technically my fourth also – and actually my only real husband."

"I met Lluís when I was fourteen. 1933. I was a spirited girl. 'Wilful' was the word my parents used. They didn't know, but I was already creeping out to go to political meetings. I was so excited about the possibilities for a new Spain, free of all the old snobberies and injustice. A lot of my excitement had to do with the fact that I was in love with the man who was preaching this new creed, but still, he was right. When I was fifteen my father announced that he'd done a deal to sell me off in marriage, as if I was a precious but expendable heirloom, to keep the family afloat. You can imagine how angry I was. I decided I was going to run away with Lluís. I got out of the house and I told him everything. I told him I loved him. I told him he loved me. You should have seen his face. I can see it now."

She gives a dry little laugh and I can hear that there is still bitterness in it, seventy years on.

"He didn't have a clue what I was talking about. He had no time for love. Not when he was going to change the world."

"So I went home and I let them marry me off. Lluís didn't want me, so what did it matter? I soon found out, of course, on my wedding night why it mattered but by then it was too late. I fell into a kind of daze, a daze of misery at what I'd done. My mother thought it quite normal. She called it 'adjusting to marriage'."

"It lasted eighteen months. Then one day I ran into Lluís and everything changed. All of a sudden he understood what I'd known all along. All he had to do was say one word, hold out his hand and my marriage was

243

over. We were together then, as we should have been from the start."

"When we married, I was so happy. So happy. Life had so much promise for us. We thought we were the first of a new epoch. The first free Spaniards."

"A few months later, the army rebelled against our government. At the beginning everything was confusion. Nobody knew what was happening. But we had the radio and we heard the news reports from the peninsula. The Republic was not going to give in. It was going to fight for its life. Of course, because it was the government the people had chosen. And we weren't going to give in either."

"Most of the soldiers on the island were for Franco. That man. It was the first time his name meant anything to me. How I wish I'd never heard it. But there's no use crying over that. I said I wouldn't tell you his story. He took enough of my life. He's not taking a minute more."

"Where was I? Yes, yes, it happened very fast. The garrison sided with the rebels and declared war. Thought that was all they had to do. Put up a few notices and take over. They thought we were meek little island peasants who didn't notice who the government was. Well, they were wrong. There was a lot of rushing about. All the parties, all the unions, the left trying to agree on something – that was a novelty – but they did it. They found weapons, guns, and they formed up columns and they marched. Lluís never slept for three days. He had a motorbike and rode between the towns, taking the news, holding meetings in different houses. I went too, out to the company of machine-gunners stationed outside Ciudadella. We got them on our side. We took back the town halls and the factories. Then we marched those Fascist bastards down to the fort at La Mola and locked them up."

Her fist is clenched above her head as she finishes the sentence with a flourish and I can see her, a young girl in a red headscarf, leaning on the side of an armoured car, filled with enough righteous zeal and sex appeal to convert any number of machine-gunners to the Republican cause.

"Then of course we thought it was only a matter of time. We thought the rest of Spain would do the same as us and the Fascists would be out on their ear within the month. Later, when we realised it was going to take longer, we believed Mother Russia would send us guns and that we'd be able to buy the rest from the French, the British and the Americans. But it didn't work that way. None of the Western powers would sell our government so much as a catapult – while Franco was getting all he needed from those other Fascists. It was so unfair. So unfair."

She glares at me, as if I am personally to blame for British foreign policy three generations ago.

"They bombed us, you know. With Italian planes based on Mallorca. Not much resistance to the Fascists over there, no. They bombed us right to the last day. If they hadn't, if they hadn't ... but I'm ahead of myself. This is supposed to be Lluís's story."

She takes a deep breath to calm herself, for Lluís's sake:

"Well, so, those early days of the war were the making of Lluís."

She smiles:

"He got a reputation as one of the decisive ones – a man you went to if you wanted something done. Until they sent Brandaris out from the mainland to be the new Governor we made it up as we went along. There were some mistakes of course. Well, they called them mistakes. I don't think many of those bastards were missed."

Ángel looks up as she says this. His eyes meet mine and I see that she has surprised us both. What did Juan Mercadal call her – a firebrand? Is that what she and Lluís loved about each other?

"Of course, they were hard years. There was less and less food each year and there were no markets for the things they made in the factories. No raw materials either, most of the time. Nothing in the shops. But they were happy years for the two of us, busy years. Lluís was in charge of collectivising the farms, starting with the ones owned by Fascist sympathisers. We were working on the harvest when that picture was taken – 1937. Lluís was redistributing wealth. Not that there was a lot of it to go around. Menorca has never been a very rich place. And we were never really ruthless enough. I mean Lluís was no Stalin. He just loved the island and he thought everyone should love it – as he said – equally. He always believed that, even at the end."

She stops for a moment and as her eyes sweep down to her lap I think I see them shine. But they are dry when she looks up.

"By the start of 1939 we knew we weren't going to win. We felt so helpless sitting here on the island while Catalunya was being crushed. There was nothing we could do, except wait and wonder when the Fascists would turn their attention on us. Lluís wanted to go to help defend Barcelona but they said he was needed here. We tried to strengthen the defences but what we had was what we had. Some anti-aircraft guns round the coast, some artillery. Not much."

"The end was like the beginning. Fast, fast, fast. It took your breath away. That's how things happen in a war. There's no time to plan. Whether you are caught or get away, whether you live or you die, it's just luck. Where you happen to be at the moment when events unfold. Luck. Good luck. Bad luck. Sometimes you can't even tell which. Not for years afterwards. Maybe never. I don't think Lluís ever knew – whether he'd had good luck, to be where he was, or bad."

"You mean to be on the Devonshire?"

"Was that the name of the ship? I never knew that. Debbenshire.

Ángel corrects her, with a glance and a smile at me, as if he is an authority on things English:

"DeVONshire. After a place in England. "

"They said it was a big ship. I never even saw it. Just its lights, that's all. It left in the early morning."

The word she uses for early morning: "*madrugada*" has a sad sound to it. It seems a good word to describe a time of parting, a time when ships, the people we love, even our dreams drift away from us.

"Why didn't you go with him?"

The question is almost an accusation and she looks up at Ángel sharply:

"This isn't my story. I told you. This is Lluís's story."

He nods reluctantly, and I see he's not prepared to fight with her:

"Where was I? Yes. It was the beginning of February 1939, this British ship appeared from nowhere and Lluís went into Mahon for a meeting – to decide what we should do. That was the last time I saw him. Everything happened so fast. That night he was gone."

"He went off on that boat. Not just him. I believe there were many. The British took them to France. I never knew who got away and who didn't. Afterwards, there was no one I could ask. I heard it said that there were executions, but there were no trials, nothing in the papers. All it took was a denunciation, someone to say you were a Red. I wasn't in a position to go asking questions."

"I don't know what Lluís did in France. Nobody does now. I doubt even his great friend Juan knows. They're lost, those thirty years or more. Did he have friends? Did he have women? Other children? What work did he do to keep himself alive? I never knew."

There is a long silence. It is a story that, at its end, merits a long silence. But it isn't finished. He didn't die in exile. He came home. To the woman he had loved. To a son.

I have to ask:

"When did he come back?"

She doesn't look at either of us. She looks at the mantelpiece and following her gaze I see, to my surprise, that she has put the photograph of the two of them in a frame and there it sits. What on earth can that mean? That she didn't betray Lluís after all? Or that she did but has managed to convince herself otherwise? I hope Juan Mercadal won't object. If the photograph belongs to anyone now, I suppose it belongs to her.

"After Franco died. Not long after."

"So it was after my ... after Joan Mascaró died?"

Ángel has a puzzled look. She glances at him and nods.

"So you were a widow. There was nothing to stop you going back to him. I was, what? Five? Six? Seven? There was nothing to stop me knowing I had a grandfather. Alive. On Menorca."

She shakes her head and I cannot tell whether it is in contradiction or pure sadness. When she speaks again I have the feeling she is talking to herself, or to someone who is not here:

"It wasn't possible."

"But why?"

From his tone, he could still be a seven year old.

"When he came back, I saw him. I didn't know he

248

was on the island. I had no warning. I was driving with your father and I saw him on the roadside. It was too much of a shock – he was an old man, limping, but I recognised him instantly. Then I realised I couldn't face him. Not without time to prepare. But he saw that I had seen him. Saw me look away. He thought I was turning my back on him."

She sighs, perhaps the heaviest sigh I've ever heard:

"It was such a tiny thing. Such a split second decision. But it was fatal. A few days later, I went to find him. It's a small island. I knew roughly where he would go. It didn't take me long to find him. I went down there to the shore, fully intending to speak to him, to explain everything. But he was angry with me. He saw me coming and he turned away. This time he turned away from me. And that was the end."

"You never spoke to each other again? In all these years?"

She shakes her head and then holds it still and straight:

"Because of the state he was in?"

"No, not that. That wasn't important. It was because of the way we had turned away from each other. Neither of us could forgive that, not on top of everything else. And besides, the music was gone."

"The music?"

She looks up and sees that something that is obvious to her means nothing to us. She shakes her head again:

"Well, now, it's not music of course but I don't know how else to say it. When we were young, there wasn't just talking, or just looking, or just touching. When we were together there was a full orchestra and a chorus – something Russian, something passionate, something revolutionary. So many glorious notes, all in harmony. That's what I had from him. That's what he had from me. That's what we were, together."

"I kept the dream of that music alive for forty years. Then, when he came back I expected the music to be there again, and instead it faded away altogether. It wasn't that I didn't still love him. I always loved him. But love was buried so deep under all the layers of dirt that life had thrown on top that I couldn't dig down to it. Maybe it was the same for him. Or maybe he'd spent all those years hating me, believing that I had abandoned him. Whatever it was he was feeling, we were both lost. All the richness, the harmony, the depth had gone. Once we had Prokofiev, Rachmaninov, Tchaikovsky every time we were in each other's sight. Now there was just silence."

There are tears on her cheeks.

"It wasn't bearable. There was no way to go back. If we'd never had the music, alright, but we had. We had. Forty years I'd dreamed of him. Twenty years I'd been afraid of saying his name aloud in my sleep and twenty years I'd slept easy, knowing I was free to dream of him all night long. And as all those years dragged by I never thought of time being important to us. I knew that he'd come back one day and then I'd hear the music like I heard it in my dreams."

"But I was wrong. That was the cruellest thing. When he came back the dreams stopped. The music stopped. Wasn't that cruel? Don't you think that was a cruel thing to do to an old woman?"

She is crying openly now and it is horrifying to watch. I feel in my pockets for a tissue but I have none. I lean forward and touch her skirt.

"Look, this is too upsetting for you. We should stop."

I glance at Ángel for support but he just looks at her intently. I see that he doesn't want her to stop and find myself surprised by his lack of kindness. She shakes her head and takes a long shuddering breath.

"No."

We both sit quiet whilst she wipes her eyes with a clean white handkerchief she had in her own pocket.

"He went to live down by the water."

She looks at me:

"You know that. You saw him. In the very place where we had promised we would stand against Franco together. A promise we were both guilty of breaking. That was typical of Lluís, to go back there. He never tried to re-write history. Never stopped taking everything on the chin. From time to time, I would hear something of him. They say he loved to grow things. He loved this island always. Of course. I was glad to think there was still some room in his heart for love. But not for people. People he preferred to hate."

"Did he hate you?"

Ángel's tone is cold but she doesn't seem to feel it. Maybe no one can be as hard on her as she is on herself:

"I don't think he ever forgave me for not being on that ship. Or understood why I went back to Mascaró. I think he thought I'd betrayed him, chosen a life on the island instead of by his side."

"How did you hear he was dead?"

I wonder if she will flinch at the word but she holds steady.

"The *guardia* came here after they found him. I am his widow, legally. That was the irony. It seems the state remarried us automatically when they reversed Franco's law that annulled divorces granted before the War. Four marriages and only one I had any say in. They told me they'd found his body at the bottom of the cliffs."

"What do you think happened?"

"I don't know. He could have fallen. He was old. It makes you clumsy. Stupid and clumsy."

251

"Or someone might have pushed him?" She looks at her grandson steadily and I wonder if she has considered the third possibility and, if she has, whether she will suggest it to him

"There were some who might have done it. He knew who had prospered under Franco. We all did. The difference was, when he came back he was still angry. The rest of us who lived here through all the grey years, we were just glad they were over. We'd finally got our freedom back, our freedom to be Menorquins, our language. People agreed to forget. We thought it was the only way. Not Lluís. He always wanted to shame the guilty men. Even though I didn't see him, I sometimes heard about it when he flared up. People talk."

"And you think he might have flared up recently?"

She shakes her head:

"The last time he got worked up about something was a few years ago, when they wanted to build on the coast down there. He claimed it was the Fascists doing it – even wrote to the newspaper. I didn't take a lot of notice. Anyone who wanted to build on the island was a Fascist in Lluís's eyes. The thing is, it doesn't matter whether he fell or whether someone pushed him. My Lluís died in 1939. The Fascists destroyed him when they drove him off this island."

I hardly know I am speaking until I hear the words:

"The way I remember him, from when I was a girl, he didn't seem dead. Sad sometimes, but not dead."

"He was dead to me."

It is an unmistakable rebuke and I realise that she believes Lluís still belongs to her and to no one else. Very quietly, Ángel says:

"Is that why you never told me about him?"

She nods. Then she shakes her head.

"Maybe. Partly. Also, I promised your father. He

252

always wanted you to believe that you were a Mascaró, and I didn't feel I could refuse him. But I was wrong. I should have let you see for yourself. Perhaps you would have seen something still alive in Lluís, like she thinks she did."

She purses her lips and folds her hands in a gesture of conclusion. We both want to hear the other stories, but the old lady will not be hurried. She sends us away with a kiss for Ángel that is almost, but not quite, apologetic.

Out on the streets of the town we wander in shocked silence past the carousels of postcards and shelves of sandals. What appeared commonplace earlier now seems surreal. Inside that spartan sitting room the island has been besieged, blockaded, bombed. Island people, the same ones who have always believed that to travel abroad is to breach their ancient laws, went into exile aboard a foreign warship. Rival declarations of war and allegiance were posted in the town square and farm-workers formed up into columns to march on rebel garrisons. It happened here, where tourists shop for yesterday's *Daily Mail* and globally-branded ice cream. There are no plaques or memorials to be seen but there are old men on their folding chairs who still remember.

39

In the matter of Lluís's death, murder seems to me the least likely explanation. But maybe I've spent more time than Ángel has on cliff tops and know how easy it would be to jump, or to stumble and fall. Getting pushed is altogether more complicated, involving at least one other person and a whole confluence of circumstances. They say you need means, motive and opportunity to commit a murder and surprisingly few people are that organised.

Perhaps Ángel prefers to believe Lluís was murdered because that would provide a dramatic ending to what we can now be sure was a dramatic life. There is pathos in the idea that Lluís was a victim of the Fascists in the end. It would make him truly eligible for inclusion in Juan Mercadal's book. But what Ángel fails to understand is that death is more usually about bathos than pathos. They don't call it a "dying fall" for nothing.

Still, he seems to think he is on the trail of a killer and has cast me as Watson to his Holmes. His contact at the town hall is helpful. Once he knows what we're looking for he goes away and comes back ten minutes later with a cardboard roll under one arm and a file of papers under the other.

"There was a model too, but they took that away. There are some photographs in the file. If you should want anything else, this is my extension number."

Ángel takes the end off the cardboard tube and shakes out a spiral of papers. They spill off the table onto the floor and we both bend down to salvage them. He takes one end, I take the other and we roll them out across the tabletop. The lines of the drawings have turned mauve and started to fade but we soon see what they show. The shapes of the cala, the islands, the rocks around the headland and the horseshoe of the neighbouring bay are represented by a faint jagged line. On the landward side of nature's ragged boundary man has drawn his rectangles, his squares and his circles.

We are looking down on the rooftops of an inchoate village. An inchoate town. Ángel draws his fingernail down the line of a coast road linking the established resort on the next bay with the village – Lluís's village, and mine – at the head of the cala. His finger stops at a roundabout on the headland. Built as shown on the plan it would be just a few yards from where we believe Lluís must have gone over the cliff.

Along the road on both sides are houses. They fill the mile of heathland behind the cliffs with a clutter of mediterraneo-suburbia. If it wasn't for that distinctive, unreplicable coastline these plans could be for Greece, Croatia, France, Turkey, Portugal, any country where white render over breezeblock can pass for vernacular architecture.

"Holy shit!"

Ángel looks across at me, wide-eyed.

"No wonder Lluís was steamed up."

"What's the date on the plan?"

Ángel flattens the scroll with his hand and reads the date in the corner. Five years old.

"Well, if they got permission they're taking their time. You didn't know anything about it?"

"Never heard of it. Five years ago I was still working in Barcelona."

"So what happened? Do you think Lluís managed to stop it?"

Ángel doesn't answer. He has opened the lever arch file and is turning the pages. After just a couple of minutes I see how the lawyer digests his brief. His finger travels down the page looking for clues. Sometimes it pauses as he reads. Then he flicks over the page and starts again. He does it fast. Half way through he comes across a polythene sleeve filled with colour photos. He unclips the sleeve from the file and tips the photos into my hands. Then he carries on reading.

The photos show a landscape I know, yet don't know. The cliffs are there but the sea at their base is unusually calm and glassy. The houses sitting proudly on top of the cliffs look brand new and yet lived in, with cars parked outside and bikini-clad figures lounging by blue pools. I feel like someone in a dream, moving through a world where I know everything is false but am momentarily unable to say why. It is the trees, finally, that give it away. Thanks to the tramuntana there are no trees out on the headland, and certainly none like the fuzzy-felt lollipops the model maker has chosen to use. As soon as I see them the illusion falls apart. The sea turns to cellophane and all the bikini wearers share identical poses and vital statistics. None of them will get up and drive away in their scale model cars. The recycling bins will wait in vain for the sound of breaking glass. The swimming pools will never need sweeping and the whitewash on the houses will stay fresh in the face of the salty northern rain. It is the perfect holiday development – so long as nobody builds it.

When I reach over to put the photos back I notice that the moving finger has stopped. Stepping behind Ángel's chair to look at what he's reading I put my hand on his shoulder. He jumps and glances round. Then he goes back to his reading. His finger doesn't move though. He doesn't turn the page.

"What is it?"

He doesn't answer.

"Ángel?"

He tears his eyes up from the page.

"What is that?"

He stands and pushes the file towards me. Then he turns his back.

The letter is written in blue ink. The handwriting is coarse but powerful, determined. Deliberately or not, the writer pressed down hard onto the cheap lined paper and even after five years the indentations are still there. There is an address at the top of the paper, an address on the cala. I don't recognise the number, but then not many houses display them. There's no postal service and most people know which house they want when they come visiting.

The letter is objecting to the development. I find myself using my finger to trace the words, not out of legal habit but to try and decipher the short blunt strokes of the pen. Before I've finished the second paragraph I understand why Ángel has fallen silent. I flick over to the second page of the letter and there is the signature I knew I'd see. I've never seen it before but I recognise it. Lluís Sintes.

I turn back and start reading again, hearing his voice tell the authorities why they mustn't build on the headland. He talks about progress and the crimes committed in its name. He tells them that the island doesn't need more touristic development. It needs its cliff tops, its birds, its plants, its butterflies. He lists the species of wildflower that grow on the scree slopes and the dry heath behind, using the Menorcan names – names I don't know but his grandson will – rather than Latin. The thorny little socarrels will be there, the sea lavender and samphire, not to mention the sky blue chicory, the asphodel, the rock roses and all the other plants that

257

won't be common for long on the cliffs if the cliffs are covered with houses.

After the list of plants there is just one last paragraph. The paper is scored even more heavily here. He says:

"I hope you find this list persuasive. I know how to make lists. I helped to make one sixty years ago but it wasn't acted on at the time. If it had been, things would have been different. Things would have been better. It would be regrettable if you should make them any worse than they are."

Ángel has come back to the table and is flicking through the photos. I point to the last paragraph:

"What does that mean?"

He translates it into English for me, word for word as I have done for myself. I still don't understand it.

He is back in front of the file now and starts again where he left off. It is my turn to wander the room and wait. Ten minutes later he flops the file closed and leans back.

"So. What happened? Did they refuse it because of Lluís?

"It wasn't refused. The town council approved it. But then it was challenged by GOB and by the time it came to court the area had been designated a nature reserve so it couldn't go ahead. The last thing in the file is the court judgment."

"What's GOB?"

"It's an environmental campaign group. It leads a lot of court challenges to proposals that would damage the ecology of the island. I've been thinking they're the sort of people I might work with one day."

"Was Lluís with them?"

"Maybe. I doubt it. His letter didn't claim to represent any organisation. I get the impression he wasn't one for organised campaigns."

"He was once. Time was when he was a Party apparatchik remember, a collectiviser of farms."

"Yes. That was something wasn't it? No wonder he stayed on that ship rather than go and fetch my grandmother. There must have been a lot of landowners after his blood in 1939."

"You think it was cowardice that stopped him going ashore to find her?"

He shrugs.

"Did you understand what he was saying about making lists? Was he threatening someone?"

"I don't know. Maybe. It sounded pretty feeble."

"Does the file say who was behind the development?"

"I found the name of the company – the developers. It didn't mean anything to me but it will. I know the architect who drew up the plans. He's done work for clients of my father's. When we get out of here I'll give him a call and ask him who the developers were. If anyone local was involved, we'll know."

"But where will that get you? Just because Lluís objected to a planning development back in the day it doesn't mean the developers had anything to do with his death. It's a long time to hold a grudge, five years, and you said yourself it was a court judgment that stopped it. Not Lluís's letter."

"You think five years is a long time. Not here. Five years is an afternoon nap here, the blink of an eye. You think there aren't plenty of grudges still being nursed here from seventy years ago? Just because nobody talks about the War? Believe me, there are things that happen under the surface here that you don't understand. People still care who was on the Right and who was on the Left even if it isn't spoken about. It goes deep. You must see that. And just think where Lluís died. Don't you think it has a certain poetry? Don't you think it might be satisfying, to throw a man off the very cliff he's fought to defend all his life? I need to know who the developers are. When I look in their eyes, when they see my face and realise who I am, then I shall know."

This is the man who complains that everybody he has ever loved has lied to him, yet still he thinks he will be able to detect the lies of strangers. I wonder that somebody so naïve can grow to manhood in a world like this. Did the young Lluís have the same certainty that things could be made to turn out right? Perhaps a man who could persuade soldiers to change sides in a war had some justification for believing that. I don't know what justification Ángel has.

"Hasn't it occurred to you that if someone did hold a big enough grudge against Lluís to kill him after five years they won't be especially keen on you asking about it? It might be dangerous for you too."

"It's the right thing to do," he says, planting his feet squarely and sticking out his chin. Suddenly, I see his grandfather and I find it hard to believe that Lluís was ever a coward.

40

Today, Catalina has sorted out some photographs of her own. The first is a studio portrait of a baby. It is mounted on stiff board, with the photographer's name in the bottom right hand corner. She hands it over to Ángel:

"Your father was born on 5th November 1939. They said the labour was not too long, for a first child. I had wanted a son so much. I wanted something of Lluís and I thought if it was a son he would be like his father. That terrified me too. Of course. I did not know what Mascaró would do if the likeness with Lluís was too strong to ignore. But there was a recklessness in me, also, that wanted the baby to be the image of his father, so that I could show him to my husband and say: 'See! Not yours. Nothing of yours in him!'"

"But it wasn't like that. When I held the baby he was not like Lluís. Not at all. Instead he was the image of my own father."

"It's my last clear memory for months, that first glimpse of him. That disappointment. Everything is fog from then on. I lost the will to live. People say that, don't they? 'I lost the will to live', but I really did. While I was carrying the baby I seemed to have strength. Everything was endurable for the sake of the child. Some instinct took over. But, after he was born, the instinct deserted me. I didn't want to live. Worse than that, I didn't care whether the baby lived either."

"I can't remember doing what they said I did. I used to try and think of it but I never could bring it wholly

261

to mind. They told me Mascaró's mother came to the house one day and found the baby in his cot with all the blankets and pillows piled on top of him. He was alive, but barely. They called a doctor then and he gave me pills that drove me even deeper into the fog."

"They thought I was mad – murderous and mad. My mother-in-law saved us. My husband wanted to put me away in an asylum but she saved me from him as she saved my son from me. She was a good woman. Religious. Old-fashioned. But a good woman. She looked after my son when I couldn't. She found a wet nurse for him – a woman who lost her own baby. The harvest failed that summer the War ended, to add to everything else. There was much disease. The poor suffered more than the rich, as they always do. The rich cared even less than usual that year. They were happy to see the poor put back in their place."

"It was the following autumn before I began to take notice of anything. Francisco was already pulling himself up on the furniture. That's my first real memory of him, grabbing my chair and hauling himself to his feet."

She rubs her hand along the polished arm of the chair:

"My husband used the time while I was ill well. Francisco's first word was: Papa. His second word was: Abi, for his grandmother. It was months later, maybe a year, before he said Mama. Long after dog, ball, milk, car. I tried to take my place as his mother, but they had made sure I wasn't essential in his life. I wasn't to be left alone with him. Ever. Those were his father's orders. Nobody must ever forget that I was not to be trusted, least of all me. The wet nurse stayed on as his nanny, and she hated me, I suppose because she hadn't been able to stop her own child from dying, whereas I, who didn't deserve a child, had a healthy boy."

"Every day I searched for some sign of Lluís in Francisco. But as he grew, tall and thin, so dark-haired, with that hawk's nose I had to admit that he had the Ciudadella look. The look of the bourgeoisie. Well, even so, I thought, if not in his looks, Lluís must be there in his character. But, if he was, Mascaró succeeded in smothering him, taking him to Mass every day, enrolling him in all the Falangist youth organisations, forever showing him how important it was to be his father's son."

She shuffles through the photographs and hands Ángel another:

"There! That's Francisco after his confirmation. Do you see how serious he is? Thinks that he and God are fellow freemasons now. You see, Mascaró's plan worked too well, in a way. Francisco was such a solemn boy, so taken in by all that mumbo-jumbo about God and Holy Imperial Spain, that he developed a vocation. A vocation at eleven!"

We stare at the pale bookish looking boy in the photograph and then look at each other.

"A vocation for the priesthood, you understand? That shook Mascaró up. Then he found he'd been too clever. I mean to have a priest in the family would have been a fine thing in his eyes. But the second or third son, not the eldest. And Francisco wasn't just the eldest. He was the only son. Despite all his efforts."

She pauses and I think I see her shudder:

"That didn't suit Mascaró at all. His wasn't an old family, like mine, but still he didn't want to see it die out. He wasn't spending all his time building up his reputation as a lawyer, making a little money even in those difficult years, so that it could all go to the church."

"But Francisco was adamant. He was always a stubborn boy and I sometimes thought that was a little bit of Lluís in him after all. He had his vocation and he

263

wouldn't be shifted. Mascaró raged and pleaded and tried to bribe him with all sorts of treats but he wouldn't be diverted. When he was old enough, he was going to Salamanca to train for the priesthood."

"But he didn't go" says Ángel.

She looks at him, surprised that his father has never even told him this:

"Yes, yes he did go. He was away there when Mascaró had his stroke. We sent word. But by the time he reached Ciudadella Mascaró was dead."

"I didn't know," whispers Ángel, "that he didn't want to be a lawyer either. He would have made a good priest."

She shakes her head:

"No, that was all over. He took up the law, served his apprenticeship and took over his father's office as soon as he could. Then, as soon as he was established, he started searching for a wife. I think he felt that was his duty to his father, too. Your poor mother. I felt sorry for her. She was an innocent thing, stuffed to the gills with the useless education they handed out to girls during those years. Sewing and Spain re-conquered for Christ and piety till it made you weep. But however naïve she was I think she soon realised that she would get no passion from your father. Duty, yes. Duty until she wanted to die of it. But no laughter, no fun, no romance. Poor thing."

"Nevertheless, he soon did his duty to Spain and made her pregnant. She was sick, miserable, not built for bearing children. We sewed things for the baby together. Francisco was uneasy about it. His father had left him with the feeling that I was not to be trusted, that there was something unsafe about me. I don't know whether he had ever been told how I had nearly smothered him in his cot – I wouldn't be surprised. But the girl, Consuela, she liked me and her own mother was dead so I had to be tolerated."

"I expected the baby to be another Francisco. I had no hopes, no expectations. I was in the room, helping the midwife, and she handed you to me while she worked on your poor mother. It was me that slapped your behind and made you take your first breath. It was me that wrapped you in a shawl and got the first look at your face. You were angry, of course, bloody, all squashed up, but as I looked into your eyes I nearly dropped you. Because I found I was holding the child I had once hoped to bear myself. I was staring into Lluís's face."

"Never in my life have I had a shock like that. It was, I'm almost tempted to say – it's only a figure of speech, mind – it was a miracle. I turned to Consuela. She was barely able to hold you, she was so weak. It had been a terrible labour – she was too narrow for babies – but she wanted to hold you and I put you in her arms. She looked at you and then she looked at me and she said:

"Isn't he beautiful?"

"He's an angel."

"I don't know where it came from – I couldn't help myself – and she said:

"Yes. Ángel. That's his name."

"Francisco always hated it. He thought it was impious. But it was one thing she insisted on, your name. Poor Consuela. She never really recovered. But less than a year later she was pregnant again. I wasn't in the room for that birth. There were two doctors with the midwife from the start. You were toddling by then and I took you out to get you away from the noises your mother was making. When we came back it was quiet. Too quiet. She was dead. The baby too."

"What was it?"

"What?"

"The baby – boy or girl?"

"A girl, I think. Yes, definitely a girl."

"My father never told me I had a sister."

He stands up and goes over to the mantelpiece, where she has placed the picture of herself and Lluís. He turns and walks to the back of the room. Then he turns again and, without a word, crosses to the door. The old woman and I watch him pass outside the window. One of us ought to go after him, but neither of us does. We look at each other.

"Go on," I say.

"I had moved out of the house in Ciudadella when Francisco married. I was happy to go. I came here, to a house that didn't hold twenty years of unhappy memories. Then, when Consuela died Francisco didn't want to stay in that old house either, though it had been in my family for so many generations. He leased it – they tell me it's a bank now – and moved to Mahon."

"I offered to come and be his housekeeper, to look after my grandson but he wouldn't have it. I think he could already see that I loved Ángel in a way I'd never been able to love him. So keeping him away from me was a way to punish me for that. The last thing he wanted was to give me a second chance, because if I succeeded in mothering Ángel perhaps that would mean there had been something particularly unlovable about him. It wasn't true of course. We just had bad luck, he and I. Too many things stacked against us. It was never his fault. But it damaged him just the same."

"So I stayed here in Mercadal. But he did bring the boy to see me. It was his duty, you see. Apart from giving up the family house he always did his duty."

"Ángel and I loved each other from the first. Of course. He was like Lluís – energetic, full of fun. He loved nature, just like his grandfather. From a tiny boy

266

he used to bring me caterpillars and butterflies in jam-jars. Injured birds. Starving cats. He was always impulsive, getting into trouble at school and with his father because he leapt into things. He had an appetite for life, just like Lluís, and he would run full-tilt at things and then wonder why he banged his head."

"It was hard for him, though, with no mother. Francisco didn't want Ángel growing up to be wild. He wanted him to be controlled, sober, a lawyer like him. He'd made the sacrifice of his vocation to follow his father and he expected his son to follow him. Ángel so wanted to study the natural world, to draw it, to understand it all. But apart from that they got along until ..."

"Until Lluís came back?"

"Yes."

"How did they meet?"

"Not through me. I knew Lluís would never be able to take his place as Francisco's father. I had seen my son clutching at the corpse of the man he believed was his father. I knew he would never accept another, especially one who was everything Mascaró had taught him to despise. That was his insurance against the boy not being his, to ensure that if he ever met his real father he would hate everything about him. And Lluís had left not knowing I was pregnant. I decided it was better to leave things as they were. To let him think, like the rest of the world, my son was Mascaró's boy. My life had been so quiet since he died that I hadn't the stomach for trouble anymore. I was a coward."

"But one day there was a knock at the door and I opened it to find my son standing there, white with shock, as if he'd seen something worse than a ghost."

"He had, I suppose. Lluís had gone to his office over some property matter. Something else he was trying to put a stop to, I think."

"Francisco looked as if he was going to fall in through the door. I put my hand on his arm but he shook it off, just looked at me with those eyes of his and said: 'Whore.' Then he turned and walked away."

"What happened then?"

"I didn't see him for a year. I tried to telephone him, at home and at the office, but he put the receiver down, or he told his girl to say that he was out. Eventually I wrote him a letter explaining that he was the son of my marriage to Lluís. I thought maybe it would matter to him to know that he wasn't a bastard. To my surprise, he answered that letter but only to say that the Church did not recognise any divorce law passed by the Red government and that in the eyes of God I had never been married to anyone but (he put) his father. So my carnal knowledge of another man was fornication. I was in fact a whore. And I had made him the bastard of a whore."

"He argued it out like the lawyer he had worked so hard to turn himself into. And, clearly, he'd done his research. There seemed nothing to be gained by disputing with him. I didn't write again. In a strange way, it was a relief. We had had very little to say to each other in the fifteen years since Mascaró died. Now, for the first time we would have had something to talk about but it was impossible. I think that's when I finally admitted to myself that I'd never loved him and I finally stopped trying. I felt sorry for him, but that was all."

"What did hurt was the way he treated Ángel. He told me Francisco was barely speaking to him. Ángel thought it was because he didn't want to study law but I knew better. I should have told the boy the truth. But I was afraid he would confront his father about it and that his father would tell him that I was a whore. I couldn't bear him to hear that."

268

"So I kept quiet. I left the boy baffled. I stuck my head in the sand."

"But Lluís and Francisco did meet again. People have told me that Lluís's son used to visit him."

"Yes. That's true. Despite everything, Francisco sought Lluís out. Maybe he wanted to measure him against Mascaró. Maybe he wanted to measure him against Ángel. He found out where he was living, I don't know how. He went to see him, in that hovel. The irony is that although the son had recognised his father almost at once, the father did not recognise the son. Francisco had to introduce himself. I imagine Lluís felt badly about that, that he could not recognise his own son. I imagine he felt it was one more thing that the war and Franco – and maybe I too – had taken from him."

"It must have been difficult for both of them. Mascaró had been very thorough. When Lluís tried to tell him about the War he would have found himself up against a perfectly schooled supporter of Franco."

She pauses:

"After a year he started coming back to visit me too. He didn't speak of what had happened, except to make me promise that I would never tell Ángel about Lluís. I felt I had no choice but to agree. It was wrong. I knew that. But it was the only thing he had ever asked of me. His visits were less frequent than they had once been but he still comes. Regular as clockwork and cold as ice. I wish he didn't."

"Why do you let him in?"

"He's my son. A son has a right to hate his mother if she fails him."

"And Ángel?"

"Oh, that boy has a right to hate me too. It's my fault he went into the law. He did it to try and win back his father's love. I could have stopped him. I could have

269

told him the truth, that it was my fault his father had stopped speaking to him. I could have told him where to find his grandfather and let him see where his love of the island, of nature, came from. But I didn't and look what has happened to him. He does a job that is utterly wrong for him. He marries a woman who has no idea who he really is (because he doesn't know himself) and despises him when she finds out. He is unhappy and confused and I've never really lifted a finger to help him even though I love him better than any other living thing."

"He said you told him to follow his heart."

"Did he? Did I? I suppose I did. But what use was that to a boy whose father was breaking that very same heart. No. I didn't do enough for him. I never have. I thought when I held him in the minutes after his birth that he was my second chance. I thought I could be a better grandmother than I had been a mother. But I have stood by and watched the damage be done, just as I did with my son. I should never have had children."

"You're too hard on yourself."

"Am I? How would you know?"

"I know Ángel loves you."

"Well, he's a fool. He always loves the wrong people, the ones who are going to hurt him."

She stares at me to see if I have the nerve to deny it. I can only bite my lip and look away.

41

Ángel is sitting outside the bar at the end of the street. There is whisky or brandy in his glass. Not much of it left. I sit down opposite him and take out my cigarettes.

"Good story?"

I pull a face as I light up and blow the first plume of smoke over my shoulder:

"It had a sort of happy ending, I suppose. She was telling me how much she loved her grandson, and how she wished she could have done more to help him when he was growing up."

"Such as by telling him the truth?"

"Such as that, yes."

"It would have been a friendly gesture, wouldn't it? What else did she tell you?"

"That she loved you from the first moment she saw you."

"Well, they all say that."

"They all? Who all?"

"Good point. Who? Mother? Dead. Sister? Dead. Wife? Gone away without leaving an address. Grandfather? He was a possibility for a while but, unfortunately, dead. You're right. She's just about the only candidate. If you leave aside my father, which I think in the circumstances we have to."

He looks at me with the same sulky self-pity he showed that first night in Mahon. I feel an awkward moment approaching and decide to try and head it off:

"You know what we didn't ask her?"

"What?"

"About the list."

He strikes himself on the temple so hard with the ball of his hand that it makes me wince:

"You're right. I can't face her again today though. Can you?"

I think about it, then I shake my head.

"Who else would know?"

"We could try your friend at the map museum again."

Ángel pulls out his phone and looks up a number:

"Efficient," I say, as I signal the waiter to bring the bill. Ángel grins, maybe for the first time today, and walks away from the table as his call is answered. I watch him, standing at the crossroads, absorbed in what the other person is saying down the phone as the little town goes about its business around him. He rubs his hand through his hair absent-mindedly and scuffs at one of the kerbstones with his foot. A truck could back right over him and I doubt he'd notice. He is utterly unselfconscious and all the more attractive for it.

A pair of young women, walking along the street, separates to go past him and when they come back together one dips her head to the other and says something and as they both giggle the second one glances back at Ángel. He is oblivious to them and I think it's a shame he believes himself to be so uniquely unlovable when nothing could be further from the truth. He's just had bad luck is all. And it doesn't seem to be over yet.

The call ends and he comes back to the table.

"He doesn't want us to come back to Mahon. He says he'll meet us at the yellow bar on the cala. At seven thirty."

I laugh.

"He's not been there for a while. It did have yellow awnings once. Twenty years ago."

As we drive back to my place, I tell him the rest of what his grandmother told me. How his father had recognised Lluís and how much it hurt him to find that the man he had revered was not his father. How he had made her promise not to tell Ángel, and how she had agreed, even though she knew it was the wrong thing to do, because she felt she owed it to him.

"But what about me?" he says bitterly as we draw up outside the house. "What about what she owed me? She knew he was trying to mould me in an image that I didn't fit – and she just let him. Exactly as she had let Mascaró mould him. She never tried to change anything second time around. Even though my grandfather was right here this time and she knew I would have seen myself in him right away – just like she saw him in me."

I put my hand over his, where it is still gripping the gear stick tight though he has turned the engine off. I know it's a mistake, but I can't help it. He is in such turmoil that it would take a dead man not to offer him some comfort.

He looks down at my hand, and opens his fingers wide so that mine slip between his and are caught. Then he leans over, puts his other hand against my cheek and pulls my face towards his:

"I think I love you," he says, and I realise it's true, what they say. No good deed goes unpunished. "Do you think you could love me?"

I feel tears spring to my eyes. For the sad fact is that the answer is yes, I could. If there was time I think I could love him. But if there was time I wouldn't be here and we would never have met. If there was time, I would still be back in my own life with my husband, watching our daughter grow up.

To stop him seeing the tears, to buy a minute before I have to answer, I kiss him. His lips are soft and warm

273

and becoming familiar now. The strangeness of kissing somebody new, after years of the same man, is beginning to wear off. The strangeness is, but the excitement isn't. His tongue finds mine and I feel the world slip again. I push my hand deep into his hair where it curls at the nape of his neck and kiss him harder, realising suddenly that, time or no time, I may need him just as much as he needs me.

He takes his hand from my cheek and feels behind him for the door handle. He has one foot out of the car before he breaks off the kiss.

"Come on," he says. "Inside." I sit there, dazed for a moment then jump out of the car and try to put the key in the front door. My hand is shaking too much and he takes it from me, fits it, turns it and kicks the door open so that it bounces against the wall. Then he grabs my hand and pulls me up the stairs. Where the landing turns, he pushes me against the wall and kisses me again, pulling my hips against him. My whole body is shaking now.

He grabs my hand and pulls me up the rest of the stairs and straight into the bedroom. He puts his hands round my neck and kisses me some more as he fiddles with the knot on my halter-neck sundress. Then it's free and he slides it down the length of my body. When he feels that there is nothing underneath, he takes a step back and looks at me.

"My God! You're so brown."

I am pleased at his surprise. It feels like I've done a party trick and I raise my arms above my head and do a pirouette, laughing, so he can see how thorough I've been. I catch sight of myself in the mirror and stop. With my arms raised I can see the definition of every rib for the first time in years, and my new skinniness makes my breasts with their nipples tanned to dark brown seem even fuller than before. My arms and wrists too are slenderer than I remember. And the tan has shaded the angles of my face, rendering it more dramatic, more striking, less softly English. Only one thing spoils the picture, only one thing stops it being the body of a healthy young woman ten years younger than me, and that is an odd distension around my belly, an odd flabbiness where everywhere else the skin is smooth over the bone. I try to pull it in, but nothing happens and I know it isn't a question of stomach muscles. It is the scrofulous blotches on my liver growing and spreading out into my abdomen.

I let my arms drop and look over at Ángel. He is still standing, frozen, with his mouth open. I step up close to him so that his view is foreshortened and start to unbutton his shirt. He rests his hands on my shoulders:

"You're so beautiful. But you should be careful with the sun. It can be dangerous."

I laugh, I have to.

"People are too careful. Life is for living. The sun makes me feel good. It gives me energy. Live fast, die young, leave a pretty corpse. There's nothing wrong with that."

"You'd leave a beautiful corpse. Stunning. But don't, please. I want you alive. I want to take you alive."

And he does.

42

We are at the bar on the mole before Juan Mercadal arrives. It is a beautiful serene evening and I sit watching the lazy way the light swoops round the tower in the lighthouse down the coast. A boat crosses the water in front of us, a white and blue dinghy with a blond boy at the helm. He looks across and sees us and I raise my arm to wave, but he just stares across the water and then alters course, turning south so that his back is to us and I let my arm fall.

I am still watching the dinghy head out through the channel when Juan Mercadal appears, not down the steps, but down the slope from the village square. He stops at the corner to stare up at the three palm trees that separate the beach from the square. A slight man with a self-effacing air, he's hardly noticeable as he stands there in his neat beige clothes and panama hat. Lluís was much more obvious, scruffy, an untidy mover, loud in a good mood, aggressively silent in a bad one. It's hard to imagine them being friends, yet in that old snapshot they looked like brothers. *Amigos-hermanos.*

After we've shaken hands and ordered coffee Ángel launches in without preliminaries. His question surprises Juan. He raises his hand to his face and covers his mouth. Then he takes it away.

"A list, you say?"

I take two sheets of lined paper out of my bag and smooth them out on the table.

Juan stares at the letter and Ángel stares at me, shocked.

I shrug. So he didn't see me filch the letter from the file.

276

So what? Does he think anyone else cares about it? I've never stolen anything before. Yet another thing I believed was bad for me. And you know what? It was fun. I'm rather proud of myself.

The old man reads the letter and pushes it back towards me. I fold the pages lengthways and hand them to Ángel. He glares at me but he tucks the letter away in his left inside pocket then smooths his hand over his lapel. When I first met him I would have thought it vanity. Now I know he is just pressing it close to his heart. Such a soft-hearted man.

There is a moment of silence, broken by the clink of coffee cups being set in front of us. I light a cigarette. Juan waits for the waitress to move to another table before he speaks:

"He did do some crazy things, your grandfather. As if it would do anybody any good to drag up the subject of the list after sixty years."

"So there was a list?"

Slowly he nods.

"What sort of list? What was on it?"

"Not what. Who. It was a list of names."

"The people who were going off in the Devonshire?"

He laughs, just once, without amusement.

"No, not them. That was another list. The list Lluís is referring to here was drawn up before that one was needed."

He stops and stirs his coffee. The spoon moves round and round in the cup, trailing a ribbon of tawny froth. The three of us watch as if we had no other purpose in being here until he taps it gently on the rim of the cup and lays it down in the saucer.

"There can't be many left who know about it now. I don't know if I should talk about it. Some things are better left ..."

Then he shakes his head.

"No, that's not right, is it? We haven't the right to complain about the Right hiding the things they did unless we're honest about the things we did. Or, as it turned out, didn't do. So, I'll tell you. It was the beginning of February 1939. Catalunya was lost, you know. We couldn't make contact with the government in Valencia any more. Soon Franco would be at the French border and we, in Menorca, would be the last place in Spain standing against the Fascists."

"How did you know – if communications were cut?"

"Well, that was an indication. In itself. When a government falls silent it's a fairly good sign that it's on its way out. Also, the Fascists were telling us. The Italians had started dropping pamphlets. Their planes circled over Mahon and Ciudadella and just as everyone ran for cover expecting bombs they let go these flocks of paper. They did look like birds, in fact, if you were brave enough to look up and see them swooping down."

"What did they say?"

"What does propaganda always say? It's all over. Blah, blah. Peace is coming. Blah, blah. Nobody whose hands are clean of blood has anything to fear. Lay down your arms. If you don't, thousands will die. Something like that. I don't know. It wasn't strictly necessary to read them. Everyone knew what they meant. They meant an invasion."

"And you couldn't defend the island?"

"Has Menorca ever been successfully defended? Did the Moors defend it against Alfons III? Did anyone defend it against the Turks? Could the British have defended it against the French even if Admiral Byng had stayed to fight? No, there are too many places to land and not enough strong points to defend. Against paratroopers? Even Italian paratroopers."

278

He shrugs and takes a tiny sip of coffee.

"So you would have surrendered, with or without the Devonshire?"

"I didn't say that. We would have fought, some of us. We had artillery on Cap Mola, some anti-aircraft guns around the coast. It's gone now of course but there were even gun emplacements round here then. There was one on that rock over there."

Ángel and I turn to follow where his finger points at an outcrop of rock that commands the beach and the entrance to the two neighbouring calas. There is nothing there now.

"Are you sure?" Ángel says.

"I've never been surer of anything in my life. We helped to build it, Lluís, Catalina and I. One of several. That palm tree didn't even come up to my waist then, more a pineapple than a palm tree and look at it now. It gained thirty feet and I lost three inches. That's life for you."

He smiles at the memory.

"Anyway. That February we were prepared to fight. We would have lost, but we would have defended the Second Republic to its end. There have been times when I still wish we had. Lived or died here together on our own ground, not scattered abroad and then crawling back one by one."

"My wife doesn't like me to talk like that. She says I'm wishing away the children, our life together. And she's right. I was lucky. She waited for me when I was in prison, when she could easily have married someone who wasn't tainted by the past like I was. But I still think it sometimes. Lluís always believed it."

"Do you think that's why he didn't go back to Catalina? Because he felt he wasn't entitled any more?"

"I don't know. Perhaps it was that – or the shadow cast by Mascaró. It must have been impossible for Lluís to think of her – with him. Maybe that's why he was so adamant about the list."

Ángel interrupts:

"I still don't understand. What was the list?"

"Didn't I say? I'm sorry. It's hard to be clear. I feel … disturbed by thinking of it. After all this time. It's difficult to explain to someone who wasn't there, who wasn't even born when it was happening. Please be patient."

"I'm sorry."

"No. No need to be sorry. Just patient."

He picks up his coffee cup and then puts it down again without drinking.

"As I said, we were ready to fight the invasion. But we knew it wasn't just a question of that. Not just a question of what would come at us from the sea, from the air. We knew there were those on the island who would be glad to see the Fascists take over. Who would be glad to help them. Those who had been biding their time ever since '36. So, when the invasion started, we knew we would need to watch our backs as well as our fronts. Do you see?"

Ángel and I both nod.

"Good, well we came up with a plan to deal with that threat. The threat to our backs."

"Which was?"

"The list. It was a list of all the people we knew to be Fascist sympathisers. The ones we thought would make trouble when they had a chance. We drew up a list and when we were sure the invasion was imminent we arrested them."

Ángel looks puzzled:

"And what, you were going to keep them locked up when the invasion started, out of the way?"

The old man picks up the sachet of sugar from his saucer and taps its edge against the table top.

"Well, not exactly. We wouldn't have been able to spare the troops to guard them all. Not when the invasion came."

"So what were you going to do with them?"

He looks around to see if anyone else is in earshot. Then he looks slowly from Ángel to me:

"We were going to shoot them."

Ángel raises his eyebrows:

"How many?"

The old man shrugs: "A few hundred."

Ángel looks at me, shocked. That soft heart again. I have to take up the questioning:

"But you didn't?"

"In the event, no. Before we had a chance, the British ship arrived at Mahon. We didn't know they were coming. After that we had only a few hours to decide whether to fight or surrender and once that decision was made it became impossible. The next night, when the ship was to sail, we freed the prisoners. We freed them on their word of honour that they wouldn't attempt reprisals on those who had imprisoned them. But they soon found guns and liquor and started to do what we had not done."

"Lluís always said it was our biggest mistake, not acting on the list. He talked about it a lot when we were in France. That's what he means in the letter. You see, the names on the list did well for themselves afterwards. Of course. When I came out of prison in 1954, everywhere I went to try for a job, I found a name from the list was in charge. It was painful to see."

"Do you remember who was on the list?"

"Some of the names, yes. Most of them are dead now, of course. It turns out the winners die off just like the losers. That's one consolation."

Ángel asks what we are both thinking:

281

"Was Joan Mascaró on it?"

Juan Mercadal looks at him for a long moment. Then he nods.

We all sit silent for a while, but I have one more question:

"Did Catalina know about the list?"

The old man frowns and finally picks up his espresso and drains it. He shudders slightly, at the bitterness, or the caffeine, or at something else and puts the cup back down:

"She should have. She helped to write it."

43

There seems nothing more to say, so I give him back the photographs (all except one), we shake hands again and Ángel and I watch him walk slowly back the way he came.

"You didn't tell me," he says as we walk up the steps together, and I assume he's talking about his grandmother and some detail of the story I've forgotten to relate. Something that will throw some light on the question of whether or not she planned to kill her own former husband.

"Tell you what?"

"Whether you could love me."

"Ah. That."

I stop. He stops too:

"Yes, that."

"Didn't I tell you before?"

"No."

I start walking again:

"Are you sure I didn't?"

"Well, not in words, no."

I look over my shoulder at him:

"In England, we have a saying: deeds speak louder than words."

"Yes, well, I've also heard you say: 'It was just casual sex. Get over it.' So forgive me if I am confused."

"I forgive you. Life is confusing. Nothing more so. I am confused myself."

"You? Never!"

"You don't think so?"

"No! You, you're so sure about everything. Do you know, I still don't have a clue who you are or where you came from. Yet you seem to have the answer to everything. You don't seem to need to work. In fact you don't seem to need anything – or anyone. Who are you, Kate? Are you even human, or did you come down in a UFO to study the human race? Is that it, are you an alien? Have I fallen in love with a fucking alien?"

"No."

"Then who are you? What are you doing here? Why the mystery?"

I don't know what to say. I am tired of lying to him, even if my lies have been ones of omission, but I can't get around the fact that there is no joy for either of us in the truth. I don't want to hurt him, but I know I'm going to – now or later. I reach out to touch his cheek and decide on later.

"There's no real mystery. I came here because I needed a break. I had enough money not to need to work for a while. This place had always stuck in my head. I always wanted to come back here."

I take a deep breath and silently apologise for the lie that has to follow:

"I was stuck, you see, in a way of being that bored me and I wanted to be someone different, someone who wasn't tied down by stuff, by getting and spending, who didn't mind what people thought. That's a very English failing, by the way, to care too much about what other people think. *Carpe diem*, I said to myself. People always think it means 'seize the day' but it doesn't, it means 'pluck the day' as if it was a ripe peach. And that's what I do now – and I like it, I like everything about it. I like being with you, I like..."

"Being with Billy?"

"I was going to say smoking, actually, but yes I did

284

like being with Billy. He's a beautiful boy. He wanted it. I wanted it. It did us both good. No animals were harmed in the making of the picture."

I'm aware that I sound unbearably flippant, but I can't help it. The situation is too heart-breaking for sincerity.

"And are you planning to pluck that particular peach again?"

He looks sour.

"You see, this is the problem. Even when you fall out of a clear blue sky, it seems that you can't hold yourself separate for very long. People aren't very good at keeping their distance from each other. That's what I've learned. And I have tried. Believe me, I have really tried. But I can't help it, I am involved now. I am involved with you."

I lay my hand on his arm and he twitches, but he doesn't shake it off.

"So you won't fuck him again – but not because you don't want to."

I take my hand away and we start walking again:

"Are you sure you aren't cut out to be a lawyer? Because you certainly can find the loophole in everything. I'm being honest with you. I'm telling you how I wanted to live when I came here and that I'm willing to compromise on that because you mean something to me. Isn't that what you wanted to hear?"

He shakes his head:

"Involved? I mean something to you? Do you think that's what Lluís was saying to Catalina when the photographer was adjusting his lens? I asked you about love and you tell me about compromise. And you think that's what I want to hear?"

He kicks a stone and it bounces down the steep drive and rolls into the water with a little splash.

"You want a love story like your grandparents, do

285

you? You want love at first sight and walking out of the market place together and a full orchestra that no one else can hear?"

We reach the house as I say this, and I turn to the door with the key in my hand but he spins me round and puts his hands round my biceps. Then he puts his face close to mine and almost hisses at me:

"I don't want it. I've got it."

He shakes me to try and make me understand:

"Don't you see? I've got it. What I want to know is, have you?"

I look into his face, into his tormented, hopeful brown eyes, and I feel like weeping for us both. Because he wants for us the life together that Lluís and Catalina planned, the life that was spoiled by the War and an enemy that could not be defeated. And he thinks just because Franco is dead that things will be different for us, that nothing stands in our way. He doesn't understand – how could he? – that there are other enemies just as implacable and other territories just as impossible to defend.

44

The road to Ciutadella is crowded with traffic and we crawl up the hill in Ferreries behind a lorry carting shoes. There are factories in industrial polygons on the outskirts of Alaior and Ferreries, making the island's buckled spine feel more like mainland Spain than Menorca. There is no shelter of old walls, fig and pine trees here, just the sun beating on a raw tarmac strip in a rocky landscape. As we drive along I feel exposed, out of my element, a traveller in a strange land.

It was Ángel's idea that we should cross the island to see the house where he and his sister were born. Where his mother died. He suggested it after we went to bed for the second time yesterday, an encounter that started as a tussle, a continuation of the argument, and changed kiss by kiss and look by look into a final silent exhausted concession that nothing mattered except this meeting in this little house on this beloved backwater.

He didn't mention her directly, just reached across the bed for his wallet and took out a tiny photograph of a woman with innocent hopefulness in her face. Maybe not all of his personality comes from his grandfather. There was nothing he could add to the picture. It was all he had ever known of his mother.

The traffic grows even denser as we approach the outskirts of the town. It is a blazing hot day. We edge slowly round several roundabouts and then turn left onto a road that skirts the old centre. We find a narrow parking space and squeeze out of the car into the afternoon heat. By the time I have locked the door I can already feel sweat gathering in my armpits.

Ángel takes my hand to lead the way and then he stops. Standing quietly by a Give Way sign on the opposite side of the road is a mounted horseman. The horse is majestic, coal black, his tail decorated with a binding of red ribbons. The rider is a boy of perhaps seventeen. He sits the horse beautifully, straight and easy. The glow on his face, between his black demi-lune hat and his heavy black riding coat, could be perspiration, but it looks more like the glow of pride.

The sight is so incongruous that I wonder for a moment if I have slipped back in time, or if I am hallucinating. Perhaps something besides the heat is making me feel feverish. I glance at Ángel to see if he is sweating too, but he looks perfectly cool and perfectly unperturbed by the vision in front of us. I try not to panic.

"Is he real?"

I'm whispering. The apparition might disappear if we startle it.

"He's real," says Ángel, glancing quickly at his watch. "It's the 23rd. Of course. I should have thought."

"Thought what?"

"That it would be *Sant Joan*. It's the biggest festival on the island. I don't know why I didn't remember. Still, it's not bad luck. It's probably the best time to see this town."

"And who is he?"

"One of the riders in the procession. They must be about to form up."

As he says it the rider touches the horse with his knee and they turn and walk slowly towards the centre of town. His face, solemn in its man's role, breaks into a boy's grin as two girls greet him from the pavement. He is serious again by the time he draws level with us but his eye catches mine and he nods his head and greets me with a soft "*Adeu*".

We follow horse and rider out onto a main street lined with shops, all closed up, and then into narrow cobbled back streets. I trust that Ángel knows his way because as the alleyways curve and twist, with the upper floors of houses leaning over them like neighbours sharing the latest gossip, I am quickly lost. Finally we turn into a street that seems different. Instead of closed doors and modestly screened windows the doors here are set open and there are people clustered in the windows and doorways, chatting and calling across the street to their friends. Underfoot there is fine golden sand.

"What's going on?"

"This is on the route of the parade. They're waiting for the horses to come."

As we walk along I notice that some of the houses have wooden barricades set up inside the doors, with the living room furniture crammed in behind. Ángel sees me looking:

"In case a horse goes into the house."

"Do they? Do they run wild? Like the bulls at Pamplona?"

He laughs:

"No, they're totally under control. It's good luck if a *cavaller* rides in through the doorway. But not such good luck if the horse takes a bite out of your furniture."

Just then a murmur runs through the crowd and, above it, I hear the steady tenor beat of a drum. A moment later I catch the high-pitched note of a flute or a tin whistle. Conversations along the street are brought to an end in a flurry of "*Bones festes*" as people move back to their own houses, or to the vantage points they have chosen. As the whistle and the drum grow louder they resolve into an urgent little phrase of music, repeated. I

289

am reminded of "Yankee Doodle Dandy", the more so when I hear the clop of hooves on cobbles and the portly figure of a man astride a donkey turns into the street. He is wearing a black tailcoat with white tie and breeches. Ribbons and coloured pompons flutter from the donkey and from the strapping on his drum. A mounted one-man band, he plays a wooden whistle with one hand and beats the drum with a stick held in the other. Yankee Doodle Dandy meets the Pied Piper of Hamelin.

"Who's that?" I whisper to Ángel.

"That's the *fabioler*. He summons all the riders from their houses and leads them through the town."

Just as he says this the first of the horses to answer the call turns into the street. Against the foreground of a fat man riding a donkey the tall lean rider is an impressive sight. Over his shoulder he carries a burgundy flag with a white Maltese cross. Behind him another horse and rider appears and then another and another. They walk steadily, proudly, along the street following the *fabioler* and by the time the leading rider reaches us there are already twenty more behind him. Straight-backed, black-haired and long-nosed they are almost indistinguishable one from the other. For the first time I understand what Catalina calls "the Ciudadella look".

I expect each horse to be the last, but they keeping on emerging from the shadow of the corner.

"How many are there?"

"Over a hundred."

"Where do they all come from?"

But I see that he isn't listening. He is looking towards the procession, staring at a rider who has just turned the corner into the street. I have been too busy watching horse after horse move past to look closely at any particular man. Now I follow his gaze and see a rider even more ramrod straight – if possible – than the others. His hat shades his face but long fingers hold the reins delicately before him and his boots are perfectly polished. The horse too looks as if he has been polished and the silver fittings on his tack gleam in the afternoon sun. There is less colour and decoration about his saddle-cloth and at head and tail than some of the other horses but he is elegant, correct. In turning out his horse, Francisco Mascaró has done his duty.

I put my hand on Ángel's arm and he turns his head back towards me. His face is pale but calm.

"It's okay," he says. "As soon as I realised what the date was I knew he was bound to be here."

Mascaró moves past and out of sight. Still the line grows longer. I count fifty, sixty, seventy, eighty, ninety, a hundred horses. And still they come. It becomes clear that position in the parade is ranked by age because although the breeches, the tailcoats, the bow ties and the hats remain the same the faces and bodies inside them grow gradually older as the parade moves forward. The boys at the front, teenagers, looked ready to burst with pride, but nervous too, terrified of disgracing themselves, conscious of the weight of tradition on their shoulders. The men in the middle ranks and middle age are more relaxed in their saddles, ready to lean down to exchange handshakes and jokes with friends. The crowd has its favourites too: a man with a luxuriant moustache; a florid old man with a face half-collapsed by stroke or palsy, each greeted with applause and cheers.

Finally, when the one hundred and twenty-ninth horse has walked past us, ridden by a little wizened nut of a man in huge spectacles, there are no more to come. Two minutes later the street is empty except for a few piles of dung.

People in the houses go back to their private parties and the itinerant crowd follows the procession. Ángel turns me aside, down another curving narrow alley and we emerge into a wider street. The houses on either side are tall but these are too proud to lean across the street and gossip. Fine carved stone door cases remind me of churches I have seen in Mexico. Ángel gestures up to first floor level and there I see long windows and beyond them the glitter of chandeliers catching the sun. At the end of the street one of the houses even has its upper storey supported on the stout shoulders of male caryatids but Ángel stops short, at a house as large but plainer than the rest. A modern laminated glass plaque fixed to the old stone by steel pins informs us that this is the corporate services branch of a bank based in Barcelona.

"Your house?"

"The house where I was born. And my sister."

The double oak door is firmly shut for the *festes*.

"Have you ever been inside?"

"Many years ago. My father would never come back here but I came one day, on my bicycle. On one of my crusades to find out who I was."

"Did it help?"

"No. How could it have? This is the house my Mascaró grandfather aspired to, isn't it? And I'm not a Mascaró. My grandmother ran away from it, and my real grandfather probably would have commandeered it for the people. How could it possibly have helped?"

The street is quiet, as if the parade has sucked the entire population of the town into its train. Shop windows are draped with pennants of the Maltese cross and many have wooden laths screwed across their plate glass, which seems abundantly cautious. We turn another corner and come out into a wide square. There are a lot of people here, sitting among the trees, waiting. A brass band is arranging itself along raised staging and the musicians are fixing flowers to their instruments.

"The *Plaça d'es Born*," Ángel says. "Let's get a drink. He goes over to one of the trestle tables set up outside all the bars and comes back with two white cups of clear liquid. He drinks his down and crumples the cup onto the floor. I do the same. It's sweet, fizzy, lemon and juniper. Strong.

"Gin?"

"Pomada. Gin and lemonade. Blame the British."

He points out to me the palaces of the old families, the tower of the cathedral that started life as the minaret to the mosque of Menurka Medina, the monument to those who died in a futile defence of the town against the Turks. He is a good guide, with his lawyer's memory for detail. But as we walk it is the street names that strike me. In Mahon the street names commemorate kings and queens, inventors and other famous Menorcans, or they describe where the streets go. From looking at old guidebooks and maps I suspect that many of the names have been changed since Franco's death, which probably means they were changed before, after the Civil War. In Ciutadella no double change has been necessary. Franco could not have objected to the street names in Ciutadella because they already reinforce the idea of a Holy Spain.

There seems to be hardly a street or an alleyway that does not bear a religious connotation: saints, popes, bishops and priests crowd in at every turning. How Ángel's grandmother must have hated living here, where there is a reminder of piety on every wall.

We find the horses, finally, in the Plaça Alfons III.

"Thank God, a square that's named after a king and not a Christian martyr."

Ángel looks at me, amused:

"Well, Alfons III did throw the Moors out of Spain and he did die at the age of twenty-five, so I think he probably counts as both."

He seems happy today, happier than I have seen him since we met. Perhaps I had no choice, but to tell him what he wanted to hear.

A horse stamps the ground, close behind me, and as Ángel pulls me gently out of the way my hip grazes his thigh and I shiver. He grins at me:

"It's not only the horses that are excited today."

Before I can think of a retort we hear the *fabioler* playing his tune and the horses begin to move into line. I pat one on the flank, just behind his stiff embroidered saddlecloth and the rider looks down and nods to me. I see the sweat gathered under the brim of his heavy felt hat and then he senses the horse in front of him move and twitches the reins to urge his own forward into the line. Gradually the square empties and we follow the procession down to the next crossroads.

"Watch this," says Ángel.

There is a gang of boys swarming round the lamp-post at the crossroads, clearly waiting for something. They let the herald, the standard bearer and the first rider go past. The next horseman is wearing a strange draped cowl – a priest? He is immensely fat, fat and ruby-cheeked, but strong looking. His horse is probably the biggest in the whole parade – and it needs to be. He is the one the boys have been waiting for. One of the gang, wearing a Cross of St John scarf round his forehead, darts out and starts pounding the roadway right in front of the stallion with something that makes a loud squeaking noise.

"What's he doing?" Ángel's eyes are on the horse:

"Just watch!"

The horse skitters sideways a few paces but the youth moves after him, crouched down and thrashing his silly day-glo hammer into the tarmac. The bishop, if that is who he is, moves away a second time but there is a smile on his face. When the youth follows for a third time the bishop lets the horse take two paces back from his challenger and then pulls mightily on the reins. The horse rears and as he does so the youth leaps up to touch its great black chest. I turn away and bury my head in Ángel's shoulder, waiting for the sickening crunch of hoof against skull. But the crowd cheers. Past Ángel's shoulder there is an ocean of raised arms. Hooters and whistles blow and looking round I see the horse stepping back steadily on its hind legs, casting a monstrous shadow. At any moment I still expect to see his front hooves come crashing down onto the road but they don't. The crowd keeps up its racket and horse and rider teeter on on two legs. It is then I realise that the rearing is not the horse out of control but the horse doing what it has been trained for.

Ángel is hugging me and laughing. I feel a fool:

"They teach them to do this?"

"They train all year for it. Haven't you seen men out in the fields at the weekends, practising?"

I shake my head.

"They're bred to it. Men and horses. They're all born here on the island. Two races of Menorquins."

The bishop is still up on his hind legs and now the crowd is throwing things under the hooves. I look up at Ángel again, glad to be in the crook of his arm, somewhere I am beginning to feel safe.

"Hazelnut shells. They're supposed to represent kisses" and he leans over to kiss me on the mouth.

"Wait here, I'll go and get us some."

But as he turns away he frowns and I see him reach into his inside pocket. He takes out his phone and puts it to his ear. Then he puts his hand over his other ear but it's clear from the way he shrugs that he still can't hear above the noise of the crowd. He melts back through the crush and I am left alone.

Finally, the bishop allows his horse to plunge back to earth. The youth with the hammer scrambles out of the way and then bows and the bishop, a little ironically, raises a hand to bless him before walking on, dignity intact. The horses behind move forward, cracking nut-shells under their hooves as they go.

I look round for Ángel but he is nowhere in sight. The crowd cheers again and I glance back to see who is being challenged now. This time it is the turn of a rider further down the line from the bishop, but his tormentor is not one of the gang of youths encamped around the lamppost. Ángel's hand is on the bridle of his father's horse. The horse keeps jerking his head up and Francisco Mascaró is pulling on the reins, trying to turn the animal away. Behind them the parade stretches down the street. Lean, long-nosed riders, a line of latter-day Dukes of Welling-ton, sit calmly with their reins across their pommels, watching the struggle. They must think it is just another young man, emboldened by the gin, pitting his machismo against the skill of one of the senior horsemen.

There is too much noise for me to hear what Ángel is shouting at his father. But it's apparent that Francisco does not, will not answer. He stares straight ahead, just like that day in his office, as he keeps on trying to haul the horse's head out of his son's grip. From across the street I can see all three of them, the two men and the animal, struggling for control. Suddenly the older man takes one hand from the reins and I spot what I hadn't seen before. He is carrying a riding crop, a thin cane decorated from tip to tip with a red silk ribbon. He raises his arm up high and at the same time the horse, feeling some slackening in the tug of war for his mouth, shakes his great long head and dances sideways.

My mouth is open to cry out and warn Ángel when I feel a tap on my shoulder and a voice shouts:

"*Bones festes!*"

I spin round and find myself looking at Billy. His eyes are sparkling and he is dripping with sweat as he grabs my face in both hands and pushes his lips against mine. I shove him away and he sways. I realise he is very drunk. I turn my head to see what is happening to Ángel, but then Billy grabs me again and throws his arms around me in a bear hug. I try to struggle free but he is too strong, even though he is so drunk he can hardly stand. His maroon T-shirt is hot and wet with sweat and the bandanna round his head makes him look like a Barbary pirate:

"Why?" he shouts at me through the din.

I push against his arms but I still can't shake him off:

"Why what?"

"Why did you choose him over me? He's old. And sad. He doesn't deserve you."

"Billy, let me go! You have to let me go."

I put both hands against his chest and push, but he just drags me closer and presses his mouth over mine, bending me backwards so that I am terrified we will both fall and be trampled by the crowd. I jab my hand against his throat and press hard. He coughs and falls back a little way. But still he doesn't let me go, just stares at me and then shouts in my ear:

"You can't enjoy doing it with him. We could go somewhere now and ... Why don't you ... Come on and ..."

His tongue doesn't seem to be able to finish what his drunken libido has begun. So he gives up trying to persuade me and instead starts to drag me away through the crowd. I twist round but I can't see the horses at all now and I know that, even if I shout, Ángel will never hear me. Billy pulls me along a few feet and then he stumbles against a wall and I take my chance, shove him hard against the stones and break free. Then I run, barging

297

my way through the crowd, tripping over a child, who wails. I glance back to see if he's following and then crash on.

As I reach the corner I hear a strange sound behind me from the crowd, almost like a gust of wind, a collective in-drawn breath and then a gasp. I don't know what it means, but it raises the hairs on my neck and I run faster – until I round another corner and the way ahead is blocked with people. They pack the road, the lamp-posts and the trees opposite. I try to push through but a surge of bodies presses me back against a shop window and I feel the plate glass flex under our weight as a horse breaks through the mêlée and gallops past, the rider re-placing his hat as he goes, to cheers.

My heart sinks. The route of the procession has looped around behind me and is blocking my way. At the street corner now another stallion appears and the crowd gives tongue like a pack of hounds as the horse rears. Its neck and shoulders come into view and then the figure of the rider, his body almost parallel with the rearing torso of the horse. It is a young boy, his face contorted with concentration and determination. He holds the reins in one hand, the other raised in the air clutching his hat. His knees are clenched high behind the horse's shoulders as he tries to urge it on, into the baying crowd and round the crucial turn. The horse, nostrils and eyes wide, takes a few steps forward on its hind legs but the barricade is too wide, too deep, too animated and despite the urging of his rider he twists, dropping to all four legs and cantering away.

The crowd jeers and waits for the next attempt. A minute or so later it comes. This time the boy's horse is flanked by two others, the brotherhood of riders anxious not to be cowed by the rabble. Again, the stallion plunges forward. Again, it snorts in terror and turns back. The two outriders try to encourage the boy on but he is already gone and they have to turn to their own task or be beaten back too. Wheeling and bucking, they ride through the crowd, shaking their heads and looking over their shoulders as they go.

The boy keeps trying but time after time he is driven back. The crowd is contrary in its desires. They want him to defy them and ride through but they make it impossible. More and more horses run the gauntlet and the boy is losing his place in the procession. Finally two riders appear round the corner together: the boy, his hair plastered to his head with sweat and his face as stricken with fear now as the horse's; and a forty year old man with a heavy moustache. The crowd screams with delight at seeing one of the stars of the procession. The man doffs his hat and bows from the saddle as his horse rears. Then he spurs it ruthlessly forward, forcing people to fall back before its hooves. The boy hauls on his reins with all the strength left to him and with one last shake of the head his horse obeys and lunges through. The boy's shoulders shake with sobs as he replaces his hat and the older man flings an arm around him and plants a kiss on his cheek as they ride off down the street together.

In the lull that follows, I launch myself through the bodies blocking my way. I fight my way out onto the road and it is only when the crowd screams that I look up and see the hooves hanging over me. Animal sweat, wet heat from a black belly streaked with white foam and two crescents of silver fill the world. For a split second I crouch in the shadow but then I find myself straightening. I reach my hand up to press it as high as I can on the horse's breast. I feel the heat and weight of it on my palm, shivering and pulsing. I feel quite calm. Resolute at last. No need to explain anything to Ángel.

No more Billy. No more watching for the disease to take its next step. All I have to do is wait for the hooves to fall.

But just as I can feel the darkness begin to fall towards me someone who doesn't understand drags me to one side and a ton of muscle in a shining coat slams down and shakes the ground.

I cling to the arm that has thwarted and saved me. A Spanish voice, shouting above the noise, is asking me if I'm okay, and I find myself already wanting Ángel again, lost what seems an age ago. My rescuer isn't Ángel. But at least it isn't Billy.

I mutter that I'm okay and stand there shaking, as the procession moves past, taking the crowd's attention with it. I step away from the noise down a side street. Soon I am in an abandoned city, bright and dark, hot and cool by turns. I have no idea of the way but my haphazard route brings me out onto the main street. When I am nearly opposite the road where my car is parked I step off the pavement and before I have taken two paces the blast of a horn and a rush of air spin me sideways. The empty street is filled with noise and colour and turbulence as an estate car corrects its swerve and speeds on. The driver turns on his siren and blue lights. I stand in the spot where the slipstream has left me, knees shaking, unable to move for a while. Then I walk away.

45

Ignoring the knocker this time, I hammer at the door with my fists until it opens. The old lady stands there, looking puzzled:

"I wasn't expecting you today."

We stand staring at each other. The drive back across the island in the heat of the sun has done nothing to calm my panic. I'm not even sure why I have ended up here, at her door, rather than pressing on home to the cala.

I can't speak, can't explain, so I push open the door and step over the threshold, uninvited.

"Where's my grandson? Isn't he with you?"

She looks down the street with the door handle still in her hand.

I shake my head, feeling a sudden pang of guilt over Ángel. Since the moment I started to run, my thoughts have been a crazy jumble: the struggle between Ángel and his father, Billy drunk and loutish, Lluís and Catalina's story. Suddenly these people are not a distraction any more. They are under my skin, a part of my life also and today, added to everything else, it has become too much to bear.

I realise that is why I am here, because I talked her into telling her story and now I need her to share mine in return.

"There's something I need to tell you. About me."

"Ah," she says, shutting the door behind me:

"Of course. Why else would you have kept coming here? I knew there had to be more to it than just a childhood memory. You look hot. Do you want to drink something?"

I nod, grateful for the old-fashioned courtesy and for time to think. When she brings me the glass I have stopped wandering the room and come to a halt in front of the old oil painting that I normally sit with my back to. It is a surprisingly fine piece of work, though in dire need of cleaning. Something about it is most definitely familiar though.

"Your ancestor?"

She nods:

"So they say. It's hard enough to tell one generation to the next, for sure. But I think he is. He has the family look. My family. The story goes that it was painted by a young Englishman who came here on his way to Italy. They say he spoiled his face in a riding accident and had to remain on the island while he healed. He wasn't rich, so he painted portraits to pay his way. I don't know if any of that is true. It's just the story that came down through the family with the picture. But I thought you'd come to tell me a story of yours, not to hear any more of mine."

She hands me the glass and I take a drink, expecting it to be water. Spirits burn the back of my throat and I burst out coughing:

"Christ! What is that?"

"Schnapps. You looked as if you needed it."

Now I know, I tip back the glass and drain it. A spreading glow in my chest and little lights exploding behind my eyes is more than compensation for the sweet medicinal oily taste. Turning my back on the painting, I find her already seated, hands folded in her lap, waiting.

"So," she says: "what is it you wanted to tell me? That you don't want my grandson to hear?"

She seems to understand what I'm doing here better than I do myself, so I sit down opposite her and take a deep breath and say the same thing Lluís said to my father, all those years ago:

"I ran away."

She nods, once, perhaps to acknowledge that I have taken the first step:

"From what? A husband?"

I should know how this works. It still feels strange, though, to be exhuming things that have been so carefully buried. This must be how she has felt, the more so since her secrets have been buried for sixty years. I wonder if I have been too impatient with her at times and I feel the colour leap into my face. She breaks into my thoughts:

"I said, was it from …"

"Yes, though not because I wanted to get away from him. He was no Mascaró. That wasn't why I ran."

"And from children?"

She is as tough a questioner as I was at the start. And just as impatient.

"Yes."

"What?"

Perhaps I didn't say it out loud, or perhaps it came out in a whisper and she didn't hear.

"Yes, from a child."

"How old?"

I can hardly bear to think about it, let alone talk about it. Am terrified of seeing her in my mind's eye. But she appears, just the same, and smiles at me. It hurts like hell and tears well up from a place I thought had run dry:

"Twelve. Thirteen in August."

She clucks her tongue:

"Boy or girl?"

"Girl." Don't make me say her name. I could not bear to have to say her name.

"Do you have a photograph?"

"No." I say, too quickly.

She looks at me for a moment, as though she knows I'm lying, weighing up what to ask next.

"Was he unfaithful? Is that why you did it, to punish him?"

I shake my head again, but it doesn't seem enough. He deserves a better rebuttal:

"It was nothing like that. He's a good man. We were pretty happy, happier than most."

"So did you cheat on him then? I mean, even before my grandson?"

It shocks me, to hear her say that. It strikes me that I haven't once considered sleeping with Ángel – or with Billy – as cheating on anyone. It's never been a question of my having run away to start a new life. I didn't come here to start anything. My life ended and this, well, this is some kind of limbo. The trouble is, limbo has started to feel as real as the life I left behind. That was never meant to happen.

"I told you. We were happy."

She frowns, puzzled:

"Why then? Why run away?"

This isn't getting us anywhere. And there's really no reason not to give it to her straight. That must be why I felt the need to come here, after all. So that there is someone who knows everything, someone who can explain it to Ángel when the time comes. I stretch out my legs in front of me and stare at my toes, like a little girl trying to think of the right thing to say to an adult. Then I put my feet on the floor and look her straight in the eye:

"Because I was dying."

304

I pause to see how she reacts. To see if she is sorry for me now. If she is, she gives no sign of it.

"Still am." I say, to drive it all the way home. To both of us.

"Of what?"

"I'm sorry?"

She is leaning forward, looking as irritated as I must have seemed every time she has havered over some detail in her story:

"What exactly is it you're meant to be dying of?"

"Cancer."

I deliver the word without hesitation. I don't want to give it the dread reverence it is so often accorded. And there's no need to hesitate for the other reason people sometimes do, for fear of shocking my listener. I'm not sure anything could shock her.

"You don't look as if you've got cancer," she says, almost peevishly. See. Not shocked. Just impatient. Which sparks me into annoyance, though whether at her or at the stupid disease I can't tell:

"No? Shall I tell you why? Because it's not the cancer that makes you lose your hair and look like hell, not at first anyway. It's the poisons they pump into you to try and stop it that do that."

"And you weren't brave enough to face that?"

I have to give it to her. She doesn't shrink from delivering a blow. But this one misses its target.

"Bravery has nothing to do with it. People 'face' it because they're more terrified of dying fast than of being poisoned slowly. Or because they think they have no choice, because those are the motions that have to be gone through. But when it's malignant melanoma with secondaries in your liver there's no earthly point in surgery. And it doesn't respond to chemo. Or radiation."

"But you had a family – they must have wanted to be

with you, for the time that was left, if it's really true that you're dying?"

"Nobody wants to be with the dying."

She snorts:

"Of course they do, if they love you."

"No. They will do it, for love. But still, nobody wants to be there."

I think of my mother, suddenly, of her face when we told her the news. I was with her when they broke the news to us about my father's stroke, and the look on her face then was nothing compared to when I had to tell her that I was dying. It was as if every fear she'd ever had for me in her life had all come true at once. As if every single cautious step she'd ever taken had been for nothing. It was the most terrible expression I've ever seen on anybody's face and I had the sense she was destined to wear it for the rest of her life.

David and Richie were hardly better, standing there with no idea what to say or do. Old enough now to feel habitually guilty about the way their twindom always excluded me, they were used to being a little awkward with me. But that minor guilt was nothing to what they were feeling now, because their overwhelming feeling was of relief, infinite relief, that if this had to happen to one of us it was happening to me and not to one of them. They knew it wasn't fair to feel that way, but they did, and they couldn't look at each other because they knew they'd read the very same feeling in each others' eyes. And they couldn't look at me either, because they feared I'd realise it too. But it was no good. I already had.

I can't even think about the others, the looks on their faces.

"So what did you tell them?"

"I left a note. They think I killed myself three months

ago. I went to a place we knew on the South coast. Left the car with some letters on the steering wheel. Took off my shoes at the edge of the cliffs. Unzipped my handbag and threw it over, with all my cards and driving licence in it. Put on new trainers and walked to the nearest railway station, where I took a train. And here I am."

"And nobody's looked for you?"

"I don't know. How would I know? The letters were clear enough. I wish I could have given them a body to find as well, for the funeral. That's my only regret."

She sits back and raises her eyebrows:

"Your only regret? When you've lied to everybody who loves you, and run away and let them think you're dead? And all the time you're here making eyes at another man. That's your only regret?"

If I wasn't hoping for sympathy, I did at least think she would try to understand my predicament. I have spent long enough trying to understand hers.

"I am dead though. *Mas o menos.* The doctors didn't give me long: months, maybe less. Weeks. My whole life. All that was left of it. All that was left of me. I just couldn't face spending it the way everyone expected me to. And if I'd told them how I wanted to finish it, I knew they'd never let me. They'd have found a way to talk me out of it."

"I know everyone is supposed to want a hand to hold as they're dying, but I didn't. I just couldn't stand it, couldn't stand being the cause of their misery. Is that so bad? So abnormal? They've all got years left, decades. I didn't. I knew they'd never understand."

"Whatever we had in common before, it was over. Done. Because I was dying and they weren't. That made everything different. All the assumptions we'd made about our lives had been proved wrong. We were no more use to each other. I wasn't going to be able to look after them any more, and I couldn't bear the thought of them having to look after me while I dropped to pieces."

"So I ran away. Alright? I ran away. I never intended to get involved with anyone else. I hardly intended to speak to another living soul. I just wanted to sit quiet in the most beautiful place I knew and wait for the right moment to end it."

She must be able to see I'm close to tears, but it doesn't seem to weigh with her. She knows just what question to ask next:

"You're not dead though. Are you? You said that was three months ago and you still look strong to me. Strong enough to have seduced my grandson into falling in love with you. You don't think that extra time would have been better spent with your own daughter?"

My stomach lurches but I refuse to let her make me cry. The awful thing is she may be right. Every day that I wake up feeling no worse I wonder if I should have stayed. Every time I smile at one of Angel's jokes or lay my head on his chest I feel guilty for being happy. But it's impossible to look over my shoulder and gaze at what I've left behind, because it's lost to me already and there's no going back. How could they ever understand what I did? How could they ever forgive me?

"I didn't know it was going to be like this. I had to leave when I still could. Do you think it would have been any easier for her to see me waste away and suffer, to watch me have fits, forget her name? Do you think I wanted her to remember me strung out on morphine, sucking chips of ice on a hospital bed in the sitting room?"

"I thought this way she would never have to pity me, or find me repulsive. She wouldn't have to eat into her store of courage being brave for me, steeling herself to come into my room, starting to wish I would hurry up and die so that it would be over and hating herself for feeling that way. This way, she might be angry with me, but she would have been angry anyway."

"I would never have left her if I didn't have to. It wasn't my choice to die. All I did was to take control of the timing. If that's a sin it's one I'm prepared to live with. I won't have to do it for long."

It is a long speech. It may be the longest speech I've made since I came to the island. I feel exhausted at the end of it. But not relieved. I hoped that telling my story would help me lay the burden down, but the old lady seems determined to add more weight to the pack, because now she says:

"What about my grandson? Is he a sin you're prepared to live with also?"

I can't sit there any longer, her dark eyes boring into me. I stand up and walk round the room again, stopping finally in front of the mantelpiece and the photo of Catalina with Lluís. The doubly familiar face makes me smile, all the more because he looks so happy: I turn around and confess something I never intended:

"I love your grandson. I never meant to, but I do. That's why I came here today. So that you would understand."

Even this doesn't move her and I realise it is not only her courage that was destroyed by twenty years of a hateful marriage. Sympathy and kindness have gone too. Everything, it seems, except cold defiance. She pushes herself out of her chair and stands facing me, with her chin raised:

"You mean, so that I can pick up the pieces when you've gone. How selfish can you be? You've torn apart your own family and now you come here and let another poor fool fall in love with you. What now? Are you

309

going to let him be the one to watch you waste away and suffer or are you going to do another disappearing act?"

"I don't know."

It's true. I don't.

"He has a right to know."

This, coming from her, is rich.

"No."

"Yes." She nods firmly. "I shall tell him the next time I see him."

I am suddenly incandescently angry and I wonder, for a moment, how hard it would be to choke the life out of her skinny old body. Something else I wouldn't have to regret for long. Wonderful how removing the threat of any effective punishment widens one's moral compass. But then I remember why I came, that she's the last person Ángel has to fall back on.

"You know that if you do that you'll be forcing me to go."

She shrugs:

"He's going to have his heart broken again, one way or the other. As you said, this way is easier."

46

We both jump when the next caller at the house uses the brass knocker. We look at each other, and know without a shadow of doubt that Ángel is standing on the doorstep. We both move to rise, but I am quicker, as if by getting to the door first I can stop her telling him what she thinks he needs to know.

But it isn't Ángel. The two men standing outside in the street are wearing the olive green uniforms of the Guardia Civil and the blank expressions of those whose duty is to bring bad news.

Before I have a chance to reply to their solemn: "*Buenos tardes, señora*" the old lady has arrived to stand beside and even a little in front of me. She stands straight and looks the policemen in the face. This is her house and if there is bad news she will be the one to receive it at the door.

Her composure is authoritative and the policemen turn their attention from me to her without any of us having said another thing. As they do so my mind races back through the day and I hear, as if for the first time, that gasp of the crowd and the sudden silence. Then my mind races forward again to the moment when I stepped off the pavement and was nearly knocked over by the ambulance.

It was an ambulance.

My hands are already pressed to my face before the older of the two Guardia speaks:

"There has been an accident. I'm sorry but it is your son, señora. We have had a call from Ciutadella. He is in the hospital there."

The old lady's self-control slips for a moment and she totters half a step before she recovers herself. In that moment I learn that she lied when she said she did not love her son. In the same moment I know for sure that what I said to her was true. I do love Ángel.

We do not speak during the journey to Ciutadella. The policemen sit in the front of the small patrol car and we, the women, sit in the back. Taken out of her own surroundings, out of the chair in which she has been accustomed to sit for sixty years, Catalina seems much smaller and older. Her clothes and her tightly-fastened hair, which have never seemed anachronistic in her own front room, do look out of place against the electric blue nylon plush of the car's upholstery and the modern world flashing past outside the car windows.

When we arrive in Ciutadella the police car noses through empty streets until we arrive at the route of the interminable procession. The car slows as it approaches the backs of a crowd of spectators and one of the guardia presses two switches on the dashboard. The siren on the car gives a long wail and heads turn to look at us. The crowd parts and I am conscious of eyes searching the car with the aimless curiosity of those whom trouble has not touched, this time.

The policeman in the passenger seat, who has his forearm on the sill of the open window, acknowledges the parting of the crowd with a series of little waves. He even reaches out to shake the hand of someone he knows as we crawl through the opening in the river of people but cuts off his greeting sharp in embarrassment when he remembers his passenger, for whom this is not a good fiesta.

They drop us in the courtyard of the hospital, telling us to ask for the intensive care unit and giving us the name of the doctor in charge. They seem relieved to have completed their duty and drive off quickly, before anything more can be expected of them.

Upstairs, outside the swing doors to the Intensive Care Unit, we find Ángel. He looks strange, pale, distracted – a colourless twin of his normal self. I feel a pang of longing for the vivacious brother. As we approach, he walks quickly over to his grandmother. He takes her hands and kisses her on both cheeks. Then he stands beside her and draws her arm through his, walking with her towards the swing doors. I see that she leans on him immediately, accepting from him the comfort I sense she would not have taken from anyone else. She speaks to him in Menorquin, a question. I guess it is: what happened? Or: how is he? His reply is in Menorquin also, very soft, and as they walk away from me I can no longer hear it even if I could understand it. Ángel has not even looked at me. I am left outside the ward, alone.

It is thirty minutes before the swing doors shudder open again. Ángel and his grandmother come out as they went in, arm in arm, but she is leaning on him more heavily now. Her normally straight back is bowed and I have the impression that without her grandson to hold her up she would fall.

"How is he?"

She does not look up at me but Ángel does, as at a stranger.

"They think it's a stroke. They're doing tests but they think it's a pretty big one."

"Bigger than the one his father had," she says, still without looking up, "and that was big enough."

Ángel and I look at each other over the top of her head. Not strangers now. We know too much of this story to act like strangers.

"You mean Mascaró?"

It is Ángel who asks what we are both thinking.

"Mascaró was his father in everything but blood. He was the only father Francisco ever wanted. He chose to live like him. What if he chooses to die like him also?"

Her legs go from under her as she says this and it is only Ángel catching her hand as it slips from beneath his elbow that stops her dropping to the floor. I grab at her other arm and there seems to be nothing there except the bunched cotton of her sleeve and a slender core of bone. Together we drag her to a plastic chair and prop her there. I run to the water fountain for a paper cone of cold water.

When I come back,\ Ángel is on his knees in front of her chair, his hands holding hers in her lap. Her eyes are open and she seems calm. He releases one of her hands so that she can take the twist of waxed paper from me and as she drinks it slops a little. She wipes water from her chin with the back of her hand and gives me back the empty cone.

"Is there a waiting room for the families?" she says, and I'm surprised to hear that her voice is already returning to its usual firmness. "There generally is in a place like this."

Ángel and I look up at the signs that hang from the corridor ceiling and see that she's right. An arrow points down a side corridor to a lounge for relatives.

"Go and tell them we'll be in there if there is any news," she says to Ángel and he stands up and goes back through the double doors.

I offer her my arm and, to my surprise, she takes it. As we walk slowly down the corridor she says to me:

"Do you think he's up to it?"

"To what?" I say, panic rising in my throat as I think she means to tell him my secret, here and now.

"To hearing the rest of my story. Mascaró's story. I want to tell it now. I want Ángel to hear it."

314

My immediate sensation is of relief, but surprise, shock even, soon displaces it. This is the last thing I expected to be on her mind.

"You can tell it to me. You've told me all the rest."

"Oh, you can stay. But I want Ángel to hear it from me. He must. You see, he thinks he is to blame for his father being in this place. He told me just now that he was having a fight with Francisco when the horse reared and Francisco fell. I said to him that a stroke can come at any time. It came to Mascaró in his chair. But he thinks he caused it. You were there. You can say what really happened."

I feel instantly guilty. My mind is still filled with other memories of the afternoon – of Billy drunk and grabbing at me, of the looming shadow of a horse blocking out the sun, of my frantic drive across the island, of my own confession. Memories of Ángel pulling on the bridle of his father's horse, of an upraised arm and a red ribbon on a riding whip fluttering in the downdraught of a blow seem altogether more remote, like remembered scenes from a film.

"I saw them arguing. His father wouldn't speak to him. But I didn't see the fall. Your son raised his arm to beat Ángel away with his whip ..."

She stares at me:

"No."

"I'm sorry. Yes."

"Then what?"

"Then ... I didn't see any more."

"Why not?"

"Someone grabbed hold of me, a youth, drunk. He was trying to maul me and I had to get away. I panicked and ran."

She grunts as if this is a wholly inadequate excuse and returns to her son and grandson.

"Why were they arguing?"

I shake my head that I don't know, but then I remember hazelnuts, a kiss on the mouth and Ángel with a phone to his ear, dropping back through the crowd. The call could have been from anyone, a client, a friend but suddenly I remember that Ángel was still waiting to hear from the architect whose firm had drawn the headland plans, the man he said would know the names of the men behind the development. Was that who was calling? Was that why he confronted his father then, when before he had been content to let him ride by?

If that was the reason then he must have been told that his father was involved. In Ángel's eyes that would be enough to implicate Francisco in murder, in patricide, whether a crime had been committed or not. And now (perhaps because of Ángel, perhaps not – the evidence of this crime being as flimsy as the evidence of that other one) his father lies in a hospital bed at the edge of life.

I look at the old lady. Part of me wants to tell her, to make her understand – if she doesn't know – how thing leads on to thing. I want to blame her for the accident, if only to clear Ángel of blame. But I can't. My fascination with her has been because she endured, she stayed put in her life though it cost her every bit of her strength to do it. I began by thinking maybe that was admirable. That maybe it is what I should have done. But now I see what it has done to her I don't want to be like her. Now I think running away can definitely be better for everybody. So I shake my head again.

She stares at me for a moment longer. Then she shrugs:

"I expect it was the same old things. That's why I have to tell him."

Suddenly she seems to be possessed by an almost manic energy. Her eyes are shining with something close to excitement – perhaps it is the exhilaration of a gambler with only the stake for one last desperate hand.

The door rattles as Ángel comes back into the room. For the first time I see that he isn't ignoring me to punish me. He is simply trapped in the events of the afternoon. He is in torment, a soft-hearted man who thinks he may be a murderer.

"You'd better tell him," I say.

"Tell me what?" he says.

47

She sighs:

"As you know, I was married to Mascaró very young. He was fifteen years older. It wasn't unusual, in those days, that kind of marriage. And most fifteen year olds didn't know what love was. But I loved your grandfather already and I knew I always would. I did Mascaró a wrong by marrying him. I did it not out of obedience to my father but to pay your grandfather back for thinking more of Karl Marx than he did of me. So, you see, in the war between me and Mascaró it was I who struck the first blow. I was stupid, and I paid the price for it. But I was fifteen years old."

"It wasn't a success, our marriage. Even he could see that. I wasn't the animal my breeding had suggested I should be. But he thought it was just a matter of schooling. He was used to breaking horses and he thought he could do the same with me. Sometimes he even used the same whip."

There is a strange little sound. When I look at Ángel, his face has reddened and he is biting his lip. I think of his father raising his arm to strike him at the *festes*. Perhaps it wasn't the first time. Perhaps he took after Mascaró in that too.

"I think he thought I'd settle down, like mares do, after the first foal. But though he covered me every night he never got me in foal. That's what upset him the most. The fear that I was barren. That he had driven a bad bargain."

"What about him?"

"Oh, men never think it's them. Or they never admit to thinking it. Anyway, he started talking of sending me to Barcelona to see a specialist. But before he could arrange it I went one day to the market. And I never came back to his house."

"That was when you put down your basket and went with my grandfather."

She nods. And smiles.

"We had three years of happiness together. War came almost at once, hunger, cruel times. Yet for your grandfather and me, so much happiness also."

"Mascaró was here, of course, on the island all through the Civil War. We knew he would be for Franco. I'd lived in his house for a year and a half. I knew well enough what he thought of the Reds. But he kept his head down and he waited. I didn't go to Ciudadella except once or twice. I didn't see Mascaró. I tried to forget he existed."

"The first time I heard his name in a long time was right near the end. The Italians started to drop propaganda. It made a change from bombs. We had no toilet paper, so it served at least one purpose."

She smiles in honour of the old joke.

"We knew the end was coming. People were scared – 'demoralized' is the word they use in wartime. But it just means 'scared'. Nobody knew what to do. Except for the Fascists. They began to crawl out of their holes then. They had been making plans for a long time. That's the strength of the bourgeoisie, you know. After any revolution they always believe it's only a matter of time before everything is returned to them."

"But we had a plan too. We thought an invasion was inevitable, but we didn't need to go getting shot in the back. So there was a list."

"Mascaró was on the list. I saw his name. Lluís didn't

say anything about it to me. I didn't say anything to him. We didn't have to. But we both knew. As soon as Brandaris, the governor, left we at the grass roots knew what we had to do. Those on the list were all picked up. They were put into the jails and when the jails were all full we used the prison ships in the harbour. But then everything happened too fast. Instead of the invasion we all expected, that British ship arrived and then the very next day the soldiers in Ciudadella mutinied and our leaders – Lluís among them – decided their only chance of continuing the struggle was to get off the island."

"Afterwards, well, but it isn't fair to hold 'afterwards' against them. They didn't know. Naturally, everyone wanted the chance to escape, including the men guarding the jails so they agreed to release the prisoners, on their word of honour not to seek revenge. It was a big mistake. Good men never made it to the harbour because they were shot by the prisoners they had just freed – some with their own guns. Never turn your back on a Fascist. I should know."

48

A pounding at the door wakes me. I open my eyes. It is still dark. The shape beside me stirs too:

"What is it?"

"I don't know. I'll go and see."

The cold in the room is a shock after the warmth of our bed and I throw on a jacket and pad over to the door, barefoot. It shakes again with another series of blows as I reach it and when I open up there is little Tolo.

"Is he here?" he says, eyes wild.

I step aside and nod. He rushes in and peers around him in the darkness. I move to light a lamp.

"What is it?"

"Ciudadella. The garrison. They've rebelled. Taken over the town and now they're moving on Mercadal with field artillery."

"What? When?"

"About four hours ago. I need Lluís."

"I'm here," says a voice through a yawn, and as the lamplight flares there he is, bare-foot like me, fastening his trousers as he comes out of the other room. He is holding his old striped shirt, the one I've mended so many times, but his chest is bare and his hair is uncombed. He looks so young and vulnerable that my heart gives a lurch, as if I am seeing him for the first time. As if I am falling in love with him for the first time, just like I did when I was fourteen years old.

"Ubiette wants a meeting. I think he's planning to surrender."

"Has he heard from Valencia?"

Tolo shakes his head.

"Nothing. He thinks they're gone. That we're on our own. And now, with Ciudadella. Well, they must be sure the invasion's on its way, mustn't they? Or else why now? They can't be reacting to the British coming – they haven't had enough time to get ready."

"So he's giving in?"

"That's why he wants the meeting. He wants to go back on board and negotiate terms. He's going to ask for safe passage off the island with the British. For all of us. But he says we have to give something in return."

"What? Apart from giving them Menorca? Our dishonour? Victory for Franco? What more have we possibly got to give them?"

"Lives."

"What lives?"

I see what Tolo means before Lluís does:

"He means the lives on the list."

Tolo nods.

"He thinks we should offer to free our prisoners, in return for our tickets out of here."

"And give Menorca back to the same old order that has kept the people in poverty for centuries? No. If nothing else, we can prevent that."

Tolo shrugs.

"It doesn't matter anymore, does it? Whether it falls back into the hands of the old land owners, or into the hands of Franco's cronies from the mainland. There's nothing we can do to stop it."

"We could fight on. We could do what we've promised to do and defend the Second Republic to the last drop of our blood."

"We'd still lose. In days or weeks. Not even months. You know it. And with how much destruction? How much bloodshed? Not just ours. Civilians."

Lluís laughs:

"There are no civilians in this war, Tolo. You know that. We are all soldiers on one side or the other. Ubiette doesn't understand that, because he's Navy. He still thinks there's a distinction between the armed forces and the people. He's never liked the idea of the list, from the moment he got here. Never understood that the men on it are Menorca's enemies just as much as if they were in Franco's battalions. If he wins, they will be. Be sure of that."

"When he wins."

Lluís glares at him hard, and then shrugs. He pushes his arms into the sleeves of his shirt and then dips his head so that his face is buried from view as he pulls the shirt over his head. When he emerges, a different mood seems to have come over him and he looks first at me and then back at the boy:

"As you say. When he wins. So, what time is it?"

Tolo takes a watch out of his pocket.

"Just after seven. The governor wants to meet as soon as possible and then go back out to see the British and Franco's messenger – you know he was Navy too, before the war – this morning. He told them yesterday that we'd decide for ourselves if we'd heard nothing from the mainland by tomorrow. But now, with the mutiny, he wants to get it settled. He's worried the ship's captain will withdraw at the first sign that an invasion is under- way and then we'll all be trapped. So will you come?"

Lluís shrugs again:

"Of course. It's the last day, isn't it Tolo? I've been here every other day. Why wouldn't I be here on the last day?"

He turns to me and takes my face in his hands. His fingers stroke my hair and he puts his lips gently against my forehead and then against my lips.

"I'll go and start the bike," Tolo says, and goes outside.

I put my arms round Lluís's waist and pull him against me, as hard as I can. We are both thin these days and I can feel his rib-cage against mine but I pull him tighter, not caring if we bruise each other, wanting to make some permanent mark to show that we belong to each other. Because he's right, this is the last day. And who knows what comes after?

"I want to come with you."

"I know. But there isn't room on the bike. Let me go now. I'll come back after the meeting, when I know what's happening. You get our things together, just a bag, and wait for me. I don't know how long I'll be. But I will come back for you. I promise. Don't go far from home today. It might be dangerous. Just wait for me, okay? Now, I need to stick my head under a tap. Wake myself up properly. Can you find my boots for me?"

They are under the bed, where he kicked them off last night before slipping in beside me late, sliding an arm under my waist and pulling me gently back against him.

"I love you, Catalina," he said, mumbling on the edge of sleep. "All my life."

I nearly told him then, what I've suspected for the last few days. As I pick up his boots and shake the laces free of their knots, I wonder whether to tell him now. But then I hear Tolo gun the engine of the motorbike and Lluís shouts from the sink:

"Have you got them?"

"Yes", I say and carry them out to where he's standing, drying his face on our ragged piece of towel.

I could still tell him as he stoops to do up his laces. But it isn't the sort of thing you tell someone as they're running out the door. Anyway, I'm not even sure. Maybe it's better to save it until I am, that way at least the

324

news won't forever be bound up with the day we lost the war.

So I say nothing, just watch him climb onto the bike behind Tolo and clap his hand on his friend's shoulder to say: "Go!" As they bounce off down the street they could be boys setting out together on an adventure and I realise that even on their way to discuss surrender they are too young and too full of life to be entirely down-hearted.

When they are gone, I go back inside and think about climbing back into bed. But without Lluís its warmth has gone, and anyway it is beginning to get light. I take off the jacket I had put on over my nightdress and then the nightdress itself and stand in front of the dressing-table mirror. I shiver in the cold and stare at my belly and my breasts. They don't look any different yet, but something feels different. There's no sickness, no tenderness, just a sense that there is a very fine wire somewhere inside me, resonating at a slightly different frequency from normal. No more than that. Just that faint, fine sense of alteration.

Time will tell. Except that there may be no time. If the Fascists come, and we're not killed in the battle, then we cannot expect mercy. We know what happened to the Republicans on Mallorca. That was three years ago. A lot of blood has flowed under the bridge since then. I find myself hoping that Lluís will not succeed in talking the governor out of his plan to negotiate with the British. Exile would be a terrible thing, but at least we would be together. Not dead, or in Fascist jails. With at least a chance of being a family.

The thought of Lluís as a father makes me smile. Suddenly I wish I had told him, after all.

I get dressed and pull an old ruck-sack down from the top of the cupboard. I fold our warm sweaters, a spare pair of my shoes. Lluís has only the boots that are on his feet. I look for the photograph of the two of us Juan took, the first summer of the war, but it isn't in the drawer. A hair-brush and pocket mirror. Couple of books. Not Marx. We can carry that with us inside, but I doubt whether the outward symbols of it will be welcome, wherever they plan to take us.

There seems nothing more to do. No point in cleaning the house, for whoever comes after us. Leave that to the landlord, who will be glad enough to get his property back. I make a last pot of coffee, what passes for coffee these days, and drink it slowly.

All morning, nobody comes. I strip down the rifle and oil it. Count the ammunition, just in case. Reassembled, it sits on the table, a museum piece from the 14–18 war.

At about one, I hear an aeroplane. Taking the rifle I go out into the street. After a couple of minutes it passes overhead – a Savoia, Italian. We've been trained to recognise them. A bomber. I duck back beneath the door lintel, but it just flies lazily around over the town. Reconnaissance, I suppose. Checking what the British are doing.

I go back inside and pace around. Where is Lluís? I want to go down to the port, but I'm afraid of missing him.

Just after two, the walls shudder and there is a low thud. I run outside again and there is another explosion and another. I count six in all – and then nothing. Other people are out in the street now. I look up but there is no sign of the bomber.

"Where did they drop them?" I say to the boy from the butcher's shop. I don't know his name.

He looks scared, is shaking a little.

"I don't know. I think it might be over the other side. Maybe the fort?"

I leave the door open and set off down the street. Five minutes brings me to a view over the water, out towards Cala Llonga and Cap Mola. Smoke is rising in a dirty plume from beyond the far hill. The butcher's boy was right. They were aiming at La Mola, probably trying to hit the naval guns on the cliffs. Which we haven't any ammunition for anyway. Still, better they waste their bombs there than on the people in the town.

The bombers come again at four. This time the anti-aircraft batteries are ready for them and it is those I hear first, before the bombs start to fall. It isn't just La Mola they hit this time. The explosions are nearer, this side of the water too and when I run out into the street, there is a greater air of panic. Word is spreading about the mutiny in Ciudadella. People are talking about an invasion. They are agitated, but no one knows what to do.

"Where's your Lluís?" asks the woman from next door. "He must know what's going on? Why aren't the soldiers defending Mahon? Have we given up already?"

I don't know what to tell her, so I go back inside. It is torture, waiting. I should have insisted on going with him. The daylight is starting to fade already and it is very cold. I pull my heavy sweater out of the rucksack and put it on under my jacket. Then I sit in the gathering darkness, not wanting to light the lamp in case it attracts the bombers.

They come anyway, just after six. The anti-aircraft batteries start up again and their manic energies are answered by one ponderous thud, and then another, louder, and a third gigantic crash that shakes the building and fills the air with dust. I ought to get under the table, but I am suddenly angry and instead I grab my rifle and run out into the street. There are no street-lights but there is a red glow darting and leaping over the roofs opposite. I run to the end of the street and turn left and left again – and stop dead.

A bomb has hit one of the tall four-storey houses that line all these streets. There is a flaming hole where the house used to be, and the buildings either side are burning fiercely, their outer walls blown away to reveal the rooms within. The street is filled with flaming rubble and the door to the house next to the crater is swinging grotesquely on one hinge. For a few seconds I think I am alone, picking my way over the smashed masonry, trying not to step on the broken glass or burning timber. But then I realise there are other people moving around, blackened, dazed figures stumbling among the debris. The scene is silent apart from the roar of the flames.

Suddenly, the darkness is illuminated by another explosion and a blaze of light. One of the blackened figures sees me in the flash and lunges at me. The hands that clutch me stink of cooking meat and I can't tell if it's a man or a woman until the voice says:

"Help me! My baby! I have to find my baby."

"Where?" I ask.

She points at the building with the swinging door.

"We're on the first floor. I never left her. I never would have left her. I don't know how I got here."

I realise that the blast must have blown her out of the side of the house. I take off my jacket, put it round her shoulders, and lead her to sit by the kerb. There are more people running into the street now, and I grab someone and ask her to stay with the woman until help comes. I leave my rifle propped against the wall and climb over the rubble to the house. Someone shouts at me to stay out of there, but I put my shoulder against the crazily swinging door and prop it up against the inner wall. There is a body collapsed at the bottom of the stairwell and I think it is an elderly woman. But I'm after a baby, so I do no more than drag the body out to the doorway and hope that someone else will come and do something for it.

The stairs are intact up to the first floor and there are two doors off the landing. The door to the left is burst open and the curtains are blowing through the broken windows at the far side of the room. Perhaps this is where the old lady has come from. The door to the right has gone altogether and so has most of the room it used to lead to. The floorboards end about two metres beyond the doorway and everything beneath is a fiery hell. There is no baby.

Rather than go back outside and explain that to its mother I turn and climb the next flight of stairs, searching for someone I can actually help.

I don't know how long it is before I finally leave the bombed street to walk back to my own, so similar this morning, now utterly different. I am most of the way there when I remember the rifle, propped against the wall, but when I get back to where I left it, clearly it's gone. Heading home again I see the motorbike from half-way down the street, and a figure sitting on the step. My heart leaps, and then falls as I see it is not Lluís but Tolo.

"Where is he? Where have you been all day?"

"Well, where have you been? I've been waiting for an hour. Have you been fighting fires? You're pitch black."

"A bomb, a couple of streets away. I went to help. Where is Lluís? Is he alright?"

"Don't worry. He's safe. He went out to the ship. The British upped anchor and left the harbour after the first air-raid. They only came back again a while ago, when they had assurances there'd be no more bombing."

"From whom?"

Tolo shrugs.

"I don't know. Who knows? Mallorca? The thing is: Lluís is still on board and they're quite a long way out by the harbour entrance. We have to get out there. We need a boat."

"Have we surrendered? Is it over?"

"It's nearly over. They radioed to say the British have agreed to take off anyone who'd be likely to suffer reprisals when the Fascists get here. Which definitely includes you and me. They're planning to sail before dawn, but it might be earlier if the Italians come back. I don't know where we're going, exactly. France I think, not England. But who knows? We're going to free the prisoners in exchange. They've given their word not to cause any trouble, but I don't trust them, do you? I think we need to get out of here, Catalina."

He stands up and walks over to the bike:

"But where are we going to get a boat?"

"They're supposed to be holding one for us, but let's worry about that when we get to the port. Come on."

I dive back into the house for the ruck-sack. I wish I still had the rifle too. Climbing on the back of the bike I say in Tolo's ear:

"Have you got a gun?"

He laughs:

"Yes, no ammo though. So cross your fingers we don't need some."

49

We leave the bike at the bottom of the hill, because everything beyond is chaos. The only light in the town is from
the fires, but the streets leading to the port are packed
with people, suitcases, crying children and panic. Word
has obviously spread. We are not the only ones trying
to leave. Tolo takes my hand and drags me through the
crowd. At one moment, I get crushed between two men
and lose my grip on his hand. I think I've lost him but
then his arm is round my waist again and he shouts in
my ear:

"They said they'd wait for us at the Customs House.
If we get separated, you'll have to make your own way
there. They should be guarding some boats. Your name
is on the list. A good list!"

We plough on. And then I lose hold of him again in a
surge of bodies and this time he is washed away by the
crowd. I look around but it is pitch-dark and suddenly
there is gunfire. At first it sounds like it is coming from
up in the town but then three shots ring out close by,
just ahead of me, and the people on the quayside start to
scream and shove more frantically. I am nearly pushed
into the water and I hear bodies falling in, splashing and
shrieking in the February sea.

I back away from the water's edge and across the road
to try and get a view down the port to where the ship is
anchored. My back is against the wall of a warehouse
now and I find a bollard to stand on, so that I can see
over the heads of the crowd. Out towards the open sea,
I think I can see a faint yellow glow that might just be

the lights of the ship. I smile, to think that Lluís is safe on board, and then I peer down the street, looking for the low tiled roof of the Customs House, trying to work out how far I have to go.

I jump down from the bollard and that's when Mascaró grabs me. He must have seen me stick my head up above the crowd and sneaked up beside me. Or maybe he even saw me with Tolo and was the one who tore us apart. Now, he puts his hand over my mouth and pushes me back against the wall. I know who it is before he speaks. Even after five years I know the smell of him.

I try to dive forward towards the water. That's my first thought. Anything but him. Anything. I realise he has a gun pushed in my ribs but I still try to fight him off. I don't care if it goes off. I half-wish it would, if I can't reach Lluís. But he doesn't pull the trigger. He doesn't need to. He knows he's strong enough. There are people running right by us, probably even people I know, who could help me. But it's dark and no one is looking my way. Everyone is intent on one thing, finding a boat. If only I could shout for Tolo, maybe he is still within earshot. But Mascaró's hand is over my mouth and when I try to bite it he just smashes my head into the stone wall.

He must realise my legs have gone weak after my head hit the wall because he looks into my eyes and smiles:

"Don't bother," he says. "He's never coming back for you."

Then he pulls me forward and flings me back against the stones again.

When I wake up I am in Ciudadella. In the marital bed. But not in the house he'd had when we married. In my father's house, which he had always wanted, to which I was always the key. Everything is quiet. There is no gunfire. The War is over. The Civil War anyway. Not our war. That is just beginning.

50

"How did he find you?"

I blink, and it is gone. That night. The most important night of my life. The girl that I was. All gone. Never to be put right. And I am just an old woman in a hospital, with her dying son.

"I said, how did he find you?"

Ángel is asking the question Lluís never did:

"Find me? Oh, that was just bad luck. Not God's will, like he said. No such thing. Just bad luck. And the list. You see, he'd been arrested in Ciudadella three days before, but there wasn't enough room for all the bastards in Ciudadella. So he'd been brought to the *Atlante*."

"The *Atlante*?"

"It was an old troop ship they were using as a prison ship. Franco used it later, for all the ones who didn't get off with the British. It was a holding prison, before they transferred them to jails on the mainland, or shot them."

"So it was bad luck. Bad luck they didn't get round to shooting him. Bad luck he was in Mahon. Bad luck I kept Tolo waiting an hour, just as they were opening the prisons. Bad luck he saw me before I saw him. Enough bad luck for a lifetime in one night."

"But you didn't have to stay with him, if you hated him so much."

This is the girl.

"No, you're right. I had a choice. I've often thought I made the wrong one. He told me the choices as soon as I woke up. 'Legally,' he said, 'you're my wife. You have betrayed me by fornicating with that Red bastard. But you're still my wife in God's eyes, and under the law of Spain now that decent government has been restored. As my wife I can protect you. Happily, I have the position to do it. If you repudiate me then I shall have to give you up to the Guardia. They're looking for Red fugitives to stand trial for their crimes. They are arresting dozens every day. Knowing who you were associated with I'd say – if things go well – you're facing twenty years in jail on the peninsula.'"

"He'd have done that to you?"

"Of course. Just as he knew I'd have let them shoot him. For all he knew, it was me who added his name to the list."

"But why did he want you back if he hated you and he knew you hated him?"

"Because he needed to show all the people who mattered to him that he was the master. I had humiliated him by leaving him and I think he needed to prove that I could be broken after all. He wanted to parade me, like one of the horses at that fiesta out there. And he did. For twenty years."

"And you let him, because of the baby."

"I told you. I made the wrong choice. I didn't have the courage to face a firing squad or twenty years in jail. I wasn't sure even where my real husband was. He had saved me once before, that day in the market, perhaps I thought he'd come back for me this time. As for the baby, I wasn't sure enough yet even to have told Lluís. I was only two weeks late on the day of the surrender."

"The thought of a baby coming had something to do with it, yes. But maybe I was just saving my own skin, or buying time. If I'd known it would mean twenty years with Mascaró I might have chosen differently. But I didn't know. I was still too young to imagine something as bad as that. Anyway, who knows why, I agreed to his deal. I agreed to be his wife again and as soon as I nodded he locked the bedroom door and climbed onto the bed to ..."

I look at Ángel but he is staring at the floor, as if he is in some way responsible. The three of us sit in silence as a nurse puts her head round the door and, not seeing the relatives she wants, withdraws it again.

"Well, then the baby came," Ángel looks up and I nod at him: "Your father. I was ill afterwards. Mascaró took to the child. Your father never took to me. You know, as a mother I was no good."

"He never said that," Ángel says it quietly.

"But you know it. He worshipped his father, the man he called his father. You know that."

Ángel nods. There is sadness in his face.

"Mascaró had most of what he wanted then. He had a wife, who hated him admittedly, but she appeared in church with him on Sunday, sat at his dinner table, lay still in his bed while he did what he wanted. He was able to believe that she had given him a son. He had his profession, which went well, despite the hard times. Because he was in league with the right people. As far as he was concerned the world was turned the right way up again."

"The thing about Mascaró was, so much of him was the look of things, the external, that it didn't matter to him that the inside was rotten. It didn't matter to him that I hated his guts and wanted to stick the kitchen knife in them every day. It didn't even matter to him that we both knew it. It didn't matter that every time I sat beside him in the cathedral he knew I was think-ing about the days when the only reason I went inside a church was to throw out the dangerous rubbish they kept inside. I remembered the day I tore the cloth off the

335

very altar we had been married in front of, tore it in two in God's own house and walked away without a scratch on me. I remembered the church in Mahon where we used to service lorries. We took down the doors and laid them on the steps to make a ramp then we drove our lorries right inside. That was, until the Italians (such good Catholics) bombed the roof in."

"He must have known what I wanted to do as I sat there beside him and he didn't care. I think he even enjoyed it because he knew I was powerless. It didn't even matter to him that every time he forced his way inside me I was trying to think of Lluís. Perhaps he thought every time he did it to me he forced me to use up one good memory of Lluís. Maybe he was right. You see, it really didn't matter to him that there was nothing but poison between us. He had won. That was all that mattered."

"The other things mattered to me though. They meant that, for me, the war didn't come to an end until 1960. Twenty years of war in a marriage is like twenty years of civil war. Hatred where there should be love, within families, or between neighbours, is a terrible thing. There was something corroding about it, just like the war – the same suspicion and distrust in the very place where there should be peace. Right there in your home. It ate at my insides until I was hollow. It would have eaten at his if he had any, but he didn't. It ate at your father's, even when he was too young to know why."

"Maybe that's why he wanted so much to be a priest. To avoid a marriage like Mascaró and I had. I told you, he was away at the seminary when Mascaró was taken ill. Mascaró was nearly sixty then, but fit. It was very sudden."

I rub my hands on the arms of the chair. The cold metal is a surprise – I expected my old armchair at home. I had forgotten where I was. Stupid old woman.

"We sent a telegram to Salamanca, but Francisco had not yet arrived home. Mascaró was in his own bed. He had been unconscious since the seizure. The doctor said there was nothing to do but wait. If he came round there would be some hope."

I laugh:

"The doctor didn't know what I was hoping for. Anyway, I sat by his bed through the night, watching his chest. He was still breathing but it was ... erratic. I kept waiting – and hoping – for it to stop. Once, in the hour before dawn, the hour when most people give in to death, I thought it had. I leaned forward to check and, just as I was sure it was over, the bastard took another breath. I put my head down on the covers and cried."

"Then the sun came up. The window was open and I heard people starting to go up and down the street and somehow I knew that he was going to come round. I knew he wasn't going to die. He couldn't bear to leave me in peace. And I was right. At about seven o'clock he opened his left eye. His right one didn't open. I think he must have been paralysed down that side. But his left one opened – and I could see that he was in there."

I look over at Ángel and I can see that he is horrified already and afraid of what he is going to hear. I think he finally knows me – knows what a terrible thing I have become.

"What did you do?" he whispers.

I look at him and say aloud words I have only ever heard inside my skull before:

"I told him Francisco wasn't his son."

Ángel lets out a sigh and buries his head in his hands.

"Thank God," he says, with a joyless laugh: "I thought you were going to say you killed him."

"Yes," I say calmly, "I did."

His face jerks up to look at me and I have to explain it to him.

"I leaned over and I said what I'd wanted to say for twenty years. 'He's not yours. He's Lluís's. You could never do it. Not before. Not since. You've been firing blanks all these years. There are no Mascarós left. You're the last.'"

"He looked at me through that one eye. I could see that I had finally hurt him. In his pride. The only place you could hurt him. He went to hit me, with his good arm, the habit of a lifetime. But when he tried to heave himself up off the bed the thing in his brain must have shifted. He fell backwards and before he hit the pillow he was dead."

51

There is silence in the room for a long time then and the old woman and I both look at Ángel. With a gesture we both must recognise as one of Lluís's he rubs his hands up over his face and through his hair. Then, slowly, he stands up.

"I'm going back in to see my father."

I move to follow him out of the room but he does not look over at me – or at her – as he walks towards the doors of the ward.

When I go back to his grandmother she is still sitting in the hospital chair with her hands on the arms, motionless. Given the way she spoke to me in the corridor before, I had expected to hear – what? shame? remorse? – in her voice when she came to her confession but what I have heard instead was relish. Satisfaction. It seems as though telling Mascaró's story has reawakened a hatred that has lain behind closed doors since before Ángel was born. Now he has been exposed to it. When she started the story she wanted some good to come of it – for her son at least – but I can't see how it can. It has turned out to be a true Pandora's box and the horrors have flown out into the air.

"What do you think he'll do?"

Her eyes move up to my face but everything else about her remains still.

"The wrong thing, probably. That's what we usually do in our family."

"But what's the right thing?"

She shakes her head and laughs, dryly at first and I

339

expect her to stop but she doesn't. Instead, the laughter grows and grows until there are tears running down her cheeks and little flecks of spittle at the creased corners of her mouth. She moves one hand off the arm of the chair to scrabble at the pocket of her dress for a handkerchief but either she cannot find the pocket in the folds of her skirt or she has forgotten to replace the handkerchief she used the other day with a clean one. Either way her hand remains empty and I pass her a pink paper tissue from a box thoughtfully left on the coffee table.

She reaches out for the tissue and I'm conscious that I don't want her hand to touch mine even through the paper tissue. There is something repellent about her, and her laughter.

I am thankful (for Ángel's sake) that she is composed again by the time he comes back into the room a few minutes later. She looks at him but does not speak, so I am the one to ask how his father is.

"They think that he's a little better. They've given him aspirin, to keep his blood thin. I'm going to stay with him."

"Is he conscious?"

"Now and then."

The old woman raises her eyes to meet her grandson's:

"Have you talked to him?"

"A little."

"What have you told him?"

"I told him that his son was here. His mother also. I told him that we both love him. That everything was going to be alright. What did you want me to tell him?"

She shakes her head and pushes herself up from the chair. It seems as if she feels that everything is done now, everything is out of her hands:

"Nothing. You did the right thing. She knew you would." She nods at me. "She had faith in you."

340

He looks at me properly for the first time since I entered the hospital and I can see that he wants to forgive me for abandoning him at the fiesta, even though he must believe that I saw the accident and did nothing to help him. He needs somewhere to turn and I am the only direction he can see that leads away from his family. His grandmother's words are giving him the excuse he needs.

Someone he loves is lying to him again and he falls for it just the same as always.

52

I have asked myself, in the days since that night in the hospital, what was the mechanism that bound up Catalina's secrets so tightly with her life.

After she finished telling her story they went out together to sit with Francisco. An hour or so later, she sent Ángel to rest in the relatives' lounge and we pushed some of the chairs together to make a kind of space where we could lie down. Without a word, he put his arms around my waist and I held his head to my chest, stroking his hair until we both slept. When he woke at dawn and went back to the ward her head was on the blankets and her hand was clasping her son's. He thought she was asleep. But when he tried to wake her, the body, though not yet cold, was heavy with absence and his father's eyes told him he understood that she was dead.

So, were her secrets a parasite, a cancer, one that had so invaded her system the damage she did in ripping it free was unsurvivable? Or had they become, after so long inside her, a symbiotic presence, a framework on which her life depended for its meaning? Her straightness, her quietness, her affectless response to the world, all the things I had taken for serenity or dignity – were they no more than a retrenchment from life, a falling back behind the barricades she had built around the knowledge that she had killed the person her son loved best? Did her heart give way in grief at what she had done forty years before? Or did it fall silent at peace because by telling Ángel the truth she had finally done something to try and help the son and grandson she had always loved and had always failed when they needed her?

His father might have been able to say how it was that she died, but the stroke has taken from him the power of speech, at least for a time. Ángel wanted to know whether she had tried to tell him her secret but when he asked the old man – and he was an old man, suddenly – if his mother had talked to him he just made a tiny gesture that could have been a shrug or a shake of the head. I wanted to know whether she had told that other secret, my secret, but if she did he has given no sign of remembering.

The old man's anger does seem to have left him though. Nobody knows, maybe not even him, whether that is the result of the catastrophe in his brain or of his mother's death. Was she able to communicate to him, with her hand clasped in his at the moment when one of them was to die, that she loved him? That she always had? Was he conscious then, or did he wake to find her head with its tightly coiled hair resting on the bedcovers? Did he think that she had offered her life in exchange for his? Did he understand her at last?

It was the doctors' opinion, their professional opinion naturally, that he was not well enough to go to his mother's funeral. But he insisted, mutely, on being dressed and placed in a wheelchair so that he could attend. He didn't need a voice to communicate that it was his duty.

And it was not, after all, just his mother's funeral. Ángel and I had assumed all along that Lluís had already been buried or cremated before we picked up his trail. Terrible detectives that we are, we never even asked the question. It was one secret that Catalina chose not to share.

It was the police who told Ángel that his grandfather's body was still in the mortuary in Mahon. They had closed their investigation shortly after the post mortem, concluding that the old man must have fallen from the cliff simply because they could find no evidence to the contrary. They said that they had written to his widow to inform her that she might collect the body of her husband for burial, but had still not heard from her at the time of her own death.

Why was that? We will never know for sure, but I think I understand now why she was so desperate to finish telling her story. She hadn't wanted to bury Lluís alone for the simple reason that she wanted to be buried with him. They were never able to live with each other again after Franco and Mascaró came between them, but now there is a place in the white-walled village of the dead in Alaior where they can lie together. And the music that surrounds them may only be the chirping of the sparrows that live in the pine trees, but it is music after all.

So that's where we laid them, the father, the son and I. Ángel even got the chance to look at his grandfather's face, for the first and the last time. Not much of a meeting, but more than he had thought to have.

Juan Mercadal Triay came to the burial too. He looked older than before, and I wondered for the first time whether he will be able to finish his work of remembrance before he too is reduced to memory. There was no mention of the list. The pact of forgetting may not last forever, but it has lasted almost long enough now. Soon, everyone who could be damaged by remembering the past will be gone. So will those who would have been helped by hearing the truth told at last.

But it was, even so, the historian who solved our final mystery for us. It was after the burial, as we waited while the ambulance lowered its tailgate for Ángel to manoeuvre his father's wheelchair back inside:

"What I don't understand," said Juan Mercadal, in a tone more conversational than inquisitive: "is how Lluís got to the edge of the cliff to begin with. I can understand that he might fall over, but I just don't understand how he got there. It's rough ground, and he wasn't good on his legs the last few years. And he never drove."

At which the old man in the wheelchair, twenty years his junior, raised his arm and made a gesture. A furious scribbling gesture.

"He wants to write," I said. "Who has a pen? He wants to write."

Ángel took a fountain pen out of his funeral suit pocket. Gently, he wrapped his father's long fine fingers round the clumsy barrel. Then he smoothed out a piece of paper onto his father's knee and we all waited.

Francisco, not paralysed on his writing side, but weakened in every limb, scratched at the paper with the pen, going back and forth over the letters until he thought they might be readable. Then he lifted the pen and let Ángel take the paper away to read:

"I took him. In my car. I did what he asked me to."

Ángel looked from the paper to his father:

"You didn't wait for him, to take him back."

Francisco shook his head and pointed with the pen at the piece of paper.

"I did what he asked me to," I read over Ángel's shoulder, and it becomes clear. Lluís and I did have the same idea, after all.

"You knew what he was planning to do?"

He stared at me implacably, happy to be mute, happy not to have to confess that he, the one-time seminarian, had knowingly driven his own father to the place where he had chosen to commit suicide.

Sometimes, it can't be easy to do your duty.

The ambulance driver was waiting now to do his and

Ángel stepped behind the wheelchair to push it onto the ramp. His father tried to turn, to look into his son's face, but Ángel stood stiffly, chin out, avoiding his gaze.

There is hope for them, I think, but only if Ángel can come to understand that the last thing his father did for Lluís was a kindness. I wonder if he is capable of seeing that. I wonder if he will ever be capable of doing as much, or as little, for me.

53

When we arrive home from the funeral, there is a plastic bucket outside the front door, with a metal lid on top, weighted down with a large stone. Ángel sets aside the stone and lifts the lid. Inside the bucket is a huge lobster, which at once starts to climb out. Ángel slams the lid down on his pincers until the creature lets go and falls back into the water. He puts the stone back on top and looks at me, inquiringly:

"Billy," I say. "I think it's an apology. Say it with fish."

Later, there is a knock at the door and when Ángel stands up I motion him to stay where he is. When I arrive at the bottom of the stairs, Billy is standing on the end of the jetty, looking out to sea.

"Hola," I say, and he turns and walks towards me, looking sheepish.

"Sorry," he says. "I was a drunken pig."

I laugh.

"You were."

I walk out towards him and we stand together, looking down into the water.

"I'm not like that."

"I know."

"I was jealous."

"And stupendously drunk."

"I've never been that drunk before."

"Or that jealous?"

"No. Or that jealous."

"You shouldn't be, you know. After all, I'm thirty-nine years old. If Ángel is old, then I am ancient."

He looks at me in astonishment. Maybe his mother isn't even that old.

"You're sixteen, Billy. We had a fantastic moment. I loved it. It made me feel wonderful, and in that sense it was important. But it wasn't the start of something. It was self-contained. We should just be grateful we had it. I am."

He squints at me in the sunshine:

"Are you?"

"Hell, yes!"

He smiles, and seems to make a decision. Telling him my age probably swung it:

"Me too."

"Good. Now will you stop giving Ángel the evil eye, and come and be friends. The two of you are the only friends I've got and I need you both."

He shrugs, but he follows me back to the house. Before we reach the door, I stop and say to him:

"Be kind to him. He just buried his grandparents."

So he climbs the stairs behind me and shakes Ángel by the hand and offers his condolences, pushing his fringe aside with his hand while he does it, as an older man might remove his hat. And I am glad that I decided not to tell Ángel exactly what Billy did to spook me at the fiesta, because from the moment they shake hands they start to be friends.

54

"We think it's about time you stopped smoking."

"We?"

Ángel jerks his head towards Billy, who is back on his up-turned bucket, the lobster having been eaten some days before. Billy squints up at me from beneath his fringe, slightly embarrassed to be co-opted, but not denying it.

They are here again, cluttering up my place. They seem to be here all the time these days and I find I don't mind it anymore. It has started to feel normal. It has started to be, and I feel treacherous to the family I left behind for even thinking this, a comfort. But maybe it's only a comfort because they don't know. They look at me and what do they see? Someone they don't entirely understand, alright, but someone interesting, mysterious, self-sufficient. They don't have a clue what I want from my life, but at least they're confident that I know. They're confident that I'm in control, and so I am.

Just not of my life. That's completely out of my hands. I still think I can control my death though. Which is not much, but it's immense compared with the alternative. For one thing, it means I may be one of the very last people alive who can smoke a cigarette without a single pang about what it might be doing to me. And, in celebration of that, I blow a long defiant plume of smoke out towards the water.

"But I like smoking. In fact, I'd go so far as to say that smoking is one of my very favourite things. Why should I give it up?"

"And drinking," says Ángel doggedly, nodding towards the beer bottle that sits beside me on the wall. "We think you should cut down on the drinking."

"Have you two joined the Moonies? Or the Mormons? Because you're acting really weird."

Ángel looks at Billy again. They have definitely been plotting together. I'm beginning to wonder if promoting this friendship wasn't a mistake. I did it because I thought Ángel would need someone to fall back on, someone who'd known me too, when I am gone. But I think I liked it better when they hated each other's guts.

"You see, we think ... we've been putting two and two together – the sickness, the tiredness, the ..." he gestures at his belly to suggest bigness and it's true, my abdomen is getting fatter, just like the doctors predicted, while everything else continues to get skinnier. I didn't think he'd noticed, but obviously he has. He stops to rummage in the bag under his chair and comes out with a small rectangular box wrapped in cellophane:

"We think you might be pregnant."

And he hands it to me. He's sitting there with this stupid, ridiculous look on his face, somewhere between embarrassment and excitement, with a little bit of pride mixed in and he hands me this box. This pregnancy test.

For a moment I think I'm going to scream.

After all that has happened, I thought nothing could surprise me any more but this is a heavy fist that punches all the air out of me and, when I get my breath back, I think I'm going to scream and run mad.

I look down at my hands and they're suddenly shaking and I want to reach up to the neck of my shirt and tear it in two. It's what people in the Bible do when a terrible thing happens: rend their garments.

350

Except it's not my clothes I really want to tear, it's my skin. I want to dig my nails in and tear it open and suddenly I realise that all these weeks, what I've been holding back, what I've been using this place and these people to mesmerise myself into ignoring, is the fear, the terror and worst of all the rage that something inside me, some part of me is eating me alive.

And it's a stupid thing, this part of me that's gone bad, because doesn't it understand, can't it see, that if, when it kills me, it dies too? It can kill me, alright, but it cannot survive me. When we go, we go together. And I want to ask it, what is the point of that?

I want to reach inside with my bare hands and rip it out and scream at it: "What is the point of that?" But I can't, because what's inside me isn't a lump, it isn't a growth. It's gone way beyond that now, from the moment it burrowed down through the last layer of dermis and dropped out into my bloodstream, to roam where it wanted. The last time I saw it, shadowy on the X-rays, it was a cluster of blobs in my liver, stupid wrong-headed cells gaining sway and crowding out the sane and sensible ones. Acting like Fascists. The triumph of evil over good, and no way to fight it. They predicted the same in my brain and my lungs, but I didn't wait around to view those photos.

I didn't wait around for the rubber sheets, for the diamorphine pump, for the droves of visitors who dreaded being there but couldn't resist coming to look at the first of their generation to die, if only so that they could go away relieved that it was not they who had drawn the shortest straw in the lottery of life.

I came here to get away from everybody who was getting ready to witness my humiliation – the ultimate loser in the only game that matters, at thirty-nine. Statistically speaking, I'm the one who has to die to let someone else get their telegram from the Queen. Do they think of that, when the envelope drops on the mat, those triumphant centenarians? Do they realise that, by the law of averages, some other poor sod had to give up their life decades early just so they can have a special celebration tea in the nursing home and their picture in the local paper?

I came here because I wanted to spend however long the malignant part of me will allow in the most beautiful place I'd ever known. I never thought it could cure me, being on the cala, never thought it would give me back my life a second time, but I thought it might be a consolation prize for all the years I'll miss.

A day on the cala, reading a book in the sun, smoking, drinking a beer with my feet in the water. That might be worth a year of normal life, mightn't it? A year in the rat race, with bills to pay, and traffic jams and rain. It might be worth two years of old age, of orthopaedic stockings and waiting in for the chiropodist and wondering what vile thing is going to come and kill you.

At least I know that. At least I know my fate. It won't be a stroke, like Francisco Mascaró's, that takes half your life in one blow and renders you impotent to control what happens to the rest. No, for me it's a question of reading the symptoms, of judging when the lethargy and nausea and shortness of breath are becoming incapacitating instead of just troublesome. It's a question of judging when I might lose the ability to make my way out over the rocks of the headland to the edge. Lluís made that judgment and he got it right. He didn't leave it too long. Well, maybe he should have done it before he needed Francisco's help, but he didn't misjudge his son, the slave to duty.

It seemed when I planned it, if not the perfect ending, then at least quite natural. I didn't regret any of it.

352

The island and the cala, with their gentle repetition of beauty, have been just the palliative I hoped they'd be. So perfect. So peaceful. Like listening to Mozart. Or to the Bach Cello Suites. And it would have been easy, I think, to take that step over the edge. In the coolness of dawn as the sun came up in a ball of fire over the islets in the channel, I think I could have taken that step with a contented heart.

Instead of which, I'm sitting on a wall holding a pregnancy test in my hand. What else is in the bag, a DNA testing kit? I wonder if they've discussed that too, this wonderfully modern two-and-two-putting-together pair of prize idiots. I look over at them and they're waiting for me to say something, though I haven't the faintest clue what.

So I don't say anything. Instead I take a last long drag on my cigarette and stub it out. Then I take an equally long drink of my beer and hop down from the wall. Walking towards the house, I scrabble at the box to find the tab that opens the cellophane. My nail finds it and I peel off the outer layer, screw it into a ball and toss it at Ángel's head. He catches it and laughs.

Then I find myself laughing too, because it is ironic, isn't it, that the symptoms of my dying are so stupidly similar to the symptoms of new life. I don't know what they're going to say, when I come back downstairs and show them that their test is negative. I don't know what I'm going to tell them, but I don't think it can be the truth. I've seen the look in people's eyes when they hear the truth, and I don't ever want to see it again.

So why am I going upstairs at all?

Because as I looked down at the box it struck me that, statistically, there must be a chance (a million to one, a billion?) that the prize idiots are right and the doctors are wrong.

Miracles do happen, occasionally. One happened to Catalina when she was handed her baby grandson and found Lluís looking up at her. And even though I don't believe in miracles any more than she did, as I climb the stairs I find myself hoping for one just the same.